UNSPOKEN

UNSPOKEN

THE LYNBURN LEGACY

BOOK 1

Sarah Rees Brennan

RANDOM HOUSE 🏠 NEW YORK

Text copyright © 2012 by Sarah Rees Brennan
Jacket art and interior illustrations copyright © 2012 by Beth White

All rights reserved. Published in the United States by Random House Children's Books, a division of Random House, Inc., New York.

Random House and the colophon are registered trademarks of Random House, Inc.

Visit us on the Web! randomhouse.com/teens

Educators and librarians, for a variety of teaching tools, visit us at RHTeachersLibrarians.com

Library of Congress Cataloging-in-Publication Data
Brennan, Sarah Rees.
Unspoken / by Sarah Rees Brennan — 1st ed.
     p. cm. — (The Lynburn legacy ; bk. 1)
Summary: "Kami Glass is in love with someone she's never met—a boy she's talked to in her head since she was born. This has made her an outsider in the sleepy English town of Sorry-in-the-Vale, but she has learned ways to turn that to her advantage. Her life seems to be in order, until disturbing events begin to occur. There has been screaming in the woods and the manor overlooking the town has lit up for the first time in 10 years. The Lynburn family, who ruled the town a generation ago and who all left without warning, have returned. Now Kami can see that the town she has known and loved all her life is hiding a multitude of secrets—and a murderer. The key to it all just might be the boy in her head. The boy she thought was imaginary is real, and definitely and deliciously dangerous." —Provided by the publisher.
ISBN 978-0-375-87041-5 (trade) — ISBN 978-0-375-97041-2 (lib. bdg.) —
ISBN 978-0-375-98918-6 (ebook)
[1. Magic—Fiction. 2. Magicians—Fiction. 3. Horror stories. 4. England—Fiction.]
I. Title. PZ7.B751645Uns 2012 [Fic]—dc23 2012001954

Printed in the United States of America
10 9 8 7 6 5 4 3 2 1
First Edition

Random House Children's Books supports the First Amendment and celebrates the right to read.

For Natasha

IOU approximately four million dollars for early-morning wake-up calls with cups of tea, listening to involved plot summaries, museum stories about daggers and teeth, company on a trip to Egypt, and company on a thousand trips to the cinema. For being excited about this book, and your eternal devotion to lady sleuths in general, Miss Marple and Veronica Mars in specific.

What do I owe you for being so awesome, and living with me longer than anyone aside from my family (who, poor souls, had no choice in the matter)? Well, nothing. That is priceless.

Contents

Part I
Lords of the Manor

Somewhere or other there must surely be
The face not seen, the voice not heard
—*Christina Rossetti*

Chapter One
The First Story

THE RETURN OF THE LYNBURNS
by Kami Glass

Every town in England has a story. One day I am going to find out Sorry-in-the-Vale's.

The closest this reporter has come to getting our town's scoop is when I asked Mr. Roger Stearn (age seventy-six but young at heart) to tell me a secret about our town. He confided that he believed the secret to Sorry-in-the-Vale's high yield of wool was in the sheep feed. I think I may have betrayed some slight disappointment, because he stared at me for a while, said, "Respect the sheep, young lady," and ended the interview. Which leaves us with a town in the Cotswolds that has a lot of wool and no secrets. Which is plainly ridiculous. Sorry-in-the-Vale's records date back to the 1400s. Six hundred years do not go by without someone doing something nefarious.

The Lynburns are the town's founding family,

and we all know what the lords of the manor get up to. Ravishing the peasants, burning their humble cottages. Fox hunting. The list goes on and on.

The Lynburns have "dark secret" written all over them. There is even a skipping song about them. Skipping songs may not seem dark to you, but consider "Ring Around the Rosy," a happy children's rhyme about the plague. In Sorry-in-the-Vale they sing this song:

> *Forest deep, silent bells*
> *There's a secret no one tells*
> *Valley quiet, water still*
> *Lynburns watching on the hill*
> *Apples red, corn gold*
> *Almost everyone grows old.*

The song even talks about secrets.

During this dauntless reporter's lifetime, however, the only Lynburn in Aurimere House was Marigold Lynburn (now deceased). Far be it from me to speak ill of the dead, but it cannot be denied that Mrs. Lynburn was a ferociously private person. To the point of ferociously throwing her walker at certain innocently curious children.

Today, after seventeen years in America, Marigold Lynburn's daughters have returned to Sorry-in-the-Vale. If the family does have any dark secrets, dear readers, you can have faith that I will uncover them.

Kami stopped typing and glared at the screen. She wasn't sure about the tone of her article. A serious journalist should probably not make so many jokes, but whenever Kami sat down to the computer it was as if the jokes were already there, hiding behind the keys, waiting to spring out at her.

Kami knew there was a story in the Lynburns. They had gone away before she was born, but all her life she had heard people wishing that someone sick would recover, or a storm would bypass the valley, and in the same breath say, "but the Lynburns are gone." She had spent the summer since she heard of their return asking questions all over town, and had people instantly hush her as if the Lynburns might be listening. Kami's own mother cut her off every time, her voice equal parts severe and scared about her dangerously disrespectful daughter.

Kami looked back at the screen. She couldn't think of a title besides "The Lynburns Return." She blamed the Lynburns, because their surname rhymed with "return." She also blamed the kids who were messing around in the woods beyond her garden: tonight they were making a sound that was almost howling. It went on and on, a noise that struck her ears hard and set her temples throbbing.

Kami jumped up from her chair and ran out of her bedroom. She thumped down the narrow creaking stairs and out the back door into the silver-touched square that was her garden at night. The dark curve of the woods held the glittering lights of Sorry-in-the-Vale like a handful of stars in a shadowy palm. On the other end of the woods, high above the town, was Aurimere House, its bell tower a skeletal finger pointing at the sky. Aurimere House, which the Lynburns had built when they founded the town, and where they had lived for generations, the masters of all they surveyed. There was no place in Sorry-in-the-Vale where you could not see the mansion, its windows like watching eyes. Kami always found herself watching it in return.

For the first time Kami could remember, every window was lit from within, shining gold.

The Lynburns were home at last.

The howling reached a pitch that raked up Kami's spine and sent her running to the garden gate, where she stood with her eyes full of darkness. Then the sound died abruptly. Suddenly there was nothing but the night wind, shushing Kami as if she'd had a bad dream and running cold fingers through her hair. Kami reached out past the boundaries of her own mind and called for comfort.

What's wrong? the voice in Kami's head asked at once, his concern wrapping around her. She felt warmer instantly, despite the wind.

Nothing's wrong, Kami answered.

She felt Jared's presence slip away from her as she stood in the moonlit garden for another moment, listening to the silence of the woods. Then she went back inside to finish her article. She still hadn't told Angela about the paper.

❧

Kami had been hearing a voice in her head all her life. When she was eight, people had thought it was cute that she had an imaginary friend. It was very different now that she was seventeen. Kami was accustomed to people thinking she was crazy.

"You're crazy," said her best friend, Angela, as the bell rang to signal five minutes before the first class on the first day back at school.

Angela had moved from London to Sorry-in-the-Vale when Kami was twelve. The timing had been perfect because Kami's first best friend, Nicola Prendergast, had just dropped her for being too weird.

"They said that about all the great visionaries," Kami informed her, hurrying down the hall to match Angela's long-legged stride.

"You know who else they said it about?" Angela demanded. "All the actual crazy people." She gave Kami a look that said she wished Kami would stop bothering her.

Normally this would not have worried Kami. Angela always looked at people with that expression, and Kami could usually talk her into doing what Kami wanted anyway. But Kami had never wanted something as much as this.

"Last summer, when we volunteered as assistants at cricket camp—"

"When *you* volunteered us without asking me, yes," said Angela.

Kami ignored this trifle. "Remember how I encouraged the kids to keep diaries, which turned into an exposé about the seamy underbelly of cricket camp?"

"I have found it impossible to forget," Angela told her.

"And remember last year when I started the petition to get Miss Mackenzie fired, and she chased me around the pitch waving a hockey stick, and we had to speak before the school board?"

"Again, unforgettable," said Angela.

"My point is, here we have an opportunity to champion truth that doesn't involve sports," Kami persisted. "It's a step toward me becoming the greatest journalist of our time. You have to help, Angela, because Ms. Dollard has this notion that I'm a troublemaker and she's only—*finally*—letting me set up a school paper because I told her you were on board."

Angela rounded on Kami, her dark eyes blazing. "You did *what*?"

"I knew that once I explained the situation, you would understand," Kami said, holding her ground despite Angela's looming over her, alarming and overly tall. She continued swiftly in case Angela was considering beating her to death with her schoolbag. "I was hoping you would agree out of real enthusiasm for the project and because you are a true friend, but if you insist on being without vision—"

"I do," Angela said firmly. "Oh, I do."

"There is one other factor," Kami said. "The office we're being given to run the school paper has a sofa in it." She paused for effect. "And we're allowed to go to the office during free periods to tirelessly pursue truth and justice. Or, say—"

"Nap," Angela finished, in the reverent tones of a knight who has finally spotted the Holy Grail. She stood lost in thought, her fingers tapping against the strap of her schoolbag. Then her perfect mouth curved ever so slightly. "I guess I do have a few ideas for articles."

They walked into class in full accord, Kami beaming

with victory. "I have more than a few. I've already started an article."

Angela slipped into a chair one over from the window, and Kami took the place beside her. "About what?"

Kami leaned across the desk, keeping her voice low. "Yesterday I was at the sweetshop talking to Mrs. Thompson about the Lynburns coming back." She glanced out the window of the classroom. Fields stretched to the south in a green blanket. To the north rose a hill steep enough to look like a cliff. On the edge of that rise stood Aurimere House, and below it were the woods, like a regiment of dark soldiers with a bright general.

She looked back at her friend in time to see Angela's raised eyebrows. "So you were basically interrogating poor Mrs. Thompson, who is probably a hundred and twenty years old?"

"I was acquiring information," Kami said calmly. "Also licorice."

"You are shameless," Angela said. "I hope you feel good about your life choices."

Kami looked out at the valley again. There were stories to be found here, and she was going to discover them all.

"You know," she said, "I really do."

They were interrupted by the entrance of Miss Mackenzie, which forced both of them, Kami smiling and Angela shaking her head, to turn to their books.

❧

It wasn't until the end of the day that Kami and Angela had time to make their way up the stairs to the second floor and check out their newspaper office. The Sorry-in-the-Vale school building—the town was so small that there was no need to have more than one—was over a hundred years old. It accommodated all Vale kids from age five to eighteen, and there were still quite a few rooms in the school that weren't used. Kami couldn't wait to use this one.

"So tell me about the articles *you* have in mind," Kami said to Angela on the first step.

"I was thinking I could write tips for people who are too busy to exercise but want to stay in shape," Angela said. "People like me."

Kami nodded. "You're always busy trying to find a napping spot."

"Exactly," Angela told her. "I can't be distracted from my search by having to do Pilates or whatever. Here's one of my tips: always take steps two at a time."

She demonstrated.

"I thought you did that just to mock my stumpy legs."

"That too," Angela conceded. "But the main thing is that taking steps two at a time is like a StairMaster workout. The result? Buns of steel." Angela casually slapped the buns she referred to, proving her point.

Angela had a perfect body. She had a perfect face too, but at least she put some effort into that, her makeup always flawless and her abilities with eyeliner unnatural. Kami focused more on clothes than on makeup. She was always forgetting to put on lip gloss as she rushed out the door, but she felt the likelihood of forgetting her clothes was not high.

Kami slapped her own ass experimentally and made a face. "Buns of corrugated tin," she said. "On a good day."

What's going on with you? Jared asked out of the blue. Kami felt his mind turn toward hers, away from his own life. It was like being in the middle of a conversation in a crowded room and having someone in an entirely different conversation among an entirely different group of people catch your eye. Multiplied by a thousand because, instead of eyes meeting, it was minds.

Beginning a new era of journalistic history, Kami told him, sending her cheer through their connection. *Also, to be perfectly honest, Angela and I were slapping our asses.*

As one does, said Jared.

And you?

There was a feeling like a shadow touching her, letting slip that Jared was unhappy, but he answered: *Just reading. Beginning a new era of being a useless layabout.* He absorbed her cheerfulness gratefully, and she could tell he was pleased for her.

Kami grinned up at Angela, who gave her a forbearing look. Kami realized that she had been standing and staring blankly for a little too long.

"Coming?" Angela asked with a small smile. She knew about Jared, though Kami tried not to talk about him too much. That was what had lost her Nicola Prendergast.

"Have I mentioned, thanks for doing this?" Kami asked.

Angela slung an arm around Kami's shoulders as they went up the stairs. "Your soul is like the souls of a thousand monkeys on crack, all smushed together," she told Kami. "But enough about you. Show me to my napping sofa."

They reached the blue door at the top of the stairs. It had a little window of clouded glass and wire mesh. Kami pulled out the chunky silver key that Ms. Dollard had somewhat reluctantly entrusted her with, turned it in the lock, and opened the door with a flourish. "Ta-dah!"

Kami and Angela peered into their new headquarters. The room was small. It had a wiry gray carpet, whitewashed brick walls, a big cupboard, several desks, and Angela's much-desired sofa. It was also filled, floor to ceiling, with empty cardboard boxes.

"I hate you so much right now," said Angela.

Kami and Angela spent twenty minutes clearing out their new office together. Then Angela gave up, gave a low moan, and fell onto the sofa, which was still covered in boxes. She lay there, her arm thrown over her eyes.

Kami kept cleaning up, whistling to herself as she folded and stacked piles of cardboard and dust fell around her like soft gray rain. Her glittery blue scarf, pencil skirt, and vintage Liberty blouse were not, she had to admit, the ideal clothes for manual labor. But she'd wanted to make a statement on her first day as a journalistic pioneer.

Kami was wrestling with a box that was determined never to fold, when there came a tap on the open door. She looked up from her giant origami creation, into the eyes of the best-looking guy she had ever seen.

There were two things about him that were more important than good looks. One was that he had a serious, substantial camera hanging from around his neck. The other was that Kami had never seen him before in her life, which meant he must be a Lynburn.

Chapter Two
The Prince of Aurimere

Kami'd always retold her fairy tales to make the fair maidens braver and more self-sufficient, but she had never had any real objection to the handsome prince. And here one was, wearing a white T-shirt and jeans instead of armor, with golden hair that curled at the ends and eyes the ridiculous blue of high-summer skies, drenched in sunlight and melted clouds.

Those blue eyes were, of course, fixed on Angela. "Uh, hi," said the Lynburn, wearing the same expression all boys did when they met Angela, as if they had been smacked in the face and were enjoying it. "Are you Kami Glass?"

Angela lifted the arm over her eyes a fraction. "Go away," she commanded. "I only date college guys."

"You don't know any college guys," Kami pointed out.

Angela's gaze went to Kami, and she smiled. "Which leaves me with more time for napping." She closed her eyes again, leaving Kami and the Lynburn looking at each other.

Kami had to hand it to the guy. Most males were in retreat or infuriated when faced with Angela's inexplicable rudeness. This guy's expression had not changed, apart from a slight widening of his eyes. She admired his self-control.

"I saw a flyer on the bulletin board about the school newspaper needing a photographer, and it said to come here after school." He had a lovely, drawling American accent: more proof he was a Lynburn.

His voice also sounded unruffled. Was he really offering to be a photographer for the paper, despite the fact that he'd just been insulted and their office was awash in cardboard?

Angela sat bolt upright and glared at Kami. "You put up a flyer? Before you even talked me into this?"

"Angela, Angela," Kami said. "We can dwell on the past or we can move into the future!"

"I can hide your body in these piles of boxes. Nobody will ever find it." Angela made a gesture of dismissal at the new kid. "Do you mind?"

He looked at Kami, who gave him a winning smile. This was how it went after Angela dismissed a guy: *then* he would take a look at Kami. Which didn't always work out for Kami. Angela was the one with the exotic beauty, which was unfair considering that Kami was the one with the Japanese grandmother. Kami's hair was black but shot with brown, not the raven's-wing black of Angela's hair. Kami's features were subtly different from her schoolmates', and her skin was pale gold, but she was betrayed by a nose dusted with freckles. Exotic beauties did not sport freckles.

The Lynburn smiled back at her. Kami liked his smile almost as much as she liked his camera.

"Seriously," said Angela. "Go away now."

There was only so much rudeness anyone could be expected to take. Kami seized Angela's arm and pulled her from the sofa. "Would you excuse us for just one moment?" she said to the Lynburn. "My colleague and I need to confer in our office." With that, she hauled Angela into the empty stationery cupboard and shut the door behind them.

In the darkness, Angela asked, "Why am I in a cupboard?"

"There are only two important things for us to discuss right now," Kami said. "The first is that to be a success, our newspaper requires a photographer."

"What's the other thing?"

"He'd be excellent decoration for our headquarters," Kami said. "You have to admit, he's very good-looking, and I need a photographer, so can I keep him, please, oh, please?"

Angela sighed. In the cupboard, the sigh was like a gust of wind. "Kami, you know I hate guys being around all the time. They won't stop staring and bothering me and giving me the sad, sad eyes like a puppy dog until I just want to kick them. Like a puppy dog."

"So you have some puppy issues," Kami observed.

The cupboard door swung suddenly open.

The new boy stood framed by the bright light of the office. "Sorry to interrupt," he said. "But I can hear everything you're saying."

"Ah," said Kami.

"Don't worry," he said. "I can take a hint. Especially if the hint is along the lines of—" He did a good imitation of Angela's dismissive gesture. "Go away now."

Angela looked fondly reminiscent. "We've had some good times together, haven't we? I'll always remember them. After you go away."

The boy's brow wrinkled slightly. "Also, you might not have noticed, but this is a cupboard."

"I admit our private office is of modest dimensions," Kami told him. "But that's the way we like it. Just because we're the editors doesn't mean we need special privileges. We're not snobs." She climbed out of the cupboard, and the new guy offered his hand. She didn't need it, but she took it all the same.

He smiled again. "My name's Ash Lynburn."

Kami beamed at him. "I thought so. We don't get many new people in town. Tell me all about yourself, and let me get a pen so I can write it down. Did I mention that you're hired?"

"Kami's always like this," said Angela.

Even though Kami knew Angela was saying it with love, she was saying it in front of someone Kami wanted to impress. She hesitated, then reached out to Jared in her mind, and uncertainty washed away in the wave of reassurance she got back. "True," Kami said cheerfully. "I am a born reporter. But you know, the old family moving back into the manor house—everyone who comes into my mother's place is talking about it." She looked at Ash. "My mum's place is Claire's," she said. "Bakery in the morning, restaurant in the evening. Best food in Sorry-in-the-Vale. We'll take you there when we have weekend staff meetings."

"I'll look forward to it," Ash said. He still had hold of her hand.

Kami shook hands firmly, then pulled her hand away and walked over to her desk: she needed it to take notes. "I'm Kami Glass," she said once she had a pen and a notepad. She waved at Angela. "This one-woman welcoming committee is Angela Montgomery. Congratulations! You're part of the team. Your first assignment is to go out to the stairs and take some pictures of Angela standing on them slapping her ass."

Angela said, "I'm going back to the cupboard."

They all ended up at the stairs, Kami coming in order to drag Angela and staying in order to interview Ash. Ash ran from the top to the bottom of the stairs a few times, trying to get the best shot of Angela (though there was no way to get a bad shot of Angela, all swishing hair, snapping eyes, and perennial annoyance), and answered all Kami's questions pleasantly, if cagily: Where had the Lynburns been? Oh, all around. Where had he liked living most? Oh, here.

"So, now that you're back, do you think you'll be staying?" Kami looked down at Ash, pen poised over her notepad.

Ash lowered his camera and looked up at her. Light flooded down the corridor, lending his hair a sheen of hazy brightness. "Sorry-in-the-Vale is where we belong," he answered, and for the first time he did not sound calm and lighthearted. He sounded as if he was making a promise, one he intended to keep. "We're going to stay here forever."

❧

Kami woke that night from a dream of being someone else, to the sound of screaming in the woods. She reached for Jared.

He answered, awake too, comforting and curious at once. *Are we going to go see what's happening?*

As soon as the silent voice in her mind asked that, the sound stopped.

Kami told herself to get a grip: she was only allowed to

be a certain degree of crazy. There were always kids messing around in the woods. These noises were perfectly normal.

Through her connection to Jared she could feel again the chill she'd felt earlier today, the knowledge that he was unhappy. *I'll be intrepid another time,* she told him. *I was just dreaming about you. How are you doing?*

Kami had to reach for him across the boundaries they had built up so they could both have their own lives and not look entirely insane. She only got bits and pieces of what Jared was thinking, especially since the summer before last. She thought of it as their decision: Kami had found it was easier to act like he was real, and they'd both made the rules.

She leaned against the boundaries between them now, venturing into his space a little, and tried to make out his feelings. His weariness dragged at her senses, like holding hands with someone who was walking slowly.

Does it matter? he asked.

Of course it matters, Kami said, and pushed at him, bullying a little. *Tell me.*

My mother asked me if I still talked to you, said Jared. *I said yes.*

Neither of them really talked about the other: hearing a voice in your head made you act weirdly enough without discussing the voices. Back when they were kids, when Kami had been young enough to send an English penny to an address she'd made up somewhere in America, their mothers had both been worried. Kami's mother had been really scared, obviously convinced that Kami might actually be going crazy. Kami had been the only child for years before her brothers arrived. She'd been brought up by young, frantic parents and her grandmother, knowing they all had to work together to make their family work at all. She was supposed to be self-sufficient. She was not supposed to be a problem child who terrified her mother by inventing an entire fantasy life for her imaginary friend.

Her mother's fear had made Kami scared as well, but not scared enough to give Jared up. She stopped asking Jared questions about his life, though, and she stopped talking about Jared to other people. He was her secret, and that meant she could keep him.

Kami did not feel comfortable talking about Jared's mother, but she knew they didn't have a good relationship. She also knew it was irrational and illogical and insane to worry about his family troubles. It was insane to care so much in the first place. He was a voice in her head, after all: she tried not to think about it too much because it made her think she really might be crazy.

Jared filled in the silence. *She wants me to stop talking to you.*

Kami did not let her dread touch him. *And will you stop?* she asked, trying to show him nothing but support.

I told her I had to think about it, said Jared wearily.

Kami curled tighter under the covers, feeling cold. Jared said nothing else. There was silence in her head and silence beneath her window, and still she could not sleep.

Chapter Three
The Secret in the Woods

The first issue of *The Nosy Parker* came out two days later. It was a huge success. Kami was unsurprised, as the entire front page was a certain picture of Angela. Since Angela was wandering around looking like she wanted an excuse to kick someone's kneecaps, Kami was getting all the compliments.

"I really liked your tell-all article about the cricket camp," said Holly Prescott, the second-best-looking girl in school. She kept up with Kami as they made their way through the riot that was the hallway at the end of school. "How old were those kids, eleven?"

"Nine," said Kami. "But old in sin."

Holly laughed. She'd always been nice to Kami, but since she mostly hung around with a succession of guys, or several guys at once, they never really felt like friends. "I've got a few ideas for articles," Holly offered, to Kami's surprise.

Kami was struck by the thought of how many copies a picture of Holly's clear green eyes and clearly dangerous curves would move. "What kind of ideas?" she asked, and smiled.

Holly grinned back and hugged her books to her chest. Ross Phillips stopped in his tracks, obviously wishing he was a biology textbook. "Well, you know I have a motorbike," Holly said. "I was zipping round past Shepherd's Corner, by the woods, you know? And there was this dead badger."

"Animals are always getting knocked down at the Corner," said Kami, not sure where Holly's story was going.

"Yeah," Holly answered. "But this badger hadn't been hit by a car. I mean, I was on my bike, I didn't get a good look at it, but I got a better look at it than someone in a car would've. It had been cut up."

Kami recoiled. "Oh my God."

"I know," said Holly. "And, I mean, maybe I got it wrong, but it just kept bugging me. I started thinking that if some horrible little kids hurt an animal, it'd be smart to put it at the Corner so it'd get run over by a car and it'd look like that's why it died."

Some subtle signal, perhaps the fact that Kami looked like she wanted to be sick, made Holly stop and backpedal. "I'm probably just being paranoid," she said hurriedly. "God, you must think I'm so strange. Look, forget about it, okay?"

"My house is right next to the woods," Kami said, thinking out loud. "We keep hearing stuff like yelling at all hours, waking my brothers. I'd been wondering about it. I'll look into this. Thanks, Holly."

Holly looked half pleased and half terrified. "No problem," she murmured. She left Kami at the top of the school steps with a wave, heading for her motorbike.

From her vantage point on the steps, Kami could see Ash Lynburn's head bent over the exposed engine of a sleek black car, expensive-looking but about twenty years old. It seemed like he was having some issues with it. She went down the steps and came up behind him. "Car trouble?"

Ash banged his head on the car bonnet. "Oh, hey, Kami," he said, giving her a smile even though she'd practically given him a concussion. "No, no car trouble. The car would have to start for there to be trouble." He kicked a tire.

Kami stepped forward to take a look. When she was a kid, her grandmother had decided their mechanic was dishonest and had taught herself and Kami the basics of car repair, and since Sobo had died Kami was the only one who knew how to fix anything at home. "Not a problem," she said. "A wire's loose, that's it. Easy fix." Kami leaned forward and tugged on the offending wire to demonstrate.

Ash puffed out a sharp, frustrated breath. "Right. I'm an idiot." Kami leaned away and he looked from the car engine to her. "I'm sorry, let me try again," he said. "Thank you. I'm in a rotten mood, but I really appreciate it."

"It's okay," Kami said. "Though I will take a favor in exchange. Since you did not spill all the incriminating details I desire in your interview, I want you to help me write an article about moving back to England."

"Moving back?" Ash asked. "I wasn't even born when my parents left."

"I'm still calling the article 'Return of the Lynburns,'" Kami informed him. "And we're taking a picture of you being all lord of the manor, outside on the hill. Do you own, like, an old-fashioned white shirt? Because you should wear it, and maybe it should be all wet, as if you were swimming in the lake."

Ash laughed. "What lake would that be?"

"Any lake. There are two lakes in the woods. Doesn't matter."

"Fixing the car wasn't *that* big a favor," Ash said. "If you want me in a wet white shirt, you're going to have to do something else for me."

Kami raised her eyebrows. "Really?"

"Show me around?" Ash suggested. "I hear this place called Claire's is good. Uh, how watchful is your mum?"

Kami let herself be swayed by his easy charm. "She neglects me horribly. It's kind of tragic."

Ash's eyes lit up. "Great."

Kami'd had exactly one boyfriend in her entire life, and Claud had been a college friend of Angela's brother and a terrible mistake with a goatee. Sometimes guys thought she was cute. But sometimes they measured her up and visibly found her chubby or dressed weirdly or—always a risk—looking like she was listening to the voice in her head.

She certainly wasn't used to attention from guys this attractive. She looked away from Ash and down at the gravel of the parking lot. "So," she said, keeping her tone casual, "why are you in a rotten mood? Someone bullying you at school? You can talk to me, I know how it is. Everyone's always so cruel to the glamorous guy who lives in the big mansion."

"My aunt and my cousin just moved in with us," Ash said, his voice back to its usual light tone. "We're still getting things sorted out so he can go to school, so you haven't had the doubtful pleasure of meeting him yet. We don't exactly get on."

Kami glanced up and saw Ash was studying her. His

habitual pleasant expression had returned. "Let me reference the mansion again," Kami said. "Put the jerk in the south wing, you won't see him for weeks at a time. Or lock him in the attic. The law will not be on your side, but literary precedent will."

Ash looked mildly puzzled, but smiled at the joke anyway. "I'll take that into consideration. Can I offer you a lift home?"

"Nah. I don't really trust your car, buddy," Kami said. "Heard you've been having trouble with it."

She always talked to Jared on her walks home. She reached for the connection to him as she left the school gates, letting him know that the next time there were screams in the woods, they were investigating.

Neither of them mentioned their last conversation.

That night Kami was so jumpy waiting for a scream and trying not to think about Jared that she couldn't sleep. As a result, she spent the following day staggering from one class to the next. Angela gave up asking her what was wrong and just steered her in the right direction through the halls. Kami was wearily relieved when the last bell rang and she could stumble home.

Kami's day wasn't over yet. Her father greeted her at the door and asked if she could watch her younger brothers while he finished up a big project. Kami was used to this. Luckily, Ten and Tomo were absorbed in front of the television, so she was able to drift in and out of a doze while curled up in the window seat.

Kami's mind was turned toward Jared, without her normal barriers up between them. She could not help thinking of how soon she might lose him, and she kept reaching for him without meaning to. If he was gone, she would stop being distracted at odd times, would be a little more normal. Her mother would be so pleased. Everyone would think it was the best thing for her. Except that Kami couldn't think of it as the best thing for her. Not when every time she thought of losing Jared, her heart beat out an insistent rhythm of sheer desolate misery and all she could think about was how she would miss him.

If she thought about him as if he was real, insane though that was, it was different. If cutting ties would make his life better, she could bear it.

I was thinking maybe . . . , Kami said, and thought about him, what was best for him, steadily so he knew she was sure. *Maybe things would be better for you if you do what your mother wants. Maybe it's the right thing to do.*

Jared said, *I don't care.*

Too many of their walls were coming down with their shared distress, blazing a channel open between them. She should pull back. She would in a moment.

I don't want to be sane. I don't want to be normal, said Jared. *I just want you.*

Kami rested her cheek against the cool glass of the window. It was as if he was real for a moment, as if he was close, with just a windowpane between them. Hardly any barrier at all.

Then Tomo laughed at something on the television. Kami turned back to the real world, to share Tomo's laugh

and catch Ten's usually solemn eyes glinting with apprecia-
tion behind his glasses, to home.

🕊

That night Kami woke to the sound of screaming again. She
flailed herself awake, knocking her alarm clock and her lat-
est mystery novel, *The Nefarious Mezzanine,* off her bedside
table in the process. Then she cast away her bedclothes and
seized her flashlight. It was exactly where she'd left it, wedged
between books and her nightlight.

Kami grabbed her coat, shoved her feet into shoes, and
launched herself down the stairs, terrified that the screaming
would stop before she could get there.

The door of their house tended to stick, but now the latch
lifted easily, the door swung open smoothly, and the night air
blew cool through her hair.

Jared, Kami said, reaching out for him. *Want to go on an
adventure?*

You even have to ask?

Kami was fiercely glad he was still there. She stepped out
onto the garden path, shutting the door carefully behind her.
Where the garden ended, the woods began. It was almost
autumn, and the trees were still thick with leaves but more
subdued, closed off as if they were keeping secrets. In the
darkness Kami couldn't see the trees for the forest. She
switched on her flashlight and the circle of light finally found
a path into the woods.

Kami set off. The night had a different quality here, as
if the trees curving over her head gave weight to the air. The
sound of screaming was fainter. It was a far-off sound, but

now that Kami was really listening she thought she heard a whine to it. She didn't know how she had mistaken it for kids' voices.

Kami hurried, feet flying over logs and leaves almost before her flashlight beam found them.

Because God forbid we miss the screaming, said Jared, growing more guarded as they drew closer, the feeling like an arm held out protectively in front her.

The sound was terrible, this near.

I don't want to miss the screaming, Kami told him. She slid her hand into her coat pocket and found her phone in there beside her keys as she ran. *I want to catch them in the act.*

Kami ducked and just missed banging her head on a low-hanging branch. She almost dropped her flashlight and the beam went wide.

The scream stopped abruptly.

The yellow circle of light caught on a wall.

It was rough wood, unpolished, the wall sagging a little. But it was a wall. As Kami drew closer, she was able to make out the shape of something like a sagging hut or maybe a shed, something that had been built.

A thought crept into her head, cold and sly as a draft beneath a door: What if this place had been built just for this?

Kami, run, Jared ordered.

Kami wanted to run, but she wouldn't. Not until she found out the truth. She crept forward.

Kami, break a branch off a tree so you can fight at least!

I can fight bare-handed if I have to, said Kami. She put her hand on the soft, weathered wood of the hut door.

It swung open at her touch.

There were candles, some burning and some blown out, their wax still running liquid and hot. There was a table covered in a white cloth. On the cloth there lay a fox. It was dead. There was blood all over the cloth. Kami knew that if she touched the blood it would still be warm, only just spilled, like the candle wax.

Jared's fear scythed through her, sharp as a blade. That, more than anything, almost made Kami panic.

Kami, run!

But she couldn't run yet. She held the flashlight in one hand and with the other took out her cell. She kept both hands steady as she took picture after picture with her camera phone.

Then she ran, stumbling faster than she had come, back through the night to the safety of home. She called the police as she went.

Chapter Four
Blood and Sunlight

When Sergeant Kenn interviewed Kami, he was very kind, told her she had done her civic duty, and even gave her a quote for the paper.

Kami closed her article on the animal killing in the Vale woods with "The police investigation is ongoing. And so, I can assure my readers, is my own." The second issue of *The Nosy Parker*—Kami had decided to put out two issues in the first week of school, to gain momentum—was even more popular than the first.

"People took home copies for their parents," Kami announced, and did a victory dance in the privacy of her headquarters. "The photocopy machine overheated and broke down. I think I can still hear the sound of it sobbing and wanting to talk about its childhood."

Ash leaned in the doorway, his eyes averted from the sight of Kami dancing. The dance involved flailing, brandishing of a vase of flowers, and most importantly the victory shimmy, so Kami could not really blame him.

"Walk you to class?" he asked.

"Well," Kami said, "sure."

Ash pushed himself off the doorframe and into the room,

toward her. "You did an awesome job out there in the woods," he said. "And with the article."

Kami beamed. "Thank you."

"But I think you and Angela should leave this to the police from now on."

"What an interesting thought," Kami said. "Thank you for sharing it with me. Let me share a thought with you: Actually, I can walk myself to class. And I can also handle myself, so I'll be doing what I want." She shouldered her bag and headed out, moving past him.

"Kami, wait," Ash called out.

She paused at the top of the stairs and looked back. The newspaper headquarters looked great, she thought proudly. The boxes were gone and the desks were shiny nut-brown. Kami had borrowed a few colorful lamps from home and had plans for a filing cabinet. The office looked great, and Ash looked great in it: arms crossed over his chest, staring at her with eyes turned dark blue with concern.

"Whoever's doing this—" he began, then switched thoughts. "What if you got hurt?"

"Here's the thing," said Kami. "Holly came to me with this story because nobody else would have listened to it. And nobody would have listened to me if I'd called the police and said, 'Oh, the kids are making too much noise in the woods.' They're listening to me now because I went out and found something. *I* found something. And it was horrible, and the only way I know how to deal with something horrible is to do something about it. This is *my* story. And I'm not going to give it up. I'm going to see how it ends. You don't get a say."

"I'm getting that impression," Ash remarked. He uncrossed his arms and walked over to where Kami stood, still undecided. "I am worried about you, though."

Kami smiled; she couldn't help it. She wasn't used to guys looking at her with concern, or drawing near her being all conciliatory and handsome. Except Angela's brother, of course, but Rusty hardly counted. "I guess you can be worried if you really want," Kami conceded. She went on tiptoe and kissed Ash on the cheek. She felt him smile, then eased back down and saw him lean in toward her.

"So, you're okay?" Ash murmured.

Kami wasn't sure, despite her exhilaration over the newspaper. The police had scared her. How worried her parents were had scared her more. She kept thinking about that night, and the blood. But her secret fears were for her and Jared: she hardly knew this boy, no matter how beautiful his smile.

She just smiled back at him. She knew her smile was not as convincing as his, but it seemed to be enough. Ash's smile spread, brighter than before, and he leaned down closer. Kami's breath snagged in her throat. She did not move away.

An explosion of noise came from the stairwell: the sound of so many people running and yelling at once that it sounded like an earthquake. Kami and Ash broke apart without ever coming together.

Kami went running down the stairs, Ash right behind her. She rounded a corner and headed down the school steps, then out the doors to the back of the school. There was a courtyard there, raised a few steps above the cricket pitch.

The cricket pitch was chaos.

"What's going on?" Ash demanded behind Kami, just as Holly Prescott came rushing up the steps.

"Your brother is fighting the cricket team," Holly announced, flushed with excitement.

"He's not my brother," Ash snapped, his cool cracking instead of just ruffling for the first time since Kami had met him.

"Who on the cricket team?" Kami asked at once, producing her emergency notebook from her bra.

"Sort of the whole team," Holly said.

Kami went forward, shielding her eyes against the sun's rays. She could only see one person not in cricket whites. All she could make out were shoulders, and a fist going into someone's face.

Miss Mackenzie and Ms. Dollard were both crossing the pitch and moving fast. Kami hurtled down the stairs and got to the combatants at the same time the teachers did. Over the noise Kami yelled: "Any comment for the school newspaper?"

Only the new boy's head turned. The sun was still in her eyes, but she thought he grinned at her over his shoulder. His teeth were dark with blood.

"Hell of a first day," he said.

Then Ash's cousin—the other Lynburn—and four members of the cricket team were marched off to Ms. Dollard's office.

Kami ran back up the steps to Holly, pen at the ready. "What happened?"

Holly looked delighted to be asked. "The way I heard it, Matthew Hughes said something and shoved him, and then the new guy punched him, and, well, you know how the cricket guys stick together—"

"Who won the fight?"

"Some of the team were still carrying their bats," Holly said. "New boy got his ass kicked. I don't mean to pry," she added to Ash. "But does he have issues?"

"Oh, Jared's nothing but issues," Ash said bitterly. "And the urge to take them out on other people." He set off toward the principal's office

"Wait," Kami said, and her voice caught on the word. "His name's Jared?"

Ash gave her an impatient glance. "Yeah, so?"

"Nothing."

Ash nodded and walked away.

It was nothing, Kami told herself. Plenty of people had that name. She just didn't like hearing it out loud.

It made her remember being in London for the first time, holding her dad's hand and enjoying the novel sensation of having nobody know her name or her entire life history, having nobody even notice she was Asian because it was an everyday unremarkable thing there. She'd heard someone shout out "Jared!" and spun around, stood up on the stone parapet of Blackfriars Bridge, and looked for him.

But Kami wasn't a child anymore, to search for him in every crowd. It was a name like any other. She still found herself feeling possessive. Jared was hers, his name was his, and it annoyed her that it was shared by some delinquent.

"Hey, he's cute," Holly said, looking after Ash. "Actually, they're both cute. The new guys, I mean. Ash is cuter, but crazy Jared might be more fun."

"Yeah, getting expelled from school and spending your life in a chain gang: such fun." Kami grabbed Holly's elbow and steered her back inside. "I need to talk to this guy."

Holly blinked. "Because he's cute?"

"Because he's crazy," said Kami. "And that's news. Besides, he's a Lynburn, and I want to know about them. That Lynburn seems a little busy just at present. But can you snag him and bring him to me tomorrow?"

"You know," Holly drawled, "I've never had a problem snagging them."

Kami felt Jared reach for her, as if he knew she was thinking about him. *I'm bored,* he said. *What are you doing?*

Talking about hot guys, Kami informed him.

Jared said, *Oh my God.*

You did ask.

It's a topic of absorbing interest, Jared said. *I'm sure. Obviously, as a hot guy myself, I wouldn't know.*

Kami laughed.

I find your skepticism very hurtful, Jared said. *I'm extremely hot. Except not so much in the face.*

If you're saying a lot of people want to buy tickets to your imaginary gun show, Kami said, *I'm very happy for you.*

His amusement rippled through her, making her smile, as she and Holly reached their classroom. Holly was giving her a strange look, which made Kami realize that she had been communing silently with the empty air for too long and had also just laughed at nothing.

"Well, thanks, Holly, you're a pal," Kami said hastily.

Holly hesitated, as if expecting something else, but Kami peeled off and headed for her usual seat beside Amber Green.

Amber gave her a brief smile through the curtain of her fox-red hair and then returned to reading *The Nosy Parker*. Kami beamed at Amber's bent head.

How do you deal with it? Kami asked Jared. *The laughing at nothing and occasionally stopping dead in your tracks.*

I have a system where when I stop, I lean casually against something, Jared told her. *It makes people think I'm a bad boy. Or possibly that I have a bad back.*

Kami laughed again and Amber gave her a familiar look that said she was worried Kami was crazy. Kami's laughter subsided and she flipped open her notebook to start plotting her interview with the delinquent.

Holly was bringing him to her tomorrow. She had to be prepared.

❧

It was dark by the time Kami got to Angela's house to discuss their future of unstoppable investigative journalistic team-work. The Montgomerys had bought their house because they thought Sorry-in-the-Vale was quaint and would be a great place to raise the kids. One year and two extensions on their house later, they both got so bored they seized any excuse to go up to London and leave the kids on their own. Angela never talked about it and never seemed to miss them.

The house had once been pretty but now resembled a sad little donkey with two oversize saddlebags. Light shone from one window, and the gate was hanging open, which was a mercy because Angela always took forever to get up off the sofa and buzz Kami in. Kami pushed the gate open farther and headed for the back door.

It had gotten very dark, very fast. She could only make out the pale side of the house and the stir of leaves that was the yew tree by the wall. Even walking carefully, Kami almost tripped over the hose.

The near miss jolted the breath out of Kami for a second. She heard the soft, almost stealthy sound of someone else breathing—which was when an arm locked around her throat and a male voice whispered in her ear: "Don't move."

Chapter Five
Listen for a Whisper

Kami's fingers bit into a pressure point on the arm at her throat. When the hold loosened, she went down low, keeping her grip steady, and used her body to trip the guy and flip him into the wall. "Rusty!" she snapped. "Quit doing that."

Rusty's eyes gleamed up at her from his crouch, laughing-bright even in the darkness. "I'm keeping you on your toes, Cambridge," he said. "Transforming you from a simple English schoolgirl to a lean, mean fighting machine."

Kami put out a hand and gave him a push on the forehead that tipped him back against the wall. "You're right, I am feeling meaner."

Rusty got up and held the back door open for her because he was a gentleman, even if he was also an incredibly annoying person who kept attacking her. Kami called out for Angela, her voice echoing off all the white surfaces in that spotless kitchen, and Rusty leaned against the doorframe as if all the exertion had exhausted him.

At first glance, Rusty was a masculine version of his sister—tall, dark, and incurably lazy. He had the same athletic frame, which he draped on walls and furniture as if simply too weak to support himself. He had the same classic features and almost the same black hair, though his was shot with the red highlights that gave him his nickname.

In reality, Angela and Rusty were markedly different. They were even lazy in quite different ways. Rusty was sleepily good-natured and thought Angela wasted energy being cranky. Angela refused to cope with being hassled by teachers, so she was brilliant at school, while Rusty had failed out of Kingston University after one term.

Rusty had also been the one to introduce Kami to her one and only boyfriend, Claud of the unfortunate goatee. She didn't hold it against him: it was hard to hold anything against Rusty.

"Oh, Rusty, why did you let her in?" Angela said. "We could have just lain down on the floor until she went away. We could've had a nice floor nap."

"Have you guys eaten?" Kami asked. "I'm starving."

"Cooking is so much trouble," Rusty said mournfully.

"You could order in," Kami suggested.

"Delivery people are so annoying," Angela responded.

Kami opened the cupboard doors and began rummaging around for supplies. She found a half-empty packet of pasta and waved it about in triumph. "I'm going to cook something."

Rusty drifted over to the kitchen island, where he sank onto a stool. "So little and so busy," he remarked with solemn wonder. "Like a squirrel."

Kami threw a piece of pasta at him. He caught it and then, as if he only worked in fast-forward and slow-motion, brought it gradually to his mouth and chewed it with great deliberation.

"Rusty attacked me in the garden," Kami announced.

"Hey, women pay good money to have me attack them," Rusty mumbled.

"That makes it sound as if you're running a one-man bordello."

Rusty leaned his chin in his hand, the effort of keeping his head upright obviously too much for him. "That'll always be the dream."

Women really did pay good money to have Rusty attack them. He rented a room above Hanley's grocery shop and taught self-defense. It was the sole thing in the world Rusty was passionate about, and that meant Angela and Kami had been jumped at regular intervals growing up.

"What do you have now?" Kami inquired, chopping onions. "Six clients?"

"Eight, counting you guys."

"You can't count us," Angela said, strolling into the kitchen. "We don't come to your stupid classes, and we don't pay you."

"My parents give me a roof over my head in return for teaching their only daughter to defend herself from predators," said Rusty. "And I teach Cambridge because she feeds me and because she'll need these skills to get out of situations she will inevitably throw herself into. It's all very equitable. Which reminds me, Angela, I'm a crazed drug dealer, desperate for the change in your jeans pockets. What do you do?"

"No," Angela commanded. "Don't!"

Rusty tackled her at the knees and Angela fell backward with a scream of rage. Kami began to fry her onions, whistling over the noise.

"So, I was looking through websites about animal sacrifice on the Internet," Kami announced to distract herself. "Apparently it's a feature in Satanic rituals."

"Wow," Rusty remarked, his voice slightly muffled. "I sure hope this conversation continues over dinner."

"Wait," Angela said, expertly twisting Rusty's arm. "I thought we were dealing with kids? Are we talking twelve-year-old Satanists?" She paused. "Actually, that makes a lot of sense. I suspect those kids from the cricket club."

Kami hadn't really expected Angela and Rusty to take this seriously. They knew what Kami had seen, but they hadn't seen it themselves: it wasn't real to them.

She aired a few more thoughts while making their pasta anyway.

"It wasn't just cruelty. It was either a ritual or staged to look like one. If it was staged, why?" Kami asked. "If it was real, people don't perform rituals, Satanic or otherwise, for no reason. I've done my research. They do it for favor from the gods, for good winds, to tell the future."

"So the answer is that they are crazy?" Angela inquired. "Shocker."

"Don't think about the answer, think about the question," Kami said. "The question is—what do they want?"

Neither Rusty nor Angela had an answer. Kami didn't have an answer herself and didn't come up with one during dinner or her walk home alone. Angela had offered to walk her home, which was so unheard of that it made Kami laugh.

"Just take care of yourself, you hyperactive midget," Angela had instructed, eyes narrowed like a cross cat, and sent Kami on her way with a shove.

Sorry-in-the-Vale by night was different, the small streets seeming to narrow and twist, the Georgian and Victorian houses becoming specters from horror movies. Above the town Aurimere House stood, windows bright but narrow, making the great black edifice look awake and aware. As if the house was a giant's head, watching them all with sly eyes, and soon the giant's hand would rise from the earth and scoop their whole town away.

Kami reached for Jared. *You there?*

Always, he said, and her uneasiness faded. Kami never really walked anywhere alone.

The next day was Friday. Kami felt strongly that Fridays should not be full of disappointments.

The disappointments started when their headmistress, Ms. Dollard, stopped by the newspaper office to say: "Friday also means that the entire school closes promptly, including Room 31B."

"I'm calling it my headquarters now," Kami said, looking around proudly.

"I'm ignoring that," Ms. Dollard said. "And I'm shutting everything up at five sharp. Do me a favor and go out and perform one of the activities I hear the youth enjoy this Friday, like defacing public property."

Kami was sad to be parted from her headquarters, but it struck her that the library had both the Internet and reference books.

The disappointments continued after school. Kami had arranged to meet Holly, who was supposed to bring Ash's delinquent cousin, on the school steps. At five sharp, she was outside the school with a notepad and pen in hand. It wouldn't take long to type out the interview later, Kami thought. She expected him to talk mainly in surly grunts.

It was one of those September days when the sunshine was mellower than summer sunshine but still warmed you. Kami was leaning against the balustrade at the bottom of the steps, basking, when she heard the doors of the school open.

Holly was on her own. She held her hands up. "I tried, boss. I did establish contact with him at lunch, had a little chat with him about our motorbikes." She smiled. "And I think I was right about him."

"That he's crazy?" asked Kami.

Holly's smile spread. "That he might be fun."

"So he's *not* crazy?"

"I didn't say that," Holly said. "My current verdict would be: Crazy eyes. Nice ass."

"I think I want that on my tombstone," Kami said. "Remember my last wishes, if I get involved in a tragic accident with a fruit cart before I can put it in writing. So, what happened?"

Holly shrugged, bouncing down the steps two at a time and going over to her motorbike, sliding her helmet over her curls. "He slipped through my fingers. We were talking about motorcycles, a friend stopped me, and then I looked around and he was gone. Let me tell you, that usually does not happen. Usually I can't lose them even if I'm trying."

"I believe you," said Kami, and sighed. "Well, never mind. We'll get him on Monday." She waved as Holly pulled into the street, then headed on to the library. Guys might disappoint, but she knew journalism would never let her down.

The Sorry-in-the-Vale library was one of the ugliest buildings in town. It was a squat brown-brick building that did an amazing impression of a bungalow from the outside and had three stories inside. The roof tiles were crumbly and a strange apricot shade. Inside, the worst part was the carpets. They were weirdly mottled orange and brown, as if someone had skinned a vast diseased orangutan.

The best part was a computer with an Internet connection that Kami did not have to share with two brothers, one intent on watching every funny cat video the Web had to offer, and the other having a star-crossed love affair with Wikipedia. It was also full of books, though that side of the enterprise proved trickier than Kami had hoped.

"Hi," Kami said to Dorothy, the head librarian, who bought bread at Claire's every morning and instantly returned Kami's smile. "Can you tell me where I could find books on Satanism?"

Twenty minutes later, she had Dorothy convinced that it was for a school project, and she really did *not* have to telephone Kami's parents. When she finally got away from Dorothy and into the nonfiction section on the top floor, she didn't find any books called *Animal Sacrifice: Why We Do This Completely Disgusting Thing and Who We Sacrificers Are Likely to Be,* but she found a few books that she hoped related to the topic. She piled them by her computer and spent time alternately leafing through them and feeding the printer change so it would print her articles as well as truly horrible pictures of people trying to tell the future with goat entrails.

Kami really didn't think what she'd seen was Satanism. Satanism seemed to involve a lot of specific symbols, and there hadn't been any of them at the hut. This left Kami with absolutely no idea what was going on, her hair frizzed up in the sticky heat of the stuffy room, and a printer coughing and stealing the last of her money.

It was closing time at the library. Kami gave up her day as totally unproductive. She gathered her giant stack of paper and the few books that seemed helpful, and decided that she would rather risk the creaky lift that was a fire hazard than the dark steps that might break her neck.

This meant, of course, that when she walked out of the nonfiction room, she saw the lift doors closing. "Hold the lift!" Kami yelled, and charged forward.

The guy inside pulled the little trick of punching the air as if it was the button to open the lift.

Kami shoved her stack of paper and books between the closing doors. "I said hold the lift, *asshole*!"

The doors opened, giving a low whine as they did so. Kami knew just how they felt.

"Oh, is this the lift?" the guy said in a bored voice. "We call them elevators in America."

Kami curled her lip at him. She couldn't retreat now. There was the principle of the thing to consider, and also the fact that she had left pages scattered on the lift floor. "Do you know what we call guys like you in England?" she asked. "Wait, I believe I may have already mentioned the word." She stepped into the lift with Ash's delinquent cousin.

Part II
Beyond Imagination

I feel that I shall stand
Henceforth in thy shadow. Nevermore
Alone upon the threshold of my door
—*Elizabeth Barrett Browning*

Chapter Six

The Other Lynburn

Holly had been right. Ash was better-looking.

Kami also saw why Holly had called the delinquent Ash's brother. They were alike enough to be brothers, but in this case the fairy-tale prince had been cast into shadow and ruin. Jared literally looked like Ash under a shadow: Ash with a tan, darker blond hair, and dark gray eyes with odd, cold lights in them. Crazy eyes, Holly had said. Cutting across his left cheek, from cheekbone to chin, was a long white scar.

"So you're—" Kami swallowed his name. Even in the cause of getting an interview, she didn't want to call this guy Jared. "The other Lynburn."

The boy crossed his arms. He looked even bigger when he did that. "The one and only other Lynburn," he said, with a bite to his voice that hadn't been there before. "Friend of Ash's, I presume? Great."

Kami stood on the other side of the lift and felt very disinclined to get closer to him. She'd never been comfortable with guys like this, guys with that deliberate angry swagger. He was a shade taller than Ash, a shade broader in the shoulders, which were straining against a battered brown leather jacket. All the shades and shadows of him added up to something that put her teeth on edge. Kami wished she hadn't taken the lift. But she wasn't going to abandon her research on the floor because some jerk had crazy eyes. She knelt down and gathered up the papers she had spilled.

The boy didn't offer to help. He did look down at the picture nearest him: a colorful printout of a squirrel with its head cut off. His eyebrows rose.

Kami met his gaze defiantly.

"I've had days like that," he remarked, his American accent all sharp consonants. His voice was rough.

"But where have you had days like that?" Kami asked. Her hands were full, but she figured she could remember the interview. "Where do you hail from?"

"San Francisco," he answered after a reluctant pause, as if it was privileged information.

Her papers collected, Kami retreated to her side of the lift, cradling them against her chest, though she had to admit the chances of him mugging her for her decapitated-squirrel pictures were not high.

The lift creaked to a halt.

The boy cursed.

"It's fine," Kami told him. "Sometimes you just have to press the button a few times."

"Great," he muttered.

He moved toward her, and Kami's heart slammed against her ribs. She stared up at him. He stabbed the button of the lift, then leaned away. His expression had not changed, but she was certain he'd noticed her reaction.

This was no way to conduct an interview. Kami tried to smile charmingly. "So, tell me," she said, reviewing her interview questions in her head and choosing one at random. "What are your three greatest fears?"

He hesitated, and she thought he was going to refuse to tell her, as if he did have some secret fear.

The next instant he answered in a bored drawl, and his uncertainty had obviously existed only in her mind. "Number three: large, unfriendly dogs. Number two: small, inquisitive people. Number one: being trapped in this elevator. Why are you asking me all these questions?"

"The people have a right to information," Kami told him.

"Well, I'm not in the mood," he said. "Leave me alone."

Kami looked around the confines of the lift. The other Lynburn was already taking up more than half of the available space. "Yeah," she said under her breath. "That should be no problem." She was deeply thankful when the lift actually moved.

They leaned back against their respective sides of the lift, hugging the walls, and Kami mentally placed herself elsewhere.

So, what's going on with you? she asked Jared. At exactly the same time, he asked her the same question.

Amusement rolled through them both. Kami found herself smiling. She saw the delinquent smile too, mouth a subtle curve. His face went grim again as he noticed her watching. He probably thought her smile meant she was flirting with him. "Don't worry," she told him. "You're not my type."

He looked away from her. "Back at you."

I'm not doing much, said Jared, warm in her mind, the amusement lingering. *Just stuck in an elevator with this creepy Asian girl giving me a death glare.*

Kami's whole body recoiled. She was just staring at him, her vision blurry around the edges with panic. When the lift doors opened, she pushed herself off the wall because this wasn't possible, because she was leaving the library and going home and never laying eyes on this guy ever again, not if she could help it.

His hand shot out and slammed down on a button. The doors closed and he slammed another hand on the lift wall, close to her head. The clang reverberated in her ears. He was standing next to her suddenly, much too close, bowed down so she was looking directly into those cold eyes. "Kami."

Kami wasn't shaking. The world was shaking her, the world was shaking apart and about to fall to pieces. Nothing made sense anymore. "Jared?" she whispered. Her voice was changed like everything else, sounding as if it did not belong to her. She lifted a hand, seeing her fingers tremble in the space between them, up to touch his face.

Jared grabbed her wrist.

They stood absolutely still for a moment, looking at each other. Kami didn't dare move. She could feel her pulse pounding against his palm. He was real. He was here, and she was scared.

He let go of her and stepped back.

They were on opposite sides of the lift again, just like before, except now he was watching her. The cold lights had swallowed up his eyes: they were pale and awful, the kind of eyes you might fear watching you in the darkness when you walked home alone. His feelings hit her, not like having someone reaching out but like someone throwing something at her. She had never felt anything like this before in her life.

It was like being enveloped by a storm with no calm center, with no calm anywhere to be found. Kami felt blinded by it, by Jared's fury and panic and, above all, his black terror.

The link between them had become an onslaught. Kami could not just tell what Jared was thinking, she could feel it. She could not escape, could not untangle the strands of herself from him. She tried to visualize walls in her head, shields that she could hide behind, feeling both exposed and lost.

"Stop it," she said, her voice catching.

"You stop it!" he whispered back.

They sounded like terrified children, and strangers who hated each other. Kami could not tell who was the most afraid.

The doors of the lift opened again with a cheerful little ping. The fluorescent lights of the library spilled in over their tense tableau. Kami could see Dorothy at the checkout desk in her fuzzy pink cardigan, squinting over in their direction. She saw a ripple pass through Jared's body, like the tremor that moved through wild animals just before they ran. For an instant she thought that he would simply bolt.

She was wrong.

First he took one step and closed the distance between them. She was trapped between the wall and his body, looking up into the strange light of his eyes.

"Stay away from me," he hissed in her ear. Then he exited the lift with so much force that it rocked.

Kami came out a moment later, blinking in the light. She was not walking steadily.

"Are you all right?" Dorothy asked, leading Kami around behind the desk and sitting her in Dorothy's own chair. "Was that Lynburn boy bothering you? He came in with a letter from Nancy Dollard saying that he needed a pile of books to get up to scratch in school and to rush his library membership through. I knew I shouldn't have let a Lynburn in. I wish they'd never come back. They don't change, and I don't believe in their laws, or their lies."

"Their laws?" Kami asked, dazed. She was aware she should be coaxing this information out of Dorothy, but her brain felt like a shattered mirror, all sharp fragments and no use left in it.

"That boy's grandparents made a law that nobody would hurt the people of the Vale."

"Isn't that good?" Kami wondered if she was hallucinating this conversation in her state of shock.

"Doesn't it make you wonder who was hurting them before?" Dorothy patted Kami's back with a heavy, concerned hand. "Tell me you're all right."

"I'm fine," Kami said numbly.

She instantly proved herself a liar by putting her head down on the cool plastic of the desk, in the cradle of her arms.

She had two choices. Either have a nervous breakdown in front of a librarian or pull herself together. After a moment with her head in her arms, she sat up and told Dorothy that she really was fine, she'd just been startled, and she was okay to walk home alone. She left the library with a weak wave.

It occurred to Kami that she might have left Dorothy with the impression that Jared had exposed himself to her in the lift. If so, it served Jared right. She crossed her arms to protect herself from the hungry bite of the night wind. She was determined to think practically about the situation, because if she didn't she was going to lose it completely.

She still found herself stumbling through the night as she cut across the Hope family's fields, colder than she should have been, lost in a familiar place. Her mind was enemy territory now. There was a stranger in it. She felt invaded and abandoned at once. She had stopped wishing for this and dreaming of it years ago. She'd had to.

It wasn't fair that he was real now. She was so angry, she felt like she wanted to kill him. She felt like he'd killed the Jared she knew, crazy as that was. She had to stop it, stop being crazy: she had to go home and put her thoughts in some sort of order, get herself under some sort of control. She kept visualizing those walls, to protect herself from him and keep him away.

She would handle this in the morning. She was going to sort everything out.

The wind rose up with a sudden shriek, the trees raking clawed fingers against the night sky. Across the fields Aurimere House glowed like a ghost in the darkness. Kami made out a black shape standing in her path. Her heart beat a frantic tattoo against her ribs until she realized that it was just the Hope Well.

She was staring straight ahead, the wind howling in her ears. It must have been some sixth sense instilled by years of Rusty jumping her from behind. She had no other explanation for why she suddenly dodged, but whatever made her do it, it saved her life.

The blow hit the side of her head rather than the back.

Kami staggered, blackness shimmering before her eyes, but she was still conscious when she was shoved between her shoulder blades. Panic cleared her head for a moment as she was airborne, the sick feeling of falling turning her stomach. Then she hit the water at the bottom of the well.

Kami! Jared shouted in her head.

Kami went under, up, and under again. She reached out and dug her fingers into the crevices between the stones. The spaces were tiny and the stones were slick, but she clung anyway. The bursts of heat at her fingertips told her that she was rasping the skin right off her hands, but the pain helped her stay aware.

Her head was a throbbing ache, but she couldn't lose consciousness. She felt her grip on the stones slipping and did not know if it was the slickness of the stones or her own grip slackening. Kami was low in the water without even being aware she'd slid down until icy water touched her lips and filled her mouth with bitterness.

Kami clawed for a higher handhold, but her palms found nothing but wet stone. She did not know if she could have grasped a handhold if she had found one. She was losing hold of everything, it was all being wiped out, panic and fury and Jared. She knew nothing but the coldness of the well water and the heaviness of her own limbs dragging her down as blackness flooded her mind and she sank.

Kami. Kami.

"Kami!"

Kami coughed well water down Jared's back, spluttering,

the taste of stale water and bile thick in her mouth, her lungs filled with searing pain.

"Oh, thank God," Jared said. "I couldn't work out how to hit you and hold on to you at the same time."

"Hit me?" Kami croaked. "I've had enough of this abusive behavior. And we've only just met! You're making a terrible first impression."

She coughed and her throat came up dry this time. She was distantly aware that she was still up to her neck in well water. She felt mostly numb, as if part of her mind was floating about halfway up the well. Kami figured that was probably a good thing, since what she could feel of her body, her head and lungs and the chill in her bones, felt so awful.

Something else she felt was Jared. He was holding her against a wall for the second time today, but as this time it was keeping her from drowning, Kami thought she might let it go. "Jared?" she said, weakly questing for information even though her mind felt pretty numb as well. She lifted her arms and locked her hands behind his neck.

"Yeah?" said Jared.

"What are you doing here?"

"Well," Jared said, his voice sounding strained, "I don't really understand it myself, but I was in this elevator—"

"I remember that," Kami said. "Honestly, Jared, one thing at a time. Why are you in the well with me? This is a really bad rescue!"

"You lost consciousness and slipped under the surface of the water!" Jared pointed out. "There was no time."

"But now we're both trapped! Now we're both going to die!"

"No, we're not," said Jared. "I called the police as I was running to the well. I'm sure they're coming."

"Did they say they were coming?" Kami asked suspiciously. "Or did you shout 'Kami's in the well!' and then jump in the well too, thus losing your phone and making sure that the police think it was some kids playing a dumb joke?"

Jared paused. He was breathing quickly, the dreamy part of Kami noticed, his chest rising and falling hard. She wasn't sure if it was because he'd had to run so fast, because he'd had to dive to grab her, or if it was panic.

"Alternate plan," Jared said. "Do you have a very intelligent collie who might communicate through a system of barks to your parents that little Kami is in the well?"

Kami closed her eyes and leaned her cheek against the wet planes of Jared's collarbone. "We're going to die." Something else dawned on her. "And where is your *shirt*?"

"Let me explain," said Jared. "I had just gone to bed, like a reasonable person, when you decided to get tossed into a well like a crazy person. And then it was a matter of some urgency to reach you. You're lucky I tripped over my jeans on the way out the door."

"You leave your jeans on the floor?" Kami asked, horrified. "You're *messy* on top of everything else? This day just keeps getting worse."

Jared had nothing to say to that. Perhaps he was overcome with shame at his slovenly habits, she thought dimly. The well water seemed to be getting warmer.

"Kami, keep talking!"

Jared's shouting hurt her head, which was inconsiderate

of him. "You're so mean," Kami marveled. "You have a leather jacket and you are just so mean!"

"Keep talking," Jared commanded. "Stay awake."

"If you were in bed, what did you do with your pajamas?"

"I don't own any pajamas."

"That is so sad," Kami said. "Boys can have pajamas too, you know. Tomo and Ten both have lots of pajamas. Tomo's favorite pair is red with trains on it." Her voice seemed to be floating away from her too, up in the air with that crucial bit of her mind.

It wasn't so bad now, Jared being real. He was holding on to her tight. She was certain he would not let her drown. She couldn't see him, which helped. She couldn't remember *why* she couldn't see him, until it occurred to her that she'd closed her eyes. Even when she pried her eyes open, all she saw was his collarbone painted ghostly gray in the well-dim light.

She gave up and laid her forehead back down on Jared's shoulder. He was shaking, she noticed, but even shaking and wet, he was still warmer than she was.

Her fingers came unlinked from behind Jared's neck, and now they were resting on the solid support of Jared's arms. She didn't think she could keep hold of him. But that was all right. He wouldn't let her drown. "Jared?"

"Yes?"

Kami closed her eyes. "Hey, Jared."

"Hey, Kami," said Jared. His voice was gentle. Everything went quiet and dark, and he was still there.

Kami was sorry when the police rescued them and she was wrenched back into consciousness and agony. Her mother was there: someone had called, and she must have shut the restaurant early. For some reason, that filled Kami with more worry than anything else, as if it was confirmation that this was serious. Her parents were not supposed to put themselves out for her. Kami was meant to be self-sufficient.

Kami curled on the stretcher, shudders wringing her body, her teeth chattering hard, and her head hurting worse and worse with every chatter. "Someone pushed me in the well," she told her mother.

"Did you see who, my darling?" asked Mum, who was not usually given to endearments.

Sergeant Kenn was asking Jared the same question, though he was not calling Jared "darling." Actually, it didn't sound like he liked Jared much. "If you weren't there, how do you know someone pushed her?" Sergeant Kenn asked.

"Well . . . ," said Jared.

"And what were you doing, running through a strange town at night?"

"I was jogging?" Jared offered.

"Without your shirt or your shoes?"

"Uh," said Jared.

The injustice forced Kami to sit up, even though Mum tried to make her lie back down. The EMTs chose this moment to load her in the ambulance, talking about taking her to the hospital in Cirencester.

Kami waved her hands at them furiously. "Stop!" she ordered. "Stop it, all of you! Jared didn't push me down the well."

Jared was leaning against the well and away from Sergeant Kenn, arms crossed defensively over his bare chest. He looked hunted, as if he did not realize Kami would take care of things.

"He would never do something like that," said Kami. "And he didn't kill his father."

There was a hollow silence. Jared looked smaller to Kami suddenly, leaning against the well with his wet head bowed, shivering in the night air.

Kami tried to go to him, but the effort made her dizzy. Her mother pushed her down flat on the stretcher. Then she was strapped down and loaded into the ambulance, despite her protests. "Mum, stop them," Kami begged at last. "I have to stay with Jared. I have to tell them—"

Mum betrayed her by climbing into the ambulance after her and taking one of Kami's cold hands in both of hers. The ambulance door shut, so Kami could not even see what was happening to Jared. Then her mother bent forward as if she was about to tell a secret.

"Kami, sweetheart," she murmured, her bronze hair falling like a veil between Kami and the rest of the world. "I know you're hurt and you're scared, but you have to listen to me. Whatever you do, never, *never* go near that boy again. It is not safe."

Kami turned her face away. "He didn't push me," she said. "He didn't."

Chapter Seven
You Are Not Safe

When Kami woke the next morning, the walls of the hospital ward, white and spotless as her hospital sheets, seemed to be mocking her. The minutes stretched on and on, but at last her dad came. He slipped in the door past a nurse, saying, "Kami, I know all the other kids are throwing themselves down wells now, but your mother and I have a firm policy of no danger sports until you're eighteen."

The nurse gave him a startled look because of the perfect English and the Gloucester accent. Jon Glass, born and raised in the Vale, gave her an amused look back.

Kami's grandfather Stephen had been the wandering soul and the last member of the Glass family, who had been farming in Sorry-in-the-Vale for years. He had sold off the farm, but he'd kept the family home, even while he spent years wheeling and dealing in Japan, where the economy was booming. He brought his Japanese wife to the Vale for a visit as they went through Europe. She was going to have a baby, and he'd thought that she should have a holiday. They stayed for the rest of their lives, which for him was less than a week. With him dead and her only asset the house, Megumi Glass was stranded in a tiny English town where everyone found her alien and suspect.

"Have mercy, Dad," said Kami. "Tell me you're here to rescue me before they break out the Jell-O."

"I even brought you clean clothes." Kami's dad held out her headband with the tiny pair of gold spectacles attached to one side.

"You are a god," Kami told him.

"All I ask in return is your eternal reverence and worship," Dad said. "Also, it would be nice if you did the ironing occasionally."

Getting out of the hospital and into the car made Kami's headache worse. She rested her head against the car window for the first part of the drive, watching the green fields roll by and be replaced by hills, curving gently on all sides. On the hill farthest away from them, as their car began the gradual drop down, was Aurimere House, witnessing her return.

"Dad," Kami asked, "what do you know about the Lynburns?" She watched him carefully, expecting something like the fear on Mum's face at the very mention of that name.

Instead her father glanced back at her, unconcerned. "Not much," he said. "The twins were a few years older than me."

This was a detail that nobody else had mentioned. Kami could not believe she had been pestering everyone else in town when her father had been willing to offer up information all this time.

"The twins?" repeated Kami.

"Rosalind and Lillian Lynburn," her father said. "I knew who they were, of course, but I don't think they ever spoke to me. They held themselves apart, being the girls from the manor. Rosalind Lynburn got together with an American and moved away, and Lillian married Rob Lynburn and they moved as well. I heard Lillian and Rob went to check on Rosalind, but I guess they went traveling, as you don't have to search for family for seventeen years. Even your mother answers her email more often than that."

Kami grinned up at him and asked, "Who is Rob Lynburn?" Aside from Ash's father and not Jared's, since Dad was talking about him as if he was still alive.

"He was a cousin, I think," Dad said. "He lived with the Lynburns. Everybody always said he was going to marry one of the twins, though Lillian was dating someone else for a while. Edmund Prescott, I think it was, but he left town. People were a bit nasty about it. Said he was running away from Lillian. I don't think it broke Lillian's heart. She married her cousin Rob a few years later."

Ash was shockingly attractive for someone whose parents were cousins, Kami thought. "Strange they'd want to move back, if they don't have any friends here."

"I know, there's nothing for them here," Dad said. "Except the mansion."

Kami snorted and her father turned Shepherd's Corner, down along the road by the woods.

"I may know why they came back," Dad said slowly. "They didn't have friends here, but you know how this place is, occasionally forgetting we don't live in medieval times. There is always a trace of that feudal worship for the lords of the manor. People never gossip about the Lynburns; they talk about them a lot in reverent tones. They won't get that anywhere else."

Kami remembered Mum's face in the stark lights of the ambulance. Maybe everyone talked about the Lynburns in hushed tones because they were afraid.

"If you want information on the Lynburns, you're asking the wrong parent," Dad added, parking outside their gate.

Kami tried to keep her voice casual as she asked, "Oh yeah?"

"Yeah. Rob Lynburn had an office above Claire's," Dad said. "He'd have lunch at the counter so he could talk to her every day. Who could blame the guy? Your mother always was the most beautiful girl in town."

Like Angela, Kami thought with a tiny sigh. It was just her luck that she spent her life surrounded by amazingly beautiful women.

"You okay, kiddo?"

Kami blinked and looked over at her father. The expression he wore was unusually serious. Her parents had been so young when they had Kami; her grandmother had always been the adult of the house, and her father mostly joked around with her as if he was Angela or Rusty, as if they were just pals together. It was strange and touching to see him protective.

Kami gave her father a piteous look. "I'm just really tired. I can't wait to go up to my room and sleep."

Dad held open the door for her. "You got it," he said. "I'll keep those mini mutants we found in the sewers and pretend are your brothers downstairs, okay?" He put an arm around her shoulders as they walked into the house, and Kami leaned against him a little more heavily than she had to. He kissed her on the forehead before she climbed into bed, and gently closed her bedroom door as Kami lay there feeling guilty.

The instant she heard him walking down the stairs, she jumped out of bed. Jared was resolutely silent in her head, all his walls up, but Kami couldn't stay furious at someone who had saved her life, and she couldn't let things continue like this. She was shrugging her coat back on when it occurred to her that she had just been in the hospital, and her parents would be legitimately frantic if they discovered she was gone. So she tore a page out of her notebook and wrote her parents a message: "Dear Mum and Dad, I hope you don't read this, but if you do, you should know that I haven't been kidnapped or abducted by aliens. I had to run an errand that can't wait. I'll be home before dark. Kami."

She left the note on her pillow and crept downstairs, past the living room, where she could hear the television and her family's voices blaring. She opened the front door quietly and slipped down the path. She went up the road by the woods, headed straight for Aurimere House.

It was a fifteen-minute walk until the road rose sharply up and away from the woods, and Kami started to feel nervous as she ascended. The road to Aurimere was so steep that anyone who made their way to the manor would be bound to arrive out of breath, hot, and already not at their best, struggling the most at the exact moment when the road curved and the wall of the manor appeared. Following the curve, Kami's line of sight hit the front of the mansion just as the sunlight struck it full force. Since the fifteenth century, the Lynburns had been building onto the house. It was a mass of contradictions: medieval and Tudor and Georgian architecture, all made of the same pale gold stone. The great bay windows blazed, the wood of the door glowed, and above the door was a carving in stone: a gate with a sword struck through it. Beneath the carving there were words engraved in the stone: YOU ARE NOT SAFE.

Not exactly a welcome mat, Kami thought as she grasped the iron knocker, wrought in the shape of a woman's head with weeds in her hair. She brought it down hard four times.

The door to Aurimere House creaked open.

Framed in the doorway stood a woman who was tall while giving the impression she was small, beautiful while giving the impression she was plain. She had long pale hair rippling from her pale face. She looked like the ghost of Aurimere.

"Um, hello," said Kami.

The woman's eyes went wide, as if she really was a ghost and she was startled that Kami could see her. "How may I help you?"

"My name's Kami Glass," Kami said. She saw the shudder that went right through the woman's thin frame.

"I'm Rosalind Lynburn, Jared's mother." Rosalind Lynburn bowed her fair head, as if admitting to a crime. "I heard something happened on Friday night," she almost whispered. "If he hurt you—if he scared you, I am truly sorry. I don't know what I can say."

Kami glared. "He *saved* me. I came to *thank* him. Is he here?"

Rosalind hesitated, wavering like a reflection in water,

then turned with a shimmer of her pale skirts. Kami could barely hear her feet on the stairs.

Rosalind had not invited Kami in, so Kami just poked her head inside and saw the wide gray flagstones and the vaulted ceiling, its arches dark with age and shadow. There were a couple of narrow windows with diamond panes that alternated crimson and clouded glass.

The sound of footsteps was clearer now, above Kami's head, retreating to the back of the mansion. Kami counted the steps and tried to measure where Jared's room might be.

The manor was all stone and arches, turning echoes into ghosts. Jared heard his mother coming long before she knocked. She didn't wait for him to tell her to come in. He'd always wondered why she bothered knocking, until he met Aunt Lillian, Uncle Rob, and Ash and saw that they all did it. Being polite and imperious at the same time was the Lynburn way.

The curtains were closed. He had actual velvet curtains like you might have at a theater. Jared thought it was ridiculous. He hadn't opened the curtains; the show wasn't going on, not today.

Jared leaned against the wall and watched his mother walk over to the window, the point of the room farthest from where he was. Rays of sunlight stabbed like golden knives through the chinks in the curtains, toward her bowed head.

"That girl is here," she said. "The one who took that tumble down the well."

It was not exactly a surprise to Jared. Awareness of her

kept tugging at the edges of his mind, as if her voice was always just on the cusp of his hearing. He had to choose not to listen, or he would be able to make out the words.

"I didn't push her," he told his mother. Not for the first time.

"Oh no," she said. "She fell down the well. Your father fell down the stairs. Funny how people fall down all around you." Her lip curled.

Jared thought of Kami, suddenly and terribly real. He'd had his arms around her in the well, knew the precise dimensions of her. She was so small he could crush her.

"I knew we should not have brought you," Mom said. "The Lynburns built this town on their blood and bones."

"That was their first mistake," Jared said. "They should've built a city on rock and roll."

Uncle Rob would have laughed, and Aunt Lillian would have smiled her chilly smile. His mother looked at him, and he saw her lips tremble with the effort of doing so, with how afraid she was.

"This town will only make you worse," she whispered. "Being a Lynburn means we hurt each other. Being a Lynburn means we hurt everyone."

Jared turned his face from the sight of his mother. He stared at the curtains, the velvet drapes that seemed black in the gloom, shutting all the brightness out. "Send her away."

Chapter Eight
Yet She Says Nothing

Kami heard the sound of Rosalind's steps returning and leaned away from the threshold, hands behind her back, trying to look as if she was admiring the weather.

Rosalind looked even more wavering than she had before. "He doesn't want to see you," she said, her voice barely there. "He doesn't want you here."

It was weird, having a parent be rude to you, even if she was just delivering someone's message. Kami flinched. "Okay," she said uncertainly. She waited for a moment, expecting Rosalind to offer excuses or apologies, but Rosalind did nothing but stand at the threshold, watching Kami with her pallid eyes.

Jared, what the hell? Kami demanded.

Jared was as silent as his mother. Kami bowed her head and retreated. On her way down the road, she turned at the sound of footsteps and looked up into Rosalind's face.

"Don't come back," Rosalind whispered, and fled. The door to Aurimere House slammed behind her.

Kami stood stricken.

How dare she? How dare Jared?

Her own mother couldn't warn her off, and neither could

his. She was not going to have a piece of her soul closed off from her. She was not going to be chased away.

Kami ran back up the road and headed around the rear of the mansion, pushing open the unlocked gate to the garden. The gate towered above her, depicting delicate wrought-iron women with flowers falling from their hair, but it swung open easily at her touch. She stumbled as she came into the garden. It had once been the kind of garden tended by gardeners. The curves and rectangles of it could still be made out, but order had been drowned in vivid floods of poppies, dahlias, and cornflowers. The deep red sunburst of a crape myrtle exploded through the dark boughs of a yew to embrace a bridal autumn cherry tree.

Kami almost fell over the husk of a tree trunk, swathed now with the red ribbons of love-lies-bleeding. She waded through the garden until she was at the back of the house. Kami didn't actually have to figure out which room was Jared's. She knew which one was his because the curtains were closed and she could feel him sulking behind them.

Kami strode through a froth of daisies to a half-fallen wall that might once have been part of a fortress, but was now a tumble of stones studded with spiky yellow blooms. She bent down, rummaging in the wild tangle of garden around her feet, and chose a pebble. A large pebble. Kami wound her arm back, took careful aim, and threw.

The "pebble" crashed through both glass and curtain.

There was the creak of an old sash window being thrust open, and Jared's head and shoulders appeared at the window. "Hark," he said, his tone very dry. "What stone through yonder window breaks?"

Kami yelled up at him, "It is the east, and Juliet is a jerk!"

Jared abandoned Shakespeare and demanded, "What do you think you're doing?"

"Throwing a pebble," said Kami defensively. "Uh . . . and I'll pay for the window."

Jared vanished and Kami was ready to start shouting again, when he reemerged with the pebble clenched in his fist. "This isn't a pebble! This is a *rock*."

"It's possible that your behavior has inspired some negative feelings that caused me to pick a slightly overlarge pebble," Kami admitted.

Jared's gaze softened slightly. His voice did not. "I saved your life, and you broke my window!"

"You had me turned away from your door like someone selling insurance," Kami said. "And I won't have it. Come down here. We need to talk."

Jared glared at her again, then glared at the ground under his window instead. "Okay," he said abruptly. "I'll come down." He glanced at her once more and amusement touched his face, but not quite a smile. "Don't break anything else until I get to you," he said, and something about his tone was more like the voice inside her head.

Kami thought for a moment that everything might be all right. But as soon as Jared came through the back door, she knew everything was still wrong. He stood in front of her, fists clenched by his sides. He was really tall, *too* tall, and his shoulders were much too wide. It made her feel on edge just to look at him. She found all her muscles locked in sheer physical discomfort. Here he was, her oldest and closest friend, and she couldn't help wishing him out of existence.

"See?" Jared said quietly. "You shouldn't have come."

"That's not true," said Kami. Their eyes met and they both flinched. Kami stared over Jared's shoulder and swallowed a lump in her throat. "It's just weird," she whispered, her voice thin.

Jared laughed bitterly. "No. Really?"

"What I mean is it's strange for *now*. All we have to do is get used to it," Kami said, gathering conviction. She knew from years of listening to him that this was the kind of situation where Jared got too tangled up in his feelings to act. It meant that she had to control her own feelings and make a plan to get them through this. "We need to take this in stages," she announced, spinning away from him. She went to stand on one side of the half-fallen wall.

"Kami?" Jared asked, sounding taken aback.

"Go stand on the other side of the wall," she said, and peered through a chink in the wall until she could see the flash of faded blue cotton that was Jared's T-shirt. "And now stoop, you ridiculously tall person."

She saw him move, the glint of his hair as he sat down in the grass. She sat down too, feeling him reach out tentatively in her mind. She reached back.

His voice in her head was familiar and soothing. *You're just tiny. It's probably why you're so bossy.*

"You know, Napoleon complexes are entirely misnamed," Kami said. "Napoleon was actually average height. He just had tall bodyguards who stood behind him all the time. Also, we should probably talk out loud as part of the first stage of my plan." She wasn't happy about having to say that to him, not when he had talked to her in her head for the first time since the well. Kami laid her cheek against the crumbling, sun-warmed stone of the wall.

"So, what's going on with you, Kami?" asked Jared, with an effort she could feel. It was a subtle difference, but his voice sounded rusty now, instead of rough, as if he wasn't used to speaking this way out loud.

Kami's mouth curved against the stone. "I'm kind of freaking out."

"Yeah," said Jared. "I don't—I hate—" He stopped.

"Talking like this is very classical of us," Kami suggested. "Think of Pyramus and Thisbe."

Jared spoke again, sounding helpless, but less like he wanted to hit something. "I might, if I knew who they were."

Kami hesitated. "You do read, don't you?"

"I haven't lied to you," Jared said, and his voice was angry again. "I read. I just haven't read that."

"They are characters in a Roman myth who had to talk through a wall. Then there was a misunderstanding about one of them being eaten by a lion."

"I hate it when that happens," Jared said. "Also, considering the way things have been going, I am thankful there are no lions in England."

There was a wall between them, but the wall of silence in Jared's head wasn't there anymore. Kami still did not quite dare to come to the place where their minds met, for fear of being shut out again. She skirted the edge of what he was feeling, and stretched out her hand so he could see it on his side of the stone wall.

After a moment, she felt the brush of Jared's fingers against hers. The light touch of skin on skin made electricity crackle through her blood so that it burned and stung in her veins. She had never been so aware of anyone in her life, or so uncomfortable.

Jared's hand closed around hers, their fingers linking. From a careful touch of fingertips, they were suddenly both clinging as if the other had fallen off a cliff and they had to keep hold or risk them slipping away. Jared's hand was a lot bigger than Kami's, fingers callused. It was just a boy's hand, blood and flesh and bone, she told herself fiercely. It wasn't such a big deal.

"I'm sorry I was a jerk," Jared ground out, sounding as if someone else had made him say it against his will. "I just—I hate this."

Kami ventured, not quite meaning to, *I thought you were going to say "I hate you."*

It was like being back in the lift again. She did not have to try to sense what he was feeling: he threw it at her and she could not hold back the storm that enveloped her.

"I don't hate you," said Jared, and *I do. I hate this, I want this to stop, how are we supposed to live with this, and how am I supposed to walk away? You're real and I hate you for it.*

"Stop," Kami whispered, her forehead pressed against the stone, her hand gripping his so hard her bones hurt. She was shaking. "Calm down. There has to be something we can do."

"What?" Jared demanded, through gritted teeth. "What can we do? How can we fix this when reality is the problem?"

Feeling was rushing through her like a tidal wave, something dark and ferocious that might knock her off her feet and drown her without even meaning to.

There weren't words anymore, just a rush of hate and love and rage and such fear, the black terror that had overwhelmed Jared in the lift, the fact that she had never been real and it had been unbearable and now she was real and it was just as unbearable. The thought that someone who existed in real life might betray you.

You were always on my side, said Jared, putting the dread into silent words. *And now . . .*

Kami felt it too, the horror of someone knowing all her secrets, every petty insecurity and small meanness she had ever felt. She felt the dread of Jared as an independent person, of what he might do, what he might think of her, and that she would have to live with those thoughts in her head. Kami wrenched her hand out of his, though he tried to hold on.

Then Kami slid her hand along his arm, her touch light, trying to be reassuring. His breathing had gone harsh and almost panicked. The soft rustle of grass and the sound of her own heart beating were loud in her ears. Her palm traveled over his elbow, followed the tense curve of his bicep, and hit the pulled-taut material of his T-shirt sleeve. She leaned forward and left the shelter of the wall.

Then there was nothing but them, unprotected and real together, both on their knees. She clenched her fist in his T-shirt, put her other arm around those too-broad, too-real shoulders. When he tried to pull away, she held on tight. Kami felt the surrender in his mind a moment before he laid his face in the curve of her neck. The whole world was so real it hurt.

Kami whispered into Jared's hair: "I'm always on your side."

Chapter Nine
Real Now

On Monday morning, Kami sat in the newspaper head-quarters, scribbling a quick list of the articles she had planned for the week. Angela was reading out the interview she'd done with the school nurse.

"So in all circumstances, she just hands students a pain pill and says to tell her if they're having hot flashes," Kami observed.

"Pretty much," said Angela.

"How about that time Ross Philips fell out of the window in the gym and cracked his skull and broke his arm?"

"Ross wasn't having hot flashes." Angela smiled. "I like Nurse Tey's style."

Kami hummed in agreement and wrote herself a note that said INFIRMARY EXPOSÉ! Then she resumed writing her list. She was chewing the end of her pencil over article number nineteen when Jared threw open the door, strode into the room, and announced, "We should date."

Kami bit her pencil in two.

Angela rose from her chair like the wrath of God in a red silk blouse and demanded, "Who the hell are you?"

"Hey, Angela," Jared said without sparing her a glance.

He shoved his hands into his jeans pockets and continued, glaring at Kami's desk. "I was thinking."

"I see no evidence of that, Jared," Kami said. "Sorry, Angela! He's crazy! Excuse us, we have to go talk in the hall." She pushed her chair back from the desk so fast that it toppled over. As she came toward him, Jared gave her a little crooked, awkward smile.

"I'm not going to let you go talk to some lunatic alone in the hall," Angela said furiously. "Who are you?"

"Jared Lynburn," said Jared.

Angela slipped out of her chair and circled Jared like a panther.

Kami intercepted the prowl and patted Angela's red-silk arm. "I'm off to go do an interview with him in the hall." She patted Angela again. "Trust me. I will explain everything." She made shepherding gestures to get Jared out of the door without touching him.

Jared let himself be shepherded, glancing at her over his shoulder as if he was uncertain she was coming with him.

You idiot, she said fondly. She saw his mouth curve before he turned his head. Kami followed him out the door, which she shut and then sagged against. "Now tell me," she said. "What the hell was that?"

In addition to leaning against the door, Kami was also keeping a firm grip on the doorknob. It was reassuring to have a firm grip on something. Jared stood in the echoing hallway as if his presence in the world was perfectly normal. Which it was, and she was going to have to get used to it.

Jared watched Kami. He was wearing the same blue T-shirt he'd been wearing in the garden, and the sight of it made her additionally uncomfortable. She wished again that he wasn't quite so tall.

"I said, we should—" Jared began.

"I heard what you said!" Kami yelped. "I guess I was hoping I'd got it wrong and you hadn't said the crazy thing you said. Since you did say the crazy thing you said, do you mind explaining it to me?"

Jared set his jaw and stared at the floor. "We should date," he repeated obstinately. "Because this whole being-in-each-other's-heads thing, there has to be a reason for it, doesn't there?"

"There has to be an explanation," Kami conceded. "Yes."

Jared glanced up, taking this as encouragement. In this particular slant of light, his strange eyes were so pale they seemed colorless.

If it wasn't for that, Kami might have called his look almost shy. She clenched her hand into a fist. One of them had to be reasonable, or they would ruin everything.

"And we've found each other," Jared continued. "So this is, like, fate. Isn't it? Soul mates. Isn't it?" Every word seemed to be dragged out of him, but now he was looking at her steadily.

Kami's voice came out calmer than she expected. "Let me get things perfectly clear. You want to date?"

Jared nodded cautiously.

Kami took a deep breath and stepped toward him, her fingers uncurling to reach out. Jared flinched, and she drew her hand back.

"As in boyfriend and girlfriend?" Kami pursued. "Sweethearts? Who canoodle?"

Jared nodded again, even more cautiously.

"Well, *mi amore,* this is awesome news! Let's get right on that," said Kami, and began to undo the buttons of her blouse. She looked down at the red buttons slipping out one by one from the black fabric of her shirt. She only had eight buttons, and there went the fourth.

Jared sucked breath out of a horrified void and shouted, *"Stop that!"* He angled himself to protect her from the eyes of a crowd that was not there. He hesitated, possibly because now he had a view directly down into shadows and curves.

Kami glanced up. Jared looked at the wall.

"Here's the thing," said Kami, doing her buttons up fast, trying to keep things casual. "I don't think that people who are freaked out by each other's physical existence should date."

"I cannot believe you just did that," Jared said. "Are you crazy?" He still looked shaken, which Kami found irritating. She was sure other girls received far more enthusiastic responses when they started with the undressing.

"Well, I can't believe you walked in and said that," she shot back. "In front of Angela!"

"I had to work myself up to it," Jared said. "I may have lost my head."

"I was acting on an impulse!" Kami said. "I still feel it was a sensible impulse."

"So what you're saying is, we're both crazy," said Jared. "Well, this is going to be fun." He risked a glance down, and the tension eased from his shoulders when he saw Kami was fully buttoned. The corner of his mouth went up again.

Kami smiled up at him. Amusement passed between them, neither of them sure which was whose.

The bell rang and Kami beamed. "Thank God, I have English class. I don't have to explain things to Angela yet!" Since the bell meant Angela would be emerging from their office any minute, Kami set off at top speed. "Come on, Jared," she called. "Time's a-wasting. We don't want to be tardy."

He followed her, keeping pace easily as she hurried down the stairs. "Look, you probably have the wrong idea about me. I mean, I read books, but I do it because I want to—because it's like an escape in my head, like being with you. I always get in trouble in school."

"That's because you're a delinquent who punches people," said Kami. "Not because you're not smart."

"I'm not smart like you are."

"You're not dumb."

"I was put in the year below you after they took one look at my records. I have to take some horrific exam called the GCSEs, whatever they may be. You sure about that?" Jared murmured.

"Yes," said Kami. "Keep up the pace. Angela moves like a jungle cat when she's riled."

"So, my class is over that way," Jared commented, making a vague gesture in the opposite direction to the one they were heading.

"So go to it," Kami advised.

Jared continued to head the wrong way.

Kami blinked and said, "I'll see you at lunch? Angela and I are meeting up at the headquarters."

"Okay," said Jared, and stopped. "No, wait. This hot girl with a bike. She asked me to have lunch with her on Monday."

"This hot girl with a bike," Kami repeated. It certainly sounded better than "this creepy Asian girl." Then she realized who he meant. "Holly. I'm an idiot." She looked up to see Jared had his arms crossed over his chest and was frowning.

"She seemed different than the way you think about her," Jared said.

"I imagine a guy would see Holly a bit differently than I do, yes," Kami said. "All the guys love Holly."

"See, like that," Jared said, and thought, *Dismissive.* "Like she's not important."

"As opposed to 'this hot girl with a bike'?" Kami said. "That was a deep observation." She heard her own voice rise and saw people passing by on their way to class glancing at them with interest.

Jared shrugged and scowled. "I barely know her. It's just . . ."

Thought and memory hit Kami, in a tangled rush, of being the kid in class with less money, being the one who people thought of as rough, dumber than the others.

"No, wait a second," Kami exclaimed, outraged. "I *like* Holly. And I've never thought about her having less money. I mean, I know she does, but I don't think about it! It's just she's more—sort of more a boys' girl than a girls' girl, if you know what I mean. She's not like you."

"I should hope not, I'm not anybody's girl." Jared raised an eyebrow. "If you're calling her a floozy, I'm by way of being a bit of a floozy myself."

"Oh, Jared," said Kami, who was well aware of his romantic experience, or total lack thereof. "You are not."

"Well, I have floozy ambitions."

Jared was leaning against the lockers now. Kami wondered if she should remind him that she was actually there, and he didn't have to pretend not to be talking to someone. She also wondered how his floozy ambitions tied in with the fact that he'd said they should go out. But it was becoming clearer by the minute that that wasn't really what he wanted.

"Maybe you could try sitting with Holly in this class, instead of letting her stick around by the door so she can watch you go off and sit with Amber again?"

Kami snorted. "You're ridiculous. And I am going to class." She headed toward her classroom like a homing pigeon for learning, and did not give Jared a backward glance. She gave him a backward thought, though. *You should go to class too.*

If you insist, Jared grumbled. *Kami? Try not to undress for anyone else today.*

Oh, hilarious, said Kami, and bumped into Holly at the door.

"Hi, Kami!" Holly turned in a sunburst of curls and wide eyes. She had been standing by the door, Kami noticed. "I haven't found Jared today. But I asked him to have lunch, on Friday. I was thinking if you wanted to catch us in the cafeteria, you could interview him then. I mean, if you don't have lunch plans."

"Don't worry about it. I found him," said Kami.

"Oh," said Holly.

"He said you guys were having lunch together," Kami

went on, and thought, *Hot girl with a bike.* "You could both come up to headquarters and have lunch?"

Holly frowned. "Headquarters?"

"Oh, Room 31B," said Kami. "We're calling it the headquarters now. Well, okay, *I'm* calling it that. But I'm sure it will catch on any day. Or, ah, you guys could have lunch together and you could do the interview yourself if you wanted? You've been doing all the running around after him; I think it's only fair. And I don't want to be in the way of your lunch with the guy. You said you thought he might be fun." There. She'd chosen her words carefully and well, as a journalist should. Giving Holly her due and not a hint of being judgmental, plus she was helping Jared with his floozy ambitions.

What is wrong with you? Jared demanded. *I thought we were having lunch.* She hadn't realized that Jared had meant he'd be canceling lunch with Holly. Possibly he'd been too distracted by the thought of Holly's hotness to make himself clear.

You are just never ever happy, Kami told him severely.

Holly snorted explosively, making her curls fly up as if in a sudden gust of wind. "The Vale's full of guys. I'd much rather have lunch all together. Would it be okay if you did the interview? I could watch and learn how to do it right. I don't want to mess up the paper. Because the paper is awesome."

"You're so right." Kami beamed at her, and took a chance to prove Jared wrong. "Uh—do you want to sit together?"

Holly lit up as if she had a lightbulb under all that hair. "Absolutely." She made an imperious motion at Eric Dawkins, who was looking at her longingly, and he hastily went and sat beside Amber Green.

Amber, despite having had a boyfriend since she was five, looked delighted. Kami began to darkly suspect Amber Green of being a floozy. Of course, she felt generally gloomy about the fact that Jared might have been right. She made for a desk in the front, and Holly slid in beside her, still glowing.

"So, what do you think about the Lynburns being back?" Kami said. "My mum doesn't seem too thrilled."

"My parents aren't either," said Holly. "I don't blame them. My uncle Edmund, I don't know if you've heard about him?"

"My dad said he used to go out with Lillian Lynburn," Kami offered cautiously.

Holly nodded. "He left town and left her. The Lynburns did not take the insult well. My dad's not all that rational on the subject, but the way he tells it, you'd think the Lynburns made his crops fail. They definitely called in debts and took a lot of our land."

The Prescotts lived on a small struggling farm outside of town. Everybody knew that Holly's father drank; Kami had put the struggles down to that.

"Not the nicest people in the world, then, the Lynburns."

"I can see why everyone's afraid of them." Holly shrugged. "They've got money and they own half the town. You don't get away from that in a couple of generations. People still see them as having all the power. I know my dad does." She glanced up at Kami. "You're not going to put this in the paper, are you?"

"And alienate one of my best reporters?" Kami said. "No way."

Holly laughed. "Thanks."

"How are you at English?" Kami asked. Maybe she could get rid of all this guilt with tutoring.

"Scored an A last year," Holly said with pardonable pride. "How about you?"

"Uh, a B plus," Kami confessed. "But Miss Stanley is really harsh. Who was teaching your class?"

"Miss Stanley," Holly said with a little smile.

"Ah."

Kami decided to be enraptured by her pencil case. It was worse than being an idiot. She felt like a jerk.

You're not a jerk, said Jared.

Are you in class? Kami demanded. *Go to class!*

If he did not go to class and concentrate, she did not know if she could. She felt so restless, his feelings all mixed up with hers, as if they were two rivers that had crashed together and now no separate course was possible. Kami pulled a hand through her hair and told herself she could fix this.

Holly leaned against her a bit to get her attention. "Lunch together," she whispered. "Should be fun."

Kami tried to put herself in Holly's shoes. Holly—who'd had curves by the time she was eleven and all the attention from guys and hostility from the girls that went with them—looked happy, about a simple lunch. Kami felt more like a jerk than ever.

Well, she could sit around torturing herself or use the time to make up for being a jerk. She nudged Holly back and grinned. "Should be."

"Oh no, oh no," Angela moaned as soon as she walked into the headquarters at lunchtime. She drew Kami into a corner away from the others. "What are these people doing here, Kami? You know I don't like people."

"Come on," said Kami. "You know Holly. Didn't you tell me you sat together in science class once?"

"When we were fourteen. I doubt she even remembers my name," Angela hissed. "And that new boy is crazy. Which reminds me: I want my explanation!" She glared across the room at Jared, who was sitting behind Kami's desk.

Jared eyed her back as if she was some sort of challenge.

I beg you not to throw down with Angela, said Kami.

I know you want us to get on, Jared replied. *But—*

She'll beat you down until you cry. I'll be so embarrassed for you.

Holly was sitting on Kami's desk, her apple on top of Kami's computer. She misinterpreted Angela's glare entirely.

"This is Jared Lynburn," she said helpfully. "Angie Montgomery. We used to sit together in science class when we were fourteen." Holly smiled. "It was always fun because the boys were sometimes so busy looking at our desk they walked into walls."

Angela scoffed, but the tips of her ears went a little pink.

"Jared," Angela commented. "Like the imaginary friend you have, Jared?"

"I used to have an imaginary friend when I was seven," Holly contributed. "A unicorn called Princess Zelda."

Kami gave Angela a wide smile. "Isn't that a coincidence?"

Angela spared a glare for Kami, and then resumed her marathon glaring session at Jared. "I'm not calling you that," she announced flatly. "It's too weird. I'm going to call you Carl."

Jared scowled. "I don't want you to call me Carl."

"That's interesting, Carl," said Angela, cheering up.

This distracted her from holding Kami penned up in a corner, so Kami ducked under Angela's arm to freedom. She surveyed her headquarters with satisfaction: bright lamps and shining desks and good people. You could take over the world from a headquarters like this. "Be a lady, Angela," she said. "No assaulting anyone until you get to know them."

"But I already feel so close to Carl."

"You'll feel closer to him after the interview," said Kami, flipping open her notebook and turning to a blank page.

Jared grinned at her and leaned his elbows on the table. "Hit me."

"What are *you* doing here?" Ash's voice rang out. He stood in the doorway, looking like Kami imagined the angel guarding at the gate of Eden must have looked at the moment he realized that the serpent had gotten past him.

Jared stood up. "I write for the school paper now."

Kami and Angela made a mutual low sound of incredulous protest.

Jared glanced over at Kami and nodded, with sudden decision. "Yes," he proceeded. "That's it. I'm very interested in affairs."

Ash's lip curled. "What do you mean 'affairs'?"

"Current ones," said Jared.

"Someone tell me this is a joke," said Ash, and cast an appealing look at Kami.

Jared swung out from behind the desk to stand in front of Kami. "And about that," he continued. "Now that Kami and I have met, she likes me better than you. So you can leave."

Kami made another involuntary sound of protest.

Jared wheeled around. "What?" he demanded, eyes resting on her again with that insistent, intent look. "You do, don't you? Kami. You *do*."

Angela strode out from her corner and gave Jared a solid push in the chest. "Look," she said. "Even if Kami said you could write for the paper, which I highly doubt she did, we run it together. So we both decide who writes for the paper, and so far, I think you're obviously unsuitable, due to the fact that you're obviously *unstable*. Give me one reason to keep you around."

Jared met Angela glare for glare. "For Kami," he snapped. "I'm going to write for the paper because Kami's here, and I'm not going to leave Kami's side. Someone's trying to kill her."

Chapter Ten
Falling All Around You

Chaos descended on Kami's headquarters. Ash gave Jared an appalled stare and shut the door with a slam. Holly jumped, her apple rolling off the computer and onto the floor.

"You maniac!" Angela got in Jared's face. "That's not funny. Where the hell do you get off saying something like that?"

"I'm not joking," Jared said coldly. "Someone's trying to kill her. Tell them, Kami!"

Everyone looked at Kami. Kami bit her lip. "Well. Yes. Someone's trying to kill me. But you don't have to make such a big deal out of it."

Now everyone was looking at her in the same way they'd been looking at Jared.

"You maniac!" Angela whirled on her. "Someone's trying to *kill* you, and you didn't tell me about it?" Her dark eyes narrowed, furious instead of being shocked or scared. That was Angela's way of dealing.

Kami grabbed her hand. "I was going to tell you. I couldn't think of how to put it, and I knew you would freak out."

"Of course I'm freaking out! Who wouldn't freak out?

Anyone would, apart from you, because you are a suicidal idiot!"

"Uh," said Holly awkwardly. "Am I missing something? If someone is trying to kill Kami, shouldn't we—um—go to the police?" She looked around at the group and gave an apologetic smile. "Just a thought."

Kami had not been looking forward to explaining this. "We can't do that; I already told the police I wasn't pushed down the well."

"Down the well," Angela repeated, and had to go sit down and hold on to her letter opener. It was in the shape of a dagger. Angela said holding it soothed her; seeing Angela hold it did not soothe Kami.

Ash cleared his throat. "And why would you say that?"

"Because when I told them I was pushed down the well, they thought Jared had done it."

Everybody's eyes swung to Jared.

"Jared didn't do it," Kami added quickly.

"Kami," said Angela, in a dangerous tone. "Sit. Explain."

Kami made for her desk, then pulled out her spinning chair, sat, and explained. It took some time, because people kept breaking in with unnecessary questions.

"What do you mean, the police were suspicious because you weren't wearing enough clothes?" Ash demanded, staring coldly at Jared. "Where were your clothes?"

Jared had his back to the wall, which Kami thought was a reflex when he was uncomfortable. She wanted to shield him. "He was doing some—Zen jogging," she claimed.

Jared flicked her an incredulous glance. "Yes," he said slowly. "Zen jogging. I wasn't wearing that many clothes because—that's part of the process. You're meant to commune with the elements. Normally, I wouldn't have worn my jeans, but I put them on because I know the English are a modest people."

"If I beat my head against this desk, maybe things will make sense," Angela murmured. "Or if I beat someone else's head against this desk . . ." She eyed Jared speculatively.

"So, anyway!" said Kami. "To recap: Someone shoved me into a well. In order to clear the name of my unjustly accused and indeed heroic rescuer"—she paused to see the effect of this praise on Angela; it seemed to be cutting no ice at all— "I had to hide this from the police. Which means we're going to have to find out who did it ourselves."

Holly smiled, as if warming to the idea of playing detectives. Angela wasn't smiling, but her anger had become more theatrical and less real. Nobody was taking Kami entirely seriously. She was used to that. She got a lot of practice with that, due to being the girl who spoke to someone in her head. It wasn't like all of this sounded plausible, even without the question of Zen jogging.

"Why would anyone want to kill you?" Ash asked in a calm, patient voice.

Kami sighed. "I have no idea."

"Doesn't it have to be whoever killed that fox?" Holly asked.

"That's what I was thinking, but why?" Kami wondered aloud. "It's not like he can stop me before I reveal all. I told the police! I put it in the paper! All has never been so revealed."

Angela put down her letter opener. "Maybe he wants revenge."

"Sure, and maybe his bloodlust has only grown stronger

until he must claim the ultimate prey—man," Kami said in the ominous tones of a horror-movie voice-over.

Angela would take her seriously enough to do what she wanted, thinking maybe there was something in it, maybe something had frightened Kami. Holly looked like she would go along with this for the excitement. Kami wished she could read Ash's face. It had been nice having a new guy around, someone who didn't know she was strange and who seemed interested. This might be the end of that.

"But pushing you, that doesn't seem like crazed blood-lust," Ash said slowly. "Pushing someone just seems like—they want to get you out of the way." He looked down at his own hands, fingers spread, and then put them in his pockets. "Is that an awful thing to say?"

"It's good thinking," Kami told him briskly. "Now, what are we going to need for this investigation?"

"I'd like a desk and a chair," Jared said.

"I can try to wheedle information out of people," Holly offered. "For which I'll need a lower-cut top."

"Good idea, Holly!" said Kami. "Let's make use of every tool we have. First, though, I'm going to print out the town register."

Angela frowned. "What for?"

"It's our list of suspects," Kami explained. "Because right now, it could be anyone in Sorry-in-the-Vale."

"This is the most exciting lunch I have ever had," Holly said fervently.

With a little effort, Kami mirrored her easy smile.

Kami was surprised when Ash came looking for her at the end of school. She'd expected him to start steering clear, but instead he was at the door of her history class. Kami saw several other girls noticing his tall golden good looks. There were a lot of his good looks to notice.

Ash strolled up to her, easy, casual, and laid his hand on her arm. She looked up into his electric blue eyes, startled anew by the sheer vividness of their color.

"Hi," Ash said, his charming smile a touch off, and fell into step with her. "So, uh, I don't know if this is any of my business, but—when did you and Jared meet?"

"Oh, er, Friday," said Kami. "At the library." Which was true.

Ash continued to give her that slightly unhappy smile. "And you two hit it off."

"Er, yes," said Kami. "We just really—clicked." Little bit of a lie, but it was for the best.

"Okay," Ash said. "I mean, it isn't any of my business, but I am disappointed."

It took Kami a few seconds to realize that while she'd been trying to cover up the whole imaginary-friend-turned-real business, Ash had simply been asking if they were dating. "We just clicked platonically!" Kami announced. "No, no. It's platonic. I've made that clear. I told him we weren't going out."

"Oh," said Ash. His smile warmed. "I wasn't sure what to make of it. I know some girls really like the idea of reforming a guy."

"Reforming him platonically!" The word "platonic" was starting to lose all meaning to Kami.

"So we're still on for Claire's?" Ash asked.

"What would you do," Kami found herself asking, "if I said I wanted to take off my shirt right now?"

She had to give Ash credit: he barely checked his stride, though his eyebrows went up.

"Give me a minute and I'll empty the hall?"

Kami forgave her mouth for saying terrible things without her permission, and smiled. "Good answer."

Ash shifted his schoolbag along his shoulder. "Look," he said. "I don't know exactly how to say this."

It appeared he did not know how to say whatever he wanted to at all. He was silent as they walked the length of the hallway.

They were going down the shadowed stairway when, as if given courage by the dark, Ash spoke again. "He's not a good guy," he said. "Kami, he's my cousin, and I don't want to say this. But I want you to be careful around him."

They reached the bottom of the stairs. Kami had been holding on to the stair rail; when she let it go, her hand was cold. "What do you mean?" she asked, her voice expressionless.

"His dad wasn't a good guy either," Ash said. "And he's dead. Someone pushed him. Just like someone pushed you."

Kami realized there was something worse than Ash not believing her: Ash believing her. Ash taking her seriously and having a suspect.

"I don't care," Kami whispered.

She spoke so softly Ash didn't hear. He bent toward her, blue eyes wide and innocent. Kami hated him for a moment.

"I don't care what anyone says," Kami said louder. "Jared didn't kill him."

Ash tensed as if he was being attacked. But when he spoke, his voice was gentle. "You weren't there."

"Neither were you!"

"You can't know what happened," Ash said.

Kami didn't know what had happened, but she knew how Jared had felt. He'd hated his father. Kami had been glad his father was gone. Now Jared was real and his father had been real and was really dead.

"You don't know what happened either," she said. She could feel Jared's rage running through her as it had in the lift. "He didn't do anything wrong."

Ash was all blue eyes and gold, a bewildered knight-errant whose rescue mission had gone off course. When he spoke, his voice was infuriatingly gentle, as if he felt sorry for her. "You can't be sure."

"I am sure," Kami lied, the words bitter between her lips because she could not quite believe them. "I am."

"You heard her," Jared said. "She's sure. So stop trying to turn her against me."

Kami's head snapped around. Jared's eyes met hers and then swung to Ash. His look created a chilly silence around them in the midst of the noisy corridor full of people preparing to go home.

Kami stepped in between Ash and Jared, facing Jared.

"Go on," Ash told him. "Prove my point. If she stayed away from you, she'd be safe."

Jared made a sharp abrupt movement, something that

would have been a lunge if Kami had moved away like she wanted to. She didn't. She held her hands up and took a step toward him, and Jared fell back.

"I am safe," Kami said, and cast a look over her shoulder at Ash. She felt fury wash through her: he could tell anyone in town what he had tried to tell Kami. "And I am sure."

She wasn't sure but she was angry, though she could not tell if the anger was hers or Jared's, and that scared her more than the way Jared had come at Ash. She looked away from Ash and back at Jared. She took another step forward and another, using his desire not to touch her to herd him down that busy corridor.

"Jared Lynburn?" said a voice. Someone touched his elbow, and they both jumped.

Nicola Prendergast, Kami's childhood best friend, stood beside Jared and smiled up at him. He didn't move away from her. "Just wanted to say welcome to Sorry-in-the-Vale," Nicola said. She nodded at Kami, giving the awkward ex-best-friend nod, and then gave Jared an expectant look.

Jared stared at her. He had a very distressing sort of stare.

Nicola bore it for less than a minute, then clearly remembered she had to be somewhere else with someone not so creepy, and darted off.

Jared looked to Kami. "Everyone either wants to welcome me with open arms or punch me in the face."

"That probably says something very worrying about your personality," said Kami. "But what?" She turned in toward him, and he almost stumbled back into an empty classroom. Kami followed him inside. The room was filled with desks and chairs knocked awry, and late-afternoon light streamed through the windows. Jared stood there still looking a little wild and completely out of place in her life. She wanted to reach out to him in her mind and get comfort in this impossible situation.

"Ash is right," she said. She watched him flinch and felt the pang travel through her as well, horrible and senseless: she couldn't stop feeling what he was feeling. "I don't know what happened, and I have to know. Jared—Jared, I'm on your side. You believe that." Jared's burning-pale eyes were fixed on her. For a moment, she did not know how he would respond.

Yes, he said in her mind.

"I just have to know the truth," Kami said. "The worst thing that's happened in my life is my grandmother dying while I was at cricket camp. You know that. I told you that. You haven't told me about this. I know you hated your father, and I know that the summer before last was bad, that you weren't with your parents. I know your father's dead. Tell me how he died."

Jared looked at her for another moment, then passed a hand through his hair and looked away. The edge of his jaw was hard, scar pulled tight over his cheek.

"My dad hated us," he said. "Me and Mom. He hated us all the time. He wasn't drunk all the time, but he was drunk often enough. The summer before last, he gave me this scar, and I ran away."

There was no emotion in his voice, stripped clean like flesh from dry bone, but Kami knew how he had felt.

"I slept on the streets for a few months, and then I got

sick in the fall, and after I was well I thought about Mom and how she always got sick. I thought about how I'd left her alone."

"You went back for her," Kami said.

Jared's mouth twisted. "I went back," he said. "It was late, and he was drunk. He didn't let me in the door. We were fighting out in the hall, he was shouting and she was screaming, and he—he fell down the stairs. Broke his neck."

"Someone pushed him, Ash said." Kami did not add, Just like someone pushed me.

"When the police came, Mom said I pushed him. She made sure they took me away in handcuffs." Jared looked at Kami again. His gaze was defiant, almost desperate, as if he was daring her not to believe him. As if he expected her not to. "There was a security camera in our building, and it showed I wasn't close enough to have pushed him. I hated him enough to kill him, but I didn't."

Kami suddenly knew how hate like that felt, the cold absoluteness of it. "I believe you," she said.

His mother had betrayed him. He'd come back for her, and she'd sent him to a cell. Kami had talked to him when he reached out for her, lonely and desperate, even though she hadn't known what she was talking him through. He had talked to her the same way when her grandmother died. Even though that had been different, had been an ordinary tragedy, an old woman with a bad heart, and this was a nightmare, she'd meant it when she said she was on his side.

"Ash isn't going to turn me against you," Kami told him. "You can trust me."

There was a flicker of warmth between them, like a match lit.

"Come on, Glass," said Jared. "I'll take you home."

Kami had told him nothing but the truth. She did believe him. She believed he'd hated his father enough to kill him. And she knew, could feel the wall in his mind, that there was something else he was hiding.

Chapter Eleven
The Haunted River

They had to swing by Jared's locker so he could grab his jacket. "A leather jacket," Kami said as he shrugged into it. "Aren't you trying a little too hard to play into certain bad boy clichés?"

"Nah," said Jared. "You're thinking of black leather. Black leather's for bad boys. It's all in the color. You wouldn't think I was a bad boy if I was wearing a pink leather jacket."

"That's true," Kami said. "What I would think of you, I do not know. So what does brown leather mean, then?"

"I'm going for manly," Jared said. "Maybe a little rugged."

"It's bits of dead cow; don't ask it to perform miracles."

Jared laughed. "Come on, I brought a spare helmet for you," he said, reaching into his locker again.

As he spoke, she reached for him in her mind, and felt the pleasure he felt in his motorbike. She could taste some of the thrill, the speed and the danger.

"Ahahaha!" said Kami. "No, you didn't. You brought it for someone else, someone who doesn't know that you have crashed that bike fifty-eight times!"

"Technically speaking, only fifty-one of those times were my fault."

"Technically speaking, you drive like a rabid chicken who has hijacked a tractor."

"Like a bat out of hell," Jared said. "Nice simile. Sounds sort of dangerous and cool. Consider it."

"Not a chance. I like my brains the way they are, not lightly scrambled and scattered across a road. And speaking of bad boy clichés, really, a motorcycle?"

"Again, I say: rugged," Jared told her. "Manly."

"I often see Holly on hers," Kami said solemnly. "When she stops for traffic, sometimes she puts on some manly lip gloss. I'm not getting on a bike."

Jared shrugged. "Okay. So I'll walk you home." He shut his locker door, turned, and made his way down the hall.

Kami felt duty bound to point out, "You can't keep following me around."

Jared frowned. "You don't—do you mind?"

"I mean, you can't," Kami explained. "You know how Angela moved to town when I was eleven? And you know how girls at that age are joined at the hip and want to do absolutely everything their new best friend in all the world does? Do you remember how long that stage lasted for me and Angela?"

Jared hesitated. "Well—"

"Two and a half hours," Kami told him. "Then Angela collapsed and started to cry. It was the only time I've ever seen Angela cry."

"Are you implying I won't be able to keep up with you?"

Kami pushed open the school door, glanced up, and found him smiling. "I'm not implying so much as just outright saying."

"I think I can manage," Jared told her.

"You're welcome to try," Kami said serenely. "I'm planning to take a shortcut through the woods on our way home." She sailed down the school steps. He was keeping up with her so far, but then, they had barely started.

"A shortcut through the woods that mysteriously brings us to the scene of a crime?"

"The woods aren't signposted," Kami said. "It's easy to get a little lost, wander about. Who knows what you might stumble upon!"

"Kami," said Jared. "I can read your mind."

"Well, that won't hold up in court," Kami informed him. "It sounds crazy."

Kami had not planned her investigative foray into the woods ahead of time, or she would've worn dark jeans and boots. But even with the disadvantage of a belted button-down red skirt and kitten heels, she was able to keep ahead of the city boy. When Kami jumped over a stile, he looked at it as if he'd never seen one before.

"I have never seen one before," Jared said, keeping close to the fence and eyeing the sheep on the other side with suspicion.

A lamb nudged its pink snub nose in Kami's direction, and she patted its white woolly head. She always meant to stop eating lamb because they were so adorable. But she always succumbed when it landed on the table, because it was so delicious.

One of the lambs fixed its attention on Jared. "Baa," it flirted.

"Boo," said Jared.

"Oh my God, Jared. Don't tough-talk the lambs."

"It was giving me a funny look," Jared claimed, boosting himself over the next stile. "I thought the countryside would have more open fields and fewer fences and barbed wire."

"So you thought all the animals wandered onto other people's land, getting run over by reckless drivers such as yourself?" Kami asked. "We like fences. And we have rolling fields. We have fields that rock and roll." She waved at the expanse of green, the landscape changing hands from tree to field until finally it all melded with the sky to become blue mist in the distance. She was surprised to find herself feeling defensive.

"Kami," said Jared. "I like it."

"You don't have to like it."

"I do anyway," said Jared.

They went over the wooden bridge over the Sorrier River, stands of bright red wolfberries waving at them from the bank.

"The Sorrier River?" Jared asked when he saw the sign by the bridge.

"It's haunted," Kami said, with some pride.

"The river is haunted?"

"During the Wars of the Roses—a big fight over who should be the king of England, Richard of York or Henry of Lancaster," Kami supplied, "Sorry-in-the-Vale stood for Richard. Henry won through vile treachery. Anyway, since Henry was a cruel tyrant, he decided everyone who had fought for Richard—who was king of England at the time!—was a traitor, and started seizing lands and squeezing people for cash."

"Classic tyranny," Jared observed. "Not very imaginative."

"So the people of Sorry-in-the-Vale hid their valuables when the king's men were going by. You know the tower attached to Aurimere? It used to be a bell tower, but the bell was carved and made of gold. Well, gold leaf, probably, but at this stage everyone says gold. Elinor Lynburn ordered that the bell be sunk in the river. What with one king and another, they didn't bring the bell up from the river until Elizabeth I was on the throne, and then nobody was able to find it. The legend goes that when Sorry-in-the-Vale is in danger, the bells in the river ring out a warning." Kami beamed with satisfaction.

Jared glanced over the side of the bridge. It hadn't rained lately, and it had been a long summer. The Sorrier was a silver trickle. "So the river is haunted by . . . bells?"

"You do not deserve an ancestral legend," Kami informed him.

They stepped into the woods under a green arch like a church doorway made of boughs. The woods had the hush of a church too. This was the real woods, and even the quality of the light was different, shadow and sunshine caught together in a net of leaves. Kami had loved the woods all her life, but without loving them any less, she could not forget seeing horror under these trees. She did not let her steps slow. Kami had found it was important not to give people time to say "Wait, is this really a good idea?"

It occurred to Kami an instant later that she was not guarding her thoughts, and with the new blurring of the boundaries between them Jared could see every fear and doubt she pretended not to have. She sent a glance that flashed resentment at Jared, standing on the gnarled roots of an oak tree.

He met her eyes, face calm. The oak leaves above him were already gilded, autumn coming to the woods like a king in a legend, touching all the trees with brightness. The rays coming through those leaves were gold on gold, firing the cold lights in his gray eyes. "I'm not going to ask if this is a good idea. I said I could keep up with you," Jared said. "I won't do that by slowing you down."

Kami's smile spread, thoughts curling around his. He didn't feel uncertain. Actually, he felt happy, the restlessness that had been thrumming through him at school stilled.

"So hurry up, city boy."

They went over fallen leaves and undergrowth that tried to tug Kami's shoes off, past a hollow tree stump covered with dead vines that looked like an elephant made of twigs, and reached the hut. It looked ordinary by the light of day, the rough brown walls leaning at an angle, the door slightly ajar.

Kami had envisioned crime scene tape garlanding the trees, but of course the police weren't going to do that for a murdered fox. They had not even taken the tablecloth off the table. It fluttered in the breeze as Kami cautiously pushed the door open. She stared for a moment at the rusty brown stains on it. She felt Jared's shoulder behind her own, warm and solid, having her back, and for the first time since the well, his physical presence was a comfort. She leaned against him and he stepped away, maybe an instant before he realized she was leaning, maybe an instant afterward.

Kami stepped forward on her own and walked around the perimeter of the hut. It was tiny, and she had studied the pictures from her camera phone obsessively. There didn't seem to be anything new here. So whoever it was had not come back, she thought. That was good to know.

She went and stood at the door with Jared, trying to find some pattern of broken twigs or crushed undergrowth to indicate which way whoever had killed that fox had fled. But the police had been here, and she and Jared hadn't been careful on their way in. There were signs of people everywhere. When Kami saw a gleam, she stooped down to the glint of white plastic automatically and without much interest. It was plastic: she assumed it was rubbish. Then she looked at what was lying in the palm of her hand.

"It's a room key," Jared said slowly. "For somewhere called the Surer Guest."

"That's a fancy guesthouse a few miles out of town," Kami said, just as slowly. Relief seeped through the shock. It could be a visitor who was responsible, then. Not anyone she knew: not someone from her town.

"Our first clue," Jared remarked. "High five."

They both hesitated, checking themselves at the last moment, and deliberately missed touching hands. The gesture was a bit like waving at each other over a distance that was only in their minds.

Kami bit her lip, then tucked the card into her pocket and headed for home, with Jared walking a careful distance away from her.

Chapter Twelve
The Crying Pools

"Something I don't understand about this place," Jared said, after a long awkward pause, "is why the stone around here, including the stone in the big stupid mausoleum I have to live in, is the color of pee."

"It's Cotswold stone!" Kami exclaimed. "And it is the color of *honey*. It's very famous. Most of the houses in Cotswolds towns are built from it. It's why they are such beauteous tourist attractions."

"Cotswolds?" Jared asked. "I thought this place was in Oxfordshire. Or Gloucestershire. Someplace ending in 'shire.'"

"The Cotswolds stretches over both," Kami said. "It's a range of hills and towns famous for their beauty. Also their sheep, but that's not the issue here. There's a quarry on the other side of the woods where the stone used to be mined, and it's been exhausted for fifty years because everyone likes Cotswold stone."

"Still looks like pee."

"Honey!"

"You can sweet-talk me all you want, baby, but I know what it looks like to me." Jared smirked at her. Kami matched up his expression to his emotions: she wanted to memorize them so she could get used to him having a face as well as feelings.

So this is the "smug idiot thinks he's funny" face, Kami observed. *Not to be confused with other "smug idiot" variants.*

And everyone told me English girls were so sweet, Jared said, and then: *Oh, hey.*

Kami glowed with pride at the success of her surprise. "I took another detour on my way home. Since you're new and everything."

The hush of the woods was changed now into the different calm of still waters, the quiet somehow enveloping rather than disturbed by humming insects or the rustle of trees.

The two lakes were laid out side by side in the clearing, two shimmering glass circles as if the ground was wearing spectacles. Kami had seen the lakes showing different colors, pearl gray under cloudy skies or blue in sunshine, but right now they were green, the green of glass bottles turned liquid and poured over pale sand. A weeping willow dipped a branch into the waters of the farthest pool, some leaves trailing on the surface and the other leaves drowned and dark.

"These are the Crying Pools."

Kami was dismayed to see a few raindrops hit the pool, breaking the silver surface, but before she could suggest taking shelter she looked up and saw the rain cloud above them melting into wisps against the sky. She looked back down to shimmering-calm water and Jared's small smile. It wasn't much, that smile, not compared to Ash's, but Kami could see the feeling behind it; she could share his pleasure and blend it with hers. It made the smile warm as a touch.

"Sorry-in-the-Vale, Sorriest River, Crying Pools," said Jared. "Is the quarry called Really Depressed Quarry?"

"Yes," Kami answered. "Also, I live on the Street of Certain Doom."

Jared drew closer to the pools. He stood looking down into one, then glanced over his shoulder at Kami.

It struck Kami that he should have looked out of place, the city boy in his battered leather jacket, but he did not. He fit here. The shadow of the trees hung over his hair, and for a moment she thought his eyes caught a green spark. It occurred to her that the Lynburns had lived in Sorry-in-the-Vale a very long time.

"I think I see something in the water," said Jared.

Curiosity made Kami forget the moment of strangeness and hurry over to peer into the lake by Jared's side. "I don't see anything."

"I thought it was a glint of metal," Jared said. "Possibly I was hoping for more rich ancestors' bells."

"Or it was the sun on the water."

"Or that," Jared conceded. "So, am I ever going to see your house on the Street of Certain Doom?"

As they wound their way back toward her house after taking the world's two longest shortcuts, Kami had to admit that she was nervous. Her house was ridiculous. Only her parents would ignore the new roof technology that had been available for, oh, six hundred years, and live in a thatched cottage. When they reached it, she swung open the gate from the woods into her garden with some misgiving.

"No jokes about Glass houses," she told Jared. "Because we have heard them all."

"What about—"

"That one too," Kami said firmly.

The gate swung open.

The Glass house was Cotswold stone too, but was a little house, resting snug on the dip of land below the woods, dark thatch over yellow stone, honeysuckle dripping down in front of the low windows. Above the door was carved *G,* and then a scar in the stone, followed by the word *House.* Kami made her way through the garden. The grass could have used trimming and she had to jump over Tomo's bicycle. A watering can was hanging on the wall.

Kami turned her house key in the door, gave it a heave to open it because it always stuck, and glanced back at Jared. He stood looking at her, then looking at the house, and in that moment he seemed strangely helpless to Kami. Which was ridiculous, because Jared was one of the least vulnerable-looking people she had ever seen. Yet something about the way he stood made her think of a kid peering in a shop window, knowing he could not have anything inside.

Jared's eyes met Kami's. His wariness flooded through her, trying to set up barriers between them too late. It was almost horrible, having what a stranger thought mean so terribly much.

Kami waved her hand. "Welcome to my humble abode!" she said grandly, and when he still stood staring she reached out her hand to him. "Jared," she said, quieter. "Come in."

He did not take her hand, and after a moment, a chill going through her, she dropped it. Jared followed her inside once she had turned away. Kami hesitated at her own threshold, about to kick off her shoes, because Sobo always wanted shoes off and slippers on as soon as you went in the door, and it always took her a beat to remember Sobo was gone and stop herself calling out "Obaa-chan!," that name she had lost when Sobo was gone, because it was a name only for family and she always referred to her grandmother as Sobo otherwise, even in her own head, because Jared was always there. She took the beat now, looked up to explain to Jared, and saw that he already understood.

She flashed him a quick smile. They walked down the hall and into the living room.

Kami had to check on the boys first thing: she shouldn't actually have taken those detours. The kids could be left alone for a couple of hours, because Ten was the most pathologically responsible child in the universe, but it wasn't like Tomo ever listened to him. The living room was a mess, as usual, and Kami almost broke her neck on one of Tomo's toy trucks.

Best if you think of this room as a minefield. Tread carefully or get exploded, she advised Jared, and then said aloud, "Hideous brats! We have a guest. Conceal evidence of your crimes."

Tomo, watching TV at ear-splitting volume, outdid the television with a shriek and turned around on the sofa. Ten, in the window seat with a book in his lap, curled in against the glass and tried to be very quiet while he assessed the situation. Kami sent him a reassuring smile and he blinked at her owlishly behind his glasses.

"Who are you?" Tomo asked Jared.

"This is Tomo," Kami said, even though Jared knew this, just so she could add, "It's been seven years since the evil fairies sent him to us as a curse. We're still not sure what we did to offend them. And this is Ten. He is ten, and yes, we know how horrible that is. We are going to throw the biggest birthday party for him the Vale has ever seen when he turns eleven."

"How many months to go?" Jared asked.

Shy Ten gathered his courage in both hands and replied in a tiny voice: "Nine months."

"That's rough, buddy," said Jared.

Ten went limp with relief. He shrugged his shoulders and bent his head back over his book.

"What are you doing here?" Tomo wanted to know. "I've never seen you before! Do you know any Snoopy songs?"

"Uh, no," said Jared. "Sorry."

"Stop bothering my guest," Kami ordered.

"If I do . . . ," Tomo began his bargain. "*If* I do. Can I have four glasses of lemonade?"

"No."

"Why not?"

"Because if you drank four glasses of lemonade, you would explode," Kami said. "Dad would come downstairs and ask, 'Where is my youngest born?' and I could only point to the floor, where all that remained of you would be a pool of lemonade and a heap of sweetened entrails. You can have *one* glass of lemonade."

Tomo gave a cheer and leaped from the sofa, heading for the kitchen at top speed.

Kami sighed. "The current theory is that he is a lemonade vampire. C'mon."

"Nice to meet you," Jared said awkwardly to Ten, who

went red and muttered something into the pages of his book.

"He likes you," Kami commented.

"Oh yeah," said Jared. "I could tell."

"He once hid under the sofa from a cocker spaniel," Kami said. "You're doing fine." She opened the door to the kitchen, and once more it was like seeing familiar things for the first time, wondering what Jared thought of them: the red stone tiles that were worn orange in places, the swags of dried herbs swinging over the wide wooden counter, the round table and the fat green sofa strategically placed in the square of sunlight that came through the window. And, of course, her brother doing what appeared to be a mystical lemonade dance.

Strangers said Tomo looked like Dad, although Dad's black hair stood up straight as a brush and he had cheek-bones that could cut glass, while Tomo had a black silky cap of hair with a face as round as a dish. They looked nothing alike, except that they both looked Japanese. Ten did not look even slightly Japanese, and Kami was the only one who looked like a mix of both, like she wouldn't quite fit in on either side of her family.

Kami stood on her tiptoes to get the high cupboard open. The lemonade was kept in the highest place they had. Keeping it in the fridge had resulted in finding Tomo curled on the floor in sugar delirium, clutching an empty bottle, one too many times.

"Here," Jared murmured. He reached up and took down the lemonade.

Kami glanced around and saw the way he'd leaned,

angled so his body would not brush hers. "Thanks," she murmured back, and went to grab glasses.

"You are a tall person!" Tomo announced approvingly, pausing mid-dance. "How did you get that scar on your face?"

"Tomo!" Kami said.

"Broken bottle," Jared told him curtly.

"I'm sorry," Kami said, once Tomo had pranced off with his glass of lemonade.

Kami, it's fine, said Jared. He looked especially tall in her kitchen, big and edgy and out of place here as he had not been in the woods. "I thought I made all of this up," said Jared, very quietly.

Kami heard what he left unspoken, the things people had said to him: *Creating a fantasy life to compensate for the situation at home, not able to deal with reality, some faraway ideal of what he imagines a home is like. Not real. Not real.*

"I thought I made you up," Jared continued, still so quietly.

"Well," Kami said. "You didn't. Want some lemonade?"

"Yeah, okay," said Jared.

He kept hovering uneasily as Kami went and sat on the sofa with her lemonade. It had been a long day. Not just because of the longest detour through the woods ever made, but because of the talk with the others in the office, having to drag into the light the thing she had been trying not to say. The thing she had not wanted to even think of: Someone had pushed her into that well. Someone was trying to kill her.

Kami was determined to solve the mystery and tell the

story. She was going to be fine. But for now she was tired, and all she could do was sit, stare out the window, and feel cold and scared.

"You don't have to be scared," Jared said, leaning against the sofa behind her. His breath stirred her hair. "I believed you."

"Yes," Kami said. "Because you know I'm telling the truth." She had not even looked at Jared while she was absorbing the reactions of everyone else at headquarters. She had not had to: your own heart did not betray you. Jared could be counted on, always. But he hadn't been real before. It was different now.

Yes, said Jared.

"It's not one-sided," he added abruptly.

Kami kept her eyes locked on the window. "What do you mean?" she asked, and her voice trembled.

He said, "I'm always on your side too."

Kami leaned back, just a little, and let the back of her head rest against his collarbone. He did not flinch away, though she heard his breath catch and thought that he maybe wanted to. He was solid, real, in her home and in the sunlight. She felt the warm curve of his neck, the catch of his breath a whisper against her hair.

"Yes," Kami murmured. "I know."

He pulled away as soon as she spoke. Kami twisted around on the sofa and looked at him. She was reminded of the way he had fit in with the woods, and thought again how out of place he seemed in her home.

"Is there," Jared began, voice rough as it had been when

they first met. He wasn't looking at her. "Is there anything I can do to make you happy?"

"I don't understand." Kami reached for him in her mind, but his walls were up and his face stayed turned away.

"Nobody's ever been happy I was there before," Jared said. "That's just the kind of effect I have on people. I want you to be glad I'm here. I want it badly. But I have no idea how to make it happen." He looked at her then, fixing her with that pale gaze. He hardly ever looked at her, but when he did his attention was absolute, and profoundly unsettling. "I'll do anything you want. All you have to do is tell me."

Kami bit her lip. "I am happy you're here."

It tasted like a lie in her mouth, when they had never lied to each other before. Kami glanced involuntarily away from him, eyes falling to her clasped hands, even though she knew that would make her look more like she was lying than ever.

She wasn't lying. It wasn't that she was unhappy he was here: it was just that it was all so complicated. He had been so safe in her head, her constant companion. Now he had come crashing into her life, a stranger with his own life separate from hers whose emotions were all tied up with hers, someone who she barely knew and who sometimes seemed cruel. She could not help being afraid of him: he could hurt her, more than a stranger should be able to, and she did not know if he would.

"You're not happy," Jared said, his voice flat, and he headed for the back door.

"Come on, I am," Kami said. "We're going to fight crime together. I totally need you to be corporeal."

He was holding the door open already, but when she spoke she felt him reach for her. She reached back, and felt his little shock of recognition, as if he had only just caught sight of her in a crowd, relief and joy spilling through the connection. She was not quite sure if it was his or her own.

"I could throw thugs out windows for you," he offered, and there was life in his voice again.

"I can defenestrate my own thugs," Kami informed him. "But you could maybe get clues for me. You know. Clues on high shelves."

Jared laughed. "You're not happy yet," he said. The afternoon sunlight transformed him into a brightly limned shadow, already turning away. "But you will be."

Chapter Thirteen
Belief and Unbelief

The back door slid open, softly and gradually, in the dark. The moonlight formed a hazy halo around fair hair, and the silhouette of a woman moved quietly as a shadow into the room.

"Boo!" said Kami, from her sentry position beside the dishwasher.

Her mother gave a little scream and dropped her parcel of baked goods. "Kami! You scared me," she said as Kami knelt down and began to pick up the contents of the parcel.

"You've been avoiding me," Kami said reasonably. "So I lay in wait for you."

Mum had known Kami since Kami was born, so she just sighed at this brilliant logic. And Kami did feel it was logical: Claire's was both a bakery that Mum opened at six and a restaurant she did not close until midnight. Mum got home to see the boys in between, but lately Kami was at her newspaper headquarters then. So midnight lurking it was.

Her decision may have been slightly influenced by the fact that Mum always brought home treats. The bakery box was mostly intact, and the pastries on the floor still looked good. Kami handed her mother the box, then picked up a chocolate chip cookie from the floor.

"Don't eat that," Mum said.

Kami bit in. "Mmm, floor cookie." She leaned against the counter and said, "Spill it."

Mum slid the box onto the counter. "What are you talking about?" she asked warily.

"Mum," Kami said, "have you met me? You tell me to stay away from someone, and you thought I'd say 'Oh yes, Mother, of course, no further questions' and sit about in the garden making daisy chains?"

"I'd like to hear 'Oh yes, Mother, of course, no further questions,'" Mum said, sighing. "Just once." She leaned forward, meeting Kami's eyes in the dark kitchen as if they were going to do a business deal. "All right, Kami, I made a bit of a miscalculation there. I was slightly overwrought. Sometimes that happens when you get phone calls saying that your child has tumbled into a well. But can't you trust me that these people are dangerous?"

"Trust you?" Kami said. "Of course I can trust you. But I want to know *why*."

Mum suddenly looked more tired than she had before. "I hoped they would never come back," she whispered. "A lot of us hoped that."

"Whatever the Lynburns did," Kami said, "Jared and Ash aren't responsible. They weren't even born."

A branch knocked on the window, its leaves silver in the moonlight. Kami and her mother both jumped.

"It wasn't what the Lynburns *did*," Mum said very softly. "It was what they *were*. What they still are. Creatures of red and gold. The whole town was terrified of them. Lillian Lynburn thought she was queen of every blade of grass in the Vale, and Rosalind Lynburn looked through you as if you were too unimportant to even notice. If she did notice you, it chilled you to the bone. But Rob Lynburn's parents were dead, and the twins' father was sick for a long time before he died. All the time we were growing up, the Lynburns were losing their grip on the land, and then Rosalind left and the others went after her. I was so glad they were gone."

Kami'd always thought her mother had a face like a woman in a Pre-Raphaelite painting. She wasn't like Angela, always fashionably dressed with flawless makeup. Claire Glass was usually in quiet rebellion against her beauty, pinning her hair up, always in loose jeans and sweatshirts. Kami had never seen her mother look tragic before.

"What about Rob Lynburn?" Kami asked. "Dad said he was the one you knew best. He said he had an office above Claire's and he had lunch early so he could talk to you. Were you afraid of him?"

"Rob?" Mum echoed, sounding startled. "I was, but I understood him better. You don't get how people felt about the Lynburns back then. We were terrified, but we were fascinated too. There were a lot of people who would follow wherever a Lynburn led. Rob Lynburn was used to having a crowd of girls after him, and he liked the attention. He expected it from all of us. He came and had lunch with me, the way men do when they're set on catching your eye." Her voice was unself-conscious as she flipped open the lid of the bakery box to examine the damage done to its contents.

It would be nice to be crazy beautiful for a day, Kami

thought, and then told herself that the way things were always happening to her—through no fault of her own—she might start a war like Helen of Troy. Being beautiful would probably be too much of a hassle.

"So, Rob Lynburn fancied you," Kami said. "And all the girls were after him, and all the boys were after the twins. So the Lynburns are hot blonds? That doesn't sound so scary."

"It didn't matter who was after the twins. Lillian never cared about anything and Rosalind never cared about anybody but Rob."

"Her sister's husband!" Kami squawked.

"Well, not at the time," Mum said mildly.

"Jared's mum was in love with Ash's father?"

Mum raised an eyebrow. "Bit of a surprise when Rob married Lillian—to Rosalind most of all. We all thought that was why she left with that American: hurt pride, a broken heart. If any Lynburn has a heart. I was hoping that the boys would act like the Lynburns usually do: that they would stay away from normal people. That you could keep away from them."

"Mum!" Kami exclaimed. "You don't know Jared. Or Ash."

"You're the one who doesn't know," Mum said. "You don't know what it's like to be in the hands of a Lynburn."

"They aren't monsters!"

Her mother whispered, "Yes, they are."

Kami skirted the counter to draw close to her mother. "Mum," she asked, "what did a Lynburn make you do?"

"Don't tell your father," Mum whispered.

Suddenly the overhead light in the kitchen went on.

"Cookies!" Tomo screeched, and zoomed across the room.

It was like the world had been flipped instead of a light switch. Their bright ordinary kitchen was a jarring contrast to secrets in the dark.

"Don't try to eat five things at once, Tomo—remember the time you sneezed lemon meringue," said Mum, relaxing and ruffling Tomo's silky black hair.

Tomo was Mum's favorite. He was the baby, and the one it was easiest to make happy. He made Mum sure of her ground as a mother, Kami supposed: he always made her smile. She was smiling now, faintly, as she reached out and patted Kami's arm.

"Please just stay clear of him," she said, and Kami realized Jared was the Lynburn her mother was most afraid of.

"Whoever he is, I agree with your mother," said Dad as he entered the kitchen. "Stay away from him. Stay away from them all until you're of marrying age. Once you reach a nice, mature fifty-four, gentlemen callers will be welcomed here."

Ten slipped out from behind him and made a beeline for the bakery box, where he politely stole the lone brownie from under Tomo's nose.

"Camilla, Henry, Thomas, you greedy monsters," Dad said. "Not a crumb left for your father? That's it, you're not my children. You're just sad, bald monkeys I won from circus folk in a poker game."

Ten retreated with his prize and went back to lean against Dad's leg. He split the brownie in two and offered half silently up to Dad.

"Well," Dad conceded, "I guess you might be my kid after all."

Ten smiled his rare smile, Mum's smile, then hid it against Dad's shirt. Ten had Mum's bronze hair, brown with gold running through it, and Mum's dark gray eyes in his thin face. He followed Dad as Dad made his way to the counter, a solemn bespectacled moon orbiting his sun.

Dad took Mum's face in his hands and pulled it down two inches to kiss her mouth. "Claire," he said.

"Jon," said Mum, "please stop calling our children by names other than their own."

Dad released Mum and grinned. "Aren't those their names? I could've sworn they were."

Mum had been the one who insisted on celebrating her children's Japanese heritage. Kami was pretty sure she'd got the names Kami, Tenri, and Tomo out of books, since Dad and Sobo had always acted like the whole thing was a bit silly.

"Let me tell you about my day, Claire of my heart," said Dad. "First the Gallagher account decided they wanted to change their logo. Your knight, slaying graphic design tirelessly for your sake, was not daunted, but then—even before my tea break—"

Mum smiled. Kami did not know if it was the memory of that last whisper in the dark, that "Don't tell your father," that made Kami wonder how well Mum had known Rob Lynburn.

Ten hovered and Dad drew him in with a hand on his shoulder. Dad loved Ten best, because Ten needed someone to love him best.

Kami stood on one end of the counter and watched her

family, who she had never thought would keep secrets from each other, her parents each with their favorite child, and felt a little bleak.

You're my favorite, Jared told her.

Kami looked out from the warmth of her kitchen and pretended that through the woods and up the hill, she could make out the lights of Aurimere House.

Yes, she told him for the second time that day. *I know.*

Aurimere was so cold at night, Jared kept expecting to step into one of the hallways and find it had turned into one of the wind tunnels the streets of San Francisco could become in winter.

Jared had been sticking to a three-stops plan for more than a week: bedroom, kitchen, and out the door. Now he was going off the map. This curving staircase was part of the empty bell tower attached to Aurimere. The stone steps were deep, the edges of a few jagged, and every step was a step into darkness. But Jared was used to blind curves. He took another step, then another, and came out blinking into what he thought for a second was yet another freezing hallway.

Then he found himself staring at a pair of frosty blue eyes. Ash's cool eyes were immediately recognizable, even in oils dark with time, in the face of a guy wearing a powdered wig and a blue satin coat. Jared took a moment to smirk at the idea of Ash in that getup, then turned away.

The gallery was lined with the accusing stares of his ancestors. They stood in two rows on either side of him, in rich frames and rich clothes. They looked like history, people important enough to have changed the future and be pre-served in time. They looked down at him as if he did not belong there.

Jared glared back at the faces. He already knew that. It was ridiculous, him even being here. Their whole apartment in San Francisco would have fit into this portrait gallery three times over. He felt as if all the cold shadows in this house wanted him to use the servants' entrance.

Jared kept walking down the hall past rows of dead aristocrats. He was looking for someone. Then he saw her name, ELINOR LYNBURN, in faded gold on black wood. She looked even weirder than the dude in the white wig. She was wearing a cone-shaped headdress with a veil, and she seemed to be bald, which was hard luck on Elinor.

Married women in that time weren't meant to show their hair, Kami told him, her mind touching his, sleepy but inter-ested. *She might've shaved it. Does she have eyebrows?*

Of course she has eyebrows! said Jared, standing up for his ancestor even though English people were crazy and appar-ently the women went bald on purpose.

Whenever he woke or went to sleep and at random moments of the day, he found himself reaching mentally for Kami, checking where she was and if she was okay. It was different now, since she was an actual girl in an actual bed.

Elinor's eyebrows were raised, her mouth drawn in a straight line. She looked kind of irritated to be stuck in a picture, as if she had better things to do.

"Hey, Elinor," Jared said quietly. "I know where you hid the bells."

"What?" his mother's voice asked behind him.

Jared crushed the impulse to jump. Showing weakness was a good way to get it kicked out of you.

She was sitting in an alcove, a little stone cup of a window and a marble seat, her long skirt flowing over the marble. The big window was diamond-paned and already touched with dew, edging the night with silver. It looked out on the dark garden.

There was moonlight shining on two pale heads below. Uncle Rob and Ash, out on one of their father-and-son bonding trips. Uncle Rob had asked Jared along a couple of times, which had made Ash dislike him even more.

"Does nobody in this family sleep?" Jared demanded.

Mom slipped along the marble seat, moving a little farther away from him. "We have been acquainted with the night," she said, with a certain lilt that he recognized as the tone she used for quoting, "for a very long time now."

She used to quote a lot back when Jared had been very young. She used to tell him she was Rosa*line,* not Rosa*lind,* and nobody told Rosaline's story. Jared hadn't understood then that she'd been talking about Shakespeare, but he'd liked sitting and listening to her telling the story nobody told. But then he'd got big and rough, and they had stopped reading together. Once Dad had ripped a book of hers into pieces and thrown it in the fire, and Mom had let out a wounded cry. She'd never cried out like that when he'd hit Jared.

Rosaline was Romeo's ex in Romeo and Juliet, *wasn't she?* Jared asked Kami.

Kami said, *Romeo loved her first, but then he met Juliet, and he thought she was better-looking.* Romeo and Juliet *is not actually as romantic a story as everybody thinks.*

125

"Were you in love with Uncle Rob?" Jared asked his mother.

Mom's eyes left the night garden and fixed on him. She was silent for a moment, and then she said slowly, "I never loved anyone but him, and my sister."

"I don't . . . ," Jared began, and stopped because all the words he could think of would scare her and it made him sick to scare her. "If you didn't love Dad, I don't understand why you didn't leave him."

Mom turned away from him, back to the garden at night. The moonlight lined her pale profile with ice. "Where would I have gone? It's the same everywhere. And it never came as much of a surprise. He said he loved me. I'd already learned that love betrays you." She left the window seat, retreating down the long hall until there was the distance she preferred between them. "Besides," she said, "I didn't have to leave him, did I? You saw to that."

Fury rose up in him again, the desire to shake her until she took it back. He forced himself to lean against the wall, and just looked at her.

"You've been talking to Claire Glass's daughter," Mom said. "I thought we agreed you weren't going to do that."

"Don't talk about her," Jared snarled, and was glad to see her flinch. "She is none of your business!"

"You don't know anything," his mother whispered.

"You never *told* me anything!" Jared shouted. "You never told me anything about any of this!"

Calm down, said Kami. She was fully awake now, reaching out, but he did not reach back. He did not want her to be exposed to any of this, to learn any new horrors about him or any secrets about his family.

"It was best for you not to know," Mom said. "Why do you think I left? Lillian was wrong to bring us back here. Our family never had a talent for happiness, and nothing will turn out the way she wants it to. The old ways are coming back again. This time, we will bring the whole town to ruin."

She turned and fled. He didn't follow her. She didn't like being chased.

Jared wanted to get on his bike and escape through the night. But there was nowhere to go, and he didn't want to go, not really. He had to stay and uncover the secrets in this house full of shadows, in the woods, in the lakes with something gold in their depths.

He wasn't on his own anymore. There was Kami to think of now.

Part III

Bring to Light

Whose woods these are I think I know.
—*Robert Frost*

Chapter Fourteen
A Life of Crime

It was before eight on Tuesday morning and Kami was already late to her own meeting when Ash, clearly also late, caught her on the stairs and said, "Can I have a minute?"

Kami hesitated. "Yes," she answered. "You can have exactly one minute. Talk fast."

Ash looked like he felt stressed out having a deadline, but he gave it a shot. "I'm sorry for what I said about Jared. I have to admit I was thrown by how tight you two seemed after knowing each other five minutes, but even if I don't like the guy, it's obvious he's had a rough time and it's good he can talk to someone."

Kami had to give him points for being mature. He looked at her, blue eyes earnest, and she had to give him many more points for being charming. "So, are we okay?" Ash asked.

"Yes," said Kami. "We're okay. So, now do you want to come upstairs and be part of my unstoppable investigative team?"

Ash ducked his head. "Yeah, all right. So . . ." He trailed off.

"Talk while you walk," Kami urged. "Time's a-wasting. Bells will soon be a-ringing."

He followed her at an easy lope while Kami hurried up the stairs. "You said you wanted to do an interview at Aurimere? I haven't found an old-fashioned white shirt yet, but I wondered if you wanted to come over tonight?"

"Sure, if I have time after we break into the lawyer's office."

"I'm sorry," Ash said. *"What?"*

Kami held the door of the headquarters open for him. "Come in. I want to explain my plan to the group."

Ash went in, casting a look that was half amused and half dubious back at her. His stride toward his desk was checked when he walked into the line of Jared's glare.

Ash gave him a chilly glance, then continued to his own desk.

Jared turned his attention to Kami. *Do you want to go out with him?*

We agreed to try to stay out of stuff like that when we were fourteen years old. You remember when we were fourteen!

Kami shut and locked the door. She'd meant her comment to Jared to be another efficient door-closing, but instead she got hit with Jared's feelings, forcing her to turn and look at him. He was leaning forward, arms folded on his desk. Kami found herself caught in the doorway looking back at him.

Yes, said Jared. *I remember when we were fourteen.*

Angela coughed into her hand.

Kami realized that to all appearances she and Jared had just been lost in each other's eyes for the past two minutes. She was used to moments of deep imaginary-friend-related embarrassment. She swallowed this one fast, then clapped her hands together and surveyed her team. Holly was perched on top of Angela's desk, face bright and eager. Angela was kicked back in her chair, looking despairing about the entire universe and Kami in particular. Ash sat forward in his chair, polite and attentive.

Kami could feel Jared's anticipation in her head. He knew what she was about to say. She told the others about finding the guesthouse card in the woods. "So we're going to have to discover who was staying in the Surer Guest on the night the fox was killed," Kami concluded. "And I thought of something else we could do: I want to know who owns the land that hut is on. It's possible the hut was built for a purpose." She beamed around at them. "Isn't this great, guys? Two leads!"

Everyone was not looking as thrilled as she would have wished.

"You want to know who owns the land, so we're breaking into a lawyer's office?" Ash asked.

"I see that you have a few doubts about this plan, Ash," Kami said. "And I commend you on your caution. But I've already tried the library and the Internet, and we don't want anyone to find out we're asking around, do we? I mean, I already got pushed into a well. Plus you don't have to worry about anything going wrong. I used to play in the office with Mr. Prendergast's daughter Nicola."

Until Nicola had decided Kami was too weird to stay her friend.

"Mr. Prendergast has all the deeds to practically every piece of property in town in his third filing cabinet," Kami said. "And it just so happens that I knocked on his door on my way home Sunday and asked to use his bathroom, and left a piece of cardboard holding his bathroom window just a tiny bit open. So this whole thing is going to be a snap!"

"This whole *crime* is going to be a snap," Angela clarified, rolling her big brown eyes.

" 'Crime' is a harsh word, Angela," Kami said. "We're *investigating* a crime. If we could make matters clear to the police, I'm sure they would look at these deeds. But we can't, so we are forced—yes, *forced*!—to do this ourselves. Morally, this is legal."

"Legally, not so much," Angela observed, and uncrossed her legs. "Okay, let's pretend I'm fool enough to go along with this."

"You really think five of us are going to break into a lawyer's office and not get caught?" Ash asked skeptically.

"No," Kami rushed to assure him. "I'll be the only one who breaks in. I mean—goes in. Via the window. I won't be breaking anything." She smiled beneficently around at them. "And all you guys have to do is be my lookouts."

Angela looked resigned. Holly looked intrigued. Ash looked unsure but as if he didn't want to back down. Kami figured that was good enough. She overcame a moment of hesitation and glanced at Jared. All the lights in his crazy gray eyes were dancing. A shiver went through her, a ripple of his delight. She felt again the way she had at the Crying Pools and at her house, the thrill of sharing your secret soul and having someone think it was wonderful.

"Aw," he said. "How come you get to have all the fun?"

The only problem with Mr. Prendergast's office was that

it was on the High Street. A lot of the postcards in Crystal's Gift Shop had some portion of Sorry-in-the-Vale's main street on it, the honey-colored buildings on the street or behind low stone walls, the casement windows gleaming. The oldest buildings were weather-pitted, spotted with lichen, like the inn, the Bell and Mist, and the secondhand bookshop run by Mrs. Pike. Most of the buildings were soft gold Cotswold stone against the bright blue of the sky, cut by random turrets and gently spinning weather vanes.

It was all very nice, but most of the people in Sorry-in-the-Vale had seen it a thousand times, so it was hardly a social whirl. Still Kami noted a few more people on the street than she was entirely comfortable with. She also noticed that a few people were giving their group strange looks, but she wasn't sure if that was because of the presence of the Lynburn boys or because she had a guilty conscience.

Kami thought about her mother telling her how the town regarded the Lynburns. People seemed to respond to them with either awe or fear, and neither made any sense. Particularly not awe directed at Jared, who was kind of a weirdo.

"You doing okay?" Kami asked, falling into step with Holly so she could give her arm a squeeze and also drop a hint in her ear.

"Yes," Holly decided after a moment, and smiled. "I'm just not hardened to a life of crime like you."

"Give it time," Kami said. "So, I'll need two pairs of lookouts, one for the front and one for the back of the place. Maybe you could"—she lowered her voice—"pair off with Jared?"

Holly looked startled, her mouth going through a variety of expressions before settling on amused. "Oh, it's Ash for you, is it?"

"What?" Kami said. "No." She found herself blushing, but it wasn't a totally awful feeling. She was surprised at how much fun it was, talking about boys with a girlfriend. Angela's steady dislike of most of the world meant that she had scorned all Kami's previous crushes.

Holly smiled as if she thought it was fun too. She lowered her voice, as if she was telling Kami a pleasant secret. "You don't have to choose one right away, you know."

"Uh," said Kami, "I'm not really hot enough to juggle two guys. . . ." Holly made a protesting noise. Kami grinned at her and went on. "But thanks for the thought. You've got the wrong idea, though. Jared is not into me like that at all. He told me that you were gorgeous."

"Well," said Holly, so used to hearing it that she didn't blush. She gave Jared a speculative glance.

"Think about it," said Kami, and hurried to catch up.

Jared shot a look over his shoulder as she did so. *There's a card up in your little sweetshop advertising Pomeranian cross puppies free to a good home,* he observed.

What's your point?

I'm not a puppy, said Jared. *You can't give me away.*

Kami and Jared were still arguing in their heads when they reached Mr. Prendergast's office. Kami waved to the broad front steps leading up to the front of the house and the plaque winking in the sun, and to the back, where a few of the buildings around shared a small common. The pairs of sentries could pick their own places. Kami had things to do, offices to break into. She couldn't decide every little thing.

You did think she was gorgeous. Which she is. She is gorgeous, and she owns a motorcycle. Holly is your perfect woman, and I am just trying to help.

Well, don't, Jared thought.

The bathroom window was on the left side of the building, caught in the shadow of the office and a little stone wall, the slate stacked instead of held together with cement. Kami scrambled onto the wall and wiggled the window. Even though it wasn't latched, it stuck slightly in the frame.

Then it was open.

Fine, since you are totally ungrateful and you hate things that are awesome, I won't, Kami thought back. She braced her palms on the sill and boosted herself up. There was a moment when her hips stuck in the frame, and she had to slither over the toilet, using the porcelain edges for handholds. She ended up sitting triumphantly on the bathroom floor.

Victory! Kami announced, leaping up and running into the office with her arms spread wide like an airplane. *If I wasn't going to be a world-famous journalist and if I didn't have such respect for truth and justice, I could be an amazing master criminal.*

I still don't see why I couldn't break in too, Jared complained.

Good luck getting in that window with, like, two people's fair share of shoulders, Kami thought. *That's part of why I would be such a great master criminal. I am so small and so nimble. Built for cat burglary!* She almost nimbly tripped over a box of files on Mr. Prendergast's floor, and decided she should concentrate on her first crime rather than mentally build her criminal empire.

The third filing cabinet, which bore a peeling yellow sticker that said DEEDS in Mr. Prendergast's looping handwriting, was tucked between two big bay windows. Kami felt that this was poor positioning. The white plastic blinds looked very flimsy.

Kami skirted around Mr. Prendergast's desk and dropped to her knees by the filing cabinet, pulling out the bottom drawer. She found some leases and went through them to check that nobody was renting the hut in the woods.

There are a couple of people standing in front of the building, Jared reported uneasily. *They're looking at us suspiciously.*

Kami closed the cabinet drawer with a slam. She instantly regretted the noise and bit her lip hard.

Retreat was impossible. Kami sprang to her feet and pulled out the top drawer. Here were the deeds of property ownership! She rifled through them, recognizing houses and farms, fields and woods.

You maybe want to get out of there, Jared advised. *These people aren't going away. If one of them spots you through the window—*

Well, do something! Kami commanded.

Like what? Jared demanded.

Like anything! Do I have to think of everything? Kami asked, hands flying through the files. This was jointly owned by Robin, Lillian, and Rosalind Lynburn, and this, and this . . . *Have a big dramatic breakup!*

Well, Jared said after a minute, *all right.*

Kami didn't have time to dread discovery or worry about the violent explosion of glee from Jared. He liked getting into trouble.

Kami liked getting results. She hadn't realized how much of Sorry-in-the-Vale the Lynburns owned. It must be half the town. Lords of the manor, indeed.

She was not surprised to find they owned the land where she'd calculated the hut stood. It didn't impress her as significant. The Lynburns owned almost the entire wood. Her fingers moved automatically, pulling out the next file. It was the deeds to the Glass house.

The Lynburns owned that too.

Kami stood transfixed.

Kami's grandmother had said years ago that she and Kami's father stayed in the Glass house because it was all they owned free and clear. Kami's parents might lie to her for her own good, the way parents did, but Sobo had never lied. She'd been a believer in the stark truth.

So was Kami. But this made no sense. This couldn't possibly be true.

Kami made her mind up fast. She drew the deed out of the drawer, folded it, and slipped it in her jeans pocket. Then she ducked down and ran, half-crouched, to the bathroom. She scrambled onto the toilet, launching herself onto the sill. In her haste, she overshot and landed on her hands and knees on the strip of grass between the building and the wall.

Kami took a moment to catch her breath. Then she stood, still dizzy, and looked into the faces of Holly and Angela. They were peering around the side of the building from the back, Holly's bright curls mingling with Angela's black waterfall of hair. They were both helpless with laughter.

Oh my God, what have you done? Kami demanded. She led the charge to the front of the building, where Jared stood at the top of the steps, looking pleased with himself.

At the bottom of the steps was a ring of amazed onlookers, and Ash with a split lip.

"Hi, Mrs. Thompson. Hi, Mr. Stearn. My gracious, Jared, is that the time?" Kami asked loudly. "We have to go!"

"Is what the time?" Jared asked, giving her a brilliant smile. The smile and the feeling that followed it flashed through her like sunlight.

Kami raised her eyebrows. *I think it's probably beat-down-for-Jared o'clock,* she said. *Once I find out what you did.*

They made it halfway up the street, to the statue of Matthew Cooper, who had died heroically sometime in 1480, and then everybody collapsed. Holly and Angela fell in a heap at the base of the statue, Ash leaned against it, and Jared leaned back against the railings that ran along the front of the inn and smiled like a devil.

"He is totally insane," Ash said, at the same time as Holly said, with equal conviction, "That was hilarious."

"What happened?" Kami demanded.

"Some people stopped in front of the office," Angela said. "I don't think they suspected anything, though; they were just looking at the Lynburn boys acting crazy."

"Who left them together at the front of the house?" Kami asked, giving Holly an accusing glare.

"You didn't say who was meant to go where," Angela said

calmly. "I don't like Jared and I am indifferent to Ash, so I made Holly come with me. It's not my fault there's no such thing as the perfect crime. Anyway, I'm glad I did it, because I—and he—" Angela's face was usually sternly beautiful. It was weird to see her sentence swallowed by a laugh.

Angela laid her head down on Holly's shoulder while Kami looked around for answers.

"He punched me in the face," said Ash, who understandably did not seem to find the situation humorous at all. "And then he yelled at me for sleeping with our personal trainer!"

"I was told breakup scenes were a good way to distract people," Jared said with beautiful simplicity.

"Ash looked so surprised," Holly said. "He had no idea what was going on. He said, 'I didn't sleep with our personal trainer! We don't even have a personal trainer!'"

Angela and Holly giggled. Ash held the back of his hand to his bleeding mouth and glared.

Jared was still grinning like a maniac. "In that case," he told Ash solemnly, "I will consider taking you back."

Kami sighed. "You are the worst team of operatives any master criminal has ever had."

Chapter Fifteen
Burning or Drowning

Kami ran home to change out of her criminal mastermind jeans into a debatably datelike dress for Ash. Dad called out to her as soon as she was in the door. "Kami, ring for a fork-lift and tell them it's the usual problem: we've got a Montgomery asleep on the floor."

Kami peeked around the door, vaguely surprised Angela had made it there so fast. Instead, she found Rusty stretched out on the hearthrug with his arms behind his head.

"You disgraceful object," said Kami. "What are you doing here?"

"I'm buying a shotgun," Dad announced. "I live in the country. A shotgun is a reasonable thing to own."

Kami abandoned the issue of Rusty's home invasion in order to run upstairs and put on a black dress with white polka dots, and red tights. Then she had to go back to the sitting room because the best mirror was over the fireplace and she wanted to check her lip gloss. "Rusty, Dad needs to work and I'm going out, so you're babysitting."

"I like that word," Rusty said, settling down for a nap. "Come, babies. Let us sit together."

Tomo sat down in the vacated space by Rusty's head and

began pulling his hair. Rusty smiled beatifically and did not open his eyes.

"Why are you putting on lip gloss, my daughter?" Dad asked. "Trip to the library? Trip to the nunnery? I hear the nunneries are nice this time of year."

"Not a date; I still remember Claud," Rusty said, and grabbed her ankle. "I forbid it."

"You introduced me to Claud," Kami pointed out.

"I'm a bad person," Rusty mumbled. "I do bad things."

"Is this true, Kami? Are you going out on a date?" Dad asked tragically. "Wearing that? Wouldn't you fancy a shapeless cardigan instead? You rock a shapeless cardigan, honey."

"I'm not going out with anyone," said Kami, almost sure it was true.

Rusty tugged at her ankle until she knelt beside him. "He sounds nice," Rusty murmured, as if mostly asleep. "And maybe it will distract you from chasing maniacs in the woods. I've been worrying about you."

"You know me better than that," said Kami. "I'm on a mission. And you really do not appear to have been losing sleep."

Rusty levered himself up on his elbows and opened his eyes. Firelight made his hazel eyes gleam; he seemed almost alert. "The stuff you were saying, about people doing rituals to get what they want," he said, "except the rituals won't work, because they are crazy and magic isn't real. I don't like thinking about how frustrated crazy people might get."

Kami was silent, because she knew something Rusty didn't. She knew about herself and Jared, and their connection. If that was real, who knew what else was? If the rituals were working, what did they do, and what else might these people sacrifice?

"I'll be careful," she said at length. "I'm just going to do an interview."

Rusty collapsed back on the hearthrug. "Have fun, and don't be home late. I get dinner out of babysitting, right?"

"I'm buying a shotgun tomorrow," said Dad. "Rusty, you might as well call your sister if we're feeding you. Kami, you really should sit and tell me more about this ill-advised social outing—"

"Gotta go! Love you, bye!" said Kami, and fled.

You had your fun for the day, Kami told Jared severely. *By which I mean that you punched your cousin in the face. That means I get to go around Aurimere House and have Ash tell me everything he knows about the Lynburns.*

Ash was the one who had asked Kami up to Aurimere. If he wanted to show her around and spend a little time alone with her, she thought that was only fair. He'd had a bad day. And if in the process he spilled any dark family secrets, she was ready to hear them. She was investigating, after all. Reporters did what they had to do to get their story. But it didn't hurt her ego that Ash seemed to actually like her. So she ignored Jared's sulking, tucked her hand in the crook of Ash's arm, and let him show off the manor.

Aurimere was all long corridors and huge rooms. Ash escorted her into one room that was drenched in light because one wall was a vast casement window. The small rectangular panes stretched from stone floor to the white ceiling, each of them yellow and filtering in the sunlight dyed twice with gold, translucent rather than transparent.

The ceiling was painted white, but its surface was raised, covered with shapes and symbols. Kami made out stars, flowers, satyrs, and a woman's face, repeated over and over until the ceiling finished with the elaborate cornices at each end. It gave her an uneasy feeling. She glanced at Ash, who smiled down at her.

"I know," he said. "It's beautiful."

Kami blinked and took comfort from the fact that not every boy could read her mind. "Settling in easily, then?" she asked as Ash led her up a short flight of steps to another room. This one had to be the fanciest parlor in the world. It had sofas with scarlet canopies.

"I've been waiting my whole life to get here," Ash said. "Ever since I was small, it's all I can remember my mother and father talking about. Once Mother found Aunt Rosalind, we were going home to Sorry-in-the-Vale. We never stayed anywhere long, and I never wanted to. We were always coming home." He gave her his charming smile. "Just taking the long way around."

"Your family's lived here a long time," Kami said encouragingly. "You must know a lot of stories." Or incriminating secrets or whatever.

"You've lived in Sorry-in-the-Vale all your life," Ash said, politely encouraging in his turn. "You must know a lot too."

"What, me? No, hardly any. *You* should tell some," Kami said. "I think your dad knew my mother back in the day. Claire Glass?"

Ash shook his head. "He's never mentioned her."

They passed through a little hall, the ceiling curving over

their heads. The light fixture hanging from the center of the ceiling was a sphere cupped by ringed hands.

Kami tried to think of leading questions, and caught sight of the Lynburn family crest over the door. It was a four-square shape. The outline of Aurimere House on a hill was in the top left, the wood on the top right. On the bottom left was a square of pale blue, and on the bottom right was a woman's profile. Cutting through the pictures was a sword hilt with a hand wrapped around it. Below the crest in gold letters were the words HAUD IGNEUS, HAUD UNDA.

"Gosh," said Kami, in the innocent tones of one who knew no Latin, none at all. "What is that?"

"It's the family motto," Ash said.

"Don't tell me, let me guess," Kami said, since Ash showed no signs of telling her. "Your motto is 'Blonds really do have more fun.'"

Another Lynburn motto possibility, if her mother was to be believed, was "Hot Blond Death."

"I think brunettes are cute, personally," said Ash. "Something like, neither fire nor water. It's meant to convey— I think—'We neither drown nor burn.' Of course, that might mean we were all born to hang."

Kami glanced up at him. His face was oddly serious. "I doubt *you* were," said Kami and squeezed Ash's arm.

"Well, thank you, ma'am," Ash remarked, exaggerating his Southern drawl. Kami laughed, delighted, even though Ash went back to being serious the next instant. "The way my parents have always talked about this place, and about what it meant to be our family . . ." He hesitated.

"Yes?" Kami prompted, and gave him a "Give me a

clue, you big, strong, handsome man" glance under her eye-lashes.

"It's a lot of responsibility" was all Ash said. "I want to do it right."

Kami sighed. "I'm sure you will."

As they explored further, Kami saw rooms that showed how long Aurimere had stood empty. In the sitting room where Ash stopped and sat in a window seat, Kami noticed the peach curtains were a little tattered. There were no sofas or chairs, and the built-in bookshelves were empty, but there was a fire guard before the large carved mantelpiece and a wooden statue of a lady in draped medieval dress with a stain in the center of her forehead like a bullet hole.

"You have now seen almost all of the house that has fancy things, like actual furniture, in it," Ash said. "I spend most of my weekends with my parents at antique fairs. Wild, I know."

Kami smiled down at him. He smiled back up at her. His hair glowed in the sunlight, and the garden was a riot of color below.

Ash smiled back and began to rise, face turned up to hers, when two things happened: Kami felt the sharp spike of Jared's unhappiness, and she saw someone walking through the garden.

Kami turned her face away. "Who's that?"

"My dad," said Ash.

"Oh, I want to meet him," Kami said instantly. "Not in a loopy 'I want to meet your parents, I want your babies' way. For the interview! Let's go."

Ash took this gracefully, giving her a rueful grin and

taking her hand when she offered it. He let her pull him from the window seat and back down the stone steps.

There was a black iron door standing open in one of the hallways, light streaming through it. All Kami saw at first glance were the flowers on the door, tiny flowers and lines as if the flowers were caught in a river, but then she made out, in the lower right-hand corner of the door, a woman's profile. She was drowning, the flowers caught in her hair.

When Kami pushed the door open, she noticed that the doorknob was a clenched fist. She didn't want to say "Wow, creepy architecture you have going on here" to Ash. There were so many times it was excellent that a boy could not read your mind. She just kept smiling as they walked into the garden, and she saw a tall, broad-shouldered man with straw-blond hair and Ash's blue eyes coming toward them, pushing a wheelbarrow.

"Hey there, son," said Rob Lynburn. "Who's your friend?"

"Kami Glass." Kami offered a hand.

Rob let go of the wheelbarrow and shook it. He had callused hands, a farmer's hands rather than the lord of the manor's hands. When he smiled, she saw where Ash had inherited his charm, though his father's was less polished. She had not expected a Lynburn to look so normal.

"Well now," said Rob. "Not Claire Somerville's daughter?"

"Yes," Kami said thankfully: information was beckoning at last! "Claire's daughter."

"Of course, of course," Rob said. "Now I look at you, I see you're just as pretty as Claire."

"Not really," said Kami. "My mother said you used to have an office over Claire's before you moved away."

"Between you and me," Rob confided, "not so much an office as a hidey-hole. Sometimes a man needs to be by himself, no matter how lovely the ladies he's living with are, and Rosy and Lillian were always that. Of course, I had your lovely mother's company for lunch every day. Claire Somerville!" He turned to his son. "We've been all over America, practically, haven't we?"

"Practically," said Ash.

"In all that time, I never saw a face like Claire Somerville's." Unlike his remark about Kami being as pretty as her mother, this Kami believed. She had seen the way men could not forget her mother and Angela, always wandering back for another look as if every man was a compass and beauty was true north.

Don't tell your father, Mum had said. Kami wondered for the hundredth time, Don't tell him *what*?

"My mother said you two were great friends back in the day," Kami lied enthusiastically. "You must have some fun stories from before we were born."

"Oh, a few, a few," Rob told her. "Come to think of it, my other boy has mentioned your name a couple of times. Kami, wasn't it?"

"That's right," Kami said, caught off guard by feeling guilty at the mention of Jared and being pleased by the way Rob called Jared "my other boy" so casually. She smiled up at him.

He used her moment of weakness to escape. "You give your mother my best, now. Ash, give me a hand with this load of clippings, and then I'll let you get back to the lady."

Ash complied, with an apologetic look at Kami. Kami was dispirited enough by her lack of investigative skills that she watched them go without protest. She followed the rockery wall, counting stones and preparing interview questions that would elicit some information. The rockery ended and a climbing frame for roses began. Kami began to count blooms.

A voice behind her said: "And who, may I ask, are you?"

Kami spun around twice, so she was dizzy when she saw that the climbing frame was in fact an arch, making an alcove of roses in the depths of the Lynburn garden. Among the roses and the shadows was a figure in black. If Rosalind Lynburn was a ghost, this was the living woman. No one had told Kami that Lillian and Rosalind were *identical* twins.

Lillian Lynburn stayed sitting, legs crossed, a picture of elegant composure. Ash might have got his charm from his father, but he had gotten his polish from Lillian. And yet she didn't remind Kami of Ash, or of her own twin. Her presence was not like Rosalind's but Jared's. She exploded into the senses like a punch in the face.

On Lillian, Rosalind's pale veil of hair was pinned up in a smooth chignon. Rosalind's soft mouth was painted red and pursed impatiently, waiting for Kami's response.

"Oh," said Kami. "Oh, hi. I'm Kami Glass."

Lillian raised her darkened, sculpted eyebrows in what seemed to be an utter lack of recognition. "All right," she said. "What are you doing here?"

"Ash invited me," Kami said uncertainly.

"Did he," said Lillian, with a vague air of surprise that Kami found insulting.

"You knew my parents," Kami forged ahead. "Jon Glass and Claire Somerville?"

Lillian's face remained perfectly blank and indifferent. "They were more likely to know me than I was to know them," she offered. "I was the Lynburn." The nerve of her, able to state such a thing so coolly, made Kami almost laugh. Lillian's eyebrows lifted; they were the only expressive feature of her face.

"My mother was right about you," Kami said.

"What did she say about me?" Lillian inquired.

"She said you used to think you were queen of every blade of grass in the Vale—" Kami stopped, horrified at herself.

Lillian's mouth curved in a slow red smile. "I still do."

Her gaze shifted to a point above Kami's shoulder. The brief warmth in her eyes, like a glint of sunlight on a frozen lake, made Kami unsurprised to look around and see Ash. She was also not surprised to see he looked alarmed. Ash put a hand on Kami's back as he came up to her, as if in apology for anything Lillian had said. He was naturally kind, she was starting to realize, which was better than being charming.

"Mother, this is Kami," said Ash.

"So I am continually informed," Lillian murmured.

"Kami, Mother," said Ash in an undertone. "Let's go see some more of the garden," he added, and used the hand on her back to guide Kami away.

"I am fascinated by gardening," Kami agreed solemnly. "Tell me about fertilizer, Ash."

"I dunno, we haven't known each other that long, that's kind of racy talk," said Ash.

They walked to the other side of the garden, where Rob was pruning, more because it was far from Lillian than because Ash had anything special to show her. There was a gate there. Kami peered over it and saw the dip and slope of the fields below the hill.

All Lynburn land, she was sure, and she thought of the piece of paper at home in her jeans pocket. She looked at the ground and saw a dark object sticking out from the bottom of the gate. It was a life-size hand, part of the gate, its fingers reaching up to Kami as if in appeal.

Kami took a step back. "Have you noticed that a lot of your décor is kind of human-hand-based, Ash?"

"Uh, no," said Ash, sounding puzzled.

Kami started to list off examples—the hand doorknob, the hand holding the sword hilt, the hands clasping the light, and now this. She refrained from mentioning the fact that the other Lynburn theme was drowned women.

They were standing by the manor wall. Ash was examining his own hands, held out before him, and calling comments over his shoulder to Rob as his father gardened, when Kami felt an impulse to turn around. Like a mental nudge.

Kami, said Jared, and then in an urgent, real whisper: "Kami!"

Kami edged toward the tower that stood nearby, joined to the manor but somehow apart from it, a bright column with a door into the dark. When she was a step closer, she saw Jared standing against the wall in that darkness.

"Come here," he said, and grinned. He was fresh from a

bike ride, hair ruffled, chest rising and falling hard, the glitter of a thin chain and a glint of sweat at the hollow of his throat. There was a thrill running through him, a feeling of discovery, something wild that crept into her blood as well.

I can't, she said automatically, and looked toward Ash.

Kami, Jared protested, just as automatically.

Kami looked back at him, and then at Ash again. *Look here upon this picture, and on this,* she thought, calling up the line from a play about an evil brother and a good one.

It was a striking contrast, Ash standing in the sun laughing and calling out to his father versus Jared in the dim stairwell like Ash's lurking shadow self, scar pale in the darkness. The worst part was that Jared saw it too, through her eyes, saw who looked like an angel and who looked like something else.

In a bleak rush of feeling, like an icy river with his thoughts tumbling jagged stones caught in the cold, Jared did not even blame her. He thought: *No wonder.*

Kami threw herself into the shadows and the stairwell. *That's not it, that's not what I meant,* she told him, grabbing his jacket.

Jared broke away from her and ran up the steep curve of stairs in the darkness. Kami ran along with him. They barely checked their steps when a storm broke out of a clear sky and sent shuddering pale reflections of lightning through a window Kami could not even see yet. Thunder followed and they kept running, even though Kami felt like the tower would be shaken by the storm at any moment. It almost made sense to her whirling mind as they ran: sunlight with Ash, and lightning with Jared.

They reached the top of the bell tower panting and breathless, Kami dizzy from the turns of the stairs. The bell was in the river, so it was just a room that had four vast glass-less windows. Rain swept in from all sides in sheets. Jared and Kami stood in the center of the room.

"I was riding my bike really fast and I saw it," Jared murmured, breath still ragged. He pointed and Kami saw it too, the dark curve of the wood from the foot of the hill where Aurimere stood, reaching in a perfect comma toward the little house at the other end of the woods. Toward Kami's house, which the Lynburns owned.

"What does it mean?" Kami asked.

Jared said, "I don't know."

A moving gleam much closer caught Kami's attention. She went to the side of the bell tower and peered into the lashing rain to see more clearly. Below, she saw Rob Lynburn abandon his wheelbarrow, Lillian emerge from her alcove, Ash lift his eyes, and Rosalind run out of the house.

The Lynburns came to stand in their wild garden, shuddering between storm-cloud darkness and washes of ghastly pale light. Their faces were turned up, tiny moons mirroring the lightning, their arms spread out, welcoming the storm.

Kami looked at Jared and saw his eyes had gone lightning-pale. His fear shuddered through her, like the ghostly light flooding the room.

What is wrong with them? And if there's something wrong with them, what does that make me?

"Jared!" she shouted over the storm. When he did not answer, she grabbed his jacket again, with both hands this time, not letting him pull away, and yelled for him out loud and in her head until he turned his rain-slicked face to hers. "Listen to me. I don't know what's going on. I don't know what any of this means. But I know this much. It doesn't matter. You're not one of them. You never were. You're not theirs. You're mine."

Jared bowed his head to hers, looked into her face, and calmed, as if he found some certainty there Kami could not find herself. "Yeah," he said to her, as she'd said to him twice before. "I know."

It was electrically uncomfortable to hold on, even only to his jacket, but she did. They stood together in the empty bell tower while the storm lasted, with the Lynburns dancing in the garden below.

Chapter Sixteen
Underwater Light

The Surer Guest was out in the countryside, north of Auri-mere as the woods were west and the town was south. Kami had never noticed before how much of Sorry-in-the-Vale was constructed with the manor as its center, and now she could not stop noticing. The guesthouse was made of Cotswold stone and looked pale as butter in the dying evening light, at the top of the long, curving gravel driveway.

The Surer Guest had hosted a wedding earlier that day. The parking lot at the bottom of the driveway was crammed. The door was ajar and much bustling was still going on inside: carts of laundry, food, and cleaning products were being wheeled through the hall from the kitchen area to the offices and storerooms. Still, there was not quite so much bustling that five teenagers could troop in undetected.

"Technically, it's older than the manor. It's built around a twelfth-century hall," Kami said, peeping in through the door. "You'll see that when we get in."

"*If* we get in," said Ash.

Kami gave Ash an uncertain glance. She had gone home yesterday without telling him goodbye, and she still wasn't sure how to frame a question about his weirdo family running out into rainstorms. She kept turning and looking at him, as if his handsome face might at any moment slide away like a mask.

"Oh, how could we fail to get in?" Angela asked, rolling her eyes. "After all, people love to see teenagers loitering around. Especially when they're dressed like ninjas."

As Kami had made the calls earlier today directing wardrobe choice, she was aware Angela's eye roll was aimed at her. "Don't worry," she told them all.

"Why?" Jared asked. "Because everyone loves a ninja?"

"Because I have a plan," said Kami, and looked brightly around at her team.

Everyone was dressed in black as she'd asked. Angela was even wearing a hat, possibly so she could roll it down like a ski mask over her face. Jared and Ash looked more alike than ever, though Jared's T-shirt was short-sleeved and worn, straining at the shoulders. Holly was wearing a black cocktail dress.

Kami said, "I want you to go in there and vamp that receptionist."

"What?" Ash said blankly.

"You know," Kami said. "Dazzle her with your charms. Rock her world. Go on."

They turned to gaze at the receptionist, a bored-looking woman with a magazine tucked not-terribly-surreptitiously under her mouse pad. She looked back at them, over the counter and through the open door, with a stare of utter apathy.

"What," Ash said, "all of us?"

"Do you want to stand around trying to guess if she likes pretty boys or rough trade?" Jared asked, gesturing lazily from Ash to himself.

"Excuse me, what did you just call yourself?" Ash demanded. "No, wait a second, I don't care. What did you just call *me*?"

"Why are you doing this to me?" Angela moaned. "I knew getting out of bed today was even more of a mistake than it usually is."

"Vamping," Holly said with conviction, "I can do."

"*Thank you,* Holly," Kami said. "All I want is unquestioning obedience, you people, is that so much to ask? I come up with the plans! I buy all the staples! I need you to do this one little thing for me."

"Oh, well," said Jared, "if it's for the staples, should I take off my shirt?"

Holly laughed and grabbed Angela's elbow. Somewhat surprisingly, Angela let Holly drag her and even answered Holly's laugh with a smile, though she seemed conflicted about it. Jared gave Ash a challenging glance and set off, while Kami made a shooing gesture as if they were geese. The whole party stumbled through the door and up to the counter where the receptionist sat.

Kami sidled out the door a few minutes later, unnoticed since every eye was drawn to the mass vamp in progress. The others followed her out soon enough.

Holly was laughing. "Jared told her he used to be an exotic dancer in San Francisco."

"My body is a gift from God," Jared said gravely. "Except for my hips, which are clearly a gift from the devil."

"I'm surprised she didn't call the police," Ash muttered. "I would have."

Angela looked traumatized, but not so traumatized that

she failed to notice something was different. Her eyes went straight to the pile in Kami's arms. "What have you got there?"

"Aprons I took from one of the laundry carts while the guy pushing it was distracted by the sight of four people making epic fools of themselves," Kami told her.

"And you couldn't just tell us to make fools of ourselves?" Ash asked.

"I didn't want you to get stiff and self-conscious," said Kami. "I wanted you to act natural. And you were all brilliant!"

"I'm concerned about your vamping skills," Holly told Angela. "You're gorgeous. You can do better. Actually, almost anyone can do better than 'Don't look at me.'"

Angela shrugged.

"We were brilliant, natural fools?" Jared asked. He was grinning, but then, of course, he was the only one apart from Kami who had known exactly what was going on. They didn't have secrets from each other.

Well. She didn't have any secrets from him.

Kami pushed the thought aside and grinned back at him, feeling his delight curl around her heart. "Especially you, tiny dancer. The Surer Guest ordered a pile of baked goods for today from my mother, so I learned they hired on a lot of staff for the weekend wedding. Staff they would not expect to recognize on sight. And the uniform," Kami said with modest pride, "is black clothes with this apron over it."

"You're a genius," Holly said as Kami passed around the aprons.

Kami preened.

The Surer Guest was like a maze. This evening the maze was crowded with people either clearing up the wedding dinner or continuing the wedding party. There was the reception hall, where the receptionist sat, still looking a bit stunned. One big door led to the ballroom; the other door opened into a corridor that led to the kitchens. The offices were on either side. Across the hall, two broad staircases led to a balcony, and from there to the guest rooms.

Kami had told everyone to spread out in different directions as soon as they were in the door, so when she headed purposefully for the offices, she was startled to find Jared at her heels. *Go investigate somewhere else!* she ordered.

No, said Jared. *Someone's still after you. I'm not leaving you to be pushed into another well.*

How many wells are you expecting to find in a guesthouse? Kami inquired.

Well, I'm not leaving you to be smashed on the head with a candlestick in the billiard room either.

Kami could tell Jared was serious, so she didn't waste her time arguing with him. She approached a door, beckoning Jared toward it, and then flung it open on a room full of cleaning supplies. A mop tipped over with a bang. Kami tried not to jump at the noise.

Next one, Jared said. He opened the next door, which led to a room full of washing machines and dryers. And a couple, the woman sitting on the washing machine, pulling the guy's shirt open and tie aside while her legs wrapped around his waist.

Kami squeaked.

Jared coughed, said "Sorry," and shut the door fast.

It was okay that she'd squeaked, Kami told herself. It wasn't that she didn't have nerves of steel. She went ahead and tried the next door. It slid open to reveal an empty desk with filing cabinets arranged around it. "I'll take the computer; you take the cabinets," Kami said.

There was a purple Post-it under the stapler with CASSIE41 written on it. When Kami turned the computer on and tried to access the Guests file, a box popped up asking for a password. Kami typed "CASSIE41" and it let her through.

Unfortunately, along with the lack of security was a lack of organization. Kami spent a while finding a lot of entries for this year's guests in last year's file. She resisted the urge to reorganize it. As the light in the windows died, she squinted at the glowing surface of the computer screen and cursed the fact that she could not turn on the lights.

Then she found the records for the night of September 10. She heard Jared turn and walk to the computer.

"Stop," Kami said. "Let me have the satisfaction of saying 'Jackpot' so you can be both startled and impressed."

"Okay."

"Jackpot," said Kami. "You can look now."

Jared leaned on the back of her chair and looked over her shoulder. Kami used the cursor to point out the names of the guests to him. "Slow night," Kami commented. "Only three guests. Jocelyn and Chris Fairchild, looking to get a romantic night without the kids. And Terry Cholmondeley—"

"With his wife," Jared said. "Madeline."

"Well, he's not actually married," Kami said. "He's from Sorry-in-the-Vale, though. So that leaves us Henry Thornton from London. Who came down alone for one night." Kami pressed PRINT on the page with Henry Thornton's details on it. The printer obliged her with a soft whirring sound.

The sound of steps down the corridor made Kami freeze, then she reached out with shaky hands to flip up the edge of the warm paper emerging from the printer. She could see half of Henry Thornton's address—she just needed one more minute. . . .

Jared spun her chair around. She glanced up into his eyes. *Someone's coming,* he thought at her. *You'd better kiss me.*

"Because someone's coming? That's so clichéd," Kami said. She stood, grabbing the printed page in one hand. They both heard a step outside the door. Jared leaned down and hesitated.

He wasn't going to do it. He always tried to avoid actually touching her.

The door opened.

The woman standing in the doorway wore a Surer Guest apron. Kami was uneasily aware of the stains on theirs. She also hoped the woman hadn't heard the sound of a computer being turned off.

"What are you two doing?"

"Dusting!" Kami exclaimed.

The woman snorted. "As if I didn't know."

"I assure you, we weren't canoodling," Kami said.

"Really," the woman said. "Then may I ask what you *were* doing?"

"You caught us," Jared announced. "Totally—uh—canoodling. The laundry room was occupied by fellow canoodlers, so we took a chance."

"The laundry . . ." The woman glanced down the hall. "You two stay right there. I'm going to have a word with your supervisor!" She set off.

Jared and Kami exchanged a look. Then they both dashed for the door, into the hall, and in the other direction from the woman as fast as they could run, and through the door at the end of the corridor. They blundered into darkness and then into several other things.

Jared cursed. "What is that?"

Kami patted the object in an investigatory fashion. "I think it's an exercise bike. My other theory, that it's a giant whisk, seems unlikely."

"Okay," Jared said in a whisper, breathless from running, and sounding like he wanted to laugh. "Just a little gym. That's okay. Let's just go through here. Take my—" He cut himself off before he said "hand."

Kami didn't take his hand. It wouldn't help; it would put them more off balance, and it wasn't like they could lose each other.

They were both silent, pretending they couldn't feel the other's discomfort, until they went through into another room and Jared fell over what Kami thought was a massage chair.

His amusement flared through her. After a moment, she said, "Lucky that door was open."

"If it hadn't been," Jared said, close by her ear, "I could have got it open."

Kami negotiated past a massage table and into what seemed to be a cupboard full of bottles, which rocked ominously for a minute. She made for the next door, visible by the dim glow in the next room, not like there was a light on but as if there was a fish tank in there.

"No, you could not have," she told Jared, smiling at him in the dark. "Not by breaking anything or jimmying any locks or indeed performing any acts of delinquency at all. Because you've reformed."

"Oh yeah," Jared said. "Obviously."

Kami fumbled for the door handle, grasped it, and turned it. "This is different. As was the lawyer's office. We're in pursuit of justice." She peered warily into the next room.

Jared came to lean against the doorframe beside her. "I just get confused," he claimed, laughing low. "Being good's only fun when it's with you."

Light reflected on the wall in the next room, a moving shimmer against the white tiles.

Kami advanced cautiously.

The room was circular, lined with pale tiles. At Kami's feet lay a square of dark water. There was a skylight above the pool. The night sky turned the pool into a mirror, dusting the water with stars.

Kami heard Jared laugh again and turned. He was taking off his shirt: the apron was on the floor. She caught sight of a slice of stomach and looked hastily back at the pool. "Jared," she said, mouth dry. "This is not being good!" She felt the inviting thrill course through her, the idea of abandoning just a little control.

"But it might be fun."

"I'm not doing it and you're not doing it either," Kami told him.

Jared dived. His body cut through the water, disappearing

in the dark with only a ripple. Kami could feel Jared's thoughts chasing through her brain: his adrenaline, the pleasure of getting away with something, something as harmless as this.

Jared's head broke the surface, his hair dark with water, the faint shimmer of light pale on his skin. "Come on," he said.

Kami hesitated for a moment and ordered, "Turn around."

Jared smiled, the little smile that went all the way through her, and did. Kami studied his shoulder blades with suspicion as she took off her apron and then the black T-shirt, being careful of the page tucked in the apron. She wished she'd worn underwear that matched, though that happened approximately three days of the year. But she wished she'd at least worn discreet black instead of a bright orange bra.

"Orange?" Jared asked. He answered her wave of indignation with a quick "Not peeking! Reading your mind!"

"I wonder what privacy would be like. Guess I'll never know," said Kami, and jumped into the water. It was a cool, lovely shock, her limbs floating in the new element. Her soft laughter echoed off the tiles and was swallowed by Jared's light splash at her face.

Kami splashed him back, shivering in the cool water. Jared was thinking of grabbing and dunking her, thinking about it mostly just to tease her. Only, it would be weird if he did, and he was a lot bigger than she was.

"Hey," said Jared, turning. The ripples in the pool as he moved washed against Kami's skin. The hair on her arms rose, her skin tingling. "I would never hurt you."

"I know you wouldn't," Kami said quickly. "It isn't that."

It wasn't that. It was the fact that he was here, which kept being disturbing, and that she was so terribly aware of him being there, all the time. She was thinking hundreds of things at once, like that they were going to get caught, and noticing the muscles in Jared's chest and shoulders without knowing what to do about the fact that she was noticing.

In spite of all that, this was fun.

Kami's eye was caught by the glint of the thin chain she'd noticed around Jared's neck at the bell tower. She saw what had been hidden by his T-shirt now: an old penny, like the one she had sent him years ago.

Kami looked up at his face.

"I told you I got it," Jared said. "I found it on the floor in our apartment."

Kami looked away from him, feeling the weight of his gaze on her. And she didn't want Jared seeing any of her thoughts, so she splashed at him and said, "Two laps. Race you."

A noise in one of the exercise rooms beyond made Kami lunge for the side of the pool. She pulled herself out and grabbed their clothes, feeling in her apron pocket for the paper. Then she ran to join Jared. He was out of the pool, trying to pull open the glass door that led to a patio outside.

It was locked.

Kami could hear footsteps by now, coming closer. She shoved Jared's clothes at his chest. *I knew this was a bad idea. Pursuing justice is good karma! Pursuing illicit fun leads to being apprehended while unclothed!*

The steps rang out, echoing clearly off the tiles and the skylighted roof.

Jared took a deep breath and said, "Kami, I'm sorry."

The glitter of stars on the pool water caught Kami's eye. She looked at it, even with the echoing steps, even while a man's voice called out: "Who's there?"

The light in the pool was so bright it seemed like there was something under the water, light radiating like underwater treasure.

What the hell is that? Jared asked.

I have no idea.

The beam wasn't a trick of the night. It wasn't their panic. Luminescence was coalescing in the air, like a curtain of crystal, stretching from the pool water beside them and reaching to the skylight. Through that gleaming curtain Kami saw a security guy, his uniform dark and his expression the same.

The guard looked around the room. He did not seem fazed by the shimmer of light in the air, or the two wet teenagers in their underwear shivering behind it. He frowned, nodded, and turned around. He hadn't seen them. He hadn't seen anything.

As soon as the man left, the lights faded, like dust motes glittering for an instant and then quenched by a sudden shadow.

Kami leaned weakly back against the glass door. "Not to steal your line," she murmured. "But what the hell was that?"

"I have no idea," said Jared.

Chapter Seventeen
Alone upon the Threshold

When they went back through the guesthouse and found the others outside, Kami was too dazed to do more than mumble something about it being good work, team, and go home. She went to bed in a state of shock.

She did believe in the paranormal, or was open to believing in it: there was no other explanation for her and Jared's link. But how could she work out something as impossible as an event that interfered with reality, that made someone blind to what was there? What, or who, had caused it?

Kami slept uneasily, plagued by bad dreams that felt as if they left stains on her mind as they passed through. She woke early, pulling herself out of bed and into the dress she'd laid out the night before. Kami slipped into green shoes decorated with daisies and went downstairs. It was past six in the morning, so her mother was gone, but everyone else was asleep.

The house was so quiet it felt like the morning sunlight had to flow in more gradually, as if the whole morning was conspiring with Kami in trying not to disturb her family. She couldn't stay here in all this quiet.

She walked to school, thinking that she would get to her headquarters and feel better, but once she was there she just found herself sitting in her chair, staring at her notebook with two words, "Lynburns" and "Magic," written on the page, and nothing else.

She didn't know how to make a plan for magic, why anyone might kill for it, or why someone might help them using it. She wasn't in control, and she didn't know what to do. She wanted the magic to stop, and at the same time she wanted Jared.

Kami reached out and felt the rush of his concern. Then she looked up at the sound of the door sighing shut and saw him. She started, but he crossed the floor toward her, eyes on hers, and she was soothed past the strangeness of it. She felt like he could put his arms around her, she could hide her face in that ridiculous leather jacket, and she would feel better.

He stopped on the other side of her desk and said, "What can I do?"

"Well," Kami said, and looked down at her notebook so he couldn't see her face, "I wish I knew what those rituals with the animals did."

"Rituals with—you think they worked?"

"Maybe," she said. "Something happened at the guesthouse last night. And there's us—we can read each other's minds. I know there's an explanation, but it doesn't seem like there's a reasonable one. So, what if the rituals do work in some way?"

"What we are isn't related to any of this," Jared said. "In any way."

The sudden chill blast of Jared's emotions made Kami flinch back. "You don't know that," she said evenly. "Logically, there might well be some connection."

"Logically, it must be magic?" Jared said, shaking his head. "And logically, what you and I have is on the same level as some sick freak killing animals and trying to kill you. That's what you think of us."

No, it isn't, Kami argued, reaching out to him with her mind, but the emotion she got from him was like a hand flung up, warning her off.

Jared's body language followed suit. He backed out of the room, his big shoulders set in a furious line, and Kami got up from behind the desk and ran after him. She resented him for leaving and for being there at all; she was angry with herself for letting it matter so much.

"You're taking this the wrong way," she told him, her voice echoing down the stairwell.

"You wonder what privacy would be like. You wish I didn't exist," Jared said. "How am I supposed to take that?"

"What am I supposed to believe?" Kami sneered. "That we're *soul mates?*"

This time Jared's fury hit Kami's own: it felt like a forest fire leaping between them, feeding off each other in a burning destructive loop. Kami was aware of what was happening and she still couldn't stop it, couldn't control it, and she hated it.

"Oh no, that wouldn't be logical," said Jared. "You always want an explanation for everything!"

"Yes," Kami snapped. "I do. What's wrong with that?

And what's wrong with wanting a little privacy? It is different now that I know you're real. It *is* hard for me to deal with."

"I'm sorry I'm so hard for you to deal with," Jared snarled.

Kami took three steps down toward him and Jared backed off, reaching the ground floor. Kami stormed down the steps after him, raging enough to think things she would never have said: *I'm sorry you've latched on to this without question because you're messed up and desperate.*

Jared turned and stalked down the hall, Kami in pursuit.

"Where are you going?" she asked. She ran to the main doors as Jared banged them open and barged through. She stood at the top of the steps as he got on his battered bike and screeched past. Kami yelled down, "Oh, be a delinquent and skip school, that's very constructive!" She slammed the door shut behind her and glared around at the students standing wide-eyed around the hall.

"That's right," she said loudly. "Stay in school, all of you. Or I'll get really riled."

She returned to the headquarters, but there was no comfort to be found there now. She turned on the computer anyway, yelling at Jared in her head.

"Uh," said Ash from the door, "are you—all right?"

"Fine!" Kami said. She typed out: "With the advent of sperm banks, women realized the sheer uselessness of men, and by the year 2100 they were largely extinct" with extreme force. "Absolutely fine, never better! Why do you ask?"

"Er, because I heard you and Jared had a screaming fight. Also, you are typing like a maddened weasel taped to a keyboard."

Kami stopped typing. "You may have a point."

"I just wanted to check and see if you were okay," said Ash. "I thought you might need cheering up."

Kami relaxed back in her chair. Ash was standing in the doorway, not leaning against it listening to invisible voices. Just standing, blue eyes concerned and voice gentle. "How were you planning to cheer me up?"

"Oh, well," said Ash, and smiled his charming smile. "How about catching a movie tonight?"

He was so nice, Kami couldn't help but think. She wasn't dating anyone else. She wasn't betraying anyone. Kami bit her lip, then smiled back, feeling the edges of her mouth strain to form the shape. "I'd love to."

Down in the dark waters, there was gold gleaming. There was no air and the water was cold as death, dragging him down like chains. There was nothing here but darkness and the unreachable gleam of gold lost down so deep. If he did not get to the surface, he would die, and yet he knew with a chill, sure knowledge that if he did not reach that golden gleam, he would die anyway. Then he saw something else, lit by the underwater shine on the metal: a woman's face at the bottom of the pool.

Jared broke the surface of the dream and woke gasping. He rolled onto his stomach and winced: he had been driving around for eight solid hours, and taken a few tumbles. He'd only eased up because he knew if he did actually crash, Kami would come for him.

So he hadn't driven his bike into a tree, and instead

Kami'd gone out on a date with Ash. That was much better. And instead of crashing his bike, Jared had stormed in here at evening time, crashed out, and dreamed about a dead woman.

Jared realized that his jacket smelled like he'd been on a bike for eight hours in it. He threw it off and headed for the shower. His bathroom at Aurimere was ridiculous and strange, each claw on his claw-foot tub clutching a tiny crystal, the showerhead a brass fist. At least the faucets worked, which was more than he was used to. It was better than he'd had in plenty of the apartments with his parents in San Francisco, and sure as hell better than the taps at fast-food places that he'd used to try to keep clean last summer.

The hot water stung on his new scrapes and bruises, sluicing between his shoulder blades. Jared cracked his neck, got out of the shower, and went to find a clean T-shirt and jeans. He left the room raking his hair back from his face, went up the steps past the tapestries, through the drawing rooms and down the long hall, calling for Uncle Rob. Uncle Rob was always kind to him, clapping him on the shoulder and calling him "son." Jared wasn't sure why he liked it or why he wanted to see Uncle Rob now, but he did.

Jared stalked into the parlor. There were no lights on, but a fire was burning, casting orange and black streaks on the windows as if the curtains were tiger hide. From the shadows, a voice said: "Can I help you?"

Jared said, "Aunt Lillian?" and turned on the light.

His aunt sat in a yellow armchair with a high back. Her hair was neatly parted, held back by a black band, which made her look like an older, evil Alice in Wonderland.

"Did you want a book?" Aunt Lillian asked. "I could not help but notice half the library has moved to your room."

Jared felt vaguely unsettled that she'd noticed. He wasn't used to adults scrutinizing his behavior. He hadn't meant to take so many books, but they were all the kind he liked, about made-up olden days when the world made sense, about death and love and honor.

"I was looking for Uncle Rob," he said, backing up. "Is he in the garden?"

"Don't go outside, Jared; your hair is wet," Aunt Lillian told him. She said it coolly, but it caught Jared off guard. It was such a mom thing to say, and something his mom would never have said. He hesitated on the threshold, and while he did, Aunt Lillian's darkened and shaped eyebrows came together in a slight frown. She repeated, "Can I help you?"

Jared came to a decision. "Yeah. Yeah, you can."

Lillian clearly did not much appreciate the word "yeah," but she nodded for him to continue.

"I was just thinking," he said, "we don't know each other all that well, do we? I mean, like—for people who are related to each other. I wondered, and this might seem strange, if you have any stories about when Ash was a kid."

Aunt Lillian blinked. Jared figured that was Aunt Lillian's equivalent of staggering back with a hand pressed to her heart. "Yes," she said, her voice chillier than ever. "Yes, I do." She rose and went to the glass-fronted bookcase at the other end of the room and took out a cloth-covered photo album with sepia roses on the front. She stood by the bookcase holding the album in her hands and regarding Jared.

Then she strode over to one of the sofas with scarlet

canopies. She sat down, her back straight, like someone trained at the most genteel military academy in the world. "You can come sit by me," she said graciously.

Jared came and sat on the couch, enough of a distance away so that Aunt Lillian had her space and close enough to see the photo album. It was possible he slumped a little more than usual.

"I am pleased you are taking an interest in the family, Jared," Aunt Lillian said. "It matters a great deal to me." She paused and added, "It is the only thing in the world that matters to me."

Jared felt a stab of guilt. He felt okay using Aunt Lillian and having underhanded motives, but it got more complicated if she actually cared what he did. It also made him accept something he really had known before. Back in San Francisco, in the last of a long string of apartments, he'd woken up to hear Mom and Aunt Lillian arguing. Mom had never lost her accent, but it had been weird to realize that he couldn't differentiate between their voices. It was like lying in the dark listening to his mother arguing with herself. Except that the two voices had very different things to say.

He'd wanted to believe it was Aunt Lillian who said "He won't be any use" and his mother who said "Of course we're taking the child. I do not care if you don't want him: I do."

But he'd known, really, that it wasn't.

Which begged the question, why would Aunt Lillian want him, and what for?

Jared leaned farther backward into the cushions, even though the straight line of Aunt Lillian's spine reproached him. "So," he said. "Tell me about Ash."

At the point when Jared relayed Ash's habit of hiding his cuddly toys in the freezer, Kami started to laugh in the movie theater.

Ash glanced over at her.

"Sorry," Kami murmured. "Just—the movie's funny."

Ash looked back at the movie, in which a small blond child was dying of leukemia.

"I have a very warped sense of humor," Kami whispered.

What she had was the deep desire to beat Jared's head in. She knew how this date should have gone. She would have sneaked looks over at Ash. A few times their gazes would have met and parted after an instant too long. She would have left her hand lying on the arm of the seat invitingly, and he would have taken it. But instead she'd been trying to maintain a poker face while being regaled with the story of when Ash was four and had stuffed a prawn up his own nose.

After the movie, Ash and Kami left the theater and meandered down to walk by the riverside. It was twilight, the moon turning the Sorrier River into a silver ribbon and turning Ash's fair hair into silver threads.

"So, that movie was . . . ," Ash said. "Uh . . ."

"Very much so," said Kami. "There's only one cinema in Sorry-in-the-Vale, and we only play one movie a week, so they pretty much know that they've got a captive audience. Not that this is an excuse for how many times I've watched *Casablanca*."

"Do they change it up?" Ash asked. "Like, one week, touching stories of love and loss and the human condition, and the next week—er—mutant killer werewolves? Not that I'm saying I personally would choose werewolves."

"If we ever got a shot at werewolves," Kami said, "I'd choose werewolves too. For the novelty value alone." She slanted a look at Ash. "Regretting your parents' rash decision to move back here, oh cosmopolitan traveler?"

"Nah," said Ash. "Everything's better here. The air is easier to breathe, and my mother's much happier. My family's—different."

"I had not noticed that," Kami told him. "At all." She thought of the Lynburns running out to soak up a storm. It was bizarre, and seemed impossible now, with Ash walking beside her in the quiet night and holding her hand in his. She could touch him, and it was easy.

Ash shrugged, and his hand tightened on hers. "Families," he said. "They can be hard. But you have to try your best for them, don't you?"

He swung Kami's hand, and they exchanged a smile going over the arch of the wooden bridge.

"So," said Ash. "What were you and Jared fighting about? I heard—"

"I don't want to talk about Jared!" Kami said, and decided to give another stab at being Mata Hari and extracting information from men with her wiles. "So . . . tell me about the difficulties in your family." She wondered if Mata Hari had ever found it tricky to know how to put things.

"Well," Ash said doubtfully, "you already said you didn't want to talk about Jared." He grinned at her again. "I don't really want to talk about my family either."

He used her hand to spin her into him a little, as if they

were doing a subtle dance. He stood looking down at her, now close, and the moonlight trembled on his lashes. He leaned down while Kami leaned against the rail of the bridge and turned her face up to his. The first touch of his mouth was gentle, light, and sweet.

Fun fact, Jared put in. *Ash wet the bed until he was five.*

Kami spluttered out a laugh against Ash's lips. Ash drew back sharply.

Kami tried not to die of mortification. "I'm so sorry," she said instantly. "I was thinking about something else."

Ash's voice had an edge to it now. "What were you thinking about?"

"I was thinking that—" Kami floundered, a fish on the dry land of shame. "That—that purple is a funny color?" She couldn't blame Ash for his look of incredulity. She was feeling something along the same lines herself. "Look, I'm so sorry," Kami said. "I'm feeling really weird. I should probably go home."

She crossed the bridge over to the road running along the woods. When she glanced back, Ash still stood on the bridge in the moonlight, looking like an outraged angel. Jared was loud in her head about the fact that she was walking home through the woods alone at night.

I'm not going into the woods, Kami snapped. *I'm not a total idiot. And if I'm alone, whose fault is that?*

Jared rolled out of bed, trying to ignore Kami's angry silence in his mind. It had been keeping him up for hours. He just had to move, as if by moving he could get past the feeling he had done something even more messed up than usual.

He pulled on a pair of jeans and took the back stairs down toward the kitchen. The landing between floors was painted red, so the first flight of stairs was like a descent into hell. He went past hell to the next flight of stairs, past one wall that was a tableau in black-and-white mosaics of a woman standing caught between Aurimere and a lake, into shadows leading down to a gray hall. There was a marble bust against one wall, a man's white profile that reminded Jared of Aunt Lillian.

Jared realized that a door was ajar and someone was awake, because he saw the slash of light bisecting the marble face. He turned toward the lit room as he descended the stairs, and he heard the murmur of voices. A family conference was going on in the library.

". . . it's clear it will not stop. We have to do something," said a woman's voice. It was Aunt Lillian, and not his mother, because she was talking about taking action.

His mother spoke next. She said, "You can't trust a half-breed."

Jared went still for a moment, and in that moment Ash opened the door all the way and slipped outside the room. He looked up at Jared on the stairs, and his blue eyes went wide.

Jared lunged from the step across the floor and pinned Ash up against the stone wall.

"Half-breed?" Jared said in a furious whisper. "Do they mean *Kami*?"

At the mention of Kami's name, Ash's eyes narrowed. "No," he said, and his voice was suddenly like his mother's, crisp and cold. "They mean you." He shoved Jared away and disappeared back into the room where they were holding the family council.

Jared didn't wait to see what Ash told them. He walked through the dining hall and then the entrance hall and out the front door, slamming it behind him. He sat on the top step of the entrance of Aurimere House, Sorry-in-the-Vale stretched dark and quiet below him.

Half-breed.

Jared had never belonged anywhere. This was the first time he had been glad of it. He wasn't one of them. He didn't want to be. He knew where, and to whom, he wanted to belong.

They could keep their secrets, as his mother wished. He didn't want to be involved.

Kami got to school the next day without any incidents like being kidnapped by pirates or having the earth open up and swallow her, which on the whole Kami thought was a pity. And on her way up to her headquarters for her first free period, she ran into the person she least wanted to see. "Ash," she said, breathless with horror.

"Hey," said Ash.

Kami stared at him with blind panic and offered: "I'm so sorry."

"Yeah," Ash said. "You mentioned that already." He fell into step with her, going up the stairs. "Look," he said.

"Don't worry about it. Really. I feel like I should be the one to apologize."

"No," Kami told him. "No, I'm pretty sure that it should be me. Over and over and over again."

"I knew you were upset. Taking you out was meant to be about cheering you up, not getting all offended and making you feel worse."

"Well, you're far too nice, and I'm still sorry for inflicting the worst date you've ever had on you."

"Oh no," said Ash. "It wasn't the worst date I've ever had. The worst date I've ever had was with a girl who had a pet fire extinguisher."

Kami blinked up at him.

"I found it puzzling myself," said Ash. "So you see."

"I could take on the pet-fire-extinguisher girl," Kami considered. "I've done some very strange things."

Ash's laugh floated down the corridor, light as Kami's heart suddenly was. Everything could be all right, she thought. "I've got faith in you," Ash said. "So—how about it? Let's give going out another try."

You'd better not come in, Jared said. *I'm in here.* He didn't hurl the comment at her resentfully. He just said it, as if he was resigned.

Kami stood at the door to her headquarters and looked in through the square of wire-covered glass. Jared was sitting at his desk, big shoulders hunched.

"No," she told Ash, and saw him blink with surprise. "I really like you," she continued, because Ash deserved to hear it. "But I've got a lot of stuff going on right now, and I just don't—I don't know how I can."

She hardly heard Ash's polite mumble saying "right" and "of course" and "somewhere to be," meaningless words strung together to get himself out of this situation. She felt awash in horror.

Kami opened the door and went into her headquarters. The half-open blinds sliced the sky into bars of light and shadow over desks and floor, red lamps and Jared's bright hair, making the room into a cage. She went over to stand at the window, behind Jared's chair. Then she gave up and leaned against the back of Jared's chair, almost touching but not quite.

"I'm glad you're real," she said. She *was* glad he was real. She couldn't wish him out of existence, or even wish he was somewhere away from her. She wanted him with her: she wanted him right here.

Yeah? Jared asked.

Kami felt his slow-blossoming relief. There was no way to live a normal life, even if he wasn't trying to interfere. She couldn't be happy when he was unhappy. There was nothing she could do. Jared's pain felt like her pain, and mattered a thousand times more than hurting Ash. There had been no way to smile at Ash and say yes to a date with a perfectly nice guy, when most of her heart lay behind the door.

Kami bowed her own head over Jared's bowed head, and hated the link between them. She didn't know if anything she was feeling was real.

Chapter Eighteen
The Water Rising

It was only half an hour after the end of school, and the Internet had already failed Kami completely. It was supposed to be a superhighway of information. She had exactly one hit on a Henry Thornton, living in Notting Hill. It was on a dating website. Apparently he was single, looking for a long-term relationship, and his interests were jazz and cricket. He had not been considerate enough to add "ritual animal slaughter" to the list.

Kami growled with frustration at the screen.

"Easy, tiger," Angela said from her prone position on the sofa. "You're wasting good aggression on computers when you could be turning it against mankind."

Kami glanced over at Angela. Angela lay serenely with her hands folded across her chest and her lashes like black lace against her white cheeks. "You look so sweet when you sleep," Kami said. "Like an emo ten-year-old's first Vampire Bride Barbie. Pull the string on the back and she says cruel things to her hardworking friends."

"Why don't you and Jared go to the library?" Angela suggested, eyes still closed. She said "you and Jared" as if they were a unit.

"Angela," Kami said sharply, "Jared and I are not dating."

Angela lifted her eyelids a fraction of an inch. "Oh no. He asked you out and now you spend all your time together, sometimes having epic fights in the hallways. Where did I get such an outrageous idea?"

"We're not and we never will!" Kami heard her voice go a little high.

Angela winced. "No loud noises. It is naptime."

Kami leaned across her desk. "I'm not one of those girls, am I?"

"Those girls who disturb my naptime?"

"Those girls!" said Kami. "You know the ones. Who are always joined at the hip to some boy and all they talk about is some boy and they don't hang around their friends anymore because they're spending time with some boy. We hate those girls!"

"I hate practically everybody," Angela pointed out.

"We should have a girls' night," Kami said. "Tonight. Hot chocolate made with cream, and a box of my mum's pastries. You in?"

Angela's eyes fell closed. "Only for the pastries."

Kami returned to contemplating Henry Thornton, who was tempting her to be an Internet Mata Hari by having a green "User online now" on his profile. She stared at his thin, serious face. "Men are nothing but trouble," she said. "Thank God for girls' night."

"Girls' night?" Holly asked from the door.

"Come," said Angela, without opening her eyes.

"Yes, do come," Kami said after an instant.

"I'd love to." Holly swept in, bringing radiance with

her. Angela slid over so Holly could sit on the sofa and lean against Angela's legs. "I'd say our best chance of getting to dance is to go to the cellar at the Bell and Mist."

Angela opened her eyes all the way. "Somewhere with other people? But other people bother me."

"I know, Angie, but I'll keep them away, and besides, they don't bother you as much as you say they do."

"Are you willing to bet on that?" Angela asked. "Like, a sizable amount? Fine, but afterward we're having hot chocolate and pastries and lots and lots of sleep."

"Cool," said Holly, and hugged her legs. "I haven't been to a sleepover in years."

Kami thought this was an excellent plan to lift her spirits. She just had to work out a few details first.

When Kami reached Angela's house that night, she found Holly parking her motorbike behind the gate. Holly looked up and smiled when she saw her. "Just give me a second."

Kami leaned companionably against the bike. "Yours is much shinier than Jared's."

"That is because the way Jared treats his is a disgrace," Holly said, with unusual sternness. "I like things to be nice. Plus I like working on the bike myself. It's a Triumph—that's a classic bike." She gave its shining blue surface an affectionate pat.

"Jared works on his," Kami said defensively. "He just uses it—I think—as a bit of an escape."

Holly shrugged. "Well, sure. That's why I got the bike myself. When things get too much and everyone is packed in yelling at each other, it's wonderful to be able to get away, to be peaceful and on your own, moving away fast. But you have to care for your escape as well. That's Jared's problem. He doesn't care about much."

"He cares," Kami protested.

Holly gave her a doubtful look, then she rose, dusting off her jeans, and Kami took her arm. Kami hadn't thought about how crammed Holly's family's farmhouse might feel, especially if the family was arguing. Holly didn't talk about her home life much. Of course she didn't: Holly liked things to be nice.

"I have a serious girls' night question for you," said Kami. "I know you're new to this, but I will require an answer quickly. Are you prepared to eat at least five éclairs tonight?"

"I don't know," Holly returned, laughing and pushing the door open as she shrugged off her jacket. Underneath she was wearing jeans and a pink backless top that was all sequins. "That's a big commitment."

They stopped on the threshold at the sight of Angela, sitting at her kitchen island being radiantly beautiful in a red silk shirt and dividing her scowls between Jared and Ash. "They were not invited," she said. "But they won't leave. Now you two are here, I'm willing to kill them if you'll help with the cleanup."

"I thought you could all use a bodyguard," Jared suggested. He looked at Kami, and she felt that he was happy to see her. She could not quite help smiling.

Kami looked away and took off her coat. She wasn't long-legged in tight jeans like Holly and Angela, but she was wearing a white dress that tied low down in front, swung bell-like about her, and had a bright pattern of apricots. She hoped that she looked pretty.

When she looked back, Jared was not looking at her. He seemed set on looking almost anywhere else. "If you keep talking to Angela, soon you will be using a body *cast*," Kami told him, more sharply than she meant to. Then she turned to her friend. "Don't worry, Angela, I expected this. Well, I didn't expect Ash."

Ash gave Jared a cold glance. "I followed him to see what he was up to."

So Ash still suspected Jared, then.

"Doesn't matter!" Kami said loudly over her own discomfort. "Boys. Listen up. We are going out for a girls' night, where there will be dancing."

Kami did an illustrative shimmy. Angela looked resigned.

Jared looked amused. "What was that?"

"You've got to dance like nobody's watching, Jared," Kami informed him.

"Have you considered that perhaps nobody's watching because they're too embarrassed for you?"

"Fine," said Kami, grinning at him. "Be a hater of dances. Be a hater of joy. I don't care. You're not invited!" She clapped her hands. "You have plans."

Hearing his cue, Rusty sauntered obligingly through the doors. "Hey, Lynburn, we're going out," he said. Then he stopped and frowned. "There are two of them," he observed.

"The other one won't need to be subdued by force," Kami assured him.

"Nevertheless, my price has doubled," said Rusty. "I'll want six dinners prepared lovingly for me in the next two weeks."

"Four," Kami told him. "And you're ridiculous. You *can* cook."

"Be reasonable, Cambridge," said Rusty. "Not doing things you *can* do is the whole point of laziness. Not doing things you *can't* do is just sensible."

Kami slapped his arm. Rusty leaned down, took her lightly by the shoulders, and brushed a kiss on her cheek.

"You look nice, Cambridge," he murmured. "Who's the blond bombshell?"

"Holly," Kami whispered. "Don't hit on her!"

Rusty laughed, sliding his arm around her shoulders and pulling her in against his side. "You know I don't hit on people," he said, ruffling her hair. "I'm Endymion."

"You're Endymion," Kami repeated.

"It is my ambition to be the Endymion of dating, yes," Rusty said calmly. "Endymion, he was a guy in myth who knew how to work it. He lay asleep forever while the goddess of the moon dropped by every night and adored him. Nice."

He doesn't have to talk nonsense in a whisper in your ear, Jared said.

As opposed to talking nonsense in a whisper in my brain? Kami asked.

Jared glared. Some people, Kami knew, had bedroom eyes. She was saddened to have to admit that Jared had filthy alleyway eyes. The thought reached Jared and he tilted his head, and Kami felt what he felt: startled and amused.

"For *killing people in,*" Kami exclaimed.

The kitchen went still except for Jared's small, strangled

laugh. Kami could not blame everyone else: it must have been a very unsettling thing to hear out of context.

Rusty remained relaxed. "Time to go," he announced. "Come on, Lynburns. We're going to the pub."

"Thank you," Ash said doubtfully.

"Not the pub where the girls are going," Rusty clarified. "The pub on the other side of town."

Jared had been edging up on Rusty and Kami, giving Rusty that edging-toward-homicidal look.

Rusty let go of Kami and grabbed Jared casually by the collar. "Come on, Blondie," he said to Ash, who moved forward propelled by the sheer force of his own politeness. Jared jerked away, and his shirt pulled tight in Rusty's hand. Rusty held on with no visible effort. "The girls don't want you here," Rusty continued, his voice light. "So you're not staying."

Kami moved toward Jared; he glanced at her and checked himself.

"Fine," he snapped, and made for the door.

"This evening with Surly and Blondie had better get me pastries," Rusty said. "You girls have fun."

He calls you Cambridge, Jared pointed out.

You knew he did that, Kami said. *It's to tease me for studying so much and wanting to do journalism at Cambridge.*

He did know. He knew everything about her, which sounded creepy even to him, but it wasn't like he could help knowing.

I could give you a nickname, Jared suggested. *I could call you Cam—Cam—* His brain refused to surrender up anything appropriate. *Camembert.*

The inside of the Water Rising was dim and brown, with stools that seemed to have old men growing from them like mushrooms from the hollows of trees.

Kami was in another pub, happy and distracted, laughing, but slightly concerned about him.

Jared felt sick of himself. The way he saw it, he had every right to hate Ash. As soon as he'd seen Ash, sitting between his mother and father and looking so much like Jared, it had given him the jolt of unexpectedly seeing yourself in a mirror. Except it wasn't quite like a mirror. It was like looking through a window into another world, a world where he'd come out right. It was fair to hate Ash, but hating another guy because Kami leaned into him with perfect trust was too close to wanting Kami to be unhappy.

"I have to tell you, boys," said Rusty. "The last time I went out with blondes who were related to each other, it went a whole lot better than this."

Jared glanced over at Ash, who was studying the table and looking more like Aunt Lillian than usual. At least Ash was miserable as well.

"This isn't really a hotbed of frenzied excitement," Jared drawled.

Rusty looked around at the two old men on stools, the elderly couple bartending who had been giving Jared and Ash apprehensive looks since they'd arrived, and the pool table with the felt curling up at one corner. "Nonsense," he said peacefully. "This is a very exciting place. They hold duck races here." Then he put his head in his arms.

"You can't seriously go to sleep here," Ash hissed.

"Seriously," said Jared. "He can."

Jared went over to the bar and got a ginger ale.

"Seventeen's old enough to drink over here," offered the woman at the bar, who Jared thought was called Mary Wright. Her husband frowned a warning at her.

"I don't," Jared said, and tried out a smile that made her look more alarmed than before. "But thanks."

He gave up, wandered back to the table, and asked Ash, "Do you play pool?"

Ash blinked, looking extremely surprised and cautiously pleased. "Not very well."

Jared smiled. "Great." He jerked his head in a summons and made for the pool table, set up a game, and grabbed a cue. Then he walked around the table, considering it from all angles.

"How about you?" Ash asked, watching. Ash tended to watch everything Jared did, as if certain the next thing would be appalling.

"I used to hustle pool in San Francisco." Jared leaned over the table and went for a power stroke. He looked up and grinned. "Sometimes I won by flirting a little. Not planning to try that here."

"You were playing pool with girls?"

Jared grinned. "Sometimes."

"What?" said Ash.

"Dude," said Jared. *"San Francisco."*

"What!" said Ash.

"What's the matter, Ash? Off your game?" said Jared, and smirked.

Ash wasn't as bad as he'd made out, but he wasn't a bold

player, and holding back at pool seldom paid off. Also, Ash steadfastly refused to make things interesting.

"I like winning something," Jared argued.

"I don't like losing anything," Ash argued back, his voice polite even when arguing.

That was when fear exploded into Jared's mind.

We can't find her, said Kami, and then her panic ran through him: Kami had heard a scream.

"Kami," said Jared. He broke his pool cue over his knee in one economical movement and ran. He saw Rusty rise from the corner of his eye, moving faster than a man who'd been napping on a table in a bar had any right to.

Ash's voice behind him came clear and sharp: "Jared, don't!"

Jared was out in the night, rain falling and the moonlight making the wet cobblestones look like shards of mirror sliding beneath his feet, by the time Ash came close enough to grab his elbow.

"Jared," Ash said, panting. He sounded desperate. "If something bad is happening, it would be best if nobody saw a Lynburn at the scene."

"If something's happening?" Jared demanded. "What could be happening? What do you know?"

"There are people in Sorry-in-the-Vale who still talk about what happened at Monkshood!"

Kami's distress was drilling through Jared's head: he gritted his teeth. "What are you talking about?"

"Oh my God," said Ash, the rain painting tears on his face. "You don't know *anything.*"

"You know what, Ash? I don't care," Jared said, and ran.

Chapter Nineteen
The Bell, the Mist, and the Knife

The Bell and Mist was a tall, narrow redbrick building, built on a little cobblestoned rise, so the floor was uneven. Across the slanting floor about eleven people were dancing, and almost every stool was occupied. This was about as exciting as a weeknight got in Sorry-in-the-Vale. It wasn't a bad night. The addition of Holly, sparkling on a barstool and clearly pleased to be there, brightened up the whole occasion.

"I think my last girls' night was when I was eleven," Holly said. "At Nicola Prendergast's place." She shrugged. "Then I got boobs."

Kami and Angela exchanged an uneasy look. They remembered: after that, it had been more comfortable for Holly to hang out with the boys, who suddenly liked her a lot more, than to stick with the girls, who suddenly liked her a lot less.

"Ah, Nicola's," Kami sighed. "That lost dreamland. She stopped inviting me because I talked to—" Kami checked herself. "Talked too much. But the joke's on her, because now she has to buy her pastries." She shot a look over at the other side of the bar, where Nicola and her friends were.

Kami hadn't even been invited to the slumber party

that Holly had mentioned, even though she'd always had best-friend pride of place before. She looked back at Angela, sardonic in red silk, and Holly, beaming in her pink sparkles. Friends who didn't care how weird she was; in retrospect, Nicola had done Kami a favor.

"I used to think about going over to Nicola and the others on nights before this one," Holly said, following Kami's gaze. "But tonight I'm happy where I am." She took a survey of the bar. "For one thing, when it's girls' night, guys look just as much, but they assume a lot less. Makes a nice change."

It would be hard to assume with Angela leaning back on her stool and drawing a scarlet nail with deliberate meaning across her throat at boys who she thought were staring too long.

"I'm pretty sure that guy just wanted a packet of peanuts," Kami said cheerfully.

"Not unless you are keeping peanuts in your bra," said Angela.

"I keep all sorts of things in my bra, actually," Kami told her. "It's always a bit of a shock when I've forgotten my phone is in there and it vibrates."

"I think Angie's right, as it happens," said Holly. "There's no way that guy was thinking about peanuts. But that's a great dress."

Kami shrugged. "Well, I work with what I have. It's not like I can pull off jeans like you guys."

"Don't be dumb, you're cute as a button," said Holly. "Of course, Angie does specialize in making the rest of us look bad."

"Don't hate me because, et cetera," Angela murmured, but her ears went pink. Kami was never going to inform Angela about that little tell.

It was soothing for Kami to have Holly confess to feeling a little overshadowed by Angela's good looks as well, especially after Jared's reaction—or conspicuous lack thereof—to her dress.

"I'll just be a second," said Holly, gesturing toward the door to the extension that led to the bathroom. "Then I believe you good-looking ladies owe me a dance."

Kami sipped her drink and glanced at Angela. Angela was watching Holly maneuver through the crowd, tall in her high silver heels, smiling and moving politely past some guy despite his clear wish to detain her. Angela's look at Holly was fond, but the gaze she swept toward Holly's suitor and then the rest of the bar was scathing.

"Why are boys such a nuisance?" Angela wanted to know, after a long pause in which she apparently brooded over this unanswerable question.

"It's hard to say," Kami answered. "I put it down to irresistible charm and sparkling wit and try to move on. Though the heap of suitors at my feet makes moving difficult." She made the straw in her drink walk across the bar, tripping over suitors that were actually cardboard coasters.

Angela raised a perfect eyebrow. "Sparkling wit?"

"Don't feel bad, Angela," Kami said. "You know guys, they only want one thing. Repartee. I can't count how many times men have admired my well-turned phrases. The shallow jerks."

"Holly's been a while; I'm going to go find her," Angela said, rising from her stool in one easy, twisting movement. "But hold that thought. I'm working on something about witticisms in your bra, and it's going to be good."

Kami waved her off and took another sip of her drink. She looked around, back at Nicola, who was talking to a guy, and then at her own reflection over the bar, in the darkened glass behind the rows of bottles. Her gaze was dreamy, drowning-dark, and strange, like she was avoiding meeting her own eyes. That was what unsettled people about her and Jared, that their eyes were so often looking at something that wasn't there.

Holly really had been gone a long time.

Kami lifted herself slightly from the barstool, because she was a lot taller from there than she was standing. She could not see Holly or Angela.

Then she heard the scream, and she knew Holly's voice. The sound cut through the cheerful noise of the bar, dead serious over all the laughter. Kami jumped off her stool and charged through the crowd toward the extension door. She was halfway there, using her elbows like paddles in an uncooperative sea, when the door burst open. Holly stood on the threshold, hair mussed and another scream on her lips, brandishing one of her high heels like a sword.

Angela was there before Kami was, coming from Kami didn't know where and grabbing Holly. Her arm locked around Holly's neck and Holly hid her face against Angela's red silk shoulder.

Kami reached them and asked the question the whole

pub was asking. Her voice was clear and made Holly's head lift: "What happened?"

"I was walking back, along the extension to the bathroom," Holly said unsteadily. "Then the lights went out. I put my hand against the wall to guide myself back, and I was touching brick, and then—I touched something else, something warm. A person. I jumped back just before whoever it was grabbed at me, so they only caught at my arm instead of getting a real grip on me. And they missed my—" Holly choked for a minute, hand pressed against her neck. "My throat," she whispered. "I felt the edge. Whoever it was had a knife."

The whole pub went still around them, as if the word "knife" was a stone thrown in the center of a lake, changing the whole surface of the water, spreading a ring of silence.

"What did you do?" Angela asked. Kami could see Angela's hands trembling—Angela!—and she clung to Jared in her mind, to his instant support and concern.

"I screamed, 'Don't hurt me,' and I tried to make my voice all shaky, and crouched down, being all—like a scared girl in a horror movie," Holly said, stumbling over the words. "Maybe it was stupid, but it was the only thing I could think of. And when I was crouching down, I got my shoe off, and I hit out with the heel, and I think I caught whoever it was in the face. I heard a shout like I did. They were taller than me, I could tell that much, but I don't know if it was a man or a woman. And then I ran."

Angela stroked Holly's hair, even though her hands were still trembling. "Think you got them in the eye?"

"No," Holly admitted.

"Shame," said Angela. "Next time."

Kami rested a hand on Holly's back and said, "I think you were really smart." She turned to look at the others with an authoritative air, because pretending to be in control made her feel more in control and less scared and useless. "Has anyone seen any strangers?" she asked, thinking of Henry Thornton from London.

The front doors of the Bell and Mist swung open, and Kami turned with the rest of the pub's clientele to see the two Lynburn boys standing framed against the night.

The crowd of people in the bar stood watching Jared, silently accusing.

Your timing is amazing, Kami told him. *By which I mean, I am amazed by it.*

Jared looked across at her, standing in a ring of space in a throng of people, like a tiny drill sergeant. Relief broke from him and toward her like a wave to shore. She was safe. Then Rusty pushed past him. Jared looked at Angela and Holly, who were hanging on to each other. This was a bad sign, he realized, because Angela was as nurturing as a barracuda. Jared looked to Kami again.

Rusty was doing a fine job of making Jared actually hate him as he went over to Kami and hugged her. Kami's arms went around Rusty's wet neck and hung on. A vaguely familiar red-haired girl stepped out of the crowd and up to the door where Jared stood, her jewelry chiming like tiny bells.

"Lynburn," she said, as if Jared and Ash were a unit, as if

she was calling on a totem or a god rather than speaking to a person.

"Yes?" Ash said softly, at Jared's elbow.

Jared gathered from Kami's mind that the girl was called Nicola. He saw Kami detach herself from Rusty and head across the floor to him.

"The people in this town are meant to be safe!" Nicola looked right at Jared. Her throat moved as she swallowed. She'd seen something in his eyes she was afraid of, Jared thought. She looked back at Ash. "Isn't that the bargain? Wasn't that the promise?"

"What do you mean?" asked Kami, which Jared could tell was partly about being a journalist and partly about insinuating herself between Jared and Nicola. As if she could glare people into not being afraid of him.

Nicola gave Kami a pitying look and shook her head, her red ponytail fluttering in the wind blowing in from the open doors. She retreated into the embrace of her friends, who welcomed her back as if she had just come home from war. Her eyes stayed fixed on Ash, imploring and accusing.

"What did she mean?" Kami asked.

Jared turned to look at Ash. The open door was a square filled with darkness, cut by silver points of rain. Ash was gone.

"I don't know," Jared said slowly. "Ash was talking about something that happened—somewhere. In a place. Monkshood."

Kami's brows drew together, dark eyes firing. "Monkshood Abbey is a derelict manor house outside of town," she said. "About twelve miles. It's been empty for years."

Jared raised his own brows. "Kids must go there all the time."

"No," Kami murmured. "No, I don't think they ever do. We never did."

"I think it might be an idea to effect our getaway," said Rusty, appearing by Kami's side. "Your friend chose an unfortunate time to make an entrance," he said in her ear. "People are looking for someone to blame for what happened to Holly. And he's a Lynburn."

"And what does that mean?" Jared demanded. "What do you know?"

Rusty glanced up at him and the alertness was wiped away from his face, blurring his features like someone breathing onto a mirror. It was replaced with the usual lazy good humor. "Nothing," Rusty said in his slow, pleasant voice. "But then, we've only been here six years. The Vale doesn't give up its secrets that easy." He looked around for his sister. Angela advanced on them, Holly rushing after her and wobbling slightly. She seemed to have broken her heel.

Jared grinned at Holly. "Hey, Warrior Princess."

Holly beamed back at him, gorgeous and flirtatious with it, as if looking the way she did it was easier to flirt than not. She stepped up to him and Jared hugged her lightly, her cascade of curls tickling the bare skin of his arm. "Sorry I'm all wet," he said.

Holly smiled up at him. "It's a good look on you." Her eyes slid around the room, making sure that everybody had seen the tearstained victim hug the Lynburn. Holly was a great girl, Jared thought as she drew back and went to hook arms with Angela.

"What's our next step?" he asked Kami.

"Leave the pub," Rusty said, urgency creeping into his drawl. "Now."

They went out into the rain, the girls pulling on their coats as they did. Kami flipped up her hood, which had teddy bear ears on it. She walked beside Jared, four inches of rain-dashed darkness between her hanging wrist and his.

"Next we get answers," Kami said. "Nicola Prendergast knows something. I can get her to talk to me." Her voice was practical and cheery, but Jared felt a ripple of wistfulness go through her. "We used to talk all the time."

"Can I get you to talk to me, Cambridge?" asked Rusty.

Jared gave Rusty a look, and then congratulated himself on being the stupidest man alive when Rusty's sleepy hazel eyes went sharp again. Kami wasn't going to like him antagonizing Rusty.

Jared slowed so he was behind the rest of the group, bowing his head against the rain. This close to Kami, able to feel what she felt, he might just as well have been sitting on her shoulder. He was able to gather what Rusty was saying, a few of the actual words floating over to him through the rain.

"—I'm older than you," Rusty said. "I know guys like this."

"—introduced me to *Claud*," Kami said.

"—worse things than Claud," said Rusty. "—just an idiot. When some guy gets all silent and obsessed—I've seen some really bad situations. Kami, watch yourself."

Kami's voice cut clearly through the sound of rain. "You don't understand."

"I've heard girls say that before now too."

"You haven't heard *me* say it," said Kami, his girl, and the chill sluicing through his shirt, the chill of knowing someone decent like Rusty could simply look at him and know that he was somehow irredeemably twisted, none of it mattered. "Trust me to know what's best for me, Rusty Montgomery, or I'll beat you up."

"Oh, please no, help, mercy," Rusty said, his voice lifting now he was no longer whispering warnings.

"Besides," said Kami, "it's not like that. It's *never* going to be like that."

They walked in silence together for a little while before Kami pulled her hand out of his. Rusty pressed Kami's hand before he let her go. It was as scary to see Rusty clinging as it was to see Angela trembling, Kami thought. She wanted to protect them both, let them relax and be detached the way they liked to be, so that they would not be hurt.

She was not as scared about being hurt herself, so she walked back to Jared through the rain falling light as petals on her hair.

She crossed the wet cobblestones of the town square, past the statue of Matthew Cooper. Jared looked up at the sound of her footsteps, eyes bright and pale under the streetlights.

"What do you want?" he snapped. He had drawn back from her in his mind: she could not reach most of his emotions. The only thing she could catch was wariness, like having a wild bird in her hands, all beating heart and wings.

Kami said, "I want to know the truth."

"Do you also want to be a little bit more specific?"

"I want you to tell me the thing you're hiding from me," Kami said. "About your father, or your mother, about your family. There's something. I know there is. Once I know what's going on, I can handle it."

"You always think you can handle everything." He said it slowly, but with no doubt.

She felt his fear for her and his faith in her coursing between them. "You think I can, too," Kami said. "Come on, Jared." She stood looking at him, near the statue under the streetlight. He turned his head away, toward the triangle of the church spire against the rain-bright sky.

"It might be nothing," he said at last. "She's my mother."

Kami was silent, willing him to continue and knowing he could feel it.

"It was a long time ago," he went on. "I was a little kid. I don't even remember which apartment it was, or how old I was. I only remember the sound of my mother crying in the kitchen, and being in my parents' bedroom. She had left her wardrobe door open. She didn't wear nice things, but she had them in her wardrobe. I liked to put my face against her fancy fur coats and think about her being happy. I was just a dumb kid."

Kami reached out for him. He avoided her touch but accepted her reach in his mind, the comfort between them like clasped hands, but not quite.

"Behind her coats and her nice shoes, there was a box. It was a long box, made of pale yellow wood, like a coffin for a child. I knew I shouldn't do it. I knew it wasn't allowed. But I opened the box."

The rain was so light Kami could scarcely feel it, but by

now she was wet through. Her coat and dress were weighted with rain, cold seeping through to her bones. "What was inside?" she asked in a whisper.

Jared said, "Knives. There were two long golden knives with grooves cut along the blades. There were handles with carvings, of ivy, I think, and one was big enough that it looked like a scimitar. Finding something like that, I should have been scared. But I wasn't. I reached out. I wanted to touch them. Only Mom came in and pulled me away."

When Jared said *I wanted to touch them,* a shiver went through Kami, down to her cold bones. She could feel he meant it, as if he still wanted to.

"When I was older, I asked her about those knives," Jared said. "She told me they were family heirlooms. She told me she threw them away."

Kami did not ask if Jared had believed his mother. She did not say that someone had come at Holly with a knife, or speculate on a family that had knives as heirlooms. Jared already looked wrung out, his shoulders braced and his body taut, as if he wanted to bolt like he had from the lift when they had first met. There were walls up in his mind, and he had hidden this from her, something that had happened to him when he was a child.

Kami wondered what else he was hiding. She had been wrong: she was scared to be hurt, and scared to hurt him. It was so close to being the same thing.

"Thank you for telling me," she said at last, voice clear and firm, trying to banish fear for both of them. "Look, you may not have noticed, but with my elite sleuthing skills I've detected that it's raining. Can a lady get a walk home, or what?"

One corner of Jared's mouth curled. "Be my privilege to escort you home," he said, in the same casual tone she was affecting. "Or something."

The light rain was turning to glistening mist above the cobbles and making her hair a dark cloud. Kami thought of knives and could not suppress a shiver.

"Here," said Jared.

Instead of slinging a casual arm around her as Rusty's would have been, Kami felt the weight of his jacket settling on her shoulders. The lining of the jacket was warm from his body, and though he was close enough so his breath stirred her hair when he spoke, he did not touch her. She reached for him in her mind and felt his deep, calm rush of relief.

He was glad she hadn't asked him anything more.

Chapter Twenty
The Forgotten Sacrifices

The next morning, Kami found Jared leaning against her garden gate. "I don't require an escort to school," she told him severely.

"Holly got attacked last night," said Jared.

"So why aren't you at Holly's house?" Kami demanded.

"Several reasons," said Jared. "One being that Holly has a motorbike, and she can run over anyone who tries to attack her. Of course, if you'd take a spin on my bike with me . . ."

"It's too dangerous. Your bike isn't equipped to drive on the ice," Kami told him. "Which I'm assuming there will be plenty of, since hell will have frozen over the day I get on that thing. I fancy a stroll through the woods to school."

The air was cool and fresh, a leaf-filtered breeze blowing. They walked under the trees, some branches making curved appeals to the sky and some held out straight as if to catch something. Before getting to school, before thinking about what had almost happened to Holly, and before tracking down and interrogating Nicola, it could just be morning. They traded off feelings of contentment, forming a loop that fed on each other. Kami would not have guessed that Sorry-in-the-Vale would suit Jared so well.

Eventually Kami said, "I'm sorry about Rusty."

"So am I, generally."

He doesn't understand that things like you looking at me and being silent are in fact you making an incredibly dumb joke in my head rather than counting all my eyelashes.

A hundred and seventeen, said Jared, his amusement teasing up the corners of Kami's lips.

"Seriously, if I couldn't read your mind," Kami said, "law enforcement would be summoned. Immediately."

They went through a glen of black trees with red-and-purple-tinted leaves. When she looked up at Jared and their eyes met, there was that shock, but she was growing used to it. Their awareness of each other hummed in the air.

The movement in the corner of Kami's eye should not have caught her attention. It was just a flutter up in the tree branches. Something about it struck her as wrong, and she found herself turning and creeping closer to the tree, with Jared beside her. They were very close by the time they were able to believe what they were seeing.

Perched on a branch, small and terrible, was a creature made entirely of eyes. It was half the size of a thrush. It should have looked silly, its body wobbling in a way no other creature's body did because so much of it was jelly, but it was disturbing instead.

Okay, either we have both been drinking before breakfast, or, that's weird, said Jared.

Hyakume, Kami thought. *Sobo used to tell me stories. Creature with a hundred eyes.*

The woods did not seem like a safe haven any longer. Kami took one slow step back, and another. Then she was running through the woods, Jared beside her. They ran for the light breaking free of the trees at the edge of the woods. There they paused, panting, in the middle of the road.

Jared glanced at her and their minds surveyed the situation together, all senses making sure they were okay. Their breathing slowed and went regular in sync. They headed up the hill to the school together, toward safety.

Kami went through the school gate first, and they saw they had escaped nothing. Horror washed through her, and from her to Jared and back again. Kami was drowning in horror. She could not breathe.

Nicola Prendergast was lying, arms outflung, on the merry-go-round in the playground. It was painted blue and yellow, cheerful colors. She was still wearing her clothes from last night, though they were cut or torn open to show her skin, all scarlet on white.

There was so much blood.

Blackness flashed in front of Kami's eyes as if she was blinking. Nicola's face was imposed on the dark. She thought of Nicola at age six, pouring mud into a teacup for Jared, before Nicola grew too old for imaginary friends and Kami chose Jared over her.

Jared turned Kami, one hand light at her waist, away from the sight of Nicola, and she was grateful. He used the tentative touch to draw her in carefully, neither of them daring to move much. Kami's fist closed on the leather of Jared's jacket. Jared leaned down and rested his forehead against Kami's, and Kami was able to breathe.

She only caught one desperate breath, one that was their breaths mingled together. Then Jared shuddered away from her. Kami turned her face to the wall that surrounded the school, not bricks and cement but slates stacked together so that they never fell. She stared at the stones and stood with her back to Jared and the dead girl as she called the police.

The police kept Jared in the station much longer than they kept Kami, who had a brief interview with kind, wire-haired Sergeant Kenn. The sergeant made her a cup of tea and patted her hand and told her that her statement was very helpful.

They kept asking Jared about his past, about his father, about his relationship with Nicola. Even though they had both said that Jared barely knew her, that they had never actually exchanged words. Everyone had heard the stories about his father. The police thought he was the one who had attacked Kami. And Kami would not be able to convince anyone Jared was innocent without proof.

Obviously there would be no school for anyone today. Kami's dad had collected her and taken her home, and she'd asked to be alone and slipped out the back door.

She went to the library. Dorothy wasn't working behind the desk, so Kami could not ask her about the new laws of the Lynburns. But that didn't matter. These weren't animals being killed now. This was a person being killed, and dead people meant records.

Kami found big bound volumes marked LOCAL HISTORY, with old newspapers fixed to the heavy cardboard like pictures in a photo album. She remembered Dorothy saying, "This boy's grandparents made a law that nobody would hurt the people of the Vale." She went back fifty years, and then a few years more, until she found a tiny note in a list of obituaries. It read, "Adam Fairchild," listed the dates of his birth and death, and said, "He will be remembered for his sacrifice." Almost every year before that date, there was a similar obituary.

Sacrifice.

Kami stopped writing notes for her article, her lists of all these deaths. She laid down her pen and remembered the children's skipping song, the one they'd sung in the same playground where she had found Nicola.

Almost everyone grows old.

She remembered Jared's story about the knives that were Lynburn family heirlooms, and her mother calling the Lynburns creatures of red and gold: red blood on their gold knives. She remembered Nicola asking for protection from the Lynburns—but protection from who, or what? Nicola had not, in the end, been protected from anything.

She sat with her head bowed over the obituaries for a long time. Then she got up and went back to the police station.

Rosalind had not gone down to the station to collect her son.

You shouldn't be here, said Jared. Kami continued sitting on the bench outside the station because he had said that at least a thousand times.

Kami, said Jared. *Look up.* Kami looked up and he was there in front of her, looking tired, with a hollowed-out feeling when she reached out for his mind.

He did not seem surprised that they thought he might have done it. He crouched down by the bench, close to her knee like a guard dog, but not sitting beside her. Kami sat with her hands folded, and they were silent outside the police station together. The people passing by knew that Nicola was dead. Everyone in town did, those who were haunting the school grounds and those who had shut themselves in their houses, like Kami's family.

Only Kami and Jared knew that there might be magic involved. A wash of light in the air, an impossible creature in the woods, being able to speak to a boy in her mind. They had all seemed like innocent things—magic that did not hurt—that Kami could dismiss even if she could not explain them. Torturing an animal was sick and wrong, but this was terrifying.

"We're skipping school tomorrow," Kami said. "We have to go to London and find Henry Thornton."

Part IV
Becoming Real

How many loved your moments of glad grace
And loved your beauty with love false or true
But one man loved the pilgrim soul in you
—*W. B. Yeats*

Chapter Twenty-One
From Year to Year

"I can't believe you wouldn't take the bike," said Jared.

"I'm sorry," Kami told him. "I have this irrational fear of fatal road accidents. Anyway, getting here by public transport was perfectly simple."

It had meant waiting an hour for the rattling bus out of Sorry-in-the-Vale, then switching to another bus, and finally catching a train at Moreton-in-the-Marsh. It would have been fine without some fool grumbling in her brain about the speed of his motorbike.

"Oh yes," Jared said. "Perfectly simple."

The redbrick walls and greenhouse ceiling of Waterloo Station gave Kami heart. She was acting at last, doing something to help. She grinned up at Jared, who was standing with his hands in his pockets and his shoulders braced. The feeling of discomfort she'd been getting from him since they got on the second bus (which she had put down to crankiness about his bike) niggled at her. She pushed at his defenses and Jared pushed back, not letting her in. He did smile back at her, though.

"Shall we be on our way?" he asked.

Henry Thornton's apartment in South Ealing was more accessible by bus than by train, so they had another walk.

"And *another* bus," Jared moaned.

"We have to work through your thing about public transport," Kami said. "Did you ever take a bus on a school trip as a child? Was it a nice safe journey, driving at reasonable speed, being environmentally sound, and leading to an educational experience? I shudder to think."

They walked over Waterloo Bridge. In the distance on either side bristled metallic buildings, like weapons in the hands of enemy forces. Kami realized whose mind that thought had come from and glanced up at Jared. The wind blew in from the river and ruffled his blond hair; his profile beneath was inscrutable.

"And here you're supposed to be the glamorous city kid."

"I just like Sorry-in-the-Vale," Jared said.

"Sure, it's nice," said Kami. "But I like London too."

Cars ran on either side of the river, every second one a black cab. Big posters stood against the sky, flickering from a picture of a bank to another picture of a woman laughing with parted scarlet lips. People went by, some with their heads down, some with their umbrellas pessimistically up despite the fact that there was no rain. There was an Indian man in a red turban, and two girls walked by talking in a Chinese dialect.

Her dad had attended only one year of college in London before he had to come back and marry her mother. The times she came to London with him were the times when Kami wondered if he regretted it. Here nobody knew who she was, that she talked to imaginary people or that she was the daughter of the son of that Japanese woman, one of theirs and not quite one of theirs. Nobody looked twice at her or Jared. It was just the two of them, passing unnoticed by the whole world.

Kami reached for Jared's hand. She barely brushed skin with her fingertips, the contact sending a jolt through her, when Jared flinched automatically back. She felt his regret a second later, but by then she had snatched her hand away.

Kami, said Jared.

Kami pointed to a spot along the concrete-lined riverbank, where there were trees starving in little cages. Kami raised her eyebrows when that thought came to her: Jared really did not like London.

"Bus stop's that way," she said, and walked ahead of him.

Henry Thornton's flat was in the middle of a residential area. They had to go past two schools, six corner shops, and innumerable houses squashed together before they found it.

Thirty-Two Cromwell Gardens did not have any gardens around it. It was an uninspiring gray block of flats, all the windows uniformly rectangular. There was a matching gray wall immediately before the building, with the gate standing ajar. Someone had grown climbing roses on the wall, but at this stage in autumn that only meant the stone was covered in dry brown twigs and thorns.

"What do we say when we press the button for Flat 16?" Jared asked, after they had stood looking at the building for a couple of minutes.

Kami looked at the way he was slumped against the wall

and realized that she had been right at the train station. The closed-off feeling she'd been getting from him, with something rippling underneath it, wasn't crankiness or anger. She did not usually look at Jared for long, stealing glances to match up with his thoughts in her mind. The reality of him always made her bite her lip and look away too soon. She studied him now; the shoulders she'd already noticed were braced, and the gleam of sweat at his hairline, darkening that already dark-blond hair.

"You're sick," she said, startled.

"I'm fine," Jared said sharply.

"We can just go. We can go now."

"We didn't come all this way to run back because I'm feeling a little peaky," Jared bit out. "Kami! Come on." He didn't say it, but that didn't matter because she heard it in his mind anyway. *I'll be fine. Nicola won't be.*

"All right!" Kami said, pushing away the thought of what had happened to Nicola, because Jared was right: she'd come here with a mission. "We'll talk to Henry Thornton. Then we'll go home."

"So, what are you going to say when we press the buzzer?" Jared asked.

"I'm not going to ring the buzzer," Kami informed him.

Jared said, *We're breaking in? I'm so happy I never have to be bored again.*

Kami slipped in through the open gate and waited, Jared beside her. She didn't have to wait long, and her luck was better than she could have hoped for. A woman came out, pushing a pram. Kami held the door for her with a smile.

The woman smiled back absently, and as she went out the gate, Kami and Jared slipped in through the door.

"Not looking like a delinquent is very helpful," Kami told Jared serenely. "Which is why you should take a step back when I knock on Henry Thornton's door. Once it's open, if we have to, we'll push our way in."

Flat 16 was on the ground floor. Kami knocked on the green door and lifted her face to the level of the eyehole with a guileless smile.

The door opened.

"Hi," Kami said warmly, and stopped, startled.

It was Henry Thornton. She recognized him from his Internet profile, dark curly hair above a thin serious face, but that was hardly a surprise. Henry's profile had said he was twenty-four, but he looked younger just now. He also looked strangely helpless, his cheeks flushed and his eyes too bright.

Henry was sick too.

"If you're here to ask me if I've accepted the love of our Savior into my heart," Henry said, "I feel awful right now and I feel Jewish all the time, so—"

Kami laid her hand flat against the door, trying to maintain an ingratiating smile. Unfortunately, that made the door swing inward just a little too much.

Henry saw Jared. His eyes narrowed. He breathed, "Lynburn." He didn't shut the door; he bolted backward from it.

Kami hesitated, her palm still against the door, uncertain whether causing it to swing all the way open would be a mistake or not. Henry might be more inclined to talk if they didn't seem too pushy.

She hesitated, but she only hesitated for an instant. Then Henry pulled the door wide open and came running through it, right at Jared. The back of Jared's head hit the wall at the same time the side of his head caught a blow from the object in Henry's hand.

Jared was on the ground, and Henry was standing over him with the gun trained on Jared's face. "Did I not make myself clear?" Henry shouted. "I want nothing to do with it!"

Jared blinked slowly, about to lose consciousness. "What?" he asked in a thick voice.

"I don't care what rewards you offer," Henry said. "You disgust me. You and all those who follow you don't deserve power. You deserve to be wiped off the face of the earth."

Kami heard a little click, like a door closing. She knew what that was. It was the safety catch on the gun.

Kami ran in through Henry's open door and right into his kitchen. She picked up the first thing she saw, which was a wooden stool. She charged back out, swinging it over her head and into Henry's.

Henry stumbled and fell to his knees. The gun went flying. Kami hit Henry across his back with the stool again before she could lose her nerve. Then she dropped the stool, dashed down the corridor, and picked up the gun.

The metal slid in her sweaty hands. Kami swallowed the lump of panic in her throat and said to Henry Thornton, her voice emerging small and calm: "I wouldn't move if I were you."

Henry sagged on the carpet.

Kami didn't understand why he'd done this, why he and Jared were both sick, but she wasn't sticking around to ask him questions when Jared needed help. She decided that Henry was unlikely to be able to assault her with any success, fumbled at the catch on the gun, and shoved it in the pocket of her ruffled skirt. Then she stepped over Henry and knelt beside Jared.

"Hey," she said, and when his eyelids did not even move, she barged into his mind. *Hey, Jared. Come on.*

Sick pain flooded through her, his pain. She wondered grimly how long he had been feeling this bad.

Jared! she shouted in his mind, blazing urgency everywhere. *I'm right here. Jared, please!*

Jared opened his eyes with a groan. They were unfocused and blurry, lashes trembling as if his eyes might close again any moment. *Kami?*

Come on, get up, Kami pleaded. *Come on, try. We're going home.* It felt like she was pulling him up with mental as well as physical effort, dragging him out of unconsciousness as she hauled him to his feet. Jared grabbed at the wall and tried to stay upright, but he was leaning heavily on her.

"You don't understand," Henry mumbled from the floor. He looked as if he was fighting a losing battle against unconsciousness as well. "You don't know what—what he is."

"I know what *I* am," said Kami. She started doggedly on her way down the corridor, fighting to keep Jared on his feet. "I'm on his side."

She got a cab to the train station, where she cajoled and shoved Jared onto the train. She even got him onto the next bus, though as they were boarding, Jared's eyes rolled to the back of his head. She had to take all his weight, and for a second she thought they would both go down.

Kami sat in the bus seat with Jared collapsed against her, his body limp though every breath was a low sob in her ear. She could feel the clammy sweat on his skin, rising hot and cooling fast on his cold face. He wasn't having very many thoughts. There was just pain, and him still trying to hold on to her.

She knew she would never get him onto the last bus to Sorry-in-the-Vale. So she did the only thing she could think of at that point. She took out her phone with shaking hands and called her mother.

Chapter Twenty-Two
Happy in the Hour

Kami was sitting on the ground by the bus stop with Jared's head in her lap when her mother's car came around the corner, raising a cloud of pale yellow dust.

Mum did not bother with parking: she stopped the car in the middle of the street and threw herself out of it. "Kami!" she shouted, bronze hair flying like a flag. "How dare you run off without telling anyone, the day after a girl died!" She strode toward them, her face white with fury.

Kami sat on the ground, hunched her shoulders, and waited for the storm to break over her head. She felt too wretched and drained to do anything else. Mum stood over her, her shadow on Jared's slack face, and was silent.

"I'm sorry," Kami said quietly. "Please let me get him into the car."

Mum sighed and knelt down. She was taller and stronger than Kami, so together they were able to wrestle Jared into the car. He tried to help, to please Kami, even though she could tell he wasn't even aware her mother was there.

After they tipped him into the backseat and the car started, Kami felt his fall into darkness. She wrenched her neck turning to look at him. Jared lay in the backseat, his hair almost black with sweat, his face pale. But she saw his chest rising and falling, so she could breathe again.

When Kami turned back, she saw her mother's face. She dropped her eyes to the crimson T-shirt that said CLAIRE'S and was smeared with dust and flour. Kami did not know what to say.

They drove until they crested the west hills and Sorry-in-the-Vale lay spread out before them, pale buildings and lights cupped in a giant's green hand. Then her mother pulled over by the side of the road.

"Mum, we need to get Jared to a hospital," Kami said.

"A hospital won't help him," Mum said distantly. "I don't think he's sick, not the way normal people get sick."

Kami thought of how Henry had been sick too, and could not argue with her. This wasn't normal.

"Kami," her mother whispered, "what were you thinking, going off with him? A girl was killed!"

Kami closed her eyes against the onslaught of images, but all the bright colors of Nicola in the playground rose up in the darkness toward her.

"I know that. I'm sorry to have worried you."

Mum smacked her fist against the wheel of her car. "I don't want you sorry. I want you safe!" she said. "Do you want to get yourself killed? Haven't I told you enough?"

"No!" Kami shouted back at her. "No, you haven't! You haven't told me anything! Nobody in this town will tell me anything! All you've done is keep secrets."

Her mother was still very pale. "Surely," she said, her voice low and shaking, "*surely* I've told you enough that you know to stay away from the Lynburns."

"I can't!" Kami said, and could not stop the tears coming. She gulped and tried to fight them back, but they burst through anyway. "I *can't*. It doesn't matter what you say. I can't get away from Jared. If something hurts him, it hurts me too. And I don't know what's going on! You haven't told me anything at all, except to do something that is impossible. You have to tell me something else! What is it that I'm not supposed to tell Dad? What did you do?" Kami couldn't stop shaking.

Her mother sat looking at Kami, and for a moment Kami thought she would simply sit there, so still, as if she was a painting with desperate eyes.

Very quietly, her mother said, "Rosalind Lynburn and I did a spell."

It was such a shock it made Kami stop crying. She gaped instead. "You did *what?*"

"We did a spell," her mother repeated, her voice clearer, almost normal but with an edge.

"So, people can do spells," said Kami.

"No," said her mother. "The Lynburns aren't people. I've told you how things were back then. The whole town was terrified of the Lynburns. We don't talk about what they are. We all knew that they weren't supposed to hurt us. But we also knew that they could. We knew what they could do to you. Nobody ever crossed a Lynburn." Mum bit her lip and plunged on. "The last person who tried was your grandfather, Stephen Glass. The family who live in the house at the edge of the woods, they're meant to have a special relationship with the Lynburns."

"The family who live in the house at the edge of the

woods," Kami repeated. "Us." She slid a look back at Jared but could only see the faint outline of his face in the shadowy backseat, turned away from her. "What kind of special relationship?"

"Being their servants," Mum said bitterly.

"Well, *that's* not happening," Kami said.

Mum did not even seem to hear her. "Doing their bidding, being their—their front guard against the world. Stephen Glass said no, struck out the word 'Guard' on our house, and left Sorry-in-the-Vale. He came back years later, thinking it was all ridiculous and that he was a man of the world who didn't believe in fairy tales. He came back to his childhood home with his new wife by his side, thinking nothing could possibly happen to him. He was dead by morning. Nobody crosses the Lynburns."

"But you weren't even born then," Kami stammered out. "How do you know he didn't just die? How could they kill him? Sobo would've told me if he was murdered!"

"She never believed in any of it. They can kill you without touching you," Mum whispered. "They can make rain fall from an empty sky. They can make the woods come alive. That's what people whisper about them. I didn't know anything, not for sure. Not until the night Rosalind Lynburn left Sorry-in-the-Vale."

The whisper came involuntarily from Kami's dry throat: "What happened?"

Shadow was falling across Sorry-in-the-Vale, evening drawing over the town like a veil. Her mother stared at the horizon, the dying sunlight reflected in her eyes.

"I was on my way home from the restaurant," she said. "I was walking down our High Street. And—I have never told anybody this, I know it sounds crazy—all along our High Street the shadows came alive."

"What?" Kami whispered. Her mother did not even seem to hear.

"Shadows unfurled from around flags and weather vanes like they had wings. They curled around gates like cats and they slithered toward me like snakes. The shadows came apart from the night and came alive and came toward me. Then Rosalind Lynburn came walking out of the darkness, pale as a ghost. She meant it as a display, you see? She meant to scare me." Claire laughed a short laugh. "She succeeded."

Rosalind Lynburn. Jared's mother, deliberately terrorizing Kami's. But she couldn't have any unearthly powers. She would have done something about Jared's father if she did.

"Rosalind came to me and she said that she thought it was time Jon showed the Lynburns some allegiance. She said he didn't want to end up like his father. Jon had just come back from London, had just given up college to marry me because—" Mum gave Kami a quick, scared look.

"It's okay, Mum," said Kami. "It wasn't my fault. It wasn't your fault. I get it. Go on."

"I *wanted* him to marry me and come back to Sorry-in-the-Vale," Mum said in a thin voice. "I loved this town. I wanted my dream here, my restaurant, and I wanted him as well. I was getting everything, but I was terrified that he'd be sorry later. And I was simply terrified for him. Nobody ever told him or his mother about the Lynburns; they were left alone because there wasn't anything they could do for the Lynburns. It was one of the things that I loved about him, that fear never touched him. Rosalind wasn't going to touch him. I said I was a Glass now too, and then she smiled. It was just what she'd wanted me to say."

"What did she want from you?" Kami asked.

"The only thing she ever wanted," Mum said. "Rob Lynburn. She knew he came to see me every day. He was marrying her twin sister, and we all knew Lillian was going to have a baby. Rosalind wanted to get as far away from her sister's victory as she could, and she chose some American tourist to carry her away, but she still wanted Rob. She said she'd do a spell so she could see him through my eyes. She said all debts would be paid off between our family and hers then."

Kami remembered that the Lynburns owned their house. Her mother had been the same age Rusty was now, and alone in the face of magic.

Mum closed her eyes. "I said I would do it. She took me into the woods, and she used a golden knife on a bird, and had me taste the blood. She cut off a piece of my hair and took it away with her. Later I told myself that she was crazy, that I'd been humoring a madwoman, but sometimes in the year after she left, just in that year—sometimes I thought I felt her. Using my soul as a keyhole to look through. Coming at me again through the darkness with the shadows in her hair." She shuddered, turning away from the car window.

"You think a Lynburn killed Nicola."

Kami reached out and touched her arm, and her mother turned to her. "I don't know. But I know any one of them might have. I know the Lynburns think our blood is their right. And so you are not going near the Lynburns again!" Mum hissed. "I won't let them touch you."

As she hadn't let them touch Dad, Kami thought. The lights of Sorry-in-the-Vale below her turned to diamonds underwater as she tried not to cry.

Mum covered Kami's hand with hers. "Do you hear me, Kami? Are you listening to me? It doesn't matter how in love you think you are."

"Oh, right," Kami said, and tears were running down her face again, beyond her power to control. She could taste them, and they were bitter. "In love. That's how it sounds, doesn't it? His heart is my heart, nobody can ever take him away from me, I keep him in here!" She thumped her breastbone so hard it hurt. "People say stuff like that but they don't mean it: they mean they're in love. All except me. I mean it. Rosalind and you made me mean it. When you did that spell, linked each other's minds. You were going to have a baby. And so was she."

She'd known there had to be an explanation for this.

Mum's hand closed convulsively on Kami's.

"You knew, didn't you?" Kami whispered. "You had to know."

"When you were a baby," Mum said, in a low voice, "I used to watch you, the way you could lie there for hours, absorbed. It never went away, seeing my daughter look off into the distance and talk to someone only she could hear. I didn't know it would happen, Kami. I didn't! I'm so sorry. I couldn't think of anything to do but try to hide it from you."

It was one of Kami's earliest memories, the look of fear on her mother's face as she watched Kami.

"I've been scared all my life," Kami said slowly. "I've thought I might be crazy all my life, and you did it to me."

"I didn't know what else to do!" Claire whispered. "I couldn't tell anyone. The Lynburns were gone, but there are others like them in this town. They don't like it when you tell secrets. I couldn't lift the spell. All I could do was try to minimize the damage the Lynburns could do to your life. They were the leaders, and without them the town seemed to settle into a different shape, a better shape. I hoped, I prayed they would never come back." She began to cry.

She'd been very young and scared, and she'd done it for love. Kami remembered how she had felt seeing magic, and the magic had not been turned against her.

Kami could not say that it was all right, that she was all right. She slid her arm around her mother's neck instead and held on.

❧

Kami refused to drop Jared at Aurimere House and pointed out that Dad was bound to notice a boy sleeping on the sofa. So her mother reluctantly agreed to help get Jared up to Kami's room.

"Unconscious guys rarely assault people's virtue," Kami pointed out, holding on tight to Jared's jacket as they hauled him up the stairs. "Besides, he almost never touches me. He doesn't want to." She looked at her mother, who was handling Jared as impersonally as she handled crates. "I'm safe with him," she insisted.

"He's a Lynburn," Mum said. "I've seen what they can do. I don't think you can trust him. And I don't think you're safe with him."

She left Kami with him, though. Kami tried to tug the blanket out from under Jared so she could cover him, but her muscles were screaming in protest. She could barely move the blanket an inch, so she climbed onto the bed and sat beside him.

He looked better, she thought, his color back, the sweat in his hair dry. She laid a hand gently against his forehead. It was hot, but it didn't seem dangerously hot.

Sleep smoothed out the lines of anger and wariness on Jared's face. He looked younger, like the child she'd never been able to reach, and terribly vulnerable.

"Hey," said Kami. "Hey. When you wake up, I have a lot to tell you." She'd known there was an explanation for all this. She'd known it wasn't that they were soul mates. She knew she would have to be very careful when she told him.

Jared turned his head on the pillow, murmuring something. It was soothing to have him there but unconscious, so she could touch him and he wouldn't flinch. She could think about him and he wouldn't know what she was thinking. She could be sure that whatever he felt was not bleeding into her feelings, that now her feelings were hers alone.

She could be almost sure.

"I wish I knew what was wrong," she murmured.

"It's nothing," Jared murmured back.

Kami jumped and let her hand drop. She looked at him: his eyes were still mostly closed, but there was a gleam of gray under his lashes.

"I always get sick like this. Every fall."

Kami thought of Jared in the woods, talking about being sick before he went home last year. She thought of the times in their lives he had reached out for comfort, and wondered how often it had been because he was ill. She leaned over him, and her shadow fell across his face.

"Don't talk," she said. "Just rest. You're safe. I've got you."

"I remember last year," Jared breathed. "I was—I remember lying on sidewalks that felt like frying pans during the day and like gravestones at night. My skin was crawling with fever and the only thing I could still do was listen to you."

"I didn't know."

Kami's throat was tight. She hadn't known what was happening to him, hadn't known that he was real. She had just talked to him, and he had needed help.

"It's all right," Jared said. His voice was still hushed, but it was very clear. "Everything's all right now. This was all I wanted."

"What?" Kami whispered.

His chest was shuddering with his fast, shallow breaths. He did not lift his head, dark gold against the pallor of her pillow. She did not think he was able to. He just lay there, the moonlight making his eyes opaque silver mirrors.

"This," he whispered back. "Nothing else ever mattered to me, and you weren't even real. All I ever wanted was you."

Now he was real, and she was real, and they were together. No matter what nightmare explanation there was, what mistakes made in blood and darkness when their mothers were young, this year was better than the last.

Jared's eyes had closed. Kami reached out, seeing her

hand tremble in the shadow and moonlight, and stroked his hair very, very lightly. She traced the curling ends of his hair with her fingertips and murmured, "I'm here now. You're safe with me."

She lay down beside him. She curled close into the warmth of his body, not quite touching, listening to his breathing smooth out and become easy and regular. They spent the night together, safe.

Chapter Twenty-Three
Waking the Woods

Kami's eyes opened and she stretched, both reflexive moves that woke her up a good deal faster than usual. The stretch brought her body into contact with Jared's, lightly touching all along one side. It was very strange to be so fiercely aware of one edge of your body.

Jared was lying propped up on one arm, looking down at her. *Good morning,* he said silently, and the two things fused together, the voice in her head and the boy in her bed. They almost seemed natural.

Good morning, said Kami. *You look better.* She should have spoken aloud. It was too intimate, morning sunlight and rumpled sheets and silence. It made Jared think—or perhaps she was the one who thought it—of when they were fourteen.

There were thoughts you couldn't help having at fourteen, thoughts they couldn't help sharing. Kami thought of them now and felt the blood wash hot into her face.

He was real now, and looking down at her, lying close beside her. The mattress dipped under his weight, so her body inclined naturally toward his. She touched his mind and saw his intense focus on her, their minds mirrors reflecting back

on each other. The shape of him was encompassable, potentially knowable, and yet terrifying and strange. She could
map out the muscles and planes of his shoulders under her
palms. It was possible.

Kami thought she could reach up and slide her palm up
the nape of his neck, and as she thought that, she heard his
breath catch.

On that sound, the door opened, and Jared threw himself backward off the bed.

"What the hell is going on?" demanded Kami's dad,
advancing with his black eyes snapping.

Jared blurted, "My intentions are honorable."

Kami sat up straight in her bed and stared in Jared's
direction. "Are you completely crazy?" she wanted to know.
"This isn't the eighteenth century. How do you think that's
going to help?"

"Well, I mean," Jared said, back against the wall like a
cornered animal. "When we're older. I mean—"

"Please shut up," Kami begged.

"I agree with Kami," said Dad. "When you're in an
abyss-like hole, quit digging." He did look marginally amused
now, rather than homicidal. "Ash Lynburn, I presume."

Jared made a face. "I'm the other one."

"Oh," said Kami's father. "The one with the motorcycle?
In my daughter's bedroom. At an ungodly hour of the morning. Fantastic. What was that about your intentions again?"

"I'm just going to go," Jared decided.

"Might be best," said Dad.

"She isn't seeing Ash."

"She talks for herself," Kami announced loudly. "Or

rather, she doesn't talk about things like that with her father, ever, at any time. And neither should anyone else."

"So, I really must be going," Jared resumed. "I have to be . . . somewhere else."

That was when Kami realized something that should have been obvious before. Jared really was completely better. He looked uncomfortable, but other than that he was his normal color, not holding himself with any trace of pain. His thoughts hummed along hers unchecked, not hiding any pain.

People didn't get sick like that, or recover like this, but her mother had said the Lynburns were not people.

Jared glanced at Dad, then back at Kami, and said, "I'll call you later."

You have never called me once in the entirety of your life, said Kami. *I'll talk to you in a few minutes.*

Jared nodded to her dad, who watched him with narrowed eyes as he went past. Kami heard Jared's steps going down the stairs before her father shut the door and cut the sound off.

"So, I know what the ladies like," Dad said. "I used to be a bad boy myself."

Kami raised her eyebrows. "Oh, you were?"

"I won't go into it, because I know you honor and respect me as your parent, and I don't want to spoil your illusions," said Dad. "Also I don't want to give you any ideas. Let's just say there were fires."

"Dad! You set *fires?*"

"Fires happened," said Dad. "And then there was your

mother. She had no time for any of that. She didn't try to reform me. She wasn't allured by my wiles."

"You had wiles?" Kami inquired, with even more disbelief than she'd shown regarding the fires.

"Damn good wiles," said Dad. "And I was smoother than that sullen blond kid too. Way smoother." There was a glint in his eye.

"You were saying about Mum?" Kami asked hastily.

"Claire was working in a restaurant and taking classes in business management when we were fifteen years old," said Dad. "She knew what she wanted. There was no reason for her to bother with me. Unless I made myself less of a bother. What I'm trying to say is, you can't change a guy. Concentrate on your own life. Someone whose hobbies include trying to break his neck on a motorcycle and slipping into a girl's bedroom first thing in the morning isn't worth bothering about."

"He's actually been here since last night."

Dad's fingers tightened on the doorknob even though his voice stayed light. "I really need to buy that shotgun."

"He was sick and needed to lie down," said Kami.

"Uh-huh," said Dad.

"He was literally unconscious, and Mum and I had to carry him up the stairs."

"Oldest trick in the book," grumbled Dad, but his brow cleared. "Claire didn't mention anything about this."

"Maybe because she thought you'd go out and buy a shotgun?"

"Maybe," Dad conceded. He left the doorway and went

over to Kami, sinking onto the mattress beside her and sliding an arm around her shoulders.

"It's not what it looked like," Kami said. "We're not like that. He's my friend, that's all." Except that wasn't all. He was always part of her thoughts, and now that he was real, he was inescapably part of her life, but it was as she had told her mother: saying he was part of her or that they were more than friends sounded like love, but it seemed like loss as well. All the words she knew to describe what he was to her were from love stories and love songs, but those were not words anyone truly meant.

They were like Jared, in a way. If they were real, they would be terrifying.

Kami did not know what Jared wanted. Kami didn't know what she wanted either, except that she was scared all the limits she'd set would be burned away, all control lost, and she would be lost too. And she was scared to want anything. It felt as if their parents had traded away so much of their children and so many of their choices on that night long ago.

"I want you safe, that's all," said her father into the silence of her thoughts, and the shadow in his voice let Kami know he was thinking of Nicola. "I want you safe in every way."

Her mother had wanted to keep them all safe. Her father didn't know anything. Kami leaned her head against his shoulder and shut her eyes. "I know."

Which was when she became aware of the current of Jared's thoughts turning cold. He was alone in the woods as he followed her memories of what her mother had told her last night.

Jared went stumbling through the undergrowth, twigs pulling at his clothes. He made for the Crying Pools. He dreamed of these lakes every night, two wide eyes reflecting the sky and hiding secrets. He didn't know why he wanted to be near them, but he did. When he reached them, he threw himself down on the mossy bank beside the pool on the left and bowed his head over his clenched hands.

Kami had been right, and he had been wrong. The link was not some undeserved but beautiful gift sent to redeem the rest of his life. His and Kami's connection was the ugly side effect of his mother threatening and terrifying hers. A shadow falling on his clenched hands and turning the lake black made him look up at the sky. There were clouds that had not been there when the sun was streaming through Kami's window, black rags like tatters of mourning cloth hiding the sun.

The skin at the back of Jared's neck crawled. He looked around, the air chill as if he was underwater. There was someone leaning toward him—a girl, her translucent green body bowing out of the heart of a tree. Jared held still, feeling like a startled animal, staring into her face.

Her eyes were hollows, green as the woods. Her hair swayed, moving like willow leaves in the wind. She leaned in close and kissed his cheek, soft as rain.

Jared shuddered, then panic exploded through him. He wanted to go back to Kami. Instead he wrenched himself up from the bank and away through the woods, up to the manor house. The double doors, above which blazed the legend YOU ARE NOT SAFE, crashed open. Jared hadn't touched them.

He strode into the echoing dark hall and came face to face with Ash at the bottom of the stairs.

"A green girl in the woods just kissed me," he announced furiously. "What is wrong with the world?"

Ash stared at him, and to Jared's amazement a look of stunned joy shone in his eyes. "You woke the woods?"

"God damn it," said Jared, and punched Ash in the face.

Ash fell back, grabbing the banister to support himself. Jared wheeled away and the doors of the library hit the walls. Inside, his mother sat by an empty fire, she and Aunt Lillian on each side of the grate like matching statues. His uncle Rob leaned against the mantel exactly between them.

"I want to know what the hell is going on," Jared demanded. "The manor, the woods, dreaming about the lakes. I know what you did to Kami's mother. I want to know what kind of monsters you people are."

Aunt Lillian broke up the tableau, rising to her feet and walking toward him with a click of heels. She raised a hand, and Jared heard the doors of Aurimere close behind him. Aunt Lillian smiled.

"We're sorcerers," she said. She reached up and laid her hand against his cheek, nails sharp against his skin. "And so are you."

Chapter Twenty-Four
Ours Is Hungry Magic

"So, now I know what kind of monster I am, what does that mean?" Jared asked. He pulled away from Aunt Lillian's hand and stalked toward the window. Black clouds were still blotting out the sun. "Did I do this?"

"I think so," said Aunt Lillian. "That's what sorcerers do, bend the natural world to their will. You caused the storm last week. We could feel it in the rain. We wondered if the one who created the storm was doing the killing."

Breath felt stolen from Jared. His lungs burned. "I didn't kill that girl," he rasped. He turned and looked at his family. Ash was at the door now, blood on his mouth. Jared's whole family watched him back in silence.

"I didn't," Jared repeated, louder. "Why would I?"

"Sometimes a sorcerer makes mistakes," Aunt Lillian said. "We're sorcerers. That means we need sources. That's what this town was built for, for sorcerers to be safe."

We neither drown nor burn, said Kami in his mind, as if this made sense to her. *They used to drown and burn witches.*

"Sorry-in-the-Vale was designed for sorcerers to live in and feed off the woods, the animals, all the life surrounding

241

us, in a place that does not change." Aunt Lillian looked at Jared, her gaze intent but remote, as if she wanted to see right through his skin to the blood in his veins. "You must have noticed that you're not getting sick this year, when the summer dies. When you always did before. The cities make you sick."

When the summer dies? Jared thought at Kami. *This is ridiculous.*

Kami said, *Stay calm, I want to know more.*

"I'm not a timid woodland creature," Jared snapped. "I don't need to be kept on a nature preserve."

"We're not making this up to upset you, son," Uncle Rob said. "None of us chose to be what we are. We just live with it."

"We didn't even know if you *would* be a sorcerer," said Ash from the door, speaking carefully; nobody had mentioned his cut mouth. "Your father wasn't."

Jared's eyes met Ash's. The word "half-breed" hung in the air between them. All his life, he'd thought of his father's blood as the poison in his veins, violence and fury. But his mother's blood was poison too. Jared could not help but think of the two bloods mingling, of what strange terrible brew they had made.

Outside the window, storm clouds boiled.

"We are not the only sorcerers in Sorry-in-the-Vale," said Aunt Lillian, and Jared thought of Henry Thornton's pale face in London, sick with the city. "We're the founders, the leaders. And we are the ones who have intermarried, so more of our children are sorcerers. We can't know which of the descendants of sorcerers in this town have power. We don't know which is the one killing for it."

"You weren't searching," Jared stated, "because you thought it was me."

"Ours is hungry magic," said Aunt Lillian. "There's power to be taken from life. From the woods, from animals. We take tokens of life, blood or hair or belongings, to focus or strengthen a spell. We can take power from certain living humans, more power than anything else, though we don't do that anymore. There is also power to be gained from death: more power, though it lasts a very short time. You wouldn't be the first sorcerer to think death was the only road to power and try for the greatest power by making a human sacrifice. All the Lynburns used to do it. The town used to let them. Every year, the sorcerers would take a death from the town to use as a source, and in return the town prospered. But we stopped accepting sacrifices before I was born."

Jared thought of Nicola lying dead. Nobody had stopped a sorcerer from killing her.

He looked around the stone room echoing with that word, "sacrifices": from Uncle Rob's kind eyes to Aunt Lillian's cold ones, to Ash with blood still gleaming on his mouth. This den of monsters was his family. "Why didn't anyone tell me?" he whispered.

His mother had not moved from her position beside the fireplace and Uncle Rob. Her hands were folded in her lap and she did not even turn to look at him as she spoke, her voice very calm. "I did tell you," she said. "I told you that you killed your father."

The storm had turned all of Sorry-in-the-Vale into the woods. The storm clouds were like dark boughs painted on the sky, and the cold, rain-laden wind hit Kami's eyes like the slap of wet leaves.

The last thing in the world Kami wanted to do was go into the actual woods, but Jared had stopped talking to her after he left Aurimere, and here was her best guess for where he might have gone. *Come on!* she yelled at him. *Talk to me!* All she got was sound and fury, a sensation as if the storm was inside her head. She shook her head, wet locks of hair whipping across her face, and plunged from her garden gate into the wild woods.

A town of sorcerers, she thought. Kami stumbled, and her knees scraped against a fallen log, but she didn't fall. She grabbed onto a branch, using it to struggle on through the howling woods.

The pools were huge twin black eyes. They stared at Kami in the glen full of whispering trees. The surfaces of both pools were still as spilled ink. Kami could not tell which pool to choose, so she just sent out an appeal to Jared, lashing out at the same time as reaching out.

Jared broke the surface of the pool on the left. He shook his head, droplets flying out into the rain as he held on to the muddy bank of the pool. His shoulders bunched and she felt his mind focus again, preparing to dive back down.

Kami lunged, on her knees in the dirt, grabbed his arms, and tried to haul him up out of the lake. Jared looked at her, his eyes not focusing. She held on hard, her fingertips biting deep into the muscles of his arms. "No," Kami said. *No.* "You're not going back down there, you'll drown, I said no." *No.*

Jared was breathing in hoarse, shallow pants: she could actually hear the scrape of his breath catching in his throat. His body was caught too, in a continuous tremor. *There's something down there I have to get,* he said. *There are people down there who want me to stay with them.*

"Well, you're not going to," Kami said. "You're going to stay here with me."

Jared said nothing, but when she tugged him up out of the water again, he dragged himself out onto the ground. He bowed his head as if it was too heavy for him to hold, and the water from his hair dripped onto her shoulder like cold tears. Kami put up a hand, her palm hitting his chest, the icy material slick over his skin.

His breath came harsh in her ear. "With you," he said. "And why would you want that?" He lifted his head and watched her, the lightning in the murky sky touching his hair with electric-pale glints. His eyes were gray hollows set in his strained face. "You were right all along," he said. "We shouldn't be—it shouldn't have happened. It's twisted and evil. I'm sorry."

"You're sorry?" Kami demanded. "You weren't even born! Your mother did it, and my mother agreed to it. You didn't do anything."

So, she did it, terrified your mother, trapped you in a cage you can't escape. She got what she wanted. She didn't care who she hurt. That's what she is. I got what I wanted too. I was fighting with my father and I wanted him blotted out of the world. I threw him down the stairs and snapped his neck. That's what I am.

As Jared spoke inside her head, the rain cascaded down in the silence, thudding into the earth and crushing the fallen leaves, breaking the blackness of the lake with glints like hidden needles.

Jared had been angry and thrown his father down the stairs, without even meaning to. He'd been angry with her the night someone threw her down the well, and she did not remember hands on her: magic could have hurled her down. Just as magic had hurled down Jared's father.

No. She wouldn't believe it.

"I'm not sorry," Kami told him. "I wouldn't go back to a time before we were born, make it right, and lose you. I wouldn't be me without you. I wouldn't, I never want to—" The crashing drum and rattle of the rain ceased, with a suddenness that made it seem like silence was echoing through the woods. Kami sat on the wet ground looking at Jared and said, on a breath—"Lose you."

Jared studied her face. The air between them felt new, the world remade by the storm. He leaned away from her.

Kami threw up walls, forbidding him to touch her mind, wanting to die if he heard this, and thought: *He's never going to kiss me. He's never going to want to.*

Jared's shoulders tensed, as if bracing for an attack.

Kami felt him misread the way she'd withdrawn. She couldn't tell him what was really going on. Instead she said, "So, we're all right? We're going to work out this magic stuff together?"

"Yeah," said Jared. "What do you want to do about it?"

Kami told him.

Part V

Direct from the Source

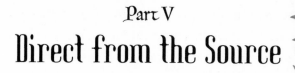

The night is darkening round me,
The wild winds coldly blow;
But a tyrant spell has bound me,
And I cannot, cannot go.
—*Emily Brontë*

Chapter Twenty-Five
These Three

Holly was the last one to arrive at headquarters, humming and carrying her motorcycle helmet under her arm.

By then Kami was already sitting behind her desk, where she retreated when she wanted to feel more secure. She was wearing a blazer because she wanted to be taken seriously, though it was possible the matching headband with the bow ruined the effect.

Angela was standing on the other side of the desk, a tower of orange silk and outrage. Jared was behind Kami, arms crossed over his chest, looking like he was her bodyguard.

"No," Angela was saying as Holly walked in, "I don't believe you. And encouraging her to spin some crazy story isn't helping me like you," she added, to Jared.

Kami stood. "He isn't encouraging me," she said. "I make up my own mind, and I'm not crazy. Neither of us is crazy. It's true."

"Oh, magic is real?" Angie said scornfully. "That's true?"

Holly's helmet slipped out from under her arm and tumbled to the floor. Everyone turned to look at her. Holly stared at the gleaming blue helmet rolling at her feet.

"Do you know something about this, Holly?" asked

Jared. There was an edge to his voice that made Holly look at him and flinch back.

Kami glanced at Jared, and then at Holly. Holly had always seemed to like Jared, to think, in her words, that he might be fun. Kami couldn't blame Holly for the way she was staring at Jared now. The remote look in Jared's eyes wasn't fun, it was frightening. Kami understood that Holly might like the *illusion* of danger and not want danger that was real. She couldn't blame her for that.

"Only what everybody says," Holly said, low.

"And what does everybody say?" Jared demanded.

"I've never heard anybody say anything," Angela announced.

"You're an outsider," said Holly.

Angela's face was both angry and hurt for a moment, before she forced her expression back into pure anger.

"You *are*," Holly told her, looking desperate to make her understand. "You and Rusty only moved here six years ago. Most of the families have been here for generations and generations. Some have been here since the start."

"The start of what?" Jared snarled. "Since the Lynburns founded their private kingdom of all the sorcerers together? Since then?"

"They're just stories," Holly said. "Stories about settling in Sorry-in-the-Vale because it was a good place, a magical place. Where we were all meant to be, and the price paid is worth it. They're just local legends, though, just stuff my dad says when he's drunk. They're not true. Nobody can really do magic! The Lynburns are gone!"

It was something Kami had heard other people from the

Vale say. They said it when they were wishing for crops not to fail and storms to pass, but she realized now she'd heard her mother say it when something happened to scare her, as if to reassure herself: the Lynburns are gone.

As if the Lynburns were genies who could grant wishes, and monsters waiting to leap, all at once.

Jared watched Holly with cold eyes. He said, "Now we're back."

At Holly's feet, her helmet shattered into pieces of crystal and bone. Holly bit her lip and looked to Angela as if she was her only possible source of comfort, as if Kami and Jared were her enemies. Angela stared at the pale and translucent shards on the floor, and her expression grew even more outraged.

Kami got up, with her hands placed flat on the desk. "You're paying for that, buddy," she said mildly.

"I don't believe you can read each other's minds. You can be a magician or a criminal or a balloon-animal giraffe for all I care," Angela told Jared, and then looked at Kami. "But you're my best friend in the world. And that controlling freak is not convincing you that he can talk to you in your head, for God's sake."

Kami could not help smiling, even though it made Angela look even more furious. Angela was asking for proof, and that Kami could handle.

"What we need to do," Kami said, "is run a test. I want you to come downstairs with me, Angela, and tell me something you've never told me before. And then Jared will tell Holly what you told me."

"I will do no such thing!"

Kami tipped up her face to look Angela in the eye. "You're so sure it's not true," she said. "Don't you want to prove it?"

Angela held her gaze for an instant longer. "Fine," she snapped, and turned, her black hair flying like a cape from her shoulders. She went for the door, her legs eating up the ground in four long, smooth strides, and stopped beside Holly at the threshold. Angela's curled mouth softened a little. "You all right?" she asked.

Holly reached out and touched Angela's hand, fingers twining briefly around hers.

"Yeah," she said, and smiled back with an effort.

Angie nodded at Holly and walked on.

"This is all going to be totally fine, I have a plan," Kami assured Holly, brushing by.

"Right," Holly said. She looked doubtful, but that was possibly because Kami and Angela were abandoning her with a guy who looked on the edge and ready to jump.

Angela did not look doubtful in the least as she and Kami walked down into the shadowy stairwell. Her high-heeled boots sounded like gunshots, going down every step.

"You're my best friend," Kami said, looking up into Angela's stern face. "I could always trust you never to think I was crazy."

"Your faith is touching but totally misplaced," Angela said. "I believe you to be a permanent inhabitant of cloud-cuckoo-land, and this year you may be getting elected mayor." She reached the bottom of the stairs and wheeled on Kami, her eyes boring into Kami's. "But you can trust me."

"So trust me," said Kami. "Tell me a secret."

Angela hesitated for a moment, looking down at Kami.

She still looked furious, but she leaned forward. Her face was still set and angry, but she brushed the hair gently back from Kami's face and whispered in her ear.

When they got back, they found Jared kneeling before Holly. Kami raised her eyebrows at the sight: Holly was pretty popular with guys, but in Kami's experience they seldom literally threw themselves at her feet. They all looked down at Jared's bowed blond head and saw he was gathering up the shards of crystal and fragments of bone in his hands, and his hands were shimmering with magic.

The air in their headquarters seemed thin suddenly, like being up on a high mountain. The Lynburns were gone, Kami thought. But not anymore.

The crystal sparkled like sun hitting snow, while the bone glowed ivory as if discovered by candlelight at night.

Jared looked up. "I can't fix it," he said. The corner of his mouth came up in a tired, crooked half smile. "No surprise that I'm better at breaking things than mending them. I'm sorry. I'll buy you a new one."

"Okay," said Holly. "I like bright colors. Maybe red or orange."

Jared's eyebrow lifted. "Okay." He stood, crystal and bone falling from his open hands. He was one of those boys who made you think about how very differently guys were shaped from girls. And now he could do magic. Kami could not blame Holly for stepping back.

"Nicola Prendergast?" Holly wanted to know, her voice very soft.

Jared flinched. "I didn't kill her. My aunt Lillian says we're going to find out who did."

He looked at Kami, and then at Angela, who nodded. Holly took a deep breath.

"What is Angela's secret?" she asked.

Kami recognized the look on Jared's face, intent and withdrawn. She'd seen the same expression on her own face a hundred times. She was grateful to him for speaking quietly, as if he didn't want to invade Angela's privacy, though Jared and Kami had so little real privacy of their own.

He said: "Angela's never kissed anybody."

Holly laughed. "What? But of course Angie's—"

Angela, standing still beside Kami, glared at Jared. Her cheeks were burning red in her pale face. Holly shut her mouth.

"What a coincidence," Jared said calmly. "Me neither."

Kami could not help a startled exhale.

Jared looked mildly surprised. "You knew that," he said to her.

"I know," Kami said. "I just hadn't—I guess I hadn't put it together."

Holly looked as if she did not care much about kissing revelations, no matter how shocking. She looked like she was concentrating on not having a panic attack. "Okay," she said, exhaling. "So the stories are true. Magic really does exist, someone magic is killing people, and Kami's imaginary friend is real too."

"There's something happening in the woods, as well," Kami said. She gave Holly a beseeching glance. "There are creatures in there. Creatures from stories. Ash called it 'waking the woods.'"

Angela was vibrating with indignation at the world. Holly

seemed as if she was about to cry. And Kami did not know how to deal with any of it: she had thought her friends would want to know the truth, that they would want to help her.

"Have you, uh . . ." Holly pushed her hands back through her hair. "Have you seen a unicorn in the woods?"

"I imagine that's next," Jared muttered.

"Right," said Holly. "Well. If the unicorn is pink, about two feet tall, with a sparkly mane, we'll know my imaginary friend is real too."

Kami blinked and then burst out laughing. She felt the pleased relief spreading from Jared to her and knew without looking that he was smiling too. She kept her eyes on Angela, and a few moments later, Angela smiled reluctantly as well.

"We did lose touch when I was seven," Holly admitted. "But Princess Zelda and I really had something back in the day."

"If we see Princess Zelda," Kami said, "I'll be sure to tell her to call you."

Kami seized a few minutes before class with Angela and Holly later, repairing to the bathroom to try to make some plans.

"We can't really go to the ladies' room anymore," Angela remarked.

"Well," said Kami, "that'll get very unfortunate very quickly."

"I mean it," said Angela. "We can't get away from guys now, not really. Not all of them. Jared will always know what we're doing. I barely know him, and he knows details from the last six years of my life that I thought nobody knew but me and my best friend."

"Imagine how I feel," Kami said dryly.

Kami saw Holly exchanging looks with Angela, trying not to be openly horrified about Kami's life in front of her. She felt her mouth twist.

Someone tried to open the bathroom door and was unable to do so because Angela had her back against it.

"Plumbing got backed up, all the toilets exploded!" Kami yelled. "Go use a different bathroom."

A voice said suspiciously, "Kami Glass, is this your idea of a joke?"

Angela kicked the door. "Go away or I'll kick you in the head."

"We're so stealth," Kami said. "It's what I admire most about us." She was sitting in one of the sinks, her legs dangling. Her hands were gripping the edge of the sink. "It's okay," she added. "He won't know what you're saying unless I tell him, and I wouldn't do that. Jared wouldn't eavesdrop on you guys either."

"I don't care about him," Angie said fiercely. "I care about you."

"I *have* to care about him," Kami told Angela.

"I can see that," Holly said slowly. "You would have to love him or hate him."

The one thing Kami could not feel was indifferent to him. The one thing she could not do was escape him. She saw Holly shiver.

"The idea of it's kind of romantic," Holly said. "But it wouldn't be, would it?"

Kami felt her cheeks burn. "It's not romantic. We're not romantic. Why do I have to keep saying that?"

"Because he wants it to be," Angela said. "Doesn't he? It's obvious you're all he thinks about."

"Yes," Kami snapped. "Yes, I matter to him. He wants to keep me to himself, he asked me to go out with him when we'd barely met, and he doesn't want to touch me."

Holly blinked. "What?"

"Him being real and me being real," Kami said. "It's been hard for us to get used to. Him having a body, it's been like being thirteen, when you can't get over how strange guys are, and you can't look at them when you sit next to them, and when your hands brush you almost have a heart attack."

"I remember that." Holly nodded. "Except I was eleven."

Kami and Angela both looked at her with raised eyebrows. Holly shrugged.

"It's been like when Holly was eleven, then," Kami said. "Except worse. Neither of us has known how to handle it, but I've wanted to. And he hasn't. I don't know what to do about someone who only wants me for my mind."

Holly slid down the wall to sit on the floor. "I can honestly say it has never happened to me."

"Yeah," said Angela. "Guys, always trying to kiss me. I have to beat them off with a stick. Seriously, I keep the stick behind the door at home."

Kami tried to smile, even as the skin between her brows pinched. "I hate you guys. And I hate talking about this. It's so humiliating."

"No," Holly protested, reaching out a hand to her.

"Yes, it is," Kami said fiercely. Embarrassment clutched her by the throat, but she swallowed and surged ahead. "Let's just talk about the investigation. Unless you guys have any leads on who might be the sorcerous murderer, I was thinking of investigating something Ash let drop. He talked about something happening at Monkshood."

"That old place?" Holly asked.

"Ever go poking around there when you were a kid?" Kami asked.

Holly was silent.

"Me neither," Kami said thoughtfully. "Time we did." She hopped off the sink and started toward the door, but then stopped. "That is," she said, "if you both still want to be part of the investigation. I understand if this freaks you out too much. I know it's a lot to deal with."

"It would be all right if it freaked you out," Holly said cautiously to Angela, as if hoping for permission to admit she was freaked out herself.

Angela had not grown up with a father hating the Lynburns like Holly had, or a mother keeping the Lynburns' secrets like Kami had. She had not had Aurimere waiting on the horizon all her life. Kami could understand it if Angela wanted nothing to do with this.

"It doesn't matter," Angela said.

"It doesn't matter?"

"What matters is Kami," Angela said, avoiding Kami's eyes. "I do not trust that guy. He looks at her as if she was his heart, made of glass and suspended on a thread that might break. If the thread breaks, I don't know what he'll do."

"His mother made me what I am to him," Kami told

them quietly. She did not want to discuss his heart. Whenever he looked at her, he looked away fast. He didn't look at her the way he must have looked at Holly when they first met.

She felt ashamed for that moment of resentment when she saw Holly's concerned expression.

"I don't want Kami hurt," Holly said.

"I won't have her hurt," said Angela. "Or you."

Holly bowed her head and hugged her knees to her chest, as if she had been hoping that wouldn't come up, that they would never have to discuss the fact that someone had tried to grab Holly the night Nicola died. Someone had meant it to be her, and they could not go to the police with a tale of magic and blood. They only had each other to solve this, and Kami did not know what she would do if Holly or Angela opted out.

There was a pause, and then Kami heard the click of Angela's heels on tile, walking across the bathroom floor. Eventually Angela's shining leather boots were touching Holly's worn running shoes.

"Nothing's going to happen to you," Angela promised her.

"Sure," Holly said, smiling up at Angela, even if her smile looked strained. "I still have several pairs of deadly high heels."

They all laughed. None of their laughs sounded particularly convincing.

"So, Angie," Holly went on, "you've never . . ."

There was a silence neither of them seemed inclined to fill. Then Angela said, "Ah, no."

"Bit hard to believe," Holly mumbled, and Kami saw her flush. "Since you're about the most beautiful person in town."

Angie's scarlet-painted mouth tugged up at one corner. "You forget one small detail," she said. "I kind of hate people."

A real laugh was surprised out of Kami and Holly both—a laugh that started out a little wild, but ended up making Kami think that only having each other might just work out.

"No, you don't," Holly said.

"I really do," said Angela, and Kami laughed again as Angela continued. "Have you met people? They're very annoying."

Chapter Twenty-Six
Monkshood Abbey

Monkshood was a good hour's walk from the town proper. The very narrow lanes meant that occasionally you had to throw yourself in the ditch to avoid a car, and once they had to throw themselves in the ditch to avoid a farmer coming by in a blue cart.

"The Americans have these inventions called sidewalks," Jared noted.

"We call them pavements," Kami said. "And we see them as luxuries that you just can't have with every road."

"You know what goes faster than us? Or even pretty, pretty ponies?" Jared asked.

"Your head, spinning through the air when detached from your shoulders after a grisly motorcycle crash?" Kami raised her eyebrows and Jared ducked his head, his ripple of amusement going through her anyway. It felt good. Not so good was the fact that Holly and Angela were rambling ahead, obviously uncomfortable about being near her and Jared. Kami could understand it. Just the fact that they could talk to each other silently must be off-putting, in the same way that speaking in a foreign language in front of someone you knew couldn't speak it was off-putting—but worse, because a foreign language could be learned.

"You were the one who wanted to tell them," Jared said, voice low as the sound of autumn-red leaves rustling on the trees along the road, whispering *hush, hush* to the sky.

"My team needs all the information available to conduct their investigation," said Kami. "And they're my friends, so I wanted to tell them the truth."

"Whatever you say," Jared answered mildly, but Kami could feel his belief that they didn't need anyone but each other.

She caught sight of Angela and Holly, standing still up ahead. They'd stopped walking and were staring across the fields at Monkshood Abbey.

Why aren't they moving? Kami thought, panic spreading from her to Jared. She walked past him, and heard him follow her.

"What's wrong?" Kami asked as she reached the other two. As soon as she drew level with them, she realized what was wrong.

Holly was the only plausible hiker of the bunch, in a padded coat with her sunny hair in pigtails. Angela in her fitted jacket and silk looked as if her sports car had broken down and she would never venture out into nature again. Both of them looked disgusted. Kami took another deep breath and wished she hadn't.

The house stood at the top of a gravel driveway, with a green field sloping up toward it and the dip of a moat enclosing that field. On the green rise, the building squatted like a glowering gnome. Emanating from the direction of the house was a thick, terrible scent of rot.

"What is that smell?" Holly asked at last.

"Could be anything," Kami said. "Might be something, you know, totally normal. The moat could be full of cat food tins."

"Yes," said Angela. "That would be extremely normal."

Kami had a strong feeling that something was waiting for them there. She expected to see a dark figure walk out, or a car drive toward them from around the back.

Kami shook herself out of her reverie with a shiver. "I know it's super creepy," she said. "But I'm not even going to pretend I'm not going in there. You two can wait outside if you like." She didn't even think about it until she saw Angela's sidelong look, then she realized that she'd said "you two." She couldn't think of a way to take it back. She could feel the same thrill coursing through both of them. She couldn't pretend to be anything but sure that, no matter what, Jared was coming with her.

They all went up the driveway together, and then circled around to the back of the house. They went no farther.

"So they kind of lock up abandoned houses," Kami said thoughtfully. "I did not know that. But it makes sense."

Both the front and back doors were barred with planks nailed in place over the entrance. The nails were rusted and buried in the age- and water-darkened wood. All efforts to pry them off would obviously be useless, as would hopeful jiggling of the windows, which were warped shut, with thick green moss growing along every windowsill.

"Aren't you supposed to be some sort of delinquent criminal?" Angela asked Jared.

"I do have aspirations that way," Jared answered. "Yes."

"Could you jimmy the lock or something?"

Jared looked at the back door, covered with its many planks.

"Or something," said Angela, her voice sharp. "Get the glass out of its frame, or scale the gutters and break in through the attic."

"Well," said Jared, "I suppose I could do *something.*" He stepped up to the nearest window, eyes narrowing. He set his leather-clad elbow against the glass.

Kami said, "Jared, no!" She spoke an instant too late.

The glass broke with a crunch and a tinkling sound as the shards fell inward.

"Sorry if it wasn't what you had in mind," Jared told Angela. "I'm not that subtle."

"Well, now we have to redeem this act of vandalism by using it as a terrible means to the excellent end of pursuing truth and justice," Kami said. "Someone give me a boost through this broken window." She already had the mossy sill in her grasp, and even though she said "someone," she was braced for it to be Jared. She looked straight ahead into the darkness of that house as he grasped her waist, hands light but firm. Despite her attempt to help herself through by grabbing at the window frame, he just lifted her and put her through, so she was past the jagged points of glass and standing in the dust-gray gloom.

Holly and Angela followed her, Angela slapping Jared's

hands away when he tried to help her. Jared got in last. A shard of glass clinging to the top of the frame caught at his sleeve when he pulled himself through, and secondhand pain shot through Kami as they all looked at the bright blood beading on his wrist in the strange light.

"I'm fine," said Jared, pulling down his sleeve.

They were standing in a very large room. The floorboards stretched in a pale expanse at their feet. There was so much dust on the floor that it had a pearly sheen.

"Even *you* could not nap on this floor," Kami told Angela.

"I don't know, a dust mattress might be very comfortable," said Angela. "Also possibly orthopedic."

They were all walking softly and close together, as if afraid to disturb the dust. There was no apparent danger: just dust, silence, and gray light. The bad smell had no source, it just drifted around them in a hideous miasma. Nothing changed even when they reached the threshold of a huge desert of a room and saw a hall with shadows along the walls and the stair banister. Kami could see nothing but darkness waiting at the top of the steps. One step was broken clear in two.

"I can get up there," said Jared. Kami caught at his arm, and when he turned to her she saw the gleam in his eye, reflecting the spark she felt kindling in him.

"No," Kami told him. "Those stairs don't look safe."

Jared grinned at her, teeth a pale flash in the murk. "Ah, but I can do magic now."

"You don't know what that means yet," said Kami, but she didn't grab him. She regretted that when he made a break for the stairs.

Kami had her foot on the first step when Angela lunged forward and caught her by both shoulders, staring down at Kami with her dark eyes narrowed.

"No," Angela said firmly. "You do not risk your life for that idiot."

"It's holding up all right," protested Jared, laughing and breathless, halfway up the stairs. He leaped lightly over the broken step.

The staircase collapsed.

There was a crash, dust rising in an explosive rush. Kami was blind for an instant. Her eyes burned with dust, and her throat burned with a scream.

Then her vision cleared. The dust was no longer moving but held suspended, glittering in the air like a curtain made of tiny beads. The stairs kept falling, but in slow motion. The disappearance of the stairs was less a crash and tumble than an escalator that went nowhere, each step waiting to take its turn to fall.

Jared twisted in midair and grabbed one of the slowly toppling stair rails. It held. He reached for the next rail, and the next, moving like an acrobat on a jungle gym. When one stair rail tumbled away from his reaching fingers, Kami reached out a hand as if she could catch it and hold it for him.

Jared's magic must have kicked in at the same time, because the rail swayed back toward him. Jared's fingers closed around it. He swung himself onto one of the remaining steps, then launched himself down the stairs as the steps fell away almost under his feet.

The last step collapsed just as Jared landed on the floor.

Kami flew at him, and he rocked back before she could grab him, evading her hands again.

"You're frightened," Jared said, his voice a little unsteady. "Don't be. Wh-why are you frightened?"

She felt his uncertain reach for her, inside their minds. Kami threw rage and love and relief at him.

Of course I'm frightened, you idiot! You almost fell to your death! Don't ever do anything like that again! I know you like taking risks—I do too, but there is a line. You are the most important person in the world to me. Don't you dare cross it again.

Dust and splinters were in Jared's hair. He had a graze and a smudge of blood on his forehead, and fresh blood welling along his arm. "I'm sorry," he said softly. "I will try."

Hearing words spoken was a shock. It made Kami abruptly aware of their surroundings and especially their friends. Angela and Holly were staring at them, looking very interested but very uneasy about the fact that a silent conversation was going on before their eyes. Under their gaze, Kami felt terribly exposed. She stepped away, avoiding Jared's eyes.

"So," Holly said, trying to smooth things over as usual, "I see this house has a cellar. Since the stairs just fell into it."

Kami beamed at Holly. She was right: there was a whole other level to explore. She moved, Jared a step behind her. He said in a low voice, "So, you like taking risks too?"

"I don't recall saying that," Kami said. "And you have no witnesses to prove I did." She went for the door on the other side of the hall and found another vast bare room. In the far corner of the room, another, smaller door was tucked like a secret.

Kami crossed the floor.

The others followed her, though Angela said, "The stairs collapsed. Which means this house is a death trap. Why do we want to explore all the fatal possibilities of the death trap?"

The little door had a handle shaped like a sword hilt. The cool metal met Kami's hand in an easy grip, and the door swung open without sticking. Concrete steps led down into the lowest floor of Monkshood House.

"What could be unstable about concrete?" Kami asked, and took a step into the dark. She hesitated and Jared's concern touched her mind, but the step held firm. She took another step down, and then another.

"Why is your first impulse to find out what could be unstable about concrete?" Angela demanded. The absence of the usual bite in her tone made it clear she was relieved.

Kami did not answer. She was busy taking each step with care, her hand pressed flat against a gray wall. She heard the others following her. She only breathed out, in a soft *whoosh,* when she reached the bottom of the stairs.

It wasn't a cellar. It was a whole other floor. In the dim light coming from the open door at the top of the stairs, Kami could see three doors in this room. One was open, and Kami went through it.

It was too dark to see much. It was empty, like every other room in the house, but Kami saw the silvery swoop of a curtain glinting in a corner. As she drew closer, Jared behind her, she saw it was an enormous tangle of spiderwebs, hanging in a pale descent from the shadowy ceiling. Kami's foot banged against a metal edge. She stumbled and checked herself, then knelt.

"Kami, are you all right?" Angela asked from the door.

"She's fine," said Jared, just as Kami said, "I'm fine. I just found something."

"You don't need to answer for her," Angela snapped. "She can talk."

"I'm aware," said Jared. "I just knew she was fine. So I told you. I always know how she is."

The metal square on the floor bore ridges that suggested strange shapes. Kami traced them with her fingers, finding the square sectioned off into four parts. She was about to raise her head to ask for light, when faint greenish light touched the metal. Jared was standing above her with his phone lit up, pointing the screen helpfully downward.

The metal square was covered in a black patina, like old grease. Beneath the grime was a house on a hill, a host of trees, a woman's profile like a profile on an old coin, and a square that looked empty. But when Kami scratched at the blackness with her fingernail, a gleaming blue was revealed.

There were words written in Latin beneath the pictures. Kami recognized the Lynburn crest. She recognized the Lynburn motto, could hear Ash's voice translating it: *We neither drown nor burn.*

Kami looked at the black grains under her fingernail. Held under the phone's light, they glinted brown and red. *We neither drown nor burn,* the Lynburns said, but everybody died.

She knew what dried blood looked like.

Chapter Twenty-Seven
In the Shadow of the Manor

Kami knew of two ways to find out why the Lynburn crest was engraved on a metal plate in a different house. One was from the Lynburns themselves, so Kami sent Jared back to Aurimere. She figured they were more likely to talk to one of their own than to Kami, turning up with a notebook and saying, "I hear you're a sorcerer. What's that like?"

The other way was to go to the people of Sorry-in-the-Vale. Kami's mother had done a spell with Rosalind Lynburn. Holly's father spoke the name of the Lynburns as if he was calling on some dread power. Dorothy Cunningham at the library had said she did not trust the Lynburns, and Nicola Prendergast had asked the Lynburns for help on the night she died.

When Holly went home and Angela and Kami split up to cover more ground, Kami realized she had not walked through her town since Nicola died. She went around the woods-bristling curve of Shepherd's Corner, nodding to a family she babysat for who were out taking a walk. She walked down the mellow golden line of the High Street, looking up at the roof of the Bell and Mist, where a weather vane in the shape of a woman's head spun gently in the wind.

Amber Green, who worked as a waitress there, was clearing the tables outside and gave Kami a friendly nod.

Kami felt as if someone was following her, their shadow on her back, and she did not dare turn and face them. It took her a few minutes to realize that Sorry-in-the-Vale was the shadow falling on her, as the manor cast a shadow over the town.

Kami had never loved or hated her town, any more than she loved or hated her shoes. Sometimes Sorry-in-the-Vale was comfortable, somewhere that fit her well; sometimes it was uncomfortable, making her feel too weird or too foreign or too ambitious. It was always familiar. She'd always thought she could trust it to be that.

The town looked different now, with blood in its past and Kami imagining secrets behind every smile. She passed by Mr. Stearn walking his elderly bull terrier, both of them walking in the same slightly jerky way, stiff legs moving in sync. He smiled at her, and she found she couldn't smile back. What was he thinking? And what might he be hiding?

Kami went into the next building on the High Street that she passed, hearing the musical jangle as she pushed open the door of Mrs. Thompson's sweetshop. It was a cheerful little cave of bright colors, shelves filled with jars of sweets: tiny apple drops in scarlet and green, tan and cream squares of toffee and fudge, black wheels of licorice, the rainbow spread of allsorts, and the speckled rounds of aniseed balls.

In the back of the candy-brilliant cave was Mrs. Thompson, small, round, and wrapped in her usual fluffy gray cardigan, looking like a very big sweet that had been dropped on a dusty floor. "Kami," she said, in the way the adults of

Sorry-in-the-Vale spoke to Kami, a little fond and a little wary, "what can I do for you?"

Kami wondered now if that wariness was all because Kami had spent her childhood holding conversations with thin air and because her grandmother was "that foreign woman." She wondered if people thought of her family as the Lynburns' servants, and if anybody knew of the bargain her mother had made with Rosalind Lynburn. Mrs. Thompson's round, wrinkled face remained the same face Kami had known for years. She just couldn't read it.

"Hi!" said Kami, with manic cheer. "I'm doing an article for the school paper on the history of Sorry-in-the-Vale, and I know you know everything there is to know about the town, so I was wondering if you had a minute?" She gestured with her notebook, as if it was the key to the kingdom of information. Then she surged on before Mrs. Thompson could speak. "I found a few old historical records that suggested the people in Aurimere House might be able to do magic. Isn't that crazy?"

"What records?" Mrs. Thompson asked, her voice sharp. "Where did you find them?"

"Oh," Kami said. "Here and there. Uh, on the Internet."

There was a pause.

"I really don't think you did," Mrs. Thompson told her. "People don't talk much about that sort of thing around here. And they would never write it down."

Kami bumped her elbow into a jar full of peppermints. The pain shot up along her arm at the same time panic shot through her chest. "Well, maybe I heard some people talking," she ad-libbed. "I think they also mentioned Monkshood

Abbey and the Lynburns. What happened to the people who used to live in Monkshood?"

"If you approach the wrong people and ask questions like that," Mrs. Thompson said, "you might find out."

The bright colors of the sweetshop were starting to look nightmarish to Kami, garish and unreal. She tried to keep her voice measured as she asked: "Are you the wrong people? Because I've known you all my life."

"And I've lived a lot longer than you have," Mrs. Thompson told her. "I remember the days of red and gold."

The days when the Lynburns used to kill people, and the rest of the town let it happen. The days that might be back again, if it was a Lynburn who had killed Nicola.

Kami thought of Jared, sick in the city with the year's passing, of the golden knives he had seen and the rhyme about the Lynburns, and the deaths recorded in old newspapers. Her stomach turned over.

"Yeah, I'm just going to go," Kami decided. She grasped the doorknob and pulled.

The door did not open. Instead the doorknob slid out of her grasp so quickly that she thought her hand had slipped, then she wasn't quite sure. She stood staring at Mrs. Thompson as the shop bell sang its jaunty tune over their heads. The walls of the sweetshop swam in a rainbow blur before Kami's eyes.

"Seriously," said Kami, her voice faint. "I think I left the oven on at home. Or the iron. Possibly both."

"Be careful, Kami," Mrs. Thompson murmured.

Kami grabbed the knob again. The metal slid against her sweaty palm, making it clear to her that the wrench of the door out of her hand last time had been different, been deliberate as someone slamming it closed. This time, though, she got the door open and propelled herself through it, hurting her shoulder with how hard she hung on to the knob until she was over the threshold and into the street.

Kami stood in the street, rubbing her shoulder where she felt she had almost torn her arm out of its socket. She'd thought she knew every shadow and corner of this town, but now the shadows were moving, and behind every corner waited another secret. She reached out for the only sure thing in the world.

Jared, she said, *I'm coming to see you.*

The garden at Aurimere was being tamed slowly. No sooner had Uncle Rob got the wild gorse bushes under control than the climbing roses had burst thorns in every direction. The grass was too long again, twining in the breeze like a woman's long hair in water. Jared had to wade through it to reach Uncle Rob, who was trying to trim the rosebushes.

Jared reached out for Kami so she could hear too, and said, "I broke into Monkshood Abbey today. Guess what I found there?"

Don't ever become a spy, Lynburn, Kami told him. He could feel her, almost at Aurimere now.

Uncle Rob's shears did not stop cutting. The sound of branches snapping and the clack of metal meeting echoed through the garden like the noise of a guillotine.

"A lesson, I imagine," he said without looking up at Jared. His uncle's broad shoulders were suddenly held more stiffly.

Jared stared at the back of Uncle Rob's head, noticing that his hair was a shade between Ash's and his own. "What sort of lesson?"

"In what happens to you if you cross the Lynburns of Aurimere House," said Uncle Rob.

Jared waited a moment, but Uncle Rob did not offer anything else. The only sound was blackthorn branches falling onto the long grass. "The Lynburn crest was in that house. Why?"

There was a long pause. Jared thought that he wouldn't get any answer except for the sound of slicing roses.

Not turning around, his voice level and dispassionate, Uncle Rob said, "Because Lynburns used to live there. My parents, and me when I was very young."

Jared was shocked silent. He'd always thought of all the Lynburns as belonging to Aurimere, but of course Uncle Rob had different parents from Mom and Aunt Lillian. "Why was it abandoned? What happened?"

Uncle Rob tossed the shears down, steel blades gaping open and hungry. Jared took a step back at the look on his face.

"My parents displeased the Lynburns of Aurimere. Our leaders, to be feared and obeyed, our judges and executioners. The Lynburns of the House came to Monkshood and killed them and took me as sorcerer breeding stock for one or the other of their daughters. I think perhaps you can understand why I never went back. And why I never wanted to come back to this town."

Jared stared into Uncle Rob's blue eyes. He didn't know what to feel: he was sorry for Uncle Rob, who had never been anything but kind to him, but he could not suppress the selfish despairing horror at yet another terrible chapter of this book of his ancestors. "They killed your parents," he said slowly. "And you married Aunt Lillian?"

Uncle Rob told him, "I learned my lesson."

Kami screamed for Jared in his head. He realized she was alone in Aurimere with his mother.

Kami knocked on the door of Aurimere and hoped, since Jared was getting somewhere with Uncle Rob, that Ash would answer. He was the best of three bad options. She was rehearsing a speech along the lines of "Let's skip the romantic awkwardness and move to you telling me everything there is to know about your sorcerous lifestyle" when the door opened.

It was Rosalind Lynburn. Her skin was paper white, her pale hair flowing, and her lips parted, like a ghost who had seen a ghost. She said, "Kami Glass."

Kami nodded. "Me again."

Rosalind stood there wavering and watching her. Kami knew Jared's feelings for his mother, the pity and protectiveness and the shame and hate too, but she couldn't reach them. She felt sorry for Rosalind Lynburn, and felt resentment for her treatment of Jared, but Kami found she could not even feel that very strongly. Feelings slipped away from Rosalind like light passing through glass. She almost seemed transparent, because she never quite seemed real. Kami wondered if that was why Rob had married Lillian in the end.

Rosalind slid the door of Aurimere House wide open and stood aside so Kami could walk in. The stone flags of the floor radiated cold through the soles of her shoes. Rosalind's hair blew in the wind rushing through the door. The ends touched Kami's face as she went past, featherlight at the edge of her eye.

Rosalind shut the door, and all the air and light outside was shut away. Kami stood in the center of the great gray hall, surrounded by arches as if each wall was a church door. Rosalind was standing in front of the door. She looked even paler against the slab of age-dark wood, almost glowing, like an angel.

Like an angel forbidding someone to pass.

"I told you not to come back," Rosalind said as Kami reached for Jared. He showed her Rob telling him what happened when you crossed the Lynburns.

Rosalind's hair blew away from her face, even though there was no wind. "Do I need to show you why you should obey me?" she whispered.

The narrow windows in the hall gleamed fierce scarlet and bright white, like blood and pearls. The lights danced in Kami's vision, dazzling and distracting. She took two steps through the sea of swimming diamonds and looked up at Rosalind. "Like you showed my mother?"

Rosalind's face remained tranquil. "I can do much worse to you," she said. "I only needed to scare her."

"And what can you do to me?" Kami asked.

"Anything I have to," Rosalind answered. "So that you stay away from my son."

The barrage of crystalline and ruby lights pounded through Kami's brain, panic pulsing through her. "I won't do it."

"I might kill you," Rosalind breathed.

"You'll have to," said Kami. She yelled mentally for Jared.

The hall was suddenly filled with cold air and glass shards as both of the windows exploded inward. The glass shards were like knives, blades the flashing red of traffic lights and blades Kami could hardly see except for where their jagged edges glittered.

They came flying at her from all directions. The air was filled with them: there was no way to duck. There were shards skimming along the flagstones and shards aimed right at Kami's eyes.

Kami put up a hand to shield herself, fury racing with the fear shivering through her blood. She spun around to face Rosalind.

"Promise me," said Rosalind, a tranquil smile on her face. "And I'll make it all stop."

The doors aren't opening! Jared shouted.

Jared's terror cut through Kami, wild as her own, and past all their shared fear Kami found a cold place in the center of her chest. Her town had been twisted into a place she hardly recognized, and now Rosalind Lynburn thought she had a right to give her orders.

"No," she said out loud.

Like a flock of birds all changing their flight pattern, the shards realigned and began to close in on Rosalind Lynburn. Rosalind's eyes met Kami's, but before Kami could decipher the expression in them, Rosalind looked over Kami's shoulder. Her face filled with terror.

The door by one of the empty windows stood open. Jared stood framed in it. Rob Lynburn was holding him back.

Rosalind retreated from Rob, leaving the door and going to the stairs. She walked through the glass shards, flying at nobody now but still suspended in the air. They caught and tumbled through her long hair like pebbles in a wave.

Rosalind sat on the bottom step of the wide dark flight of stairs and put her face in her hands. "I never wanted you to know," she said, sounding almost forlorn.

"Know what?" Lillian Lynburn demanded from the top of the stairs.

Ash was beside his mother. He looked at his aunt, at Kami, at the hall with its empty windows that the wind was whistling through, and at his father. Ash's eyes went wider and wider: he looked scared.

Kami was surrounded by broken glass and Lynburns, terrified and exhilarated and never alone, the fierce beat of Jared's focus on her like a second heart that echoed the first.

Rob's grasp must have slackened. Jared was able to wrench away and run into the hall. The glass in the air between him and Kami fell to the stone and shattered, glittering points of star white and sunset red scattered over the gray floor.

Are you all right? Jared asked.

For a moment, she thought he might grab her, as she'd tried to grab him at Monkshood, but he simply hovered close. She looked up into his tense face and his pale blazing eyes. *I'm all right.*

"I don't understand," Lillian said furiously.

"Look what they're doing," Rob told his wife. His voice was rough. "Look! Can't you see what's going on?" He looked at Kami as if he hated her.

Jared aligned himself with Kami, pushing his shoulder in front of hers, and glared back at his uncle.

Kami was the focus of all Lynburn attention: Rob's burning look, Lillian's icily baffled stare, Ash's scared eyes, and Rosalind's distress. Jared on her side but not knowing, any more than she did, what was happening.

When Rob Lynburn spoke, his voice was grim and accompanied by the sound of Rosalind sobbing. "This girl is a source," he said.

Chapter Twenty-Eight
A Heart in Your Hand

The Lynburns escorted Kami into the parlor, as if because she was a source—whatever that might be—they were willing to use company manners. Lillian placed herself on one of the canopied sofas at the back of the room, like a queen receiving her subjects. She sat in the center of the sofa, so Rob was stuck sitting to one side, like a royal afterthought. Rosalind was on the other sofa, still weeping. Ash was standing at the door as if he was uncertain of his welcome, or uncertain that he wanted to be there, or both.

Kami sat on the window seat, a dull gold curtain obscuring part of her view of the room. Jared was on the floor at her feet, close but not touching her as usual. He had one leg drawn up to his chest and was acting so much like a guard dog Kami thought he might snarl if any of his family drew near.

"So, you're all sorcerers," said Kami. "And I'm a source. What does that mean?"

"We use natural things as sources for our power," Lillian told her. "The woods. Animals. Whoever killed that girl was using her death to fuel his power."

"But I'm not dead," said Kami.

"Indeed," Lillian returned. "Sorcerers get one burst of power from death, but a continuous flow of power from life. We get power from this town, from the woods, and especially from the lakes. We can use someone's hair or someone's blood to focus a spell. And in special cases, with a particular kind of person, a sorcerer can form a link that will magnify their power tenfold. But people born capable of being sources are very rare, and we do not use them."

"Because the power is not worth the cost," Rob broke in. "A sorcerer is bound to their source and can never break away. It is a disgustingly imbalanced form of magic. If the source dies, the sorcerer dies. If the sorcerer dies, it makes no difference to the source."

The weight of their combined accusing stares pressed down on her. "It would make a difference to *me*," said Kami.

"Be that as it may," said Lillian, "two things are known among our kind. One is that a sorcerer with a source has great power. Power to wake the woods," she continued, eyeing Jared. "Power to change the world."

"And the other is that in the end, the source controls the power," said Rob. "The sorcerer's power might be magnified, but now it all pours out through the source. The source could decide to cut the sorcerer off from their own magic at any time and leave them with nothing. The magic does not even really belong to the sorcerer anymore. What use is it to have world-changing power, just to put it in someone else's hands?"

Kami thought of being hidden at the pool, seeing things in the woods, turning the glass against Rosalind. Had *she* caused all of that herself? Had she taken power Jared was born with and used it, used him, without ever intending to? She touched Jared's mind. He didn't feel angry with her, only surprised, his mind turned to hers naturally, like brushing the back of someone's hand and having him link your fingers together.

Lillian looked at Kami speculatively. "Some might say it was worth it, having a partner in order to be able to change the world. They write stories about sources and sorcerers. They become legend. They say King Arthur was a source."

"So I'm Merlin?" Jared asked, sounding incredulous.

"The story is unclear," Lillian conceded. "There is also mention of a woman on Arthur's side who could do magic. The Lady of the Lake."

"Uh," said Jared, "I'd rather be Merlin."

Lillian smiled a small scarlet smile. "A sorcerer has to go through fire and water to reach their full power. Especially water. I think the Lady was the real sorcerer."

"You see how it works," said Rob. "We all know the name of the source. We can never be sure who the sorcerer was. The sorcerer does not matter. There has not been a sorcerer and a source in Sorry-in-the-Vale since 1480 for a reason. I don't want that kind of life for my nephew."

"I'm okay," Jared said. Kami felt him reaching for her and knew he said it more for her benefit than Rob's.

From the look on Rob's face, he knew that too. "Are you? Or are you just saying what she wants to hear? Sources influence your emotions as well as control your magic. You haven't known about sorcery long, I know, but you have to understand how serious this is. She could cut you off from your own magic any time she liked. You have to understand that she has absolute power over you."

Kami sat stricken.

"*You* have to understand," said Jared, "that that's what I want."

Rosalind's ragged breathing caught on another sob. "I didn't mean for this to happen," she told Rob. "I would never do anything to upset you."

That piteous appeal made Kami look not at Rosalind or at Rob, but at Lillian, to see how she took this evidence that her twin sister was still in love with her husband. Lillian had not turned a hair. She was looking at Jared, her blue eyes narrowed with interest. "My sister did this to you?" she inquired. "I understood that taking a source was voluntary."

"She did this to us," said Jared. "She put a spell on Kami's mother to see through her eyes before either of us was born."

"I didn't know what would happen," Rosalind said sharply, lifting her tear-wet face from her hands. "That woman, Claire, she wasn't a Glass. There was no way she could have been a source. I didn't know she was having a baby, or that you could find a source that way, across distances, without saying the words. I just wanted to make a bridge from me to Sorry-in-the-Vale."

"And instead you made a bridge for a source to your son," Rob said. He was the only one in the room who looked concerned for Jared.

So *this* was why the Glass family had a house built where

the Lynburns could keep their eye on it, why the family was meant to stay where the Lynburns could keep their eye on them.

"I didn't know what I was doing," said Rosalind, swallowing another sob. "I didn't know anything. Not until he was born, and he was such a terrible baby. The city was like a cage. There was nowhere to go, but then there was another Lynburn with me. But he wasn't ever like us. He was always talking to someone else. He used to turn his face away from me. It was as impossible to love him as it was to love David."

"Rosalind," Lillian snapped. "He was a child. You linked his mind with another child's. And you are Lynburns. You had somewhere to go. As soon as you realized what you had done, you should have come to me."

"I didn't do it," Rosalind said, and looked beseechingly at Rob. Her fingers were white on the arms of the sofa. "Not really. It was Jared. He chose to make the connection. It was Jared and that girl."

Lillian's voice crackled, impatience breaking up the smooth flow of her commands. "I wish you would take some responsibility for once!"

"And what about you?" Rosalind demanded. "What about what you've done? What about what you did to me?" She rose from the sofa, one hand wrapped around the walnut wood bolster that held up the canopy.

Lillian tilted her chin and regarded her coolly without getting up. "I do not regret anything I have ever done. That is a policy of mine."

"You have no heart," Rosalind said, low. "You never did."

"The mistress of Lynburn does not need a heart," Lillian told her.

Rosalind cast a look at Rob, as if expecting something. When Rob stayed silent, she ran from the room. Ash side-stepped fast, bowing his head, to get out of her way. She had not looked once at Jared.

Lillian had scarcely looked away. Kami did not much like the way she looked at him, the appraisal of the woman who thought she owned every blade of grass in the Vale.

"None of this is Kami's fault," said Ash. His head stayed bowed.

"Of course not," Lillian said absently. She leaned forward, eyes narrowed and her focus solely on Jared. "We could test the limits of your ability."

Rob shifted away from his wife and rose to his feet. For a moment, Kami thought he would run out the door after Rosalind. "We know the limits of his ability!" he said. "Rosalind chained his powers to someone else before he was born. I would never have believed she would do such a thing. I will not allow it to continue."

The room blurred before Kami's eyes, the Lynburns pale gold spots in her vision as if they were made of light. "It doesn't have to continue?" she asked. "There's a way to stop it?"

"A way to sever the connection? Yes," said Rob Lynburn. "I beg you to do it."

"How—" Kami began.

At the same time, and far more loudly, Jared said, "No."

Kami let her fingers brush Jared's shoulder: it was tensed, hard and unyielding as stone, but stone would not have flinched away from her. "I think we should hear what he has to say."

"*No!*" Jared repeated. He wrenched himself up to wheel on Kami.

For a moment, he was just another one of the Lynburns. All of them were staring at her now, the creatures of red and gold, with demands in their eyes, and the only thing she wanted was to escape.

But I can't escape you, can I? she asked him. *And that's why I think we should listen to your uncle and weigh our options.*

I don't want options, said Jared.

Now Kami was angry. Jared said things like this all the time, as if—and then he didn't do anything about it. He didn't seem to want to touch her, ever. So why did he talk like that? She could read his mind, so he should make more sense! "Jared and I need to talk this over alone."

"Why?" Ash asked, his voice unexpected in that hushed room, his eyes fastened on Kami. "Why do you need to be alone?" he asked. "You can read each other's minds."

"Thank you for pointing that out; I wasn't aware," Kami told him. "And yes, it would be fantastic to have a silent conversation with all of you looking on." She stood up. It didn't give her much of a height advantage, but she glared up at Jared and over at Ash anyway. "None of this was Jared's fault. None of this was my fault either. You may think I don't matter because I'm not a sorcerer, but I don't care for being threatened or being ignored. And you know what? I'm going to go."

I'll go with you, Jared said.

Do what you want, said Kami. She passed Rob and Lillian

without looking at them. She was radiating so much fury that it acted as a force field, because Ash took a step back and blinked in surprise.

Jared did not back off, of course. As Kami stormed out of the sorcerers' parlor, he was right behind her.

Once out of the parlor and down the couple of steps, Kami hesitated. She didn't want to walk back through the hall of cutting wind and glass. The room she was in now had a window, floor-to-ceiling pale yellow panes. The garden spread out beyond the glass, transformed into smooth bright lines.

Kami went for the side door, tucked narrow and dark against that wide light expanse of window. When she clutched the doorknob, another fist-shaped one, the black iron knuckles pressed too hard into her palm. The door opened and the sunshine hit Kami, flooding warm over her hair and skin. She felt pure relief as she emerged from the cold manor.

Kami went and leaned against the wall attached to the rockery. She was staring at the ground and saw Jared's shadow falling across hers before she saw him.

Doesn't any of this freak you out? Kami asked.

No, said Jared. *You are the source of everything for me. Why should magic be any different?*

Sometimes I feel like I don't know the shape of myself without you, Kami thought. She felt almost desperate. *Sometimes I feel like you don't know the shape of yourself.*

"I know what I'd be."

She looked up when Jared spoke. His jaw was tight, his eyes lowered: his hair falling on his brow, his lowered lashes a fringe of shadow on his cheekbones. The sunlight struck his hair and made it burn gold, but his face was all shadow.

"You wouldn't be like your father," Kami said. "You wouldn't be like them." She opened her mind to Jared. She tried to make it like opening a book so he could see her faith as clear as carmine and gold glowing on a page.

Who in the world would believe that but you? Jared asked. *And how would I know you believed it, without this?*

"You could trust me," said Kami.

I do trust you, Jared told her. *But I don't understand why you want this gone.* Kami felt the struggle in him and saw him swallow. He spoke painfully aloud again. "Is it something I did? I can—"

"No, Jared," Kami said. *No.*

Confused pain radiated from him. Kami wasn't sure if he was angry at her or at himself; she supposed it hardly mattered. That was the problem. Kami looked about the autumn garden, ruby and gold leaves making the trees look as if they were hung with treasure. She looked back at Jared. She saw the way he fit into this scene, as he had fit into the woods the first time he had stood by the Crying Pools, joking with her about the Sorrier River.

The Sorrier River, of course, was the sorcerer's river. Sorry-in-the-Vale was sorcery in the vale. This place had been made and meant for him, so perfect that living in a city was like poison to him, while this place sent power coursing through his veins. She had access to that power now. According to Rob, she had control over it. She could reach out and touch it, the same way she could touch his mind. Except that she didn't want to.

"I meant what I told you," she said slowly. "By the Crying Pools. If I could go back, if I could change everything, I wouldn't. I would never want to lose you."

Relief washed through him, though confusion lingered. "So—"

"We can't lose each other now," said Kami. "I know you're real, and you know I am, so we won't lose each other. I think it would be worth listening to what your uncle has to say. I'm not saying I want to do it. I'm saying it might be worth considering."

Jared's voice was blistering. "Being cut in two?"

"Being individuals for a change!" Kami said, her voice low. "Being alone, for once in our lives." She pushed off the garden wall and stepped away from Jared, watching her shadow slide away from his, while building walls in her mind, forbidding him to pass.

Jared looked up at her as she moved away, his eyes pale and disturbing as they always were in the grip of intense emotion. She knew that now, had learned him by heart well enough to recognize the color, like seeing a gray sky turn storm white through a pane of glass.

She looked at his face, the shadows and angles of him, and had such a vivid thought that she could almost imagine she was acting on it: walking to him across the waving grass, feeling his body, so separate and so different from her own against hers, muscles and sinews shifting against hers. She imagined her fingers on the warm nape of his neck, drawing his head down.

Only she could not do it with all her feelings laid out before him: this would not just be her telling a guy how she felt with no assurance of a return. There would be no way for her to escape afterward. Human beings were not meant to be bound together like this. She did not know how to bear it.

"Do you remember what you said to me the third time we met?" Kami asked. "That we should date?"

Jared did not answer, but his eyes went shocked silver.

"If we cut the connection," she said, "I would." Even with her walls up, she could feel his anger. Of course, she thought, of course she would say something like that and he would be angry. She wondered what he could sense, what might be slipping past her wall.

"I wish you hadn't said that," said Jared. "It's like blackmail."

"It's like you have no other use for me but this connection," Kami said. "Without it, what would I be to you? Just some ordinary girl. Nothing special about me at all." She remembered the first time he had seen her. He hadn't been impressed by her. She looked away and saw birds bursting from the trees, taking wing from the sorcerer's wrath or just fleeing because winter was so close.

"That's ridiculous," Jared said curtly. "And this whole conversation is ridiculous. There's a murderer on the loose. If we weren't linked, you would have died in that well. We can't afford to break the connection now."

Kami could see the fact that there was a sorcerer killing people was a great relief to Jared. She thought of Nicola Prendergast and felt nothing but fury.

"So we have to keep it for now," she said coldly. "We can break it later. I want to find out how." She turned her back on him and strode back across the garden before he could answer, through the iron door with the drowning woman on it, and back through the stone corridors to the flight of steps that led to the parlor.

Lillian Lynburn's voice echoed clearly against the stone. "Now Jared's powers are explained, and we have no idea of who is killing people in my town."

Kami stood still, Jared beside her. Despite how desolate and angry she felt, she reached out in her mind and he reached back. They stood at the bottom of the steps under a light shaped like a caged star, soothing each other with their thoughts as they had done for years and years, since they were swapping lullabies in cradles across an ocean.

Jared's family had believed he was Nicola's murderer all this time.

Chapter Twenty-Nine
Yours to Break

Kami woke the next morning while Jared was still asleep, his dreams chasing each other in the back of her mind. Sunlight, strained by autumn leaves, left a lacy pattern of shadows on her pillow. Kami uncurled from the warmth of her sheets, her toes making the unpleasant journey from bedclothes to fuzzy slippers, and found her giant pink robe, which she only wore at the times she was most in need, because it made her look like a bright pink woolly mammoth. She went downstairs wrapped in comfort.

Even if there was a shadow town lurking beneath the bright surface of Sorry-in-the-Vale, home was safe, she thought. Then she opened the door of the kitchen and saw Rob Lynburn sitting at the table with her mother.

Kami raced across the floor, grabbed his arm, and tried to haul him to his feet. "No!" she snapped. "Whatever you threatened her with, whatever you want, she's not going to do it. This family doesn't serve the Lynburns anymore."

Kami saw her mother's hands tighten on her coffee cup, but Rob's gaze was calm and steady. She suddenly felt ridiculous for descending on him like an avenging angel with pink flannel wings. Or a very short, fuzzy version of Batman.

"I wish it didn't," Rob said. "I have never hurt or threatened your mother. We've always been good friends. Haven't we, Claire?"

"If you say so," said Mum, as easy to read as the Mona Lisa. She reached out a hand to Kami.

Kami took the hint and let go of Rob's arm, let her hand be clasped in the strong comfort of her mother's fingers.

"Well," said Rob, sounding regretful, "as good friends as we can be, under the circumstances."

Mum lifted her head and smiled a smile as bright as winter sunlight, and about as warm. "That depends on what you want with my daughter."

Kami had seen her stiff posture when Kami had come in. Mum was afraid of this Lynburn, as she was of every Lynburn, but she was trying to protect Kami anyway. She sent her mother an encouraging smile. "It's okay."

"I mean her no harm," said Rob Lynburn. "I just want to undo what Rosalind did to you both. Let me have a word with Kami in private."

Kami had to protest again that it was okay and pull her hand out of her mother's grasp before Mum let them go out into the front garden, but she did let them go. Kami figured Mum couldn't turn down a chance to have the connection severed. Kami could see the pale curtains in the kitchen moving as she stood against the garden gate.

Kami looked at Rob Lynburn, who was gazing down at her in a kindly way. In some ways, he seemed the most normal of the Lynburns, but she remembered his upturned face, wakened to magic hunger by Jared's thunderstorm. She'd do best to keep in mind that none of the Lynburns was all that normal.

She focused on the words cut into the stone by her gate, ivy hanging over the blurred message. THE G——HOUSE, it said. Kami had grown up assuming that the "G" stood for "Glass." Her mother had known all along that it stood for "Guard" and that the word meant heavy responsibilities and dark consequences.

"Well," Kami said, "what have you got to say that you didn't say yesterday?"

"Only this: that yesterday I was very impressed by how sensible you were being," Rob told her. "Many young people would be drawn to the thought of such power in their hands. But you see that the magic does not belong to you. I wish Jared could see as clearly, but he's blinded by the connection. I was so glad you had realized that the emotions that come with the connection are not real."

Kami pulled ivy leaves savagely off the stone. "Not real?" she asked, trying to keep her voice neutral.

"Not entirely real," Rob qualified. "How could they be? A connection like this would make anyone feel close to anyone. Yours is the worst case I can think of. All the links I've heard about contained some element of choice. You were children."

Kami looked at the movement in her kitchen window and thought about what their mothers had done.

"My boy is lonely and impressionable, and now that you two are together, magic is flooding to him through you. I'm not surprised he got so worked up when we suggested the severance. But you're wiser than that. You're sensible to know the connection you feel is based on nothing but magic misused, and any power you gain would be tainted and not yours by right."

Jared was lonely. She'd known that all her life, that she was the only important thing to him. "I have no interest in power of any sort," Kami snapped.

"Of course," said Rob Lynburn soothingly.

He ticked Kami off. She didn't want to hear him telling her how mature she was, praising her because he thought it would make her behave the way he wanted. Only he'd called Jared "my boy" twice now, and he seemed to mean it. He was infuriating, but he might want the best for Jared. So did she.

"I believe you care about Jared," Kami said.

"I do," said Rob. "Show me that *you* do."

"I told Jared it was something I might want to consider," she continued slowly, trying to be reasonable for Jared's sake. "He didn't want to hear it."

Rob looked at her, and a breath of cold air snaked in even over the collar of her thick robe. He looked like a scary sorcerer for that one moment in time, able to command wind and shadows.

"But it's not up to him," he said. "It's up to you."

❧

"It's part of why sorcerers don't like having sources," Kami explained to Angela and Holly that afternoon. "Apparently sources can say, 'Sorry, buddy, you're cut off' anytime, but once linked, the sorcerer can never get away."

"I say you do it," said Angela, her voice echoing in the hall. Kami and Holly both looked around to see if anyone had overheard, but people were just making their way to class, oblivious.

"Oh no, she couldn't do that!" Holly said, shocked. "It would be such a betrayal."

That was what Kami had said to Rob. He had not agreed: he had seemed sure that this would save Jared from worse betrayal later on, when Kami got used to having power over the world and power over Jared. He'd been angry when she refused.

"Holly's right," Kami said. "Besides, Jared was right too. It isn't safe to break the connection right now, not when it might save one of us. It already saved me once."

"There's this wonderful new invention," Angela said. "It's a device that you can carry in your purse, or even in your pocket, and using it you can communicate with people from a distance and let them know if you feel unsafe. Not just people: I believe you can also contact the constabulary! I hear it's quite simple to use."

Holly, who was standing close to Angela, elbowed her in the side. Kami gave her a grateful nod.

"Fine," Angela said ungraciously. "But if you're not going to do it now, you have to do it sometime. Tell him you're doing it, soften the blow, and pick the time or whatever you have to do, but you can't live like this, Kami. Not forever."

"She can decide this for herself," said Holly, and looped her arm through Angela's. "Besides which, while you're standing around laying down the law, we're going to be late for Political Science."

"You people make me tired," said Angela. "I mean that quite literally. I want a nap. Well, I guess that's what Political Science is for."

"Don't drool on our notes," said Holly, and dragged Angela off.

They were laughing as they went. Kami felt a slight, unworthy pang of jealousy. Angela was *her* best friend and not Holly's. Angela had always made her preference for Kami's company quite clear by openly disliking everyone else's; if Angela liked someone else, Kami could not help but worry about being replaced. It wasn't like she could read Angela's mind and be certain she still had the best-friend spot.

Kami shook her head at herself and made her way upstairs to the headquarters.

Holly and Angela had not mentioned one important reason for Kami not to break the link.

Without it, what would I be to you? Just some ordinary girl. A connection like this would make anyone feel close to anyone.

Even if she could read someone's mind, she could apparently still be scared of losing them.

Kami was in no mood to enter her headquarters, her sanctuary, and find Ash sitting at her desk. He looked up from a map of Sorry-in-the-Vale, on which Kami had marked the houses with the families who had been in town longest according to Holly's mother.

"What are you doing?" Kami asked sharply.

"Waiting for you," Ash said.

Kami strolled in, closing the door behind her. "I could've sworn we gave you a desk of your own."

"Well . . . I happened to see the map," Ash said. "And I wanted to—it sounds stupid, but I wanted you to see that I wasn't working on the paper or anything. That I was waiting for you."

It was silly, so silly it was almost plausible. But then Ash, with his bright clear voice and his bright clear face, always seemed so very plausible. Kami rubbed the spot between her eyebrows. She was sick of drowning in uncertainties. "Why were you waiting for me?"

"I wanted to talk about you being Jared's source. It explains—a lot about you, and you and him. And us. I understand why you couldn't tell me before."

"Because you were being so frank and open with me about the magical details of your life," Kami observed.

Ash ducked his head in abashed assent, and Kami felt guilty for snapping at him.

"I guess I can understand that too," she conceded.

"We both had a lot of things we had to hold back," Ash said. "But now we don't."

He was gorgeous and sweet, and his sudden reawakening of interest in her was making Kami suspicious. She was either becoming a paranoid freak or having a perfectly reasonable reaction to the world going mad around her. "Yes, openness is a beautiful thing. You do realize we have a murderer to catch."

"That's what I wanted to talk to you about."

"That was not the impression I was getting," Kami said slowly. Unless Ash had been about to confess that he had some sort of fetish for sassy girl detectives. Maybe he'd read Nancy Drew at an impressionable age.

"I think you should cut the connection between you and Jared," Ash said.

Kami stilled, halfway across the room. She laid her hands down gently on the surface of the nearest desk, Holly's, as if it was breakable. "Oh?" she said.

So that was what all this was about.

"Haven't you considered," Ash asked softly, "that you are not safe?"

"Why would I be less safe than anyone else?" Kami returned defensively, but even before Ash replied, she knew. Nobody had tried to take her, nobody had wielded a knife to sacrifice her for power. But somebody had tried to push her, tried to eliminate her. Somebody else knew about her and Jared's connection and did not want a Lynburn to have such power.

"This sorcerer doesn't want anyone else to have power," Ash said, echoing her thoughts. "Why *should* anyone else have power? Why should you, when the sorcerer is the one killing for it? If they kill you, they kill Jared. Source and sorcerer, taken out with one blow."

So that was Jared's excuse for staying connected gone, Kami thought. He wouldn't like that. He already didn't like it. She could feel his anger and his fear for her, chilling her own blood.

"Working out a motive is progress," she said, her voice shaky in her own ears.

Ash's expression cracked. Beneath the broken surface of his calm, Kami saw emotions more desperate than she'd ever suspected Ash felt. He dropped his gaze back to the map. "I don't care about progress," he said in a low voice. "I want you safe. And as long as you're his source, you're not safe."

"And I'm sure pure chivalrous concern for her safety is your only reason for wanting the connection cut." Jared sneered from the doorway.

Kami did not know why she was surprised. Naturally

Jared would skip out of class to go after Ash for this. He was standing in the doorway bristling, hair going in all directions. He looked as if he'd run all the way there.

Ash stood up. Kami saw Jared's eyes flicker, felt his ripple of suspicion, and knew he'd seen both the fact that Ash was sitting at Kami's desk and the map.

"What do you mean by that?" Ash asked in a soft voice. He did not rise to Jared's challenge, his tone staying level. It gave him a dignity that made Jared look bad.

Jared heard Kami's thoughts. Their feelings tangled together. She felt his fury flame higher and tried to keep control. "Uncle Rob told me more about sources last night," he said. "People who are suitable to be sources are rare. Interesting that you're so anxious to free Kami up."

"You think I want to use her for power?" Ash demanded. He looked sick. "I agree with my father. He says that sorcerers who use sources are no better than leeches. He says they're pathetic. And weak."

"Weak?" Jared tilted his head. "Really?"

Now that Kami knew what was happening, she could feel him do it. The sensation was as if he was leaning on her for balance, but with his mind and not his body. It was just a slight pressure. The map rolled up in front of Ash, and then lifted and laid itself at Kami's feet, unrolling there like a carpet.

Ash's mouth curled. The light on Kami's desk turned on by itself. Her glass full of pens tipped over with a clink and all the pens rolled out. Then a box of paper clips turned over. Pens and paper clips spread out, made a glinting and colored pattern below Ash's spread palms.

Kami had only seen Jared, whom she trusted, and Rosalind, whom she hated, do magic. She had felt wonder with Jared and fear with Rosalind. She did not know how she felt seeing Ash do it. Disturbed, perhaps, seeing the world be so manifestly different from the way she had always believed it was. She was not sure she could trust Ash's magic any more than she was sure she could trust Ash. But she wanted to.

Ash moved his hands and the paper clips rose, folding themselves out into little hooks that danced through his fingers. The threat was clear.

"You're not the only one who's a sorcerer, cousin."

Kami took a step closer to Jared. His mind reached for her, welcoming as a hand held out to catch hers. It was the only way she knew that he registered her move toward him, because he was still glaring at Ash.

One of the paper clips unfolded completely, stretching into one long needle-thin, needle-glittering strip of wire. It moved like a tiny bolt of lightning, a too-bright flash in the air and across Ash's face. It left behind a dark streak of blood, welling from the same place Jared's white scar stood raised against his cheek, and Ash flinched back.

"No," said Jared. "But I'm the only one with a source."

Kami stumbled away from him, wrenching her mind from his, not putting up any walls, just wanting distance. She lifted a rejecting hand, and map, paper clips, and pens all hit the wall. She took three more strides, making for the door, and threw a furious look back at Jared. "You might not have one much longer."

Part VI
Closing the Storybook

So dawn goes down to day.
Nothing gold can stay.
—*Robert Frost*

Chapter Thirty
Source of Light

Kami couldn't go home to the mother who loved her but had lied to her, and she certainly couldn't go into town. So she went into the woods where she had seen her first death instead. There was nowhere safe left, and she could think there at least.

She sat down by the lip of what Jared had joked was called "Really Depressed Quarry." The hollow of Cotswold stone looked like half of a pear with its flesh scooped out. On her other side, the trees stretched out, plum and yellow and red in the graying light. She could hear though not see the Sorrier River, water rushing and leaves rustling together like people whispering secrets: *Shhhh, shhh, shhh. Sorrier, sorrier, sorcerer.*

Kami drew her legs up to her chest, under her long skirt patterned with yellow bees and red flowers. She pulled the material tight around her ankles.

You shouldn't be out there alone, said Jared.

But I'm never alone, am I?

Her constant companion was silent. He was sorry, and still angry, and Kami could understand both those things but she couldn't understand him lashing out and making Ash bleed for no reason.

For trying to separate us!

He's entitled to an opinion, Kami said. *So am I.*

Jared had no answer for that but fear that she would want to be separated, and his rage. The rage that had cut Ash's skin. The rage that had sent his father tumbling down those stairs to his death.

No, Kami said. *I didn't mean that. You didn't know what you could do then. It wasn't your fault. But now that you know what you can do, you're responsible for it. You can't hurt anybody else.*

I'll do whatever you want. As long as she didn't leave him. *And I won't let anything happen to you,* Jared promised. *You do not need to worry about anyone coming after you because you're my source.*

I wouldn't cut the connection because I was afraid. I wouldn't do anything because I was afraid.

Yeah, said Jared. *I know that.*

Kami was as close as she could get to alone, but she still sat wrapped in someone else's thoughts, his watchful affection and concern. It was not so bad at this precise moment.

Shadows were gathering in the gold cup of the quarry. Kami looked down and could not see any of the curves and spikes of the quarry where she and Nicola Prendergast had played hide-and-seek when they were kids. When Nicola was alive. Kami closed her eyes for an instant and then rose.

Now she could see the river through the trees, a snake of silver motion fringed with the jewel colors of the leaves. She saw something else as well. Delicate as something painted on china, balanced on one leg at the edge of the river. It was a heron, but not an ordinary heron. Each line of it, the thin legs and the curve of wings and neck, burned bright blue, like the hottest flame from a Bunsen burner.

Sobo had not been the kind of grandmother who loved to tell stories, but Kami had heard one or two and interpreted them in her own way, shaping the legends of a country she had never seen into her private personal stories.

Aosaginohi. Blue heron fire. A night heron, softly illuminated against the darkening sky.

She had not thought much about Ash's words to Jared, about waking the woods. Certainly not in connection to herself. Only here was the *aosaginohi.* Now Kami thought about the little creature made of eyes. *Hyakume,* guardian with a hundred eyes.

Jared had not woken the woods alone. She had done it too. Source and sorcerer, creating a storybook land out of Sorry-in-the-Vale. Only the stories were different this time, because they were her stories too. For the first time, Kami saw what Rob Lynburn had feared she would see: the lure of power.

Kami's mother was home for dinner every Tuesday, so the rest of the family was always home then as well. Dad had made lasagna, and they all sat around the table and fought over the dregs of the lemonade. Tomo won, of course.

Ten primly drank ice water and focused on his salad. "I am considering becoming a vegetarian," he announced in a low voice. "Not that this isn't excellent and nutritious," he told Mum, blinking worriedly. "But I might owe it to my conscience."

"Whatever you want," Mum said.

"I do half the cooking, and by 'half' I mean three-quarters," Dad pointed out. "And if you're going to turn up your nose at all my carnivorous delights, ingrate child, you can sit under the table and gnaw sadly on a raw Brussels sprout at mealtimes."

Ten smiled a tiny smile. He always knew when Dad was joking, though strangers' jokes puzzled him.

Kami reached for the salad dressing and met her mother's fingers stretching across the table for the same thing. Kami pulled away. Her mother's hands were icy cold. Her mother's gaze met hers.

"How was your day, Kami?" she asked, and picked up the dressing.

"Oh, fine," Kami said. "The paper is going well. I'm working on a really big issue right now. I'm going to do an article on the old families of the Vale." She looked at her parents.

Her father raised his eyebrows at her, and her mother's gaze trembled and slid away.

"I heard that some of the old families were very powerful," she added. "Can either of you help me? Any word about families who've got their own way a lot over the years?"

"That'd be all of them, wouldn't it?" Dad said, rolling his eyes. "Especially the Lynburns. The other families say, 'My way or the highway.' The Lynburns say, 'I am unfamiliar with the concept of the highway, so that leaves you with only one choice.' Ha-ha." Dad's voice softened then, as it did every time he spoke of his mother. "She always said they weren't important: that they knew so little they thought this small town was the world."

Kami thought about the Lynburn boys, fighting over her as if they were dogs snarling over a bone and she had no choice in the matter. "Forget the Lynburns," she said sharply. "Who else?"

Who else might be able to do magic? Who else might have wanted to kill Nicola?

"A lot of families in the Vale intermarried over the years," Mum told her, staring at her focaccia. "There's no real way to know who has inherited what, or who is descended from whom anymore."

"Which brings us to the least sexy word in the English language, kids," Dad said, kicking back in his chair. "Inbreeding. Avoid it. Think about dating outside the Vale."

Mum sat with the line of her back so straight that it looked as if her spine was made of steel. Dad rubbed a hand over the curve of her shoulder. "You have a migraine, Claire?"

Mum gave him a faint smile. "It's not so bad." Stress brought on Mum's migraines. Kami wondered how many of her headaches over the years had been about sorcerers and secrets. Mum looked back at Kami and said, "Some families were important once and aren't anymore. Like the Prescotts. Power fades with time. All power but the Lynburns'. They're the ones to watch. For your article."

"Article," Kami said. "Right."

Dad reached over and pulled a lock of Ten's wavy bronze hair. "Do you get the feeling that they're talking about something other than an article?"

Kami stared at her fork, lying forlornly askew on her plate. "I don't know what you could mean! You are talking crazy!"

"They are talking about boys," Dad told Tomo and Ten. "I believe your mother may have concerns about Kami and a Lynburn boy. Possibly in a tree. Potentially k-i-s-s-i-n-g. I couldn't say."

Kami stood up from her chair. "Not likely." And how true that was.

Her dad whistled cheerfully at her as she went out the door. Kami heard Tomo taking up the whistle as she climbed the stairs, and the murmur of her mother's voice. She went to her bedroom and sat on her window seat, looking out the mullioned window. Through the old triangles of glass, she saw her town on one side. She saw the dark curve of the woods, starting from her home and ending with the manor.

Sorry-in-the-Vale, the Sorrier River, sorry, sorrier, sorcerer. Her town, and now she knew the truth of it. She'd helped shape her town with magic, added something new to the world with her story. Kami had never wanted to do anything but these two things: discover truth and change the world. What she needed to do now, before anything else, was discover all the truth.

The Prescotts, her mother had said. Holly's family.

Kami found herself trying to figure out exactly *when* Holly had become friendly with her. She only had Holly's word for it that Holly had ever been attacked. The Prescotts had once been powerful, her mother had said, and Holly had told Kami about the Prescotts' grudge against the Lynburns. A Prescott might want to kill, and might choose the time of the Lynburns' return to do it so a Lynburn would be blamed for the murder. A Prescott might be born a sorcerer. Power might tempt Holly, if she had the opportunity to take it.

Kami rested her cheek against the glass and shut her eyes against all the light and darkness of Sorry-in-the-Vale.

The next day, Kami couldn't find a single member of her team in school. She didn't have class with any of them on Wednesdays, but she didn't see anyone in the cafeteria and her headquarters were deserted.

It gave her room to think.

By the time Kami cornered Holly in the corridor at the end of the day, she had already made up her mind how to behave. She smiled, determinedly bright. Holly smiled back, and Kami wondered if the smile looked a little fixed, a little false.

"How's it going?" Kami asked.

"Fine," said Holly. She had the same coloring as Ash. Kami wondered how much more likely it was to be a sorcerer if you had a few drops of Lynburn blood in you. "How are you?"

Why was Holly turning Kami's questions back on her? Kami thought wildly. Then she told herself to get a grip. "Also fine!" she answered. "Thank you for asking!"

Holly squinted at her, but she didn't ask Kami if she was all right. Kami found that suspicious too.

"Where's Angela?" Kami asked in desperation. She didn't think she could bear to stand here doubting her friend for an instant longer.

Holly's face shut like a door, leaving her eyes glittering and cold. "No idea," she snapped. "I'm not interested in where she is or what she does."

While Kami was still staring, Holly turned on her heel and walked down the corridor. Other people saw Kami getting the brush-off. A wave of murmurs hit her as she turned and walked the other way, trying to pretend nothing was wrong.

Kami ducked into a bathroom as she went, pulling out her phone and calling Angela. She stood in the center of the white tile floor, listening to the phone ring until it went to Angela's voicemail.

"I'm too lazy to answer messages," Angela's recorded voice said, tinny and far-off in Kami's ear. "Don't bother leaving one."

Kami hung up and rang Angela's home phone. When she heard the soft click of the phone being picked up, she breathed out in deep relief. The breath froze on her lips when Rusty's sleepy, good-natured voice said: "Rusty Montgomery's emporium of pleasure. Tell me you're good-looking and then tell me how I can serve you."

"Rusty, for God's sake," Kami said. "What if it was my mother calling?"

"Your mother is a very nice-looking lady," Rusty observed. "Though I'm not sure why you think she'd be calling me."

"What if it was the grocer, then?"

"Mr. Hanley has a very individual but compelling charm."

Kami could not force herself to laugh. She didn't even know how to pretend to be normal, not when she couldn't stop seeing how sweet, friendly Holly's eyes had turned cold. "Is Angela there?"

"No," Rusty said, his casual drawl coming an instant too late to be natural.

"Well," Kami said, "do you know where she is? She's not answering her phone."

Rusty hesitated again, the scrape of his breath sounding like another door shutting Kami out.

"Rusty," Kami said, "Angela shouldn't be disappearing off on her own. It's not safe."

"She hasn't told you anything?" Rusty demanded. His voice was suddenly sharp, which Rusty's voice never was.

Nobody was acting normal. Kami felt disoriented, everything familiar made strange. "What are you talking about?"

"Nothing," said Rusty.

"Nothing?" Kami repeated. "Though you are a master of deceit, somehow I see through your cunning story."

Rusty drew in a deep breath. "Look, Kami, Angela is fine. I promise you. I think she's just gone off to be by herself for a while. She's a little upset."

"Angela doesn't get upset," Kami said blankly.

Kami had seen Angela at thirteen years old, when her parents went on a five-month trip. Angela had set up an old armchair as a punching bag in their garden and beaten it into rags and splinters before Kami's eyes. Then she had gone and taken a nap.

Angela got angry and got even with the world by pretending she didn't care. She didn't run off to take some personal time and have a little cry.

"Everyone gets upset," Rusty said, his voice soothing,

as if that was likely to calm Kami, as if generalizations ever really applied to anyone. "She probably went for a walk in the woods."

A walk in the woods, Kami thought. The phone slid a little against her damp palm. "Rusty," she said. "There is something you're not telling me."

"What would make you think that?" he asked.

It was horrible, hearing Rusty's voice shift into caginess. Rusty was always so simple, as if he couldn't be bothered to be complicated. The idea that even Rusty was keeping secrets from her was a terrible one. She thought about the Montgomerys moving to Sorry-in-the-Vale, a place where they knew nobody and clearly were not very happy. She thought about Henry Thornton, a sorcerer who had come down to Sorry-in-the-Vale from the city.

"What do you know, Rusty?" Kami asked, dropping the pretense that this was an ordinary conversation. Her voice sounded tinny and desperate in her own ears.

"What do *you* know?" Rusty shot back, his voice harsher than she'd ever heard it, a man's voice, not a lazy, charming boy's. "I don't know what's safe to tell you. I don't want to tell any of Angela's secrets."

So, Angela had secrets.

Kami wasn't even curious; she just felt sick. "Rusty," she pleaded, "she's my best friend."

"I know," Rusty told her. "But she's my sister."

Kami stared at the murky underwater green of the bathroom tiles.

"Maybe you should come over," Rusty suggested. His

voice sounded normal again, which was even more disorienting.

There was a knot in Kami's throat, tightening with her fear, like a snared animal who only drew the snare tighter by struggling. "Why would I come over if Angela's not there?"

"Come on, Cambridge. You're my friend too." It was the nickname that made her hang up so abruptly she found herself startled by the sudden emptiness in her ear. She couldn't stand to hear that pet name turned against her.

The phone rang while it was still pressed against her ear. The sound made Kami jump. She turned the phone off with shaking hands and slid it into the pocket of her jeans. She didn't want to stay in the bathroom, so she turned on her heel and left.

The first thing she saw was Ash, walking down the corridor toward her, his head bowed. The lights in the classrooms were out, only the fluorescent lights overhead illuminating their school at all. In the shadows and stark light, Ash looked more like Jared than ever.

It wasn't just the light, Kami thought as she drew closer to Ash. It was seeing Ash through new eyes. The first time she'd met him, she'd noticed how perfectly put together he was, always saying the right thing, looking the right way, every word and movement controlled. She had admired that. She hadn't thought it meant he was hiding something.

But now she knew everyone was hiding something.

Ash's calm blue eyes were shadowed, dark as the lakes where Jared had almost drowned. He was walking too fast, as though he wanted to get away from something.

Kami kept walking toward him. "Ash?" she said. "What's wrong?"

Ash blinked and checked his own step. Kami reached him and stood staring up at him. He stood with the lockers in a metallic line at his back, and the look on his face sent a ripple of unease through her.

"Ash," Kami said urgently, "tell me. I'll help you."

Ash stayed frozen, gazing down at her. Then he leaned down and kissed her. His mouth was sudden and hot against hers, catching the gasp of surprise she made. He grabbed her wrists, pulling her toward him and against his body fast. It wasn't at all like their last kiss. This wasn't sweet or romantic.

Kami had heard of having your breath taken away, but she'd never lost hers before. It was partly that it was so fast and she was so surprised, and it was partly something else. The kiss went deeper and he let go of her wrists, and she found herself sliding her fingers into his hair, stroking and trying to soothe. He drew away and looked into her face, eyes beseeching, as if he had a question and needed the right answer.

Kami, a little dazed, had a question of her own. "Why did you do that?"

That was clearly not the answer Ash had been searching for. He stepped away from her. Kami's hand fell from his hair.

"Isn't it obvious?" he asked, then he pushed past her and walked away.

No, Kami wanted to shout after him. No, it wasn't. She wanted to run after him and demand answers herself. She let him go, the front doors of the school swinging open to let him pass, everything in Sorry-in-the-Vale made to obey the sorcerer. The doors fell closed behind him, one last slant of sunlight falling across the floor.

Kami was still trembling, cold all over except for her mouth. It had been obvious Ash was in search of some sort of comfort. She didn't know how much of her response to him had been about who he looked like, not who he was, and that was a terrible thing to find yourself doubting. It was a terrible thing to do to anyone.

Kami had a wall up automatically between Jared and these thoughts, but there hadn't been a wall during the kiss. So everything was even more complicated than it was already. Everything was always more complicated because of this terrible link.

Kami could feel Jared's emotions, so tangled that even he wasn't sure which one was prevalent, jealousy or anger or confusion, as he recognized that she'd responded to the kiss. Kami did not know what to say to him.

The door of the school creaked open again. Kami looked up from the floor. She saw fingers of shadow creep in, like the shadow of a giant's hand. As she watched, everything the shadow touched was consumed by its darkness.

Jared! Kami screamed silently. She backed away and the darkness came inexorably closer, taking pieces of the corridor in sharp hungry gulps. It was as though Kami's world was made of paper and someone was hacking at it with a vast pair of scissors.

Kami backed up another step, breath sobbing in her throat. She knew Jared was coming for her, running, but he was sure to come too late. Her back met the cold wall, and she felt Jared reach for her in his mind. It was all he could do.

It gave her a moment of warmth and calm. It was enough. She thought of facing Rosalind across a sea of flying glass. She thought of how she had felt seeing the *aosaginohi,* blue heron fire, and afterward, when she had sat at her window and looked outside. Built for sorcerers, woken woods and all, this town was hers too. She was a source of magic. This was just an enemy too cowardly to show their face.

"No," Kami said to the shadow crawling toward her, feeling the magic flow through her, from her to Jared and back again. She held out her hand and saw light fill it as if she held water cupped between her palms. The light brimmed in her hands, glowed between her fingers. She let a little light slip from her hand. The tiny points glittered like grains of sand turning into stars as they tumbled through the air toward the creeping dark.

"Don't you dare," Kami commanded. "I'm not scared. I'm the source." She let her hands fall open. The light poured from her palms and rolled down the floor, the color of sunlight on stone in her town. It washed the shadows away.

Chapter Thirty-One
Trust the Sun in Me

Kami stood panting and shaking. Then the door opened again. The creaking sound sent horror flashing through her, making every nerve burn. Against the pale sky outside, there was another dark shape, casting a long shadow on the shining floor.

Kami was terrified for a split second. Then she felt the brush of emotions not her own. When she turned toward the touch, it went all through her like sunlight: relief and love and joy. She ran down the corridor, down through the fading glow of magic. For once she was simply glad that Jared was real, his feelings flooding through her and her arms sliding around his neck.

She closed her eyes and held on, as she had when they found Nicola. This time she was able to keep holding on, her cheek laid in the curve of his neck, cool leather and warm skin on either side of her face. He had his arm around her, his breath was stirring her hair, and for a long moment they were both safe and warm in a space with no walls between them.

Then Jared stepped away from her, held her back with his hands on her shoulders. "You're all right?" he demanded.

Kami's walls all went back up. She said, knowing he could tell that she was lying, but not why: "I'm fine."

"Being able to hold whoever this is off with magic doesn't matter," Kami said, once they got to her headquarters. "Whoever this is could still go after anyone in town who doesn't have magic, or after one of us when we're asleep. Who has the most magic chops is irrelevant. What matters is finding out who the sorcerer going after us is. Which means that what matters, lucky for us, is elite investigative reporter skills."

A flash of Jared's amusement, subdued like lightning seen from far away, made Kami look up from her notebook. She was sitting behind her desk because she felt better there. Jared was on Angela's napping couch, one knee drawn up and his arm around it, watching her.

Only Kami's desktop lamp was on, the better to stay in school after hours without being discovered. She was sitting in a pool of light and had to blink to make him out. The light was dying outside the window, caught in the gray time between sunset and twilight. Jared was all in shadow, except for his eyes. They shone colorless as glass with moonlight striking it.

Kami brought her mind closer to Jared's, questing. She came in contact with a wall as high as hers. She blinked again.

He never mentioned her walls. She could not comment on his.

"The problem is," Kami said, and heard her voice crack, "I keep panicking. I thought that being a reporter would mean being able to—keep some distance from the story, that it would all be really interesting and I would care a lot, but it wouldn't be personal. Today I couldn't stop thinking that

Angela or Holly might be the sorcerer. I can't suspect the people I care about, but I can't seem to trust them either, and I have to trust someone."

"You can trust me."

Kami tested the wall again. She could not read a thing from him. "Yes," she answered all the same, and they both heard uncertainty in her voice. "But I can't just trust the people whose mind I can read. The list is somewhat limited."

"I don't see a problem with that," Jared said. "I only trust you. But if you want to be all emotionally healthy about it, I'll try to understand. That's just the kind of relationship we have."

Kami smiled. Then she glanced down at the frantic scribbles in her notebook, the black loops of letters tangling like briars. She'd worked out ways to suspect everybody in town.

"Maybe the problem is that you're too close to it," Jared said. "The idea of Angela or Holly just has you rattled. It doesn't mean you're not an elite investigate reporter."

"Damn right," said Kami.

"So make it a story," he suggested. "Step back from worrying about Angela and Holly and think about it. If it was something on the news or in one of your mystery novels, who would you think did it?"

Kami looked down at her notebook again and tapped the page with her pen. She let the pen drop from her fingers and tried to imagine that this was just another story. The kind of puzzle she'd always wanted to solve. "All right," she said slowly. She got up from her chair and walked the boards of her headquarters, reached the wall, spun, and came back. "Holly got attacked at the Bell and Mist, or at least she said she did. She might have been lying. But if she *was* attacked, then the people I could see at the Bell and Mist aren't the sorcerer. I was with Angela most of the time. It wasn't her, unless there's more than one sorcerer."

Rusty's voice came to mind, obviously uneasy, knowing a secret of Angela's that Kami did not. Kami kept walking. "We can't forget the timing of all this either. The dead animals, me being tossed into a well. The attacks began around the start of the school year—the same time the Lynburns arrived. The only people we know for certain are sorcerers are that man Henry Thornton, who hasn't been in town since that one night; Mrs. Thompson, who has had seventy years to decide to start murdering people in a crazed bid for power; and the Lynburns. The ones with the knives, the ones with the past of red and gold."

She was going full speed ahead now, almost bouncing off the walls as Jared stayed still and watched her. "It's either a frame job or it really is a Lynburn. And in real life, unlike in mystery novels, the murderer isn't always the one you least suspect," Kami continued. "It's usually the one the evidence points toward. Henry Thornton looked at you and knew you were a Lynburn. He saw that you looked like someone else, someone he was afraid of. I'm not sure. I can't be sure. But if you ask me who I think did it? I think it was a Lynburn." She stopped then. She was alone in the dark with a Lynburn.

"So we have four suspects," Jared said slowly.

Kami thought, *Five.*

Jared stood up, and his shock rippled through her, with rage just behind it.

"I didn't mean for you to hear that," Kami said.

Tell me you didn't mean it, said Jared.

"I don't think it's you," Kami told him. "I don't believe that, but—" She didn't want to be the girl who just believed in the guy she liked, no matter what extenuating mind-reading circumstances existed. She didn't want her feelings to blind her. She didn't want anything to blind her. She did not know what her feelings were, or what his were, or how to separate the two. She did not want to drown in what was between them and lose control, or lose who she was.

Thinking about this objectively, things looked very bad for Jared. He was the one who hadn't known how sorcery worked, the one who got furiously angry and wanted to take it out on the world. He had admitted to seeing those knives, admitted that he had killed his father. He had been the sorcerer who was furious with her the night she was thrown down a well. She didn't know when they had last been completely open with each other. Maybe they never had been.

"Fine," Jared said explosively, and Kami realized how much she had let slip in her distress. He took one step toward her. Kami had to tilt her chin to look up into his face. She could feel the warmth and tension of his body.

"Are you scared of me?" Jared whispered.

Kami whispered back: "I've never been as scared of anyone as I am of you." She shivered, but the fear felt almost familiar. After all, she had been alone in the dark with him her whole life. Nobody could hurt her like he could.

"Take down your walls," Jared said, his voice low and urgent. "I'll take down all of mine." He lifted a hand, fingers curled a fraction of an inch from her cheek.

Kami almost turned her face into his palm, but instead

she held still and waited to see if he would touch her on his own.

"Kami," Jared said. His voice was soft: she barely recognized it, and she realized this was what he sounded like when he was begging. "You are the only thing in the world that matters. You can trust me. Please."

He did not touch her. She did not take down her walls.

His fury hit her like a blast of heat, strong enough to make her take a step back.

"I'm sorry," Kami told him. "I can't."

"Fine," Jared said. He didn't linger, didn't look at her again, just turned away and left her standing in darkness with his rage burning in her mind.

Kami tried to call Angela again that night, but she only got her voicemail. She tried the house, and when Rusty answered she hung up.

She woke up the next morning, the dawn light brushing the treetops outside her window with silver, more luminescence than real light. She could feel Jared's unhappiness, even in his sleep. Kami picked up her phone.

Ten minutes later, she threw on a gray woolen dress and her winter coat. She ran out of her house and uphill through the fields that stretched away from the woods. The world was cold in the morning time, autumn drawing to a close. When Kami jumped a stile, the grass crunched, stiff with frost.

She had to trust someone.

The fields glittered as she crossed them and the sun rose higher in the sky. The morning light was still so pale that for a moment the farmhouse looked wrapped in mist. The door of the house swung open. Holly came out as Kami hesitated at the last fence. Holly's hair was sleep-rumpled, and she looked tired and apprehensive. Kami knew the feeling.

"Hi," said Holly faintly, and came down to the fence to meet her, shrugging on her fleece-lined jacket.

Kami glanced up into Holly's face and took a chance. "I like you," she blurted out. Holly flinched. "I know we haven't been friends very long," Kami continued, looking at the frosty fields. "And I know you were maybe trying to be friends for a while before, and I didn't realize, and I'm sorry about that. I was being dumb. But I think you're great, and I'm glad we're friends now." Kami took a deep breath so she could start explaining that she had suspected Holly for a moment.

Holly spoke. "Really?" she asked, and her voice was trembling. "I'm really your friend?"

"Holly, of course."

"You're not just putting up with me because Angela likes me?" Holly said.

"What are you talking about? Why would I do that? Angela likes a lot of stuff I don't like. Angela likes documentaries about deadly spiders and having eighteen hours of sleep a day. I'm pretty comfortable with not liking everything Angela likes."

Holly gave a small laugh, which made a brief frosty cloud shape in the air between them. "Okay," she said. "Okay."

Kami reached out and put her hand on Holly's where it lay on the fence. Holly turned her hand under Kami's and linked their fingers, holding on tight. "Can you do magic?" Kami asked.

Holly blinked.

"Can Angela do magic?" Kami asked. "You said that you weren't interested in where she was or what she did, and Rusty said he didn't want to tell any of Angela's secrets. I feel like I can't trust anybody. I wrote down a list of suspects and it was the whole town. Anyone could have magic, anyone could be trying to hurt us, but I have to be able to trust my friends. Will you please tell me what's going on?"

Holly's hand clasped Kami's tight. "Angela tried to kiss me," she said.

It was Kami's turn to blink. "What?"

"I wasn't expecting it," Holly said. "Maybe I should have been, I mean, I'm meant to be the girl who knows about all that stuff, but I—but I don't. I wasn't trying to lead her on or anything. I didn't even know she liked girls."

"What?" Kami repeated. She was truly the worst investigative reporter in the world.

"I've had guys I thought were my friends turn out not to be after their real friend decided I wasn't so great after all," Holly went on. "I guess I'm not sure how it works with girls. I was confused and I got angry. Look, I'm sorry. Is Angie all right?"

"I have no idea," Kami said. "I mean, I literally had no idea about any of this. I thought Angela's secret might be that she was a sorcerer."

She and Holly stood staring at each other. Then Kami pulled her hand gently out of Holly's grasp, pulled out her phone, and called Angela's house.

Rusty answered on the first ring. "Angela?"

Kami hung up the phone. "Angela didn't answer her

phone all day yesterday," she told Holly, speaking slowly because she didn't want to bring her thoughts any closer to reality. "She didn't come home last night. I might not know everything about her, but I know her. She wouldn't run away, even if she was upset. She's stood and fought everything she ever came up against her whole life. She's not with Rusty, and she's not with me, and she wouldn't go anywhere else."

The color drained from Holly's face. She was very still. The light of the sun caught her hair at that moment and made her look like a marble statue crowned with gold. Only her eyes looked alive and afraid.

Kami said what she hadn't wanted to say, what she had been too scared to say. She felt cold, as if by uttering the words out loud, she was making them true: "Someone has her."

Chapter Thirty-Two
Shine and Entwine with Me

Holly and Kami raced through the woods. Holly was faster than Kami and she had to keep pausing, hanging on to tree branches and gasping, for Kami to catch up. Kami was running as fast as she could without stopping. Her lungs were burning, her heart was hammering, and she could not stop herself from thinking of what could be happening to Angela, of all the things that could already have happened to her, while Kami had been busy suspecting her best friend of being a murderer.

There was no time to feel guilty. Kami kept running, twigs snagging on her clothes like children catching at the material with small clinging fingers. Ahead of her, she saw Holly, and past Holly she saw the hut where she had found the fox.

There were thin bare branches between her and the hut, dark lines that fragmented the world, as if she was looking through a window where the glass had shattered but not fallen out of the frame. Holly waited for her to catch up. Kami could not blame her for not wanting to go into this place of potential horror alone. She joined Holly as quickly and as quietly as she could. They tiptoed toward the door of the hut in silence.

The only sounds were the dry crackle of twigs and dead leaves beneath their feet, the dry rasp of their breathing. Kami put out a hand and pushed the door of the hut in. It was empty, the tabletop dusty, and leaves blown in on the dark floor. It did not look as if anyone had been in there since she and Jared had found the Surer Guest key card.

Angela was not there.

Which meant they had no idea where she was.

Kami turned away from that dark little room. She looked at Holly and saw the same desperation there that she felt.

"What we need are reinforcements," Kami said. She remembered her fight with Jared and stopped cold. She hardly dared reach out to him. It was like holding out her hand in the dark, uncertain as to whether he would take it, or if he had his back to her.

The answer came as soon as she let her walls down, showing Jared what was happening. Support was hers, absolute reassurance, a hand—his hand—catching hers in the dark and holding fast.

Come here, Jared's voice said clearly in her mind. *You think it's one of the Lynburns? Time to find out which one.*

"Come on," Kami told Holly. "We're going to Aurimere."

I'll wake the family, Jared said. *Let them know that we're expecting guests.*

Kami's thoughts ran through his mind, her terror turning his throat dry and making his head pound. Jared could not get Kami's visions of Angela in that dead girl's place out of his head. Except that Kami, of course, was planning as well as panicking. He wasn't going to let her down.

Jared came out of his room and into the corridor with its arched stone roof. It was like walking through a church every day, this place, as if he was always coming to confess his sins. "Mom!" he yelled. "Aunt Lillian! Someone!"

There was no answer. He went down the stairs three steps at a time, past the doors to the library and through the parlor. His voice, calling for his family, echoed off the wall of windows.

"Jared, this is not an appropriate time to run around screeching your head off," his aunt Lillian remarked, shutting up a large dark desk-slash-table in swift, economical movements. "In fact, I'd prefer if you refrained from screeching at all times."

"Another girl has disappeared," Jared said.

Aunt Lillian's eyes narrowed. "All right. Let's go get the others. I would lay a considerable amount of money that the sorcerer will be doing this in the woods. We're all drawn to the woods."

"Kami already checked the hut where the dead fox was found," Jared told her. Aunt Lillian blinked at him, and Jared rolled his eyes. "My source."

"Oh," said Lillian, already moving, a blur of black and blond heading straight for her son's room.

Jared ran after her. "Kami and I were talking. She thinks the person killing people is a Lynburn. I agree with her."

"That's utter nonsense," Lillian said contemptuously.

"Is it?" Jared asked. "You thought it was a Lynburn too, until you found I had a source."

Aunt Lillian turned on the step to face him. Jared, climbing the stairs after her, was pulled up short, her blue eyes on a level with his. He backed down a step: his mother would not have wanted him this close.

"Jared, *don't*," his aunt said, and Jared blinked at her, not sure what she meant. "I did not want to suspect you."

Jared raised an eyebrow. "But you did."

"You're my responsibility," Aunt Lillian said. "This whole town is, but especially my family. I know how you grew up, with a city poisoning you and with your parents both hating you. I wanted to take you back here, back to our home. I wanted to make things right for you."

Jared looked away from her face, too like his mother's but wearing an expression his mother would never have worn, at least not when talking to him. He wanted to please her, like he wanted to please Kami: he wanted it so badly it hurt to think about. He just didn't know how. "It's fine," he ground out. "I get why you thought it was me. I wouldn't trust me either." Even Kami did not trust him.

"I do not believe it was you anymore," Lillian stated. "I do not believe it was one of our family at all."

Jared looked away from the stone wall and back up at Aunt Lillian. "Or is it just that you still don't want to suspect us? You do know about the knives?"

"Rosalind took them and threw them away to punish me for a wrong she thought I had done her," Aunt Lillian said. "Maybe I did. It doesn't matter."

"It does," said Jared, "if she didn't throw them away."

His aunt held his gaze for an instant longer, then snapped to attention like a soldier, returning to her mission up the stairs. "You will see," she informed Jared, each word punctuated by the slap of her boot heels on a step. "Ash—" She went still on the threshold of his bedroom.

Ash's room was always neat, which Jared thought was unnatural but also very like Ash. In the early morning, that perfect room was so perfectly still, so absolutely empty, that it was frightening.

Lillian's face went white and her eyes looked blind as a creature's that had lived underground all its life and only now emerged into the horror of the sun. Jared stepped up and cupped a hand under her elbow. She walked away from him, into her son's room.

"I am not going to faint. I would never dream of fainting. There is a perfectly good explanation for this. I know my son. He would never hurt anyone."

Aunt Lillian stared at Jared as if daring him to speak. He said nothing. She did not look reassured. Instead she glanced furtively back at her son's bed, so obviously not slept in, and then she walked past Jared as if he was not there. That felt familiar to Jared at least.

"Rosalind," Lillian said.

Jared started. She wasn't reading his mind, he realized. She was simply calling for her sister because she was in trouble, and she was sure Rosalind would help her.

Aunt Lillian moved fast. She was halfway down the corridor before Jared decided to follow her again, despite the fact that she was seeking out his mother. Mom had chosen to live in a different wing from the rest of the family. Lillian had to go up and down a set of the back stairs, past a tarnished suit of armor.

Jared, following her, saw a light in the wall casting a black shadow in the shape of a hand on her fair hair. Aunt Lillian ran on, not even noticing it.

"Rosalind?" she called out again once she was in the right corridor, the one above the portrait gallery. "Ros . . ." It was not a nickname. The name had died, half formed, in Aunt Lillian's mouth.

The door to his mother's bedroom was open. Light from a small window in the corridor across from the room cast a pattern of diamonds and dark diagonal lines on her empty, rumpled bed.

"Where is she? Where is everyone?" Aunt Lillian demanded, turning on Jared as if he might have abducted her sister and her son both.

"What's happening?" It was Uncle Rob, standing behind them in the corridor.

Jared couldn't take his eyes off the light and shadows playing on his mother's sheets. As soon as Kami said she thought the murderer was one of the Lynburns, he'd thought of his mother. He had feared it behind the walls he put up, and now he realized it could not have been just fear. He had seen the knives in his mother's possession. He must have known all along, really.

His parents had *both* been monsters, then. No, his whole family were monsters, but his parents were the worst. There was nothing but poison in his veins, and the potential for violence. He thought of lightning cutting a wound across the sky, and all that blood on the girl's skin. When he did look away from his mother's bed, he saw Aunt Lillian standing by Uncle Rob, her hand on his arm, as if she was reaching out for help. He had never seen her touch Uncle Rob that way before.

But she was not looking at Uncle Rob. She was looking at him. "Rosalind is your mother," she murmured. "Yet you're not surprised."

The sound of a door opening made them all start. The girls' voices made Aunt Lillian's shoulders slump for an instant as her brief hope was taken away.

Jared walked past Aunt Lillian, who was stiff with despair, and Uncle Rob, looking both confused and concerned. Jared stopped at the top of the stairs that would lead him to Kami and looked back at his aunt's pale face, the mirror of his mother's. "No," said Jared. "I'm not surprised."

Jared's feelings were like a beacon in Kami's mind. His distress burned so brightly she barely saw the stone hands and drowning women of the manor. Holly had to run after her up the stairs, then across flagstones and to the corridor where Jared stood with his aunt and uncle.

Kami did not look at the open door and the empty room. She ran to Jared and Jared lifted his hand, warding her off.

I'm so sorry, she told him, trying not to care. *I'm so sorry, but it's not your fault. Nothing your parents ever did was your fault. You misunderstood me last night, but you have to understand me now. I know you're not like them.*

Jared had so many walls up, she could not tell what he

was feeling, except that the burning beacon of his distress had gone dark. *And how do you know that?*

Because I know you, said Kami. *Nobody knows you like I do.*

Jared tipped toward her, as if they were reading something together, and she pictured again her thoughts as an illuminated manuscript. Kami needed some things to be clear to him. Her heart was almost an open book.

Jared could tell she was holding back, and something dark passed from him to her, like drops of ink in running water, even as he made an effort and smiled at her. "No," he said. "Nobody does."

You're all right?

You're here, said Jared. *So I'm all right.*

"Jared," said Kami. "We have to—"

"We have to find Angie," Holly finished, before Kami could say it.

Kami looked at Holly, who was staring warily at Lillian and Rob Lynburn. Kami took her first real look at them, Rob standing by his wife, Lillian with her pale face and wide cold eyes. They were sorcerers, sorcerers Kami did not know and could not trust.

"The woods," Lillian said abruptly.

"What?" Jared asked.

Kami realized that while he hadn't touched her, his body was angled toward her, aligning himself with her and Holly. She glanced at the other Lynburns and saw the same realization passing over Lillian's face, turning her eyes into dark lakes. Kami could tell that she didn't like seeing one of her precious Lynburns on the side of the lowly mortals, not at all.

"Don't pretend you don't know, Jared," Lillian said, her voice low. "You have the same blood in your veins as the rest of us. It draws you to the same end. Don't pretend you are not drawn to the woods. If Rosalind has the girl, she has her there."

"If Ash is with her," Rob told her, his big hand closing on her thin shoulder, "it will be all right, Lillian."

Lillian nodded sharply once, staring out the window into the woods.

Kami glanced over at Holly, who was glaring defiantly at the sorcerers, trembling with eagerness to be gone. "Do you mind if we stop talking about Ash?" Holly asked. "And start thinking about the person he might hurt? None of you Lynburns seem to care about Angela at all. Or is it that you don't care about anyone but yourselves?"

"There's no time for this!" Kami shouted. Everybody looked at her and she lifted her chin. "They're in the woods?" she said. "Let's go. There are five of us. Four of us can do magic, and two of us can read each other's minds. We can split up. If my group finds Angela, I'll tell Jared, and if the other group does, Jared will tell me."

A flash of protest went through Jared as she suggested separating, but he knew when she was determined, and he knew sense when he heard it. She felt that he hated it, at the same time as she watched him nod.

"You should all stay here. Rob and I will handle this," Lillian said. "You're children. Jared hasn't done the ceremony of the lakes, and that means he doesn't have the magic we do. He wouldn't be able to stand against Rosalind." She said her sister's name forcefully, as if she was terrified she would not be able to get it out.

"Jared has a source," Rob reminded his wife. "They will be able to stand against Rosalind. We might need them."

Kami did not wait for Lillian to argue. "Then it's settled. Jared and another magician should go with Holly; one magician come with me."

"Go with her, Uncle Rob."

Kami looked up at the tense sound of Jared's voice, saw his eyes, and said quietly, "You protect Holly."

"I don't care about being protected!" Holly shouted. Tears and fury together made her eyes glitter. "I only care about Angela."

Kami spun away from them all and headed for the stairs, down toward the woods. She heard Jared and Holly fall into step behind her. She heard Lillian's whisper echoing against the manor walls: "It may be too late for Angela."

Chapter Thirty-Three
Red and Gold

Jared could feel the lure of the lakes as if there was a magnet in his chest, pulling him toward metal. Pulling him toward the cold waters of the Crying Pools. Something kept telling him there were people waiting for him there.

"You have the same blood in your veins as the rest of us," Aunt Lillian had said. *"It draws you to the same end."*

He resisted the impulse. He reached for Kami instead, touched the scared uneasy hum of her mind from all the way across the woods.

They were combing the woods to save Kami's best friend from his mother. Jared wanted to punch somebody when he thought about that: he could feel something building inside him that wanted to be a storm. He locked every muscle in his body and stood straining, looking up at the sky. There were wisps of cloud forming against the blue, like the curls of steam from a kettle. He knew that he had created those clouds. Surely he could use all this power they said he had, and do something useful for Angela.

He wanted to send out envoys, conjure up goblin scouts or magical messengers, anything that would help them search this forest. As he thought that, he saw the tendrils of smoke slide out of the sky into the woods, spilling through to the brown tangle of the undergrowth, rasping with a dry whisper through the bright leaves. They went combing through the forest. Jared could feel them going searching.

He heard a soft indrawn breath and looked at Holly. She was looking at him, blue eyes wide and her mascara smudged by tears she had been brushing away as they walked, surreptitious as if she was stealing.

"Looks like an octopus made of smoke," she said, and gave him a sliver of a smile.

"I was feeling like a pretty badass sorcerer until you said that," Jared told her. He could feel something else in the air hunting through the forest. For a moment, he thought that the searching thing was what they were looking for, but then he glanced at Aunt Lillian's face, intent as his mother's when she was reading a book. The cool, searching air felt like Aunt Lillian looked.

Holly's hand gripped Jared's arm, startling him. Her fingernails dug into his skin. "Can you please hurry?" Holly said tensely. "We have to *find* her."

Lillian nodded in unexpected agreement. "It has to be us who find her."

Jared nodded and tried to concentrate. Holly's hand on his arm was anchoring him to his body, and airy messengers were coursing through the woods because of his power, but Kami's thoughts were the most important thing of all.

Jared, Kami said in his head, and he could tell she was wary. *Ask Lillian why.*

"Why—" Jared said aloud, and then caught up with Kami's thought. "*Why* do you want it to be us who find her?"

He glanced at his aunt, her restrained profile that should have looked out of place in the woods and yet did not.

She regarded Jared with a considering air. "Rob wants to be the one to do it," she answered slowly. "If a sorcerer goes rogue, turns vicious—it's the responsibility of the Lynburns at the manor to deal with it. It's the responsibility of the Lynburn heir, and that's me. Rob would want to spare me."

Spare you . . . , Kami prompted.

Spare her from killing Ash, Jared thought bleakly back to her. *Isn't it obvious?*

There was a sense of urgency in Kami's fear, a cold current in the stream of her thoughts.

"Spare you . . . ," Jared prompted, echoing Kami.

"Spare me from executing Ash and Rosalind," Lillian said. "Rob knows what I'll have to do. There's a place outside Sorry-in-the-Vale called Monkshood Abbey. Rob's parents used to live there. You might call them the cadet branch of the Lynburns."

Jared knew all this, but he tried to look encouraging and repeated Kami's thoughts: "What happened to them?" he asked quietly.

"They wanted more power," Lillian answered, just as quietly. "They broke the law Aurimere made and started killing people in the cellar of their house. My parents had to go and fight them to the death to stop them. My father died a year later; my mother was never the same again. But they had to do it. It's our duty to protect the town. Nobody else can."

Jared thought about the crest of the Lynburns fastened in a cellar floor, covered in dried blood. He thought of Uncle Rob saying that his parents had displeased the Lynburns of Aurimere, and not mentioning that they had done so by slaughtering people. He'd called the Lynburns of Aurimere judges and executioners.

"Rob would know what has to be done," said Lillian. "He's been there before. He understood then."

The Lynburns of Aurimere had come to Monkshood and killed his parents, Uncle Rob had said, and taken him "as sorcerer breeding stock for one or the other of their daughters." It didn't sound to Jared like Rob had understood all that well. Horror pierced Jared as he thought of what that meant, and who he had trusted with Kami.

Kami! he said. *Run!*

A wall between them fell. Jared saw what she had been concealing from him, what explained the urgency she had been feeling and why she had been forced to interrogate Lillian through him.

Rob's not here, she told him. *I turned around and he was gone. I don't know where he is.*

Kami was alone in the woods. Of course, she told herself firmly, that was a great deal better than being in the woods with the man who might have killed Nicola. This was absolutely fine, in fact.

A rustle to her left made her spin around, and she saw a bird burst from the trees in a flurry of wings. Her heart felt as if it was trying to copy the bird. Kami pressed a hand to her chest and told herself to calm down. She could feel Jared coming, Holly and Lillian with him.

Kami reminded herself that she was a source and could

send shadows away on her own. But just because she could do it by herself did not mean she wanted to be by herself. She saw light sifting and sparkling through the autumn leaves, and thought of Nicola Prendergast's eyes, staring blindly up at a different sky.

A crack of wood made Kami spin again, waves of heat and cold breaking over her. Sweat prickled at her temples. Leaves played in the wind over her head, mocking her in soft whispers. She did not know where the magical threat might be coming from. The only thing being a source did for her was let her know it was near.

Panicking would not help. What might help, Kami thought, laying out her thoughts in a logical process, was finding a weapon. She knelt down amid the dry leaves and the snake-coils of tree roots and reached for a fallen branch. Her fingers did not get the chance to close on it, as someone grabbed her hair, pulling her head back.

She felt the sharp, shocking cold of a knife edge along her throat.

Kami gasped and tried to bite the gasp back. Suddenly nothing seemed as important as being terribly still.

The scrape of the blade against her skin felt hungry. The voice scraping in her ear sounded hungry too. "Not so brave now, source."

Kami's breathing was as shallow as she could make it. All she could see was the canopy of leaves. All she could feel was the touch of that knife. She reached out desperately for Jared, but she could only feel his stark fear for her. Rob Lynburn's breath was hot against her cheek, a Lynburn knife cold against her neck, and if she did not control her own terror and Jared's as well, she was going to die.

"Don't even think of trying any magic, or I'll cut your throat," Rob instructed, and illustrated the point: she felt the knife slice in.

For a moment, all she felt was shock and a flare of heat, and then the pain came. She couldn't move. She felt the burning sensation of blood, blotting out the chill of the knife, running down her skin. She felt Rob's chest rumble against her back with a laugh and knew that her blood was giving him power.

Kami focused on a point directly above her head, on amber-colored leaves like gold lace in the sky. She disobeyed the madman with the knife to her throat and used magic. Above them, leaves rustled, clouds chased each other through the sky, and boughs creaked as if they might break and come tumbling down on both their heads.

Kami felt the jerk of Rob's body as he looked upward, and felt him go slightly off-balance. Then she acted, because all the magic had been was a diversion. Kami reached up and seized his arm, digging her nails hard into a pressure point. She leaned into him, using her body and his weight to flip him over her shoulder and into the leaves.

A handful of her hair went with him, ripped out of her scalp. The pain made her vision blur, but she didn't hesitate. She scrambled to her feet, lurching. Rob grabbed for her leg but she evaded his grasp and ran.

We're coming. Jared urged her to keep running, pouring encouragement into her veins as she blundered through the woods. She had to find a safe place until they were here. She had to hide. Kami dashed toward the sound of the river. Twigs grabbed at her clothes and stabbed at her eyes. The woods were turning against her, doing the sorcerer's will, fueled by her own blood.

Kami struck back in her mind, all of Jared's rage behind hers. She heard Rob Lynburn cry out. It bought Kami time to reach the quarry and climb down, shoving her feet into the hollows and handholds she knew from childhood. Even this playground had been tainted.

At the bottom of the quarry was Angela.

She lay under a morning-bright blue sky, the tree above her dropping autumn leaves in shining drifts, like a shower of coins every time the breeze changed. Her hair was spread in a black pool on the stone around her, and her face was very pale. She was wrapped from head to foot in iron chains.

Kami ran toward her, and Angela opened her eyes.

"Angela," Kami gasped out, fear and love closing up her throat so she could barely breathe. "Don't worry. I'll help you."

"Don't," said Angela.

Kami stared. "What?"

"Don't help her," said another voice.

Kami turned to see who was in the quarry with them.

Ash sat with his legs drawn up to his chest, hands hanging empty between his knees, and his eyes wide and staring, fixed on Angela and not blinking. He looked as if he was in the grip of a nightmare. He also looked resigned: his face as set as it was gray, as if he had accepted he was not going to wake up.

"What are you doing here?" Kami asked very quietly. She didn't want to hear it; she didn't want to believe it.

Ash said, "I'm supposed to kill her."

Kami placed herself in front of Angela. "And why is that, you *incredible asshole?*"

Ash looked away. "To get more magic," he answered in a defensive voice. "I wouldn't expect you to understand."

"Good. Because I never will."

"What's the alternative?" Ash asked.

"Oooh, hard to say," Angela sneered behind Kami. "Other than live without magic like everybody else, you loser."

"We're not like everyone else, though, are we?" Ash demanded. "You didn't spend your life chasing some guy who my mother knew would hurt my aunt, because one of yours always ends up turning against one of ours. You didn't spend your life being sick every fall, living in a different house every time, because we couldn't come back home. We can be more powerless than your kind could ever be. We should be more powerful than your kind could ever be. And it's not fair."

It was Rob's logic in Ash's mouth, that sources should not be powerful, that nobody should be powerful except the sorcerers. Rob's poison in Ash's ears, and Rob's rage that had sent Kami tumbling down a well, because she and Jared were better off dead than linked.

"Your father sent you to us, didn't he?" Kami asked. "That very first day. Rosalind told you both everything about me and Jared as soon as you found her, and gave you the Lynburn knives. You came asking for Kami Glass."

Even Ash's feet looked restless and guilty, shifting on the

ground as if he was climbing and could not quite find purchase, as if he was going to fall. "He only told me to watch you," Ash said, low. "I didn't hurt you. I liked you. I didn't hurt that girl Nicola either. I never wanted to hurt anyone."

Kami looked over her shoulder at Angela. She was still now, but Kami could see her wrists and how she had struggled against her chains, the skin raw and sore. "Oh, no?" Kami asked.

"I'm not the one who set the price for power," Ash said softly. "I would never have made it blood. But that's what it is." Something about the way he said it was like the sound of the chill, turning-to-winter wind, running through leaves that were dying by turning to gold.

The hair on the back of Kami's neck was standing up. Ash and Rob, and maybe Rosalind. Maybe three sorcerers. She did not know if she could fight them all, not when she felt so weak and strange since the Lynburn knife had shed her blood. But she had to.

Ash's face was still turned away, his profile like something on a coin. Kami remembered what she had thought about him once, that he looked the part of a fairy-tale prince.

"You helped your father kill animals," she said.

It was strange when Ash glanced at her and his face changed from picture-perfect to something human and guilty. "When you kill, power floods through you," he said. "You feel like you're finally, finally all right. That at last you are what you were always told you were supposed to be. It wipes away what came before, it makes everything right, and then it fades so fast. I know you don't understand. I just want to explain to you—that I'm sorry." Ash's voice faded as he spoke, passion dying into wistfulness, then silence and the sound of the river.

"Don't be sorry," Kami said. "Don't do this."

"But if he doesn't kill me," Angela murmured, sounding almost relaxed about the whole business, "someone else will."

Ash moved then, and Kami saw what had been concealed by his body before: the other Lynburn knife, long and glittering gold in his hand.

"What do you want me to do?" Ash demanded, and his voice was as cold as the blade looked, light washing up and down the steel, as cold as the sweat that slicked Kami's body.

"I want you to choose," said Kami. "Stop being a coward and apologizing to me and act. Show me what you're going to do, Ash. Show me who you're going to be."

"I've already chosen."

"Kami!" said Angela, and her voice was fierce. It made Kami turn her back on Ash and his knife. "Kami, will you trust me? Promise me something. Will you please hide and stay hidden—no matter what?"

Kami looked down into Angela's clear brown eyes. Angela did not look afraid, even now, when Kami felt so scared and so worn by terror it seemed like she had been scared for years.

Kami nodded.

She had hidden in the quarry before, more times than she could count, but it had been years ago. Sobo, Dad, or Mum would call for her to get out of the woods, and she would be curled up in one of the crevices in the quarry wall, giggling to herself and Jared in the small space.

Kami stepped into the shadow cast by the quarry wall

and wormed herself into her old hiding place. She was far bigger than she had been the last time she had tried this. Every extra inch of her was in pain, her head jammed painfully against her knees, but she was hidden just in time.

Rob Lynburn did not climb down into the quarry. He leaped, and landed on his feet on the quarry floor, knife in hand.

Chapter Thirty-Four
The Last Words

Rob landed lightly for such a big man. Kami saw grit, the color of sand, crunching beneath his heels.

He had one hand braced on the side of the quarry as he leaned over his son. Out of the corner of her eye, Kami saw Rob's hand: big, square, rough, and capable. She forced herself to stay quiet in her hiding place. She saw Angela lying perfectly still beneath her chains.

"You couldn't do it?" Rob Lynburn sneered.

"I know her," Ash said in a low voice. "I can't . . . hurt someone I know."

Kami heard the hesitation, the way he could not bring himself to even say "murder" or "kill."

So did Rob.

"I wonder if you'll ever have the strength to be a real sorcerer," Rob said. Ash flinched at every word, as if each one was like his father was piling stones on his chest. "You have to understand they're not like us. They would take control of us if they could. Would you want to be a slave to one of them like your cousin?"

Ash lifted his head. "No," he said hoarsely.

Angela went tense. So did Kami.

Rob echoed their fear in a voice full of anticipation. "So have you changed your mind?"

Kami hated Ash for doing this to Angela, but something about his anguished face did make her wonder. What would have to happen, what pressure would have to be applied by someone who was supposed to love you, before picking up the knife seemed like your best option?

Ash's restless, glittering gaze met Angela's, wavered, and held.

"No," he said. "I haven't changed my mind."

"Then I'll have to do it," said Rob, and pulled the larger Lynburn knife from his belt. It shone like treasure in the sunlight, marred by dark lines across the grooved blade. Kami realized the lines were her own blood.

The weapon made a bright arc as Rob swung it down toward Angela.

Angela rolled out from under the chains, gathering one up and wrapping it around her fist even as she whirled. She swung her chain into the side of Rob Lynburn's head.

"Go on and try," she suggested.

Now Kami understood what Ash had meant when he told her he had already chosen, when he told Angela that he had not changed his mind. He had set Angela free before Kami even entered the quarry, and they had arranged her chains to look like she was still bound.

Rob staggered. Angela hit him again.

Rob fell on his face and Ash scrambled away, dropping his knife as he retreated from his father. Kami watched as Angela stood braced, centering herself as Rusty had taught them, and brought the chain down in another unstoppable arc.

The end of the chain struck Rob on the face, laying open his cheek. There was blood on the stone now, but not the blood Rob Lynburn had been planning on. He would never have anticipated that an ordinary human could attack him like this. Angela brought the chain down again hard, splitting the skin of Rob's back.

The floor of the quarry trembled, a crack running between Angela's feet, and Angela pivoted and slammed her foot down on his neck.

"I don't think so," she said, and rained down blows.

The wish for revenge burned fierce in Kami too, along with Jared's, protective and furious. Even so, Angela looked almost terrible. When Angela's arm was caught and her next blow fell short and useless, she nearly snarled in thwarted rage, blinked and focused on Ash.

Ash was panting. "You can't beat my father to death!"

"Can't I?" Angela panted back. She let her mouth curve more fully, into the shape of a scythe. "Watch me."

Ash did not let go of her arm. Angela looked down at Rob Lynburn.

Kami had promised to stay still and be quiet, no matter what. She believed in Angela enough to keep her promise. Rob was down, Ash was on their side, and Jared and Lillian were coming. They could contain Rob.

Angela flicked her gaze from the father back up to the son and stepped back abruptly. Then she offered Ash the hand not holding the chain.

Ash glanced at her upturned palm, then back at her face.

"You unchained me so I had a fighting chance," Angela said. "Which, as you can see, is the best kind of chance. So you can come with me and Kami, if you want. Or you can stay with him."

They both looked down at the murderer, lying sprawled in his own blood at the bottom of the quarry.

Ash put his hand in Angela's.

Angela turned, with a chain in one hand and Ash's hand in the other, toward where Kami was hiding. "All right, Kami," she called out, and moved toward her. "You can come out now." Her eyes were blazing with pride and fury.

Kami was so proud of her, and so sorry about what she had to tell her.

"Angela," she said. "Look behind you."

Angela and Ash both whirled around. The blood was still there, scarlet trails over stone. But Rob Lynburn was gone.

Kami had only looked away for an instant. She had not considered how the wild power of the woods and a source's blood might help a sorcerer heal.

Angela took a deep breath and said, low and calm, keeping her grip on Ash and her chain, "We should run."

"You both run," Kami told her. "Go get Jared and Lillian and Holly; they're coming toward us. Find them and bring them here."

"Why can't you come too?" Angela snapped.

Kami saw fear under her anger for the first time. Angela was never, ever scared for herself. Kami looked at Ash's face and saw he understood.

Kami kept her voice steady. "Because the rock has closed in on me. Rob did it, and I'm trapped. I can hold him off, I'm a source, but you need to go get help. Angela, I trusted you, please trust me now. Please go."

Angela hesitated, then whirled around and left. She used her grip on Ash's hand to help him as they scrambled out of the quarry, Angela more familiar with the terrain. She stood on the lip of the quarry and pulled him up to stand beside her with ease.

Kami watched their heads, one dark and one bright, going into the woods, until they disappeared from her sight.

Angela did not know Rob had spilled Kami's blood with that knife. She did not know how weak Kami felt, trembling in her stone prison. She would be furious if she found out that Kami had made her leave when Kami could not defend herself, but Kami wanted to be sure Angela was safe.

Kami drew in a slow shuddering breath, and reached out for comfort where she could always find it. *I can hear him coming back,* she told Jared. *I'm scared.*

One of Rob Lynburn's boots hit the heap of chains with a dull clang. Kami looked at him stepping over his own blood and shivered.

Don't be scared, Jared told her. *He won't touch you. I'm coming, and I'm going to kill him.*

Kami swallowed. Her breathing was so loud in this small space, hissing and furnace-hot, like the roar of a dragon in its cave. She was afraid Rob might hear. Kami turned her head as far as she could and looked at the dark stone instead of at Rob Lynburn. She turned her mind toward Jared. *Come soon.*

The hollow closed in tighter on her, like a stone fist. Stone pressed against her back, her sides, and her face, cold against her lips. Its grip seemed to go right through her flesh and promise to grind her bones to powder. She could not help it: she let out a small, stifled sound of agony.

Rob Lynburn made a soft, delighted noise. "Come out," he called.

Kami stayed where she was. The stone tightened around her. She did not know if she would be crushed or suffocated first. Jared's cold, clear terror cut through the dark confusion of her brain.

If she did not get out of here, she was going to die. She had to take her chances with Rob.

"Come out," Rob repeated. "Or be buried alive."

She tried to will the stone to open and free her, but she had no air and he had her blood. Kami made a small, strangled sound of assent. The stone grip released her, easing by just a fraction. She turned her face toward the light and began to drag herself out on her raw, bleeding hands and knees.

Rob stood over her, smiling against the sun and looking like Jared's dependable uncle. The knife was shining in his hand.

Kami looked up at him, her vision hazy so his golden hair blurred with the autumn leaves. She cleared her throat and whispered, low and hoarse, every word painful: "I'll cut the link."

❧

Jared was running through the woods, trees and light going by in a blur. He could hear Holly and Aunt Lillian running after him, neither of them able to keep up. Holly was still shouting questions somewhere in his wake. Aunt Lillian had given up asking.

Jared's heart was louder in his ears than their footsteps or their voices. Most of him was with Kami, stone on all sides and closing in. He thought nothing would be able to stop him, and then Angela and Ash burst out of the trees.

Angela's hair was tangled with twigs and leaves. Her mouth was a snarl, and from one of her hands a knotted chain swung. She looked ready to use it. Her other hand was in Ash's. He looked as if he had gone wild too, but wasn't adapting to it as well as Angela. His face was distorted and marked with signs of tears.

For a moment, they all stood staring at each other.

Then Holly shattered the stillness by throwing herself at Angela. "God, Angie!" she exclaimed, arms locked around her neck. "What happened?"

Angela started and went still, seemed about to say something and checked herself. Her face changed, the snarl dropping away. She dropped Ash's hand and lifted her own hand to gently touch Holly's bright hair.

Ash looked very alone. Jared felt a presence at his elbow and glanced to see his aunt Lillian had drawn level with him. She had her eyes fixed on her son.

"Yes, Ash," she said, her voice horribly, ferociously calm. "What happened?"

Ash swallowed and suddenly looked innocent, a storybook hero beholding horror in the woods. Jared wondered exactly how much practice he'd had looking innocent for his mother. Nicola Prendergast had died the night she asked Ash for help. Jared was prepared to bet that Ash had told his father.

"Your husband is the one killing people," Jared informed her flatly. "I'm guessing Ash knew it. And I don't care which of our nest is the worst monster, because he has Kami. We have to get to the quarry now!"

Angela's eyes narrowed, the snarl returning. She looked eager to use that chain. Jared felt in perfect accord with her for the first time, and his lips curled in a silent snarl back.

Then they were all running, Angela holding Holly's hand and carrying her along with them, Ash and Lillian at their backs. And still most of Jared was with Kami, alone with a murderer and trying to make a bargain.

Oh God, please don't do it, he begged her. *Please hold on. We're coming.*

❧

Kami spoke rapidly, ignoring her cracking voice, trying to replicate her usual reporter's tones, sweeping someone into an interview with the force of sheer conviction. "That's why you came to my house and told me I was the one who could break the connection. You've been recruiting sorcerers who you thought would agree with you about the best way to get power—you tried to recruit a stranger from London; why wouldn't you want your own nephew? If I die, he dies. But you came to me and asked me to cut the link because you didn't want him to die, and you didn't want his powers to be chained to me. You want him free? I'll free him."

Kami could see the sudden calculation in Rob's eyes. He had to believe she had a reason for severing the connection.

"I told you it was something I might want to do already, in my garden," Kami went on. "I had no reason to lie. I might get magic out of the deal, but people shouldn't be tied to each other like this. I don't want either of us to be a parasite. I don't want his voice in my head, his feelings running through me like a disease. I want to be my own separate self. I was thinking of cutting the connection anyway. I swear I'll do it." She stopped, out of breath, her throat one long, silent scream of pain.

Jared was quiet in her head now. She'd had to be convincing, and truth was the most convincing thing of all. None of what she'd said she felt, none of what she'd said she wanted, had been a lie.

"Do it right now," Rob commanded her.

Kami hesitated.

"I would rather my nephew was dead than your slave," Rob said. "And I am not waiting for you to recover and hurl your stolen magic at me." He picked up Ash's knife from off the quarry floor, smaller but with similar carvings on the hilt to the one in his hand. He offered it to Kami, blade first. "So do it now. Or I'll free him by cutting your throat."

"I don't understand what you want me to do!" Kami eyed the knife and weighed her chances of fighting Rob with it. Nonexistent, she thought, with his strength and reach.

"Take this," Rob instructed her. "And do what I say."

Kami took the knife, holding it very lightly. Her hands wanted to shake, but she refused to let them. No matter how little chance she had of defending herself with this, it was a weapon, and she was not planning to let it go.

"Do you see your shadow?" asked Rob.

Kami looked up at him and remembered how she'd seen him look like a sorcerer in her garden. He had the same wild, powerful look about him, but now he looked vicious as well. There was blood in his hair and an open wound on his cheek.

Someone had been able to hurt him, and that had maddened him: he wouldn't feel in control again until he had hurt someone else.

And here she was.

Kami lifted her hands, the empty one and the one with the knife in it, saw how he tensed as she moved, and gave up the idea of a lunge. She obeyed him, finally, looking down at the quarry floor and the trembling dark shape of her own shadow. Her shadow was lying across the bloodstained stone, touching the chains.

"Lay the knife at the tips of your fingers," Rob commanded. "So close you can feel the blade against your skin. Then cut the shadow away."

Jared had been silent in her head. Now Kami turned her mind to his and let his thoughts and feelings flow through her. It was like being on a boat watching your homeland receding in the distance, seeing it for the last time under rain and thunderclouds.

Kami, please, please wait just another moment, Jared begged. *I'll save you, and later I'll be better, I'll do anything you want, be anything you want me to be. Please don't do it.*

His desperation and misery swept her up like a storm capturing the sea. She turned her mind to even these feelings, because they were his, like his terrified rage in the lift when they had first met, being wrapped in his arms in a cold well, being dazzled by his wonder at the woods and her home and her. Like being a child, awareness of him the morning chorus that woke her and the lullaby that sent her to sleep, his thoughts always her first and last song.

I love you, Kami told him, and cut.

Chapter Thirty-Five
Nothing Gold

The smoke Jared had created raced through the leaves ahead of them, spreading out dark tendrils. They were the shadows of retribution, coming for Rob Lynburn.

It was the only thing Jared could think of: rage and retribution.

And then Jared went down. The crash startled Angela and made her spin to one side and turn on him, chain clanking in her hand. Jared did not even care. He wished she would bring the chain down, beat him unconscious, and end the wrenching pain and echoing silence in his mind.

"Easy, Angie," Holly said. "Jared, what's wrong?"

Jared lay on his stomach, struggling to lift himself on his elbows. He could hear his breath rattling in his throat, a terrible uneven sound.

"Where are you hurt?" Holly demanded, moving closer to him without letting go of Angela's hand.

"I'm not," Jared began to lie, and then bowed his head, shoulders hunching in agony. He could taste earth, bitter between his lips. He could feel the woods, the whole world, twisting and going wrong around him. "It doesn't matter! Get Kami."

Angela leaned down and looked into his face.

Jared gritted his teeth and stared back. "I'll catch up," he promised, and dropped his head again. He made a pathetic sound, crying out like a dying animal. "Leave me!"

Angela stood straight and said, "All right."

Behind her were Ash and Aunt Lillian. Jared was distantly amazed to see how concerned they looked, and furious that they seemed to have forgotten anything else was happening.

"You want that scum to kill another girl?" Angela demanded. "I'm going."

"So am I," Holly said.

Angela began to run, Holly holding on to her hand, and Ash ran after them.

Aunt Lillian stooped down and touched Jared's hair. It was the strangest thing: only Kami had ever touched him like that before, so gently.

"Go," Jared snarled, and turned his face away.

She did. She left him on the ground, struggling and failing to get up.

❧

Kami had not expected it to hurt. But it hurt worse than anything she had ever experienced in her life. She supposed through the haze of red agony that it made sense. This was surgery, after all, surgery of the soul or the mind or both at once. And she had done it to herself and to him. Worse than the pain was the sudden wrongness in her mind and in her bones, in every part of her.

Silence filled Kami now, like the silence after words failed and someone stopped breathing. She was gasping, lost as a fish thrown onto dry earth, lying on her side on the chains and scrabbling on the rock trying to get up, because in spite of all this she knew what was coming.

Rob Lynburn's shadow fell on her, blotting out the sun. She could not see his face, only darkness, and the bright light of the knife as he brought it down. Only the blow never fell, because Rob staggered and had to catch at the quarry wall to keep his footing.

"Rob," said Rosalind Lynburn. "You can't kill her."

"Rosalind!" Rob exclaimed furiously. "I asked you to go to the town and wait there."

Rosalind flinched away from his tone, even though she'd had the strength and conviction to hurl herself at him and force down his arm. Kami could see, suddenly, the ingrained habits of a lifetime. She saw how Rosalind might have chosen a violent man to take her away, because men who hurt her were the only ones she knew how to love.

"I went to the town," Rosalind murmured, her fair hair hanging like a veil before her face. "I did what you told me. Then I came back, and I'm sorry, but you can't kill her!"

Every muscle of Rob's bloodied, wounded face went tight. Kami recognized, with a cold crawling feeling, that he had been crossed too many times today. She forced herself to sit up and pushed herself staggering to her feet. She still had the knife in her hand, even if all the magic in her was dead and lost.

"That's right," said a voice at the lip of the quarry, a voice that was used to obedience without question. "You're not going to kill her. You're not going to kill anyone."

Lillian Lynburn cast a look at the loose rocks of the quarry, and they rolled to form rough steps. Behind Lillian, coming like an army of one, was Angela swinging a chain. Behind her came Holly, and then Ash.

"Lillian, I'm your husband," said Rob. "Listen to me."

"You're a criminal," Lillian told him. "You broke my laws, in my town, and I am going to execute you. Step away from my sister."

Rosalind shook her hair away from her face. It flew back like gossamer. Lillian held out a hand to her. Rosalind did not take it, but she did move toward her twin. A look passed between them like a spark, fire traveling from Lillian to light Rosalind's eyes.

Angela walked over to Kami and stood beside her like a guard. Holly came to stand at her other side, cupping Kami's elbow. Kami had not realized how unsteady she was until she had some support.

"Ash!" Rob bellowed.

"I'm so sorry," said Ash, and lifted his head. "Kami," he said, "I know you'll never forgive me. I can't blame you. But I truly am so sorry."

Wind and dust rose behind Rob, a small storm but large enough to envelop them all.

Lillian glanced at her sister and her son, and they both copied her as she lifted her hand. The storm dispersed, turning into dust motes that shone in the red light of the sinking sun.

"Rosalind," said Rob, "you would never betray me."

"If you kill her," Rosalind said, her voice very low, "you kill Jared."

"You don't understand," Rob told her. "I knew you didn't, I knew you couldn't, or you would not have done this. I made her cut the connection. I would never allow harm to come to Jared. He's free."

"Oh," breathed Rosalind.

"Enough!" snarled Lillian, and lunged for Rob. She moved so fast she almost had him, but he had his knife, and he struck without hesitating.

Rosalind and Ash both screamed as the knife came down. The dust storm rose again, this time flying into Rob's eyes, surrounding him. Angela dashed forward into the melee and hit Rob from the back with her chain. When the dust cleared, Lillian and Rob were circling each other. Lillian's shirt was torn, a scarlet stain spreading down one side. But she had Rob's knife.

"Your parents' son after all, aren't you?" she asked, and spat at his feet.

"And proud of it," Rob snarled back. "I had such hopes for you, hopes that you'd understand. But I was deceived in you. I married the wrong sister. You are your parents all over again, those sanctimonious murderers."

Lillian grinned. Seeing her with her hair coming down was somehow stranger than seeing her bleed. "And proud of it."

Everyone was watching the confrontation. Kami was as fascinated by it as any of them. But she'd tried to become a skilled observer, trained herself to notice anything strange. She found herself looking around.

Nobody else had noticed the quarry was filling up with threads of insubstantial grayness, slipping out from the woods from every side. "Lillian!" Kami called out. "Watch out!"

Lillian glanced around, and Rob leaped forward. He did no magic: he just stepped forward, seized his wife's hair, and cracked her head against the quarry wall. Lillian crumpled. Rob stooped to pick up his knife, while Ash ran forward and put himself between his parents. The quarry was like a cauldron of mist. Kami could barely see Lillian slumped on the rock. She grabbed onto Angela's free hand and she, Angela, and Holly stood linked together.

"I could never have dreamed I would be so disappointed in you, Ash," said Rob.

"Look," Kami said softly.

Through the mist rising from the quarry, she could dimly make out silhouettes. People coming out of the woods from all sides.

"What the hell?" Angela whispered.

"They're reinforcements," Kami whispered. Now she knew what Rosalind had been doing down in the town.

Rob had failed to recruit Henry Thornton. But how many sorcerers had he succeeded in recruiting? Kami could not make out most of the faces through the mist, but she saw the two nearest her: a woman she had never seen before and Sergeant Kenn. One of the officers investigating Nicola's murder.

Kami held on tightly to Holly's and Angela's hands and started counting sorcerers under her breath. She was up to twenty-six before Rob Lynburn spoke.

"Sorry-in-the-Vale is mine," he said quietly. "You just

don't know it yet. I have more sorcerers than you, and we will do whatever it takes to get more power. Any of you Lynburns can come join me in the town tonight, and all this will be forgotten. Any of you who do not come . . . Well. This is a real sorcerers' town now. And there are new laws."

Rob looked from his wife's unconscious body, to Rosalind, and at last to Ash, who stood trembling in front of him, "Those who turn traitor and break my laws," Rob said softly, "will be executed." He walked away, up the path of rocks Lillian had made.

The dark figures drew away. Even the mist was receding by the time Jared appeared, walking slowly through the pale shreds of mist, as if they were ghosts who loved him, clinging to him and refusing to let him pass. He looked as drawn and sick as Kami felt. He did not look at Kami, but he looked at the chains and blood, at Lillian unconscious, at Ash and Rosalind shaking as if they had fevers.

"What happened?"

"We had a moment of triumph," Angela informed him. "Unfortunately, it was short-lived, and you missed it."

They all went back to Aurimere House, passing through the arched doorway bearing the warning YOU ARE NOT SAFE. Ash carried his mother up the wide flight of stairs from the hall to her room. He did not come back.

Kami sat in a chair in the parlor, aching all over, and fell into an uneasy, exhausted sleep. When she woke, Jared was gone. Holly and Angela were stretched out on the canopy sofas, both asleep. Angela's chain was still knotted in one hand. Kami stood over her best friend and touched Angela's shoulder lightly, just enough to feel her there, solid and real and safe. Then she tiptoed out of the room. Her whole body felt like the empty place where a tooth used to be, a phantom ache that she had to keep investigating.

She went down a set of steps, across a hall, and into the library. There was no light except the dying sunlight from the bay windows. Kami passed the glass-fronted cabinets full of leather books and armchairs with backs high as thrones to sit on the window seat.

The library was on the ground floor, on the side of the manor near the cliff. Kami could not see the path, but she could see Sorry-in-the-Vale. Everything about her, body and mind and soul, hurt. She didn't know what to do about it.

Except she knew they all had to do something. She had to think of something. She wished Jared was with her. He had stayed by the door of the drawing room, not looking at anyone, while she was awake. She had not known what to say to him in front of the others.

She could go and find him. She remembered that morning in her bedroom, and she thought she could rest if he was there, if they were together. Only she was not sure of her welcome.

They were not linked anymore, Kami told herself, and suppressed a pang of desolation. The tiny creak of the door made Kami look up.

Jared had never surprised her like this before. She breathed in fast, taking a gulp of air to ease the shock. It was terrible to see him and have him so far away, all his thoughts and feelings locked to her, as remote as a star. It reminded her of when they had first met, and how his physical presence kept startling her. Now that was all she had.

He was here, though, and that was what she wanted.

He looked the same, gold hair in shadow, scar the thinnest of white lines, and gray eyes at their palest and most disturbing. The harsh lines and angles of his face looked harsher tonight: he must be in as much pain as she was. She wondered how she looked to him and how, with everything so changed, they would manage to comfort each other.

At least he was here. At least, now that he was with her, comfort seemed possible.

Kami forced herself to smile. "Is Lillian awake?"

"I don't know," Jared answered. His voice sounded very loud in her ears, now that she knew there was no way for him to speak to her silently. His mouth twisted. "But my mother's gone."

Kami opened her mouth to ask where, and then closed it. She turned her head back toward Sorry-in-the-Vale, where Rob waited for the other Lynburns to see the error of their ways and come to him.

She, like Jared, knew perfectly well where Rosalind had gone. "I'm sorry," she told him. She wanted to reach out and console Jared, but she did not know how to any longer. She couldn't reach out with her mind, and he had always shied away from her touch. She did not think she could bear for him to do that now.

"It doesn't matter," Jared said. "Except that it means there's another sorcerer out to get us."

"At least we know who she is and what she looks like," Kami murmured. "There are at least twenty-six other sorcerers."

"You counted them?" Jared's mouth curled at one corner, and the ache in Kami's chest turned almost sweet, the sudden force of hope a welcome pain. "Of course you did."

"They might be people from Sorry-in-the-Vale, or they might be newcomers. I saw one of each. If they're new, we can find out about them, but otherwise—we have to find out which of our neighbors are secretly sorcerers who want to kill us, and I'm not sure where to start the investigation." Saying it that way lifted her heart. It all sounded slightly more doable. Kami thought she knew how to handle an investigation.

"I'm sure you'll figure it out," Jared said.

Had his voice always been this hard to read before, and Kami had never noticed because she knew how he felt? She thought he sounded detached, but perhaps it was that he was so removed from her. She didn't know. Kami decided to take his words at face value and smiled at him again, though her lips were trembling and it was oddly hard to do.

Jared crossed half the room and then stopped, leaning against one of the glass-fronted cabinets full of books. Even when he was walking slowly and she knew he was in pain, he was graceful. She had never noticed that before either.

"Jared, I want to talk," she began, and stopped helplessly. She did not want to talk. She wanted it not to be necessary to talk.

"Let me say something first," Jared said. "Thank you."

Kami blinked. She had an absurd impulse to tell him

that he was welcome, but she said nothing. She could see his reflection in the glass cabinet, an iced-over doppelgänger of Jared, turning his eyes white and the curl of his mouth cruel. She felt it would be as impossible to reach out to this Jared as it would be to reach through the glass and touch that one.

"You were right to sever the connection," Jared continued. "You were right all along."

Kami was numb. It seemed for a moment as though by cutting away Jared, she had cut away every part of her that felt anything. All she could think of was what Rob had said to her in her garden one morning: that the emotions that came with the link, Jared's emotions, were not real. "Was I?" she whispered.

"Here we are without the link," Jared said. "And what am I to you? What are you to me?"

"I don't know." Kami's voice sounded muted, pressed flat by the way he was looking at her, as if he was seeing a stranger.

He answered his own question. He did not seem upset. He seemed puzzled, as if looking back at his past self and wondering how he could possibly have been so stupid.

"You're nothing special."

It was as simple as that.

Kami kept looking at him, even though she wanted to look away. It made no sense, she thought, that someone who seemed so distant from her could hurt her so much.

"So thank you," Jared told her. "I see things far more clearly now."

"I'm glad to hear it," Kami answered at last, her voice shaking out of control. She had been so scared of losing control with him. She had never really believed she could lose him, and in losing him lose so much of herself. "And you can go to hell now, for all I care."

"Who knows," said Jared, not taking his icy gaze off her. "Maybe I will."

They looked at each other for a few moments longer. Kami's whole body had gone tense, as if she was going to fight him. Then Jared smiled at her, a small savage smile that pulled his scar tight, and he turned around and left. He shut the door with a vicious slam.

All the warmth seemed to leave the room with him. Kami hugged her knees to her chest to try to control her shivering and turned away from the door. She sat there, on the top of the cliff with no path in sight. She stayed looking out of the window, watching darkness fall over her town.

For the first time in her life, she was alone.

Acknowledgments

How do you thank people for saving your book? Kingdoms and the hand of the princess seem to be in order, but since I'm short on princesses right now, I will make do with offering my deepest thanks.

First and foremost, so many thanks to Mallory Loehr. From the moment I met her and she said the magic words ("I love Diana Wynne Jones" and "dangerous books" being among the most magical), I had the mad secret ambition to work with her. I never dreamed I'd be lucky enough to work with her on the very same novel I was wailing about to my friend on that very weekend. Thank you for being even greater than I imagined, Mallory!

And many thanks to Phoenix Valentine, with apologies for distracting her. . . .

Thanks also to Suzy Capozzi, Michael Joosten, my wonderful copy editor Deborah Dwyer, and everyone else at Random House Children's Books.

Thank you for my cover, the most beautiful cover in the world (sorry, all other covers, you tried, but it *just wasn't enough*), to Jan Gerardi and Mallory Loehr, who worked—including me every step of the way; it was like a miracle—through two false starts and balefire to get such a wonderful image. Thank you to Beth White, artist extremely extraordinaire, for creating it: I love it more than I can say.

Thank you to my amazing agent, Kristin Nelson, always for every book, and especially for being so happy about the cover. Thank you, everyone at NLA—particularly Lindsay Mergens, who helped a lot with my publicity fretting!

Thank you to Venetia Gosling and the team at Simon & Schuster UK—so happy to be having another go on the merry-go-round with you! It's an honor and a privilege.

And thank you to my amazing foreign publishers, one and all.

Thank you, Holly Black, for being the friend I wailed to about this book—incessant, incessant wailing—and the first person to read the whole thing. The email you sent me about it is one of my treasures.

Thank you, Saundra Mitchell, for being a first reader and for being the friend I wailed to about covers—and thank you to my other first readers, Justine Larbalestier, Karen Healey, and R. J. Anderson.

Thank you, Delia Sherman, for coining the phrase "Sassy Gothic," and to Cassandra Clare and Robin Wasserman for naming *my* Sassy Gothic.

Thank you, Maureen Johnson, for playing Jared (or were you Kami and I was Jared?) in a dark, closed swimming pool. Memo: I am not in love with you. Though you are a most attractive lady.

Thank you to the Book Club—Zoe Cathcart, Joanne Lombard, Emma Doyle, Karen Pierpoint, Aileen Kelly, Jessica Barrett, Stefanie O'Brien, Clare Lynch (and Isabelle). Especially for the time you lovely ladies thought you were coming to have, you know, a book club—and ended up being there on the night *Unspoken* sold to Random House, and dealing with me in a fit of joyful hysterics, and also my dad arriving with champagne. (Total shamer.)

Thank you to my father for the champagne nonetheless, and my mother, my brothers, and my sister, Genevieve, who was one of the early fans of the cover.

Thank you to all my friends: in Ireland, in England, and in America, and the best one in Slovenia. You all now know far more than you ever wanted to about being a writer. I know how much I owe you for putting up with me!

Thank you to all the Gothics I now love—among others, all three Brontë sisters, Daphne du Maurier, Edgar Allan Poe, Mary Stewart, Barbara Michaels, Victoria Holt, Madeleine Brent, and Jennifer Crusie—and to all the sassy reporter ladies I've always loved.

And you, the one who picked up this book, looking for something to laugh at, something to cry at, something to interest you, something to remember: I hope you found it. Thank you.

SARAH REES BRENNAN was brought up on a dark, storm-wracked shore where clouds hang over a stone-gray sea and sailors meet their doom. (Irish weather: not so good.) Her house was full of secrets, not the least of which was what her parents were feeding the kids for them all to end up being six feet tall! She grew up to live in New York, where she was almost murdered by sinister thieves and was saved by handsome firemen, and then London, where she found the grave of a pirate dead from plague. In the midst of all this she wrote her first book, *The Demon's Lexicon* (an ALA-YALSA Top Ten Best Book for Young Adults), and *Team Human* (a vampire novel, written with Justine Larbalestier).

Sarah has never done as much research as she did for *Unspoken,* during which she was almost murdered in the woods (admittedly by a goat) and went to a Gothic manor, where she suffered a horrible fate: sitting on the tallest gravity fountain in the world. She never had an imaginary friend as a child, but now she writes about all the imaginary friends she has as a (sort of) grown-up and hopes you like them. Visit her on the Web at sarahreesbrennan.com, or write her at sarahreesbrennan@gmail.com to tell her all your imaginings.